BLACK DIAMOND DOGS

Suzi Wieland

Twisted
Path
Press

For my Chewie, who will never see the inside of a ring.

Chapter One

The Day Before

Tikal National Park, Guatemala

Cody hoped the memories of these two days would carry him through his week of hard labor. Tomorrow he'd be helping build a well for a small Guatemalan village, but today he was hanging out with the gorgeous Aline, exploring ancient temples and having tons of fun.

"Are you going to open your eyes, or do I need to call a doctor?" she asked in her sexy accent, thrusting a bottle of water into his hands. Cody's legs ached, and his heart pumped from the jaunt up the staircase of the temple at Tikal National Park, and he'd taken pains not to look around as they climbed to the top of the stone face. He wanted to open his eyes and see the stunning view above the treetops from over two hundred feet in the air.

"I'm okay." The cool water soothed his throat, and he downed half the bottle in seconds. The scorching ninety-degree temperatures were baking him, but he'd better get used to it. "I don't want to look until I can take the whole scene in." He ran his hand over the rough limestone block built by the Mayans over twelve hundred years ago. The history surrounding these temples was amazing.

Finally he opened his eyes.

The sea of green extended for miles; the clouds scattered about as the sun ruled the sky from above. Some other stone giants poked through the canopy of trees a half mile away, but it felt like so much farther. "Wow. It's…"

"Not for the faint of heart." She grinned.

He laughed and took in her full body, the red tank top clinging to her curves and her long, lean legs. A light layer of sweat glistened on her forehead and chest, nothing like his drenched shirt. That girl had thighs of steel.

"You're in great shape," he said.

"Of course I am. I work out and do yoga every morning."

He should've figured as much. She'd been pretty limber last night in bed.

Cody leaned forward and peered down. They couldn't see over the edge to the ground, but it was a long fall. "Did you know they've only uncovered a fraction of the ruins? Around thirty percent, they estimate. Think about all the ancient artifacts beneath the jungle floor?" The thought of the hidden treasures filled him with awe. "It makes me wonder how many creatures the jungle is hiding that haven't been discovered."

"Maybe you'll discover something new when you're building that well." Her dark brown eyes glimmered, and she lifted her fancy braid and fanned her neck.

"Maybe." He grinned.

"You're so generous. Helping that poor village to have clean water."

"It's no big deal."

Sitting on a beach with other spring breakers would've been nice, but building this well in a remote village would be an interesting challenge. Besides, he'd done the tropical thing before.

"It's a good start for a future veterinarian."

He'd never see her again, so his little white lie wouldn't hurt anyone. After he finished his senior year this semester, he'd be starting at veterinary school, but he had no desire to work with animals. He wanted to work in a lab and search for new medicines to help the animals or find cures to diseases. Most people gave him the are-you-crazy? look when he said he wanted to get a veterinary degree to sit behind a microscope, so he'd told her he was just going to be a regular vet.

"So I was thinking," Aline said, "since you had no plans now, we should clean up and have some dinner. And then we can take a nice swim later."

"Sounds like a plan." He was glad she'd spent the morning working, the reason for her trip here, and he got in a little zip-lining excursion. The rest of his day was open though.

They enjoyed the views a bit longer and soon made their way down the wood steps lining the side of the temple. The shade of the trees gave him great relief, and he listened to her talk about Brazil—or Brasil, as she'd called it, dragging out the A sound and making it sound more like an S than a Z.

"So Manaus should be your first stop, and don't even think of visiting Rio. It's over-rated, and there's so many better places to visit." She wagged a finger at him with a small smile on her face. "My business is almost done, and I can't wait to get back to my dogs. I didn't show them to you yet." She took out her phone and opened the pictures. "Here are my dogos. This is Silva and Braz." She flipped through some pictures of the dogs she bred.

"Nice dogs," he lied. They sorta looked like an all-white boxer, a type of dog he'd never been fond of. Labs were more his style. "They look fierce." Maybe it was the pose of the dogs.

"They're spectacular hunters, but they're soft and gentle too, and we place most with families." She hadn't shared much with him about her breeding business last night, and once they got back to her hotel room, it'd been more action than talk.

Action he wanted to repeat tonight.

Aline waved the phone at him. "I've got a few calls to make when I get back to the hotel, but then we can swim."

"Work stuff?" he asked.

"It never ends." She gave a dramatic sigh and smiled. "I'm actually here for my father. We're trying to recruit a friend of the family to work in Belém. I don't know how I got dragged into this, but my father knows I'd handle the situation better than my brother. He's too impatient. He doesn't understand that business deals take time." She sipped her water as she led Cody to the shuttle buses—well, rickety conversion vans that hardly looked road-worthy.

"My father was the one who suggested this restaurant we can go to," she continued. "He said it was spectacular."

"I'm up for anything."

Aline wound her arm around his waist and squeezed. "Then you're just my type of guy."

*

The waiter led them to a table in the outdoor patio and asked about drink orders. Cody was a little underdressed in his khaki shorts and plaid shirt next to her sleek emerald green dress, but she hadn't seemed to mind.

"I think a bottle of Merlot would be good. Don't you?" Aline barely waited for an answer and told the waiter which one she wanted.

The drinks arrived, and Cody sipped at his wine.

"Good, isn't it?" Aline nodded at his glass.

Reds were too bitter for him, but he could tolerate it for one night.

"Very good." *Anything to impress a woman.* DeShaun would've rolled his eyes at Cody. Of course, he had a girlfriend he'd be marrying in a few years, so he didn't get the whole dating scene.

"So are you working with your mother after you graduate?" This was the third time she'd brought up him and the veterinary thing since he first mentioned it. "I bet she'd love to have you by her side at her clinic."

"I really don't know. Maybe if she wants me there." He grinned to show he was joking. He'd actually love working with his mom, and if he were going to practice veterinary medicine, he would, but that wasn't his passion.

"I could use someone like you at our facility. Someone who loves our dogs as much as I do. It takes a special person to be a vet."

He should've told her from the start that research and development were more his thing, but there was no need to burst her Cody-is-awesome bubble.

"I guess we're both following in our parents' footsteps. You started your own business like your father, right?"

"My breeding business has grown greatly even though my competition is always trying to discredit our dogs. But that's how it is with any business."

"Pretty cut-throat?" Cody joked. Why in the world would dog breeding be so competitive?

"You'd be surprised," she said in all seriousness. "But my dogos are the best."

"What kind of dogs did you say they were?"

"Dogo Argentino. They're beautiful dogs. So majestic and strong."

She talked about the dogs again, repeating some things she'd said earlier, but he didn't care. He enjoyed listening to her talk, the confidence in her voice, her cute accent.

Eventually the waiter brought the bill, he paid, and they returned to their rooms to change. He waited down at the pool and replied to an email from his buddies. Texting was too expensive, but the wi-fi was free.

Not long after Aline arrived, Cody glided through the refreshing water, trying to keep his mind off the half-naked woman swimming with him. Those small pieces of fabric on her black string bikini barely covered her body, and he wanted to see it all over again. But this was a respectable hotel, and he couldn't go all horn dog in the pool with others around.

"Why are you staring at me like that?" Aline splashed him lightly. She dove underwater and swam until she reached the shallow end. The evening was quiet, and they surprisingly had the pool almost to themselves. A few people sat off to the side, but they were busy drinking and talking.

"Are you sure this isn't a topless pool?" he asked.

"No." She shook her head in mock disgust. "And it's probably a good thing because once I take my top off, you'll lose control."

"It could happen," Cody joked and glanced away from her to clear his mind so he wouldn't sport a woody. "We can talk politics. That'd cool me down a bit. Except I know nothing of Brazilian politics, and I assume you're not familiar with ours either."

"No. I've urged my father to get involved, but he says he's too busy." She leaned against the edge of the pool. "He does so much for the community, and he'd be a terrific leader."

"That works too." Cody grinned.

Her cute nose wrinkled. "What do you mean?"

"Talking about fathers shuts everything down."

She grabbed his hand and tugged him close. A laugh erupted from the table across the way.

Screw it, Cody thought. They were paying no attention, and no kids were around. He wrapped his arms around her waist.

"My father would love you," Aline said. "Many of the men in Brasil are lazy, and it's hard to find a quality man."

"I find that hard to believe. Brazil is huge. There's got to be plenty of men. I mean, this is *you* we're talking about." He raised his hands and waved to her body to prove his point.

She laughed. "True, but the problem is not me. Men are often intimidated by strong women, or they want me for my money."

"Money, huh? If I'd known, I would've made you buy dinner tonight." He nudged her in the shoulder. A wealthy, beautiful woman and crazy sex. He'd never been with a woman who took control and told him what she wanted. Too bad it didn't happen at the end of the trip because he was afraid this week's hard work would wipe out those memories.

6

"Maybe you'd like to skip out on this little thing of yours tomorrow. You should run away to Brasil with me. You'd love it there."

He pretended to think about it. "Tempting… very tempting, but Mom would probably miss me."

She cupped his cheeks, her mouth inches away from his. "But I'd miss you more."

Her lips overtook his, and for a moment he forgot where he was. Until raucous laughter broke out at the table off the pool again.

"I think we should head back to your room," he whispered. He had to get up early tomorrow for his long day, and he needed some sleep. But not before he got a few more hours of Aline.

"I think you're right." She gave him one last kiss. "Why don't you go get a bottle of Merlot from the bar. I've got to make a call, but I'll be done by the time you get to my room."

"I'm on it."

They climbed out of the water, and he watched her dry off. She walked away with a smile, and he rushed to the bar. Another Merlot. He just wanted something that wasn't so damn dry, but it's not like he'd drink much.

Just one and then he was done. Missing the bus in the morning was not an option.

Chapter Two

Day 1

Location Unknown

Every muscle in Cody's cramped body ached as he woke. Damn. He'd fallen asleep. Thankfully no light peeked through the windows, so he didn't miss his bus to the worksite.

The bed felt rock hard though, and the stiff muscles would be an annoyance on his first day. He tried to stretch his arms, but they stuck together. He wasn't even lying down.

He jacked open his eyes. What the hell. One small light barely lit the room, and the hum of a machine was too loud to be the air conditioner. Cody jerked his arms again, but they didn't move. He tried to kick out his legs, but something restrained them. Why couldn't he move?

He thrashed around, his eyes adjusting to the light. Thick straps shackled his arms and legs to a metal chair. His muscles strained as he tried to twist, to wriggle out of the bindings, but the straps dug into his skin.

Slow down. Think, Cody told himself. *Just a dream. No, a nightmare.*

He closed his eyes and lay back, taking deep breaths, expecting to wake up, but it didn't happen. Instead, the cold air penetrated his body to the very core. He fingered the thick strap around his wrist. He'd never break out of these.

A wave of dizziness swept through him. Where was he? Why was he here? Who did this?

A raspy voice said something, and another light flicked on. Cody's eyes shot open, and he squinted at the brightness. His surroundings came into view: the hard metal floor and the low ceiling, small boxy windows lining each side of the narrow room, the muted roar of jet engines.

He was on a plane.

He bore down on the floor with his feet and thrust backward, but his chair butted against a wall.

Then he saw the two men staring. The buzz of the engines covered their quiet words, but they were watching him. One wore a red t-shirt, jeans, and sneakers. A big scar ran from his cheek to his chin, and tattoos covered every inch of skin on the bulging arms leading to enormous hands that could squeeze the life out of Cody's neck in literally seconds.

The other guy was straight out of corporate America in his navy dress pants and shoes, and long sleeve button-down shirt with not one wrinkle. His hair was slicked back, and he was clean-shaven.

Cody was on a plane, maybe not even in Guatemala anymore.

Aline. Oh my god. They'd better not have hurt her.

"Where am I? What did you do to me?" He tried to act tough, but Cody's voice shook like the nerves in his body.

One of the guys said something, but it wasn't English.

Drug. Maybe they'd make him smuggle something back to the U.S. If he said no, they'd slice open his throat and toss his body where nobody would find it. Or maybe they kidnapped him for ransom. His parents weren't rich; they couldn't afford to free him. Cody choked down the panic.

The big guy with the shaved head stood. He took three steps to Cody and knelt down to check the straps. Cody tried to kick out, but his tethered feet wouldn't move more than an inch. The guy snickered and slapped Cody in the arm.

"Relax, boy." He stretched up and towered over the chair.

Cody shut his eyes. *It has to be a dream.* But the sound vibrating in his chest and the smell of stale cabin air told him this was real. He yanked his arms again, throwing his whole body to the side. The leg of the chair raised slightly, and he did it again—harder. The third time the momentum tipped him over, and his body and chair clattered to the floor. A sharp pain flashed through his skull, and Cody laid his cheek on the cold metal floor.

The two guys righted the chair with little effort. Fancy Pants frowned, but Baldy wore a smile.

Fancy Pants said something, and Cody strained to figure out what they were saying, but his Spanish was limited to a few words from one high school class years ago.

Baldy spit out more gibberish and shrugged, looking to his buddy—his boss maybe. Or more likely the lawyer who just sprung him from prison.

Fancy Pants frowned and mumbled something.

"Where am I? Who are you?" Cody tried again.

"I'm Daniel, your escort for the day," Fancy Pants said in a crisp, clear voice like Cody was on some sort of tour. "And this is Felipe. Andressa will discuss everything with you when we arrive home."

"Who's Andressa? Where are you taking me? What does he want from me?"

"I said you will find out when we reach Andressa's," he growled, while Felipe sat there grinning like a maniac. "And I suggest you pronounce the name right. It's An-drays-sa."

Cody shook his head, not even remembering how he'd said it.

"Am I still in Guatemala?" They could be anywhere. It could be hours later, days later.

"You're in the air right now," Baldy said. "We're heading to paradise. A little place we call—"

"Felipe. Andressa..." Daniel continued on with foreign words Cody didn't understand, his voice calm. Cold. The smile fell off Felipe's face. Cody stared around the plane for an indication of where he was, but there was nothing. Only boxes and empty space.

"We'll be landing soon," Daniel said, and Cody leaned back against the chair, scanning his memory for anything he remembered of the night. He wanted to crawl back into bed and wake up again, have breakfast, and head out to help the villagers.

"What did you do with Aline?" He summoned the tough-guy voice even though his nerves were jelly. The plane wasn't that big, but maybe she was in a different room.

"Aline, huh?" The two guys exchanged a look, and Felipe grinned. Cody needed some superhuman strength, a shot of adrenaline. He'd never take down the hulking Felipe without it.

"Aline's fine. Don't worry about her," Daniel said in a bored voice. He walked to the cockpit and poked his head inside. Cody couldn't see anything, or understand the words the men were speaking.

He returned shortly and said something to Felipe.

"Please stow away your tray tables and put your seats back. We will be arriving soon," Felipe said with a laugh. Daniel rolled his eyes and sat in his cushioned seat, buckling himself in.

Cody could take Daniel… maybe. But Felipe, no way. The guy was a damn bruiser.

The plane landed roughly, and they stopped. Slowly the jet noises faded.

"Ahh, finally home." Felipe stretched, strutted over to Cody, and snapped a pair of handcuffs around one wrist. He untied the other arm and forced Cody's other wrist into the cuff before yanking on them, cutting into his skin.

"You kick me. I kick your ass," Felipe grunted, flexing his bulging arms. "We don't want to hurt you, and we won't if you don't make us." He stared Cody down, a challenge not worth taking at the moment.

After another few minutes, Daniel opened the aircraft door, and Cody peeked out the doorway, the sweltering air smacking him in the face. Holy hotness. And muggy, way more humid than Guatemala.

A limo waited at the bottom of the metal steps, not far away from a hangar. Signs were posted around, but he couldn't read them. A few people roamed around the other hangars. Maybe he could trip Felipe and run to get help.

Felipe jabbed something hard into Cody's back. "Just so you don't think of trying to run."

All the fight drained out of Cody. He didn't know where he was or who had him. And Aline—what had they done to her?

Felipe escorted Cody down the steps and into the car with its pristine leather seats and tinted windows. Drug dealers didn't kidnap people and transport them in limos. At least he'd never imagined they would.

Once Daniel climbed inside, Felipe slammed the door. "Don't bother trying to jump out. We'll stop for you. Won't we, Daniel?" Felipe said, and Daniel nodded.

"Put this on." Daniel held out a black hood, but Cody hesitated. "Do you want Felipe to help you? He's not that gentle." Daniel sighed, and Cody pulled the hood awkwardly over his head. At least the material was breathable.

They drove for a while, and Cody slumped in his seat. Ironic how his first limo ride he was held captive and tied up with a scratchy bag over his head. One day he'd laugh about this with his buddies.

If he got away.

No, not if.

He couldn't think like that. He'd get home to his parents, to his friends. He'd see DeShaun and JJ and Trev, and he'd repeat the story of his escape over and over, getting more dramatic each time like JJ did with his stories. He would escape.

The bag over his head seemed to shrink, and he tried to pull the fabric from his mouth with his handcuffed hands. It was so damn hot in here.

Stay calm and use your brain. Panicking doesn't help, his mom always said. She'd never been kidnapped at gunpoint though.

She always worried about Dad traveling to the Middle East and getting taken hostage by terrorists, and now Cody was the one kidnapped. Dad would be the first one on a plane to look for Cody.

If he could only call somebody for help... His phone! He patted his front pockets, knowing it wouldn't be there, and the handcuffs kept him from reaching around the back. The last thing he remembered was lying in bed naked with Aline. Then nothing. But he was dressed now. They must've broken in and knocked him out.

Daniel told him to take off the hood. Cody tossed it to the floor and looked out the window. Foreign cars and foreign buildings and foreign languages. The streets contained a mix of high rises stuck in with small houses, stark white buildings with others painted green or blue or a muted orange. Even red.

The roads were busy, and pedestrians walked around, people who might help him, except they didn't know the limo held a prisoner.

They drove in silence, Daniel tapping away on his phone, Felipe staring so hard that Cody wondered if he'd have burn holes in his head. The pistol lay on Felipe's thigh—black and ominous—and his smug look gave Cody the willies.

"Are you admiring my gun?" Felipe caressed the barrel. "It's a beauty, isn't it? Lots of power behind this shot. Not like Daniel's wimpy gun." He laughed, and Daniel gave Felipe the stink-eye. "You a gun man, Cody?"

He sighed. "Not really. Handguns, I mean. My dad and I hunt, so I'm more familiar with rifles and shotguns. I've shot a pistol before at the range."

Maybe they'd see him as a person, relate to him, and maybe let him go.

"What do you hunt?"

"Deer. Pheasant and duck mostly."

"I've never been hunting." Felipe let out a guffaw. "Well, other than people."

Cody's head jerked up. Felipe smiled, but it wasn't the I'm-joking kind of smile. Cody turned and stared out the window, and luckily Felipe didn't talk anymore.

They drove past ramshackle homes packed together tighter than sardines. Half-naked children stared at the limo as they played on the crumbling streets. Some homes were windowless, while others were covered with bars, and lines of clothes were strung out in front of the houses.

Daniel knocked on the window not long after, the car slowed to a stop, and he crawled out the door and held it open for Cody. They wouldn't let him go, no way. Cody stepped out, Felipe behind him.

Cody held his breath, squinting in the bright sunlight. The stifling heat only took seconds to make the sweat form on his forehead. Dilapidated buildings with tin roofs and bars on windows lined the potholed-laden road. Garbage littered the sidewalks, and it smelled, a rancid mix of trash, human waste, and who knew what. A burnt-out shell of a building stood down the street—its walls stained black, and a dog with its ribs showing dug through the garbage out front.

"You want to leave? Go ahead. Either way." Daniel waved his hand nonchalantly. Cody glanced at Felipe, but the gun wasn't out anymore.

They wouldn't kidnap him just to let him go. Maybe this was like one of those movies where bad guys snatched people off the streets to be hunted by crazed maniacs.

Who was he kidding—this was real life, not a movie.

Up the street, a guy screamed at a woman dressed skimpier than a stripper. He stopped and glared at the limo and yelled, pointing his finger, then ranted again. The crack of a hand hitting a cheek fired down the street, and the woman cradled her face.

Not that way.

Across the street, a group of teenage boys smoking cigarettes and drinking from large glass bottles scowled at the limo. Cody felt them sizing him up.

Down the other direction, a group of rough gangbangers with hard eyes gawked at them. Cody was a mouse, and they were a bunch of hawks circling above.

"See those guys there?" Felipe said. "They don't like us, but they recognize me, so they won't mess with us. But you…" He cleared his throat. "They'd love to have some fun with you. And do you know what they do when they want to get rid of a body?"

Cody's skin prickled, every hair standing up on end.

"They toss it in the river. You ever see a piranha tear apart a human? It's not pretty." Felipe laughed insanely.

"Make your choice, Cody." Daniel covered a yawn. "Andressa's plans don't include death, but those guys aren't as civilized. Your decision."

Cody took one more glance at the men down the street. Some of them who'd previously been sitting were now standing, like they'd started inching their way toward the limo. The angry man up the street was still yelling at the cowering girl. Cody didn't know where he was, and even if he did, he'd never get away.

The cold air of the limo was still hitting his legs. The leather seats. The professionalism of Daniel. He didn't know what this Andressa-guy wanted with him, but right now it meant he wouldn't die… Yet.

Cody crawled into the limo.

"Good choice, man." Felipe punched his shoulder and scooted to his seat. "Andressa said he was a smart guy."

Daniel handed Cody the hood again. "Put it on," he said, and Cody hesitated. "Now! I don't want to go through the whole threat thing again." He pointed to Felipe, who flashed his gun. Cody complied with the request, and as the limo sped away, he sagged back into the seat, wishing to wake up from this nightmare.

Wait a damn second. He shot back up. "You said piranha. Am I in South America?" They didn't live on any other continent except for South America, as far as he knew.

Cody heard a chuckle, and then Daniel's gruff voice. "I said Andressa will explain it when we arrive."

It was a piece of the puzzle, but a minor one. What the hell was he doing in South America?

Chapter Three

Day 1

The Amazon Rainforest, Brazil

The limo stopped, and the engine died.

"Ahh, nice to be home again," Felipe said. "I would've preferred a few nights stay in Guatemala, but no such luck."

Cody's heart was about to burst out of his chest. This was it. He would find out who Andressa was and why he wanted Cody. Or maybe he'd soon be dead. He didn't want to think that though.

Daniel ordered Cody to remove the hood, and the bright light blinded him once again. He stretched his stiff body from the long drive, over an hour, maybe two. He couldn't really tell.

The car sat atop a long asphalt driveway. Palm trees stood at regular intervals along the drive, sentries guarding his escape, but right behind them was the overgrown forest filled with all shapes and sizes of trees and bushes. A modern two-story white house with a clay-tiled roof loomed over him. Something waited for him behind that orange front door… someone.

Daniel tapped his foot while looking at his watch, and Felipe eyed Cody curiously. None of this made sense. Kidnappers didn't pause to let their prey check out their surroundings. Unless…

He backed up and hit the limo behind him. Unless they knew he wouldn't be leaving. He wanted to go home, to see Mom and Dad.

Cody had to be strong, had to put up a fight. He checked out the rest of the surroundings. A second garage sat off to the side of the house, and the driveway led both ways, even though he didn't know which way was out. They were in the middle of nowhere—maybe close to two hours out of the city.

Daniel cleared his throat and nodded at the house. Cody clenched his sweaty hands. *Stay calm. Don't panic.* They'd said Andressa didn't want to kill him.

Felipe held the door open, and they walked into a large foyer, Daniel leading the way. Umbrellas filled an ornamental stand near the door—possible weapons. The spiral staircase blocked his view of the rest of the house, but he could see into the office just off the foyer.

The door shut behind them. If he had a chance to escape, he'd trail the road and slip into the shelter of green trees if a car appeared. He'd better damn well pick the correct direction the first time because otherwise he'd get caught.

That's all he had. Not much of a plan, especially since Felipe and Daniel both had guns. Daniel was probably a crack shot too, despite his pretty-boy looks. Shooting someone running through the trees wouldn't be easy though.

They entered a large, neatly organized office with a computer on the desk. Maybe he could get an email out, and help would be on the way.

"Sit down." Daniel thrust him toward one of the two seats in front of the desk and pulled on a suit coat. "Andressa will be here soon." He and Felipe stood guard at the door, and Cody peered at the giant fish tank built into the wall of the room. A lone silver fish no bigger than his hand swam among the plants, its scales sparkling under the lights. Strange because the tank had to be at least a hundred gallons or more and could hold a ton of fish.

"Cody!" A high-pitched voice squealed, and Cody jumped up.

Aline. Where had she come from—was she okay? He searched her body for bruises but saw nothing. Aline yanked him into a giant hug. Thank god she was okay.

"Thanks for coming. I'm so happy you're here," she said.

Huh—back up. Cody stepped away. Aline's brown eyes shown with delight, her hair styled in an intricate braid, and she wore a tailored suit and pants with a bright orange shirt underneath. She and Daniel would make a good couple.

Cody shook away the idiotic thought, and her words repeated in his head. *I'm so happy you're here.*

"What's going on?" He glanced back at the two guys in the doorway. "Where am I?"

"You can call me Andressa now. Everybody else does." She pointed to the chair.

Andressa—she's the Andressa they were talking about. Not a guy. He wasn't even sure if they'd said Andressa was a man. Not that it mattered. She brought him here for some reason. His brain tried to sort out this puzzle, but too many pieces were missing.

He sat.

"Did the boys treat you well? I warned them they'd better." She drew her gaze to the two men. "Daniel, you didn't hurt him? He's not acting like himself."

"No, Andressa."

Aline brought him here. Andressa.

Cody's throat closed off, and he gritted his teeth. She slipped something into his wine and threw him on a plane. "You drugged me, kidnapped me, and brought me to Brazil." He gripped the armrests tightly.

Andressa leaned over, patted his knee, and perched on the edge of the desk so elegantly. She crossed one leg over the other, reminding Cody of the woman he first saw at Tikal.

"I hope they weren't too rough with you. It was necessary. But now that you're here, it'll be wonderful. You'll love Manaus. Once you get settled, I'll bring you there."

This wasn't happening. It couldn't be real. Women didn't just kidnap men from hotel rooms.

"I'm not staying. I'm supposed to be in Guatemala, helping people. They're expecting me."

She clasped her hands together on her knee, her smile bright. "They'll be fine without you. We need you more. I told you I was in need of a vet."

"I'm not a vet," Cody spit out.

"Not yet." Her smile was so damn normal, and her eyes sparkled, not like those of a deranged kidnapper.

"Not ever. I'm going to work in research. In pharmaceuticals. I…"

He had to convince her to let him go, and her earlier words replayed in his head. *But I'd miss you more.* More than his mom, she'd said. Holy hell—his parents. Mom would freak when they said he hadn't shown up.

"That's what I love about you, Cody. You have such big plans, such drive. You'll be a welcome addition around here."

"You can't keep me here," he barked.

"Why are you so angry? We won't work you to death. We're equals in this relationship." Her voice remained so calm, the complete opposite of his frenzied tone.

"What relationship? It was just sex."

"And it was wonderful sex." Andressa sighed, staring out the window dreamily. "You and I are perfect for each other in so many ways."

The anger clouded his vision, his head pounding. He wouldn't sit here and listen to this crap.

"We're not in a relationship!" Cody jumped to his feet and reached for her, but the handcuffs shackled his wrists.

She leapt off the desk and clasped his hands. They were face-to-face, and he felt Felipe's presence behind them, but Andressa waved him off. She pursed her lips and stared before speaking.

"If you can't behave properly, we can leave these handcuffs on for a while. But if you choose to be a gentleman, Felipe will remove them." She nudged Cody back into the chair, and he rubbed at the red welts on his wrists. "Daniel will show you to your room. You will

20

stay there until you're ready to join us at dinner." Her voice had taken on an eerie calm, and he shuttered the chill running up his back.

Andressa swept out of the room, her heels clicking on the wood floor.

"So will you be a good boy?" Felipe nodded toward the cuffs. Cody gave him a quiet yes, and Felipe unhooked the cuffs and let Cody stand.

"Don't bother trying to escape. You're a long way from civilization and besides…" Daniel glanced at Felipe and opened his suit coat to show Cody the holstered gun. "We've got excellent aim. Andressa doesn't want us to hurt you, but only she can grant your freedom, and we're under orders to keep you here. Dead or alive, it doesn't matter to me." He stared Cody down until Felipe set a thick hand on Cody's shoulder and pushed him out the door.

Daniel led the procession up the grand spiral staircase and down a hallway of the quiet house. "We're in the middle of the Amazon. We're a hundred fifty kilometers to the next town, no neighbors for half the distance. And they're not the nicest people anyway. Not as bad as those guys we saw earlier, but they don't like Americans."

Felipe patted Cody on the back. "And don't even think about the jungle. You'll get lost. Unless a jaguar or caiman gets you. Or an anaconda. Squeezed to death and eaten might not be as bad as being bitten by a pit viper though. Their venom is pretty painful." He pinched at Cody's neck, and Cody jumped forward. Felipe laughed.

That scar on Felipe's face. He'd probably gotten it in a knife fight, or while trying to kill someone. If that's how Felipe came out of a battle, he didn't want to see the other guy.

Focus on something else, Cody told himself. *One, two, three…* Cody silently counted the doors they passed.

"Don't worry though, man," Felipe continued. "As long as you stay out of the jungle and listen to Andressa, you'll be fine."

She'd needed a vet, so she'd kidnapped him and acted like they were dating. Sure, they'd had fun together, but it'd mostly been the sex.

The sex. She'd brought him here to be a sex slave, but didn't that only happen to women? And it was seedy sex traffickers and drug dealers who enslaved women—not a professional woman who owned a dog-breeding business.

Daniel led him into a bedroom with mint green walls and brown woodwork. A white comforter with green trim covered the bed, along with fringed pillows.

"Here's your room. Clean up and make yourself comfortable. The bathroom's through there." Daniel pointed to a doorway. "Take a nap, whatever."

Cody almost snorted. "You want me to go to sleep? Are you kidding?" He glanced toward the large windows framed by lace curtains overlooking a pool and grassy backyard.

Daniel gave him a death look. "I'd drop the attitude. It'll make your life much easier. Andressa's patience does not last long."

He spun around and shut the door, but Cody didn't hear a click. He was in the middle of nowhere. In Brazil. He might've had a chance with Middle Eastern terrorists, knowing the politics and cultures, thanks to Dad, but Brazil... he was lost.

He stepped over to the French doors. The balcony hung over a concrete patio, which meant a good chance of breaking his leg if he tried to escape. Cody returned to the bedroom door and peeked into the hallway. Felipe smirked at him, and Cody slammed the door. He returned to sit on the cushy brown ottoman at the end of the bed.

His parents would be so pissed if he had to make up the semester. He'd wasted his first two years of school and got crappy grades, which meant retaking a ton of classes to get into veterinary school. He was finally almost there, in his final semester.

Cody hung his head in his hands. Making up classes was the least of his worries right now.

He needed to find a phone but saw none sitting out.

A check of the dresser drawers showed a lot of women's clothes folded neatly, some men's underwear and socks, and a box of condoms, but nothing else. Clothes were bursting out of the giant closet: women's dress shirts and skirts took up about three-fourths of the space, plus men's clothes. He hadn't gotten a vibe that Daniel was Andressa's boyfriend. He checked out the tags on the clothes.

Daniel was tall and lanky—these clothes were more Cody's size. He didn't want to think about what it meant.

In the bathroom, products with words he couldn't translate lined the shelves, but nothing looked out of the normal. Chrome fixtures, a walk-in shower and separate tub, and white towels filled the sizable bathroom. Cody used the toilet and returned to a plush chair in the corner of the bedroom. A book sat on an end table. He couldn't read the title, couldn't even figure out the genre from the cover.

Even if he found a phone, he didn't know how to dial out of Brazil. They wouldn't have 911, and besides, he didn't speak Portuguese, so how could he tell someone what was wrong? He had to try though.

The sun shined on his face through the door to the balcony. He'd see how things went today, and tomorrow he'd tie the sheets together and scale the balcony. The animals wouldn't be as bad as Felipe said.

He was about to sit down and figure out a plan when someone knocked at the door.

Chapter Four

Day 1

Daniel popped his head through the doorway. "Andressa's waiting for you at dinner."

Cody hadn't even given a thought to food with everything going through his head, or maybe he'd been ignoring the hunger pangs.

Floor-to-ceiling windows looked out into the backyard patio on the main level, bathing the large family room with light. A plush leather couch and other furniture faced a large screen TV, with a wet bar setup in the corner. Granite countertop, leather-cushioned stools, and shelves filled with glasses and bottles—she must do some entertaining in this room.

Andressa jumped up from the couch and flung her arms around Cody. Her business attire was gone, and now she was wearing a more casual dress that showed off her tanned legs. Her strong grip held him close, and he breathed in her sweet scent, bringing him back to the two previous nights he'd spent with her.

A lot had happened since then though. He backed away, and a frown flew across her face, but she quickly recovered.

"Thank you for joining me." Her hand grabbed his, but he didn't pull back. She wanted something from him, but what?

She couldn't have kidnapped him because he'd said he was going to be a vet—that wasn't rational—and then got these two guys to go along with her crazy scheme. He had to gather his wits, figure this place out, and then take off.

She dropped his hand and headed to the table. "I chose a Merlot for you." She filled two glasses with a dark purple wine and brought him one.

Cody stared at the glass in his hand. The bottle had already been open before he got here, but he witnessed her pour her glass first, so she must not have slipped something in the bottle. Still though, he waited until she drank from hers before he tried it, just in case.

One last glass of wine, she'd said last night. One more blasted glass of wine, and less than twenty-four hours later, a delusional bitch was keeping him captive in Brazil.

A large fish tank on the opposite wall drew his attention. This one held ten or so dull gray fish, similar in shape to the silvery one in the office.

Felipe strutted into the family room, beer in hand. He plopped down on the couch and flicked the TV on, the outline of the gun visible under his t-shirt. Daniel coughed in the corner and glanced at Cody before speaking in Portuguese.

Andressa set her hands on her hips, annoyance marring her face. "English, Daniel."

"Yes, Andressa," he muttered and slunk away. Andressa eyed the smirking hulk on the couch before facing Cody again. "Don't worry. It's only the two of us for dinner tonight. Felipe doesn't usually stay at the house, but since it's your first day here, he'll stick around to make sure everything goes *smoothly.*"

Felipe patted the holstered gun under his shirt. "Think of me as the problem solver. When Andressa has problems…" He shrugged. "I solve them."

Cody didn't want to become a problem, not before he had a chance to escape.

Andressa motioned for Cody to follow her into a dining area off to the side. A large table for two was set with china and more silverware than he ever used. Just like Christmas dinner at home as a kid. He'd hated when Mom made him set the table up all fancy at holidays, and right about now he was wishing he was home with them sitting down to eat.

"Have a seat." Andressa stuck her head through a doorway and said something before returning to the table. She sipped from her wine and unfolded the cloth napkin. "I'm so pleased to have you staying with us. Most of the men I date are so juvenile. That's why I'm glad I found you."

Again with the relationship thing. He clenched his teeth. "We're not dating."

"Cody, please." She tsked tsked him like he was an errant child. "Don't ruin dinner." The dark look disappeared, and her voice softened. "It's fate really. You and I running into each other after I decided to hire a full-time vet."

The door swung open, and a short grandmotherly woman dressed in a gray uniform rushed into the room with a tray of food.

"Vera prepared steak to make you feel more at home. She's a wonderful cook."

The woman didn't acknowledge the compliment and unloaded the food, never once looking at Cody. The house had to be around four thousand square feet, but it was a long ways from being a mansion, and Cody hadn't expected to see servants. Daniel seemed more like an employee, and Felipe... maybe a bodyguard. Or henchman.

"Is Daniel your butler?" Cody glanced toward the office as Andressa helped herself to food and passed it to him.

She laughed. "No. He's my personal assistant. He came highly recommended by my father."

"Is it just you here?" He had to get his bearings, didn't want to run into some random person when he tried to escape.

"Of course." She threw up her hands as if not understanding. "Why would the help live in the house? He lives in the barracào with some of the others."

"The barracào?"

"Vera and the other maid live there. I've built my staff very comfortable accommodations. They don't realize how lucky they are to have such a generous employer."

"Does Felipe live there?" Cody would never get anywhere with that goon around all the time. Maybe he could take Daniel—without a gun of course—but not the human bull. Cody finished his wine, and Andressa poured another glass.

She swallowed her food before speaking. "Oh no. Felipe's my cousin. He lives down the road, but he'll be staying here for several days. However long it takes you to get settled in."

Cody cringed at the way she said settled. At least she didn't plan on killing him, but how long was she expecting to hold him? He took another sip of wine—it was going down way too easy.

"Am I staying there? In the barracão?" he eeked out. He wouldn't be staying here for long. As long as she didn't tie him up at night, he'd be out of here.

Her lips parted into a laugh, and she reached across the table and patted his hand. "Why would my boyfriend stay in the barracão?"

Cody about choked on the steak in his mouth. *Boyfriend.* He had to get out of there… tonight. He didn't care if he walked for days until he ran into somebody.

"We'll give you a tour of the barracão, and you'll see the dogos later."

"Dogos?"

"Yes, my dogos." She shot him the unhappy look again. "We talked about this before. You'll take wonderful care of my dogs. You seem to have the touch."

But you haven't seen me around any animals. He opened his mouth to say the words, but slammed it shut.

Her eyes lit up as she continued talking. "I'm so excited to have you here with us. I have so much to share with you about our vibrant city. You'll love Manaus, and someday you can see it."

Cody downed the rest of his wine. He only half-listened as Andressa jabbered on about the culture and nightlife: museums, art, and colleges. They sat for over an hour after finishing, drinking glass after glass of wine. He needed it to numb the reality of the situation.

"Time to retire." Andressa grinned. Sleep. Cody needed it since he'd ruined his shot at escape tonight with too much drinking, but tomorrow he'd make a run for it.

Besides, she'd probably lock him into the bedroom or have Felipe stand watch over him.

He piled the silverware and crushed cloth napkin on his plate, picked it up, and pushed his chair out to stand.

"What are you doing?" Andressa asked, the disapproval seeping out of her voice.

"I'm bringing my plate to the kitchen."

"It's Vera's job. Let's go."

Cody stood, and the blood rushed to his head. He leaned on the chair to get his bearings. Just a bit buzzed. Or maybe a little drunk. Andressa didn't seem to notice as she led him to the stairs, his hand in hers.

The spiral staircase seemed to wind on and on, but eventually they made it to the second floor. Andressa stepped into the bedroom behind him. "How do you like my room? I've been told I have a flair for decorating."

"Your room?" But this was his room.

"Oh Cody." Andressa slung her arms around his neck and pressed her chest into his, her wine breath mixing with his own. "I can't believe you're here with me." Her mouth covered his, prodding him to kiss her. He got lost in her sensuous lips, the heat of her body pressing into his, her roaming hands.

"You'll love it here," she whispered. Her words cleared his fuzzy head.

"No."

He pushed her back. This wasn't the beautiful, sexy woman he met in the bar. This was his kidnapper.

"What do you mean, no?" she barked, her eyes small slits.

Liquid courage filled his veins. "I mean, don't touch me. What do you think I am, your… your…" Sex slave. God, he couldn't even say it. "You can't keep me prisoner. You have no right."

Andressa's face twisted into something nasty, her chest puffing up. "You are a guest in my home, and you will live by my rules."

"Screw your rules," Cody shouted.

Her hand flew out and slapped his cheek. He touched the stinging flesh and backed away.

"You will not disrespect me in my own home." Fury filled her brown eyes, her hands gripping her hips. She stomped her foot and pointed to the door. "Get out of my room!"

"I can go?"

"Yes, you can go find your own room. Get out of mine." She flung open the door and grasped his shoulders. With more force than he expected, she thrust him into the hall, and he stumbled to his knees.

The door slammed, and Cody stared down the empty hallway at the other doors. Maybe he should try to run. All he had to do was follow the road. Eventually he'd get somewhere.

Cody scrambled to his feet and fled to the stairs, steadying himself with the handrail. Daniel waited at the bottom with a menacing frown.

"Don't even think about it," he growled.

I can take him. Daniel was tall, but lean—probably not many muscles on his skinny arms. Cody took the first step.

Felipe stalked around the corner, his flinty eyes zeroing in on Cody. He positioned himself behind Daniel, legs planted wide, tattooed arms flexing. "What's going on?"

There was no way Cody could fight both of them, not without getting his ass kicked. Or shot.

He turned around and flung open the first door—a bedroom—and collapsed onto the bed.

*

A knock woke Cody up, and he glanced at the clock. The door swung open, and Felipe filled every damn inch of the doorway.

"Hey," Felipe said with a curt nod, his jaw set. "Andressa said we have a little problem." He folded his arms, giant masses bulging with muscles.

"No, no problem." Cody's mouth went dry. The closet wasn't far. He could run and lock himself in.

"I like you, man, and I don't want to hurt you, but Andressa's in charge."

"There's no problem, really. Not anymore." Cody whipped his head around, looking for any weapon. The only thing close was a bunch of pillows. His heart sped up. "I'll do whatever she wants."

"I believe you, but Andressa said you need to learn your lesson." He stepped into the room. "It'll go much faster if you don't fight. Let's go."

Cody trudged to the door, not knowing what else to do. "Where are you taking me?"

"Nowhere."

Felipe wound up, and his fist slammed into Cody's stomach. Cody doubled over, the pain spreading. He had no time to react, to protect himself, before Felipe punched him again. Cody toppled to the floor. Pain flared through his chest, along with a stinging in his throat. Puke poured out of his mouth onto the carpet, the stench of wine and digested food filling his nose.

Felipe's cold laugh filled his ears. If Cody'd had any strength, he would've jumped Felipe, but instead he lay weak on the floor. The laughing stopped, and when Cody lifted his head again, Felipe was gone. He needed to find the bathroom and clean up, but his stomach throbbed with each small movement.

A warm washcloth pressed into his head.

"Cody?" Andressa said. "Oh, sweetie. You had too much to drink. Is that why you were acting funny?" She continued to wipe Cody's brow as he lay still. She hunched over him in her silky black robe and tugged on his hand. He sat up. "Let's get your clothes off."

She helped remove his puke-stained shirt and escorted him to her bedroom. She handed him a pair of pajama pants and shirt. He changed, jerking the top over his sore skin, and winced.

"I didn't realize you had so much to drink. That's the problem with alcohol. You need to be more careful."

Cody didn't say a *screw you* as she tucked him into bed. He didn't say it when she cuddled up behind him. And he didn't say it when he heard her soft, relaxed breathing.

But he sure as hell was thinking it.

Chapter Five

Day 2

"Rise and shine, dumbass." The light flicked on, and Cody blinked, his eyes trying to focus on Daniel. "Get your butt out of bed."

Six a.m. and no Andressa. He stuffed the pillow over his head and rolled over, trying to burrow under the covers. His tender skin ached, and he stopped moving.

Daniel jerked the blanket off. "So you pissed Andressa off last night. Not smart." He chuckled. "She's not very forgiving."

This couldn't be another beat down; Cody's poor stomach couldn't take it.

"Get showered and dressed and come downstairs to the kitchen."

"What if I don't want to?"

"If you don't, then Felipe will help you." No emotion showed on Daniel's face, but he raised his brows. Cody gulped, running a hand over his tender skin. Daniel pointed to the clothes hanging on the door. "Andressa provided something to wear, something she picked out *for you*. Or you can choose whatever you want. The choice is yours."

Cody nodded, and Daniel slipped out the door.

He studied the clothes: polo shirt, khaki pants, and loafers. At least she had taste. In the bathroom, a piece of paper lay on the counter, her name embossed on the top in gold. *Andressa Cardoso*. He almost laughed. She'd called him her boyfriend, and this was the first time he'd seen her last name.

Cody,
I didn't know what products you use, so help yourself.
Love, Andressa

He scanned the brown bottles neatly organized on the counter, opened one at a time until he found one that seemed like shampoo, and took it into the shower.

Downstairs, after cleaning up, Felipe waved him toward the kitchen, where he found Daniel eating breakfast and Vera at the stove. No Andressa. Cody cleared his throat, and Daniel's head flew up. Vera didn't even glance back.

"Vera," Daniel said, "get Cody his breakfast." He motioned to Cody to sit at the small table. A light rain peppered the windows, gray clouds masking the sky, and Cody studied the backyard, a big open area but then a mass of trees.

She hurried to retrieve a plate piled high with scrambled eggs, bacon, and two pieces of toast. Her head stayed down when she served the plate, didn't respond when he said thanks.

"Can I have something to drink, please?" Cody asked tentatively.

She didn't move, and Daniel sighed. "Andressa said you are only to speak with me today. Get him juice, Vera."

Cody ate in silence while Daniel read his newspaper, and Vera continued with her cooking. Once his stomach was full, he stood and picked up his plate and glass.

Daniel grabbed his arm. "Vera will get it. Come with me."

"Thank you, Vera," Cody said once more, but her head stayed bowed, staring at the stove. "Where's Andressa?" Not that he wanted to see her.

"She's working out right now." He didn't elaborate, and Cody didn't question him anymore.

Daniel strode past Felipe and into the office. On the desk was a framed picture of Andressa and an older man. She had one picture with people in it in the whole house—he was pretty sure he hadn't seen any others. Daniel plopped down behind a desk and opened a laptop, giving no further instructions. Cody stared at him, then took one of the chairs against the wall.

"Don't think I'm happy about this," Daniel said. "You messed up last night, and now I have to be your babysitter. I've got things to do, so you can just sit here."

He couldn't be serious. "What am I supposed to do?"

"I don't care what you do. Just do it in the chair because you're not leaving."

"How... what?"

Daniel gave him a dirty look, and Cody stayed silent.

And he sat.

And sat some more.

Maybe Cody could use the letter opener and three pens on the desk to stab Daniel. Maybe give him a bad paper cut with those Post-its. Cody sighed. He wouldn't get far with Felipe in the other room.

"Where's Andressa?" he asked.

"At the kennels now, I suppose." Daniel didn't look up.

The hands on the decorative wall clock crawled so slowly. Taking a nap in the chair would be nice, but Cody's brain was too wired. Hopefully somebody had alerted his parents when he didn't show at the meet site. Dad would fly to Guatemala to search for Cody. He'd probably demand to see the hotel room and wouldn't give up until his mother had to drag him home.

"Maybe I could send a message to my parents and tell them I'm safe."

No answer.

Cody tilted his head back and thumped it against the wall lightly, getting no reaction from Daniel. First chance he'd get, he'd use the sheets to scale the balcony in Andressa's room and hit the road.

Shit—his passport. Maybe she hid it somewhere in the house. She was smart enough not to have left his stuff in the hotel room. Cody scanned the office for a safe, not like he'd know the combination.

When he got away, he'd have to find the U.S. Embassy to get help. They had to have an embassy, right? He stared at the pictures of buildings on the wall behind Daniel: a few tall buildings and other multiple-story structures that looked like they belonged on a college campus. The way Andressa talked, Manaus sounded big, so it must have an embassy.

By eleven, Cody had an achy neck in addition to his still-sore stomach. "Um, can I go to the bathroom?"

Daniel pursed his lips. "Felipe," he called, but there was no answer.

"I gotta go now. What, you think I'm going to run?"

He might, if everything played out right.

Daniel tossed his pen onto the desk. "Go ahead. Walk right out the front door before Felipe arrives. At most you'll make it to the gate before he catches you. But even if you did, you wouldn't get out the gate. Raul's there." He picked up his phone and sent off a text. "This is a professional operation, Cody. Andressa's got plenty of security, and nobody is unarmed around here."

Cody slumped in his chair as Daniel smirked and returned to his work.

Ten minutes passed before Felipe poked his head in the doorway. "What's up, man? I heard you have to take a piss. Need me to hold your hand?"

"He wouldn't let me leave," Cody muttered, but Daniel pretended to be busy reading something on the computer screen, and Cody followed Felipe down the hall. "I don't need a babysitter."

"I know you won't run." He patted the gun hidden under his shirt. "And Daniel knows you won't run, but Andressa… Well, she's the boss, so it doesn't matter what the fuck we think." Felipe slapped Cody on the back so hard he almost stumbled. "Sorry," Felipe said with a shrug.

In the bathroom, the cool water refreshed him. He was thankful this punishment didn't involve pain. After peeing, he stared out the window, thinking about his escape.

"You fall in the toilet?" Felipe chuckled.

"No." Cody wasn't in the mood to see Andressa, but staring at the walls in the office was getting old.

He barely got out the door, and Felipe spoke again. "I'd invite you to watch the game with me, but Andressa wouldn't approve."

"I won't tell if you don't." Watching TV was way better than a stuffy office. And despite being nervous about Felipe, Cody almost wanted to be around him, more than Daniel. At least Felipe talked to him.

Felipe left him at the office door and sauntered off toward the family room. Cody slunk down in the chair. Daniel huffed and shook his head. Cody wanted to ask about Felipe, if he'd ever killed anyone. He'd certainly alluded that he had, and Cody was almost sure it was true. But did he really want to know?

Yes.

No.

They all acted as if Cody being here was the most normal thing in the world. Maybe this wasn't Andressa's first kidnapping.

Daniel worked for a little longer and finally looked up from the computer, then stood. "I need to talk to Vera about lunch."

Cody would have a few minutes alone here, and he could get to the internet and send an email. He had Andressa's last name, and somebody somewhere could find her.

As soon as Daniel left, Cody shot to the computer.

His chest tightened. The log-in box was the only thing on the screen. All hope slipped away.

Something swished by the door. Daniel peered in at him and smirked. "I told you Andressa's security is tight. She doesn't want *any* of the help getting access to the internet."

"I wasn't..."

"Sure you weren't." He strode in, and Cody scraped by him. On the wall was a large aerial photo, and he stepped closer to study it. Several buildings dotted the middle of the picture. A house— probably this house, with the extra garage. A long, skinny building lay around the bend, not far from Andressa's house, and a road continued to wind through the trees until it reached two more long, thin buildings. Green trees enclosed everything, bordered by a river on three sides. The house was the farthest away from the water, but those two identical long buildings weren't far from the river's edge.

The driveway at the house led north until it was out of the oxbow and met up with another road.

"Is this the Amazon?" Cody asked. He could follow the river until he reached another house. The hope swelled again.

"No." Daniel sighed. "We're on a tributary of the Negro, which joins the Solimões and forms the Amazonas."

"But this is us. We're almost surrounded by water."

"Yes. And I wouldn't recommend a swim. You've no doubt heard about the piranha. But they're not the only creatures out there. The electric eels and caimans are especially vicious, and—"

"What's a caiman?"

"Our version of the alligator. Except they're bigger and meaner." Daniel studied him intently. "Don't forget about the poisonous frogs and dangerous insects. And tarantulas."

Cody's head snapped up.

"Or maybe an anaconda might find you. Either way, we're so far from the city… from anybody, so you'd die of dehydration. The sun can be pretty intense here."

Okay, the road would be his first option. The river a last resort. He had no doubt Daniel was playing his warnings up a bit, but those animals were out there, and as freaked out as he was to be with Andressa, one part of him was amazed. He was in the middle of the Amazon rainforest, the largest rainforest in the world. Home to thousands of species of animals and plants and bugs, and indigenous tribes untouched by the modern world. The Amazon was the place that might hold the answer to cures, for treatment of diseases for animals and people. He might be the one to discover those cures.

If only he'd come by his own choice.

Fifteen minutes later, Vera appeared with food. Again, she didn't acknowledge Cody's presence. He ate quickly, and after she took his plate away, he realized he should've eaten more slowly because Daniel forced him to sit once again.

And sit. And sit.

Twice, he nodded off and woke to Daniel laughing at him. Cody rubbed his neck, hoping for this day to end.

When six o'clock rolled around, Daniel shoved a drawer in the filing cabinet shut and stood. "You can go to your room and clean up for dinner."

Cody's face heated. "I haven't done anything. I don't—"

"Those are Andressa's instructions." He swept by Cody. "Dinner's at seven. Don't be late."

Upstairs, Cody fell onto the bed and closed his eyes. He never imagined sitting in a chair all day doing nothing would be so exhausting, but he felt like sleeping. Instead, he washed up as Andressa requested, wondering what the hell she had planned for him next.

Chapter Six

Day 2

Andressa stood in the corner in deep discussion with Daniel, probably getting a report about Cody's behavior. She spun around, her face bright. "Cody, you're here. How was your day?"

Her heels clicked as she approached him, and she grasped his hand and kissed his cheek. "You look handsome. I see you're wearing the outfit I bought."

She dismissed Daniel and motioned for Cody to sit at the table set with burning candles, cloth napkins, and wine—did she eat this way every night, by herself even? Maybe he was one of the many guys she kidnapped, except what had happened to the previous guys? A chill ran down his spine—they were at the bottom of the Amazon.

She filled his glass with red wine and sat back.

"I had such a busy day. I had to catch up on everything that didn't get done while we were in Flores, plus meet with prospective clients." She took a sip of her wine and babbled on about her day.

He didn't even know what time it was at home, didn't know if his father was finishing up work at his office with the students who stuck around for spring break. Or if Mom was staying late to care for an animal someone brought into her vet clinic five minutes before it closed. Or maybe his parents were sitting down to their meal talking about their days, not knowing Andressa had kidnapped Cody.

No, they had to know he was gone.

Mom probably freaked out when they called to say he hadn't shown up. He hated putting her through the agony of not knowing if he was alive. "I need to tell my parents I'm safe."

"Not now, Cody," she spat.

"But I have to. They might go to Guatemala to look for me. Who'll run her clinic? Who will take care of those animals?"

"We'll talk about this later, I said," she snarled. "Please don't ruin dinner."

She seduced him and abducted him, snuck him into Brazil. She was ruining his life, and he didn't care about her damn dinner.

He threw his fork down, and it clattered on the plate. "Did you go to Guatemala looking for someone like me?"

"I told you I was there on business. It was pure luck bumping into you, fate. You... Me." She closed her eyes with a satisfied smile. "I knew the first night I took you to bed that you were the one."

"So you decided to kidnap me on the spur of the moment?" The bitterness seeped out of his voice.

Andressa's eyes popped open and quickly narrowed. "I didn't kidnap you. You said you wanted to come to Brasil. You and I are meant for each other." She set down her fork and sat up straighter. "You are just what we need here... Just what I need. And you'll love it here. Tomorrow I'll introduce you to everybody."

It was too much to hope that any of her other employees would help him escape—of course they wouldn't. They'd follow her rules like Felipe. They'd beat him if she asked. Nobody would help him, and he'd be stuck here forever.

Andressa talked all through dinner, and they retired to the couch in front of the TV. She cuddled up to him, and he resisted the urge to push her away.

"I have a surprise," she said, grabbing the remote. "I got satellite channels for you. Movie channels and others based out of the EUA."

"What's the EUA?"

"Nos Estados Unidos." She stared at him for a moment, but when he didn't respond, she sighed. "The United States. Your TV isn't as good as Brasilian, but maybe you'll feel more at home."

He bristled. "Have you ever watched any American TV?"

"No. Why would I watch something inferior?" She looked at him like *he* was the crazy one. "We have so many celebrities of our own, so I don't pay attention to your Hollywood actors. Last year, Beatriz Par and Alberto Senra filmed a movie in the Amazon. They actually used one of my father's buildings for some scenes. It was a big deal. Beatriz and I still keep in touch."

"That's—"

"If it wasn't for me, Beatriz and Alberto might not even be together. I gave them a spectacular thank you gift, for using our building, and she told me it was my bottle of wine they got drunk off of. And got together for the first time." Andressa flipped through the movie guide, rambling on about the celebrity couple, as if anybody else would care how her father let them use an empty apartment to film their movie.

She tucked her legs under her and grasped his arm, laying her head on his shoulder and giving him a good whiff of her vanilla-scented hair. His body tensed, but she didn't seem to notice.

"They even asked me to be a stand-in for the movie. It didn't have any lines, so I declined. It was a silly comedy, and if I am starring in a movie, it should be something more dignified."

Yeah, more important to match your ego.

She set the remote down. "Did you see any movies you like?"

He'd spotted the *Jurassic Park* listing, and he'd seen it a hundred times, but all he wanted was a little familiarity, a link to the place he missed so much. They spent the next two hours in blessed silence, the only problem being the leech stuck on his arm.

"What a stupid concept," Andressa huffed at the end. "Who would breed killer dinosaurs?"

"They didn't mean for them to kill people. It just—"

"But they did. They should've foreseen the consequences."

He started to argue with her but had little energy. She'd argue with him no matter what, might even get pissed. It wasn't worth the fight. "Yeah, it's a dumb movie," he said.

"Next time, I'll pick the movie." She smiled. "Especially if all Hollywood movies are like this one."

Yes, all American movies are about bringing dinosaurs back to life. He covered a yawn.

"Oh, is my baby tired?"

The spacious room suddenly felt cramped, the air oppressive. He had to get away from her.

"I'm beat," Cody said. "Can I go to bed?"

"Of course we can. A proper night's rest is very important." She squeezed his shoulder and led him away. They passed Felipe sitting in the office in front of a TV on the way. Upstairs in the bedroom, she patted the bed. "I'll be out soon. You can use the bathroom after me."

It was more like twenty when she came out, and Cody was half-asleep in the dark room. She flicked the light on. "All yours." Her hand waved toward the bathroom, and he squinted in the bright light. She was standing before him in a silky blue robe.

"I'll wait until the morning."

"No," Andressa snapped. "You'll go now. Bad brushing habits lead to cavities. Trust me, we've had enough employees who don't take care of themselves. Besides, I don't want to kiss your yuck mouth."

Cody froze.

She pulled off her robe and hung it up. Her black nightie clung to her body, accenting her chest and her hips. His head was a war-room with a fight between the body that remembered all the things Andressa had done to him at the hotel and his mind that knew exactly who Andressa was.

Cody peeled his eyes away and shot off to the bathroom. The cold water cooled him down. What the hell was wrong with him? He shouldn't be considering sleeping with her. She forced him here at gunpoint, threatened him if he tried leaving.

He did a very thorough brushing and took his time washing up.

"What's taking you so long?" Andressa called from the other room.

He had to come up with a reason why he couldn't have sex.

"Cody, I'm waiting."

"Coming." He sighed before forcing a neutral look on his face. She was stretched out on the bed, and his gaze followed the curve of her body… her beautiful body… to the end of the lacey fabric on her thighs.

No! He shook off those feelings.

"I'm so tired." He faked a huge yawn, even though it was true.

"Come warm me up." Her sexy grin was back, and he looked away as he climbed into bed.

"I'm tired, Andressa. It was a long day." He rolled over so he wasn't facing her.

"And whose fault was that?" She scooted behind him and kissed his neck. Her hand slid up and down his side. "Being in a new country is overwhelming, but we have each other, and you can depend on me to help you get through it."

Her arm wound around his waist, and her hand slid down to his waistband.

"Don't," he said, fighting what was coming.

"Don't what?" Her voice hardened.

"I can't." Cody rubbed his temples. "My head is pounding." It was all he could think of.

"What? Do you get migraines?" She popped up.

"No," he said quietly. "I just have a really bad headache. I didn't want to say anything when we were watching the movie, but…"

Andressa leaned over to kiss his forehead. "My poor baby." She ran her hands through his hair and pressed her fingers into his skull. "Where does it hurt? Up here?"

Cody closed his eyes as she massaged his head. "At the top."

"Headaches are horrible. I know how bad they are. Do you want something to help with the pain?"

"It doesn't work. Usually it'll just go away after a while." Not until she fell asleep though.

"You close your eyes and relax."

He did as she commanded. His excuse worked tonight, but it wouldn't work twice in a row.

Chapter Seven

Day 3

Cody woke to Andressa's hand trailing up his back. Her lips pressed against his shoulder. His body coiled so tightly he felt like he'd never relax.

"Good morning, sleepy." She nibbled at his neck, her soft hands wandering over his side to his boxers, under the thin fabric. She'd barely groped him, and his dick twitched. His mind replayed the sex they'd had in the hotel—hot and sweaty bodies rolling around in the bed.

Dammit. He tried clearing his head. He didn't want this. Didn't want her.

"Did you sleep well?" she purred.

"Yes."

She nuzzled her nose into his neck, her hot breath on his tingling skin. Her naked body pressed into his back, and she wound one leg over his. "Make love to me, Cody."

No. His heart thumped, scared of what she might say. She couldn't do this to him. She couldn't make him have sex with her.

"I can't." He screamed at himself to ignore her touch, but his body wasn't cooperating, and he stiffened under her warm hand. "I can't," he choked out.

"Your body says you can." She rolled him onto his back and climbed on top of his legs, staring at his hard-on and pushing his t-shirt up his chest.

He didn't move.

Andressa's eyes dimmed, and her head tilted to the side. "Relationships are fifty-fifty, Cody. I'm providing you with everything you need. The least you can do is to fulfill my needs. Is that so much to ask?"

She kidnapped him and brought him to Brazil against his will. Threatened him with a gun. Had him beat. "I didn't ask to come here, you crazy bitch."

She jerked her hand out of his shorts. "What did you say?"

The hard edge was back, an edge that could cut his skin. But even if she made him sit for days on end with Daniel, he would.

"I said no. You can't force me to have sex with you."

She chuckled darkly, and a cold shiver soared through his back. He didn't know what she was capable of. Maybe he shouldn't have denied her.

"I'm a very forgiving woman, but you'd be wise not to cross me."

No. He wouldn't give in. She wanted someone weak, someone who would listen without questioning, and he needed to stand up to her. "I'm not going to have sex with you. You need to let me go. This isn't right."

"You and I were made for each other." Her voice remained under control. "Why can't you admit that?"

She'd get tired of him denying her and would let him go. "What don't you understand? I said no."

Andressa towered over him. "I won't tolerate insolence. You should be grateful for what I've done for you. You're the one who said you'd love to come visit me, to see Brasil. I brought you here, and you're acting like an ungrateful child. Get out of my room!" She crawled away and rolled to her feet, her face blazing red.

Cody shot out of bed, and Andressa leveled her gaze, pointing to the door. "Now," she shouted.

He slipped out of the room, short of breath, shuffled down the steps into the quiet family room, and headed toward the fish tank built into the wall. The dull gray fish, all about the size of his hand, swam through what appeared to be live plants. He'd never seen this type of fish with the red running down their bellies and along the lower fin. They were almost the shape of a football, except their face was fairly rounded. The ugly things were trapped, just like him.

Today's mind-numbing silence with Daniel would be hell, but he would stick it out until she gave up. She would send him home, and he'd get back to real life. He'd give his parents a big hug and would return to school and move on with his life, leaving Brazil in the deepest recesses of his mind.

Cody heard a soft click and then hard, steady footsteps on the floor. The tiny hairs on the back of his neck stood, but he didn't move. His eyes roamed the room. The door to the kitchen wasn't far away; he could reach it quickly, get outside.

But who was he fooling? He wouldn't even get to the road, and they'd shoot him. He should've left when he had the chance, slipped out the back door.

It was too late now.

"Cody, man," Felipe said from behind him. Cody wiped his damp palms on his shorts. "We've got things to discuss. Let's go outside."

No weapon was in sight, the lamp too far away. The fish had so many hiding spots, little caves made of rock, bushy plants, but Cody had nowhere. Several large rocks dotted the bottom of the tank, but by the time he reached inside to grab one, Felipe would be on him.

Felipe motioned for him to follow. This time would be worse. She'd beat him harder and longer until he gave in… or died. He'd never visit Mackinac Island again, Mom's favorite vacation spot, he'd never sit in the stands cheering on the Brewers with Dad, and he'd never again split the colossal buffalo chicken pizza at Uncle Luca's with DeShaun, eating so much they wanted to puke.

Cody followed his executioner through the patio doors by the pool.

"You don't learn, do you?" Felipe glared, his thick tattooed arms seemingly growing into logs. Another guy lumbered around the side of the house to join them.

"Felipe." Andressa stuck her head out the door. "Remember what I told you."

"Sure do. Don't touch his face." The door slammed, and he turned to Cody. "What Andressa wants, Andressa gets." Felipe's arm jabbed out, a battering ram hitting his body.

The pain roared through Cody's stomach, and he doubled over, dropping to his knees. The other night's hits hadn't been so bad, but he'd never felt pain this sharp. The second guy wrapped his arms around Cody and hauled him back to his feet.

Felipe wound up again. Cody tried wriggling away, but his arms were locked tight, his stomach, the target, waiting to be hit. What had he ever done to deserve this? He'd never hurt anyone, never did anything to warrant getting his ass beat. All he did was have some fun with a beautiful woman.

Cody gasped for breath as Felipe pummeled him two more times, and the other guy dropped him. Cody fell to his knees, curling up into a ball, wanting to die. Tears filled his eyes, but he blinked them back.

"Each time it'll get worse," Felipe said. "It's your choice. You're a cool guy, but Andressa comes first."

They dragged him upstairs and threw him into bed, and Cody lay there wishing to go home.

Chapter Eight

Day 3

Cody groaned and stretched his body a few hours later, crying out in pain. The thick pillows swallowed him but gave no comfort. Never once had he gotten into a real fight, and now twice he'd had his ass beat. All due to one crappy mistake. He'd never wanted his mom more than right now, the woman who cared for him when he was sick, who hugged him through his tears when he was a kid.

He should've taken Tae Kwon Do all those years ago. If he had his black belt like DeShaun, he might've been able to defend himself better. As soon as he got home, he would take a class, and he wouldn't quit until he had that black belt.

The clock read almost noon. The bed was empty, but a note lay on the end table telling him to take a shower and come downstairs. It was signed *Love, Andressa.*

Cody wanted to show his love for her with a jab to her stomach—to knock her flat on her ass, pound her head into the floor, and throw her to the piranhas.

He swung open the door and stepped onto the balcony. The humidity dampened his skin, and he swore at the heat. Dark clouds hovered in the sky, no sign of the sun. The edge of the forest lay so close, the singing of the unseen birds reaching him.

His stomach ached so badly, but he had to forget it. Rest. Gain their trust. Don't get beat. Those were the things he had to do, and soon, he'd be out of there, maybe even make it home before spring break was over. When he escaped, he'd better bring water with, just in case, and maybe food—he'd have to think this through a bit. Taking off without a plan would get him dead.

After a long shower that didn't help his aches and pains, he dressed in the clothes sitting in the bathroom. Each step down the stairs induced another cringe, but he kept going.

"Sweetie." Andressa jumped up from the table and tossed down a folded napkin onto her plate. "How are you feeling? Are you okay?"

Why are you even pretending to care?

"I'm fine."

"Vera, Cody's arrived," Andressa called toward the kitchen. Seconds later the woman appeared with a tray of food. His stomach growled. Andressa watched him as he took a bite of the roast beef sandwich. Tangy and delicious. He wouldn't give her the satisfaction of knowing how good it was though.

He took a mini-banana off the plate. Yuck. If he was home, he would've thrown this brown banana in the garbage.

"You'll love Brasilian food. It's much healthier and tastier than the processed food you Americans eat." She reached across the table and patted his hand. "Your body needs to detox. You'll feel much better when you eat more natural foods. Plenty of fruits and vegetables. We'll get you healthy again."

She knew nothing about what he ate. He bit back the comments and stared at the banana. Despite being brown, it didn't feel mushy.

"Please, Cody. It's a banana-maçã. There's nothing wrong with it."

He removed the peel and took a bite of the apple-flavored banana as she continued talking about the benefits of eating healthy. Andressa cleared her throat, and he looked at her. "Huh?"

"I need to catch up on work that's fallen behind because of you, but I've made a list of the things you need to do today so you won't be bored. Tomorrow, though, we'll spend the day together."

Today, tomorrow. He'd be there no longer than a few days.

"I should call my parents to tell them where I am," he said nonchalantly. He still hadn't seen a phone anywhere around, other than in someone's hands.

She sighed hard and heavy. "I know it's difficult for you to leave behind your friends and family."

"I didn't leave them behind. You—"

Andressa whipped her hand up to stop him. "It's best to walk away. You'll make it harder if you keep worrying about the people you left behind."

Cody slumped in his seat. "You said we'd talk about it later. My parents. They'll worry when they don't hear from me. Wouldn't you want to tell your dad if it was you? Wouldn't your mother worry?"

Mom would go through all worst-case scenarios—imagining him lying dead because some drug-crazed Guatemalan robbed and beat him. Or that he'd gotten into an accident at the jobsite and somebody covered it up.

She stroked the back of his hand with her red nails. "We're your family now."

The fork lay on his plate. So close. Jam it into her hand and run.

But Felipe was around. If Cody hurt Andressa, he wouldn't live to see tomorrow.

"I'll tell you what," Andressa said, pulling back her hand. "Why don't you write them a letter explaining everything. How you met the woman of your dreams and decided to take a chance on love." Andressa gave him a dreamy look, and his stomach soured. "I'll mail the letter for you."

"You will?" A little hope filled him. He didn't want Mom wondering and worrying over him—crying every day because she didn't know what happened to her son. Even if Andressa forced him to lie, his parents would know he was safe.

"What a wonderful idea. I'll print out some pictures from your phone, and we can include them."

"You still have my phone?" All he needed was a few seconds to call for help or send his location with a GPS signal.

"Yes, but don't bother looking for it. I changed your password. I anticipated you might get homesick, and this is our special time together. Our time to get to know one another. Sort of a honeymoon." She grinned. "Besides, you have so much to learn at the kennels. You'll be very busy."

"Vera," she called, and the woman appeared in the doorway. "Cody and I are finished."

"Yes, ma'am." Vera nodded and stacked the dishes. Felipe busted through the doorway, stuffing food into his mouth. Cody backed away, staring at those fists of steel, but Andressa was already out of the room.

"Looks like you're stuck with me today." Felipe laughed. "Hey, I'm a fun guy. Don't let our previous experiences prejudice you."

"What are we going to do?" Cody asked.

"I'm your tour guide for Casa de Cardoso and the rest of the grounds. Andressa said you haven't explored the house yet."

"That's because she kept me locked away." Cody clamped his mouth shut, trying to temper the frustration.

"You saw the kitchen already," Felipe said and strutted the other way. "Andressa's into that healthy eating crap, but Vera can find you better food when you're sick of smoothies and granola." He laughed at himself and headed past the fish tank. Cody was about to ask what the fish were, but Felipe led him through the family room and to Andressa's personal gym that held a treadmill, elliptical machine, and more.

"Vera's a fine cook. Everything's made from scratch. But Andressa doesn't allow anything unhealthy in this house. If you get dessert, savor it because we rarely have any. Dessert apparently makes you fat and lazy." He chuckled again. "Do I look like I'm fat and lazy?"

"No."

Felipe looked like a bull on steroids.

"I'm sure Andressa will encourage you to use the gym."

Cody eyed the weights. Even if he used a dumbbell as a weapon, he wouldn't have much of a chance to hurt Felipe. He'd have to catch Felipe off guard and crack him in the head, but Felipe was keeping an eye on him.

They returned down the hall and grabbed umbrellas from the front stand, then stepped outside. The fresh rain, the clean smell, and the cooler temperatures invigorated him, and with no wind, the umbrellas kept them dry. The rain pounded the leaves of the trees, and Cody didn't have time to take the whole scene in as he tried to keep up with Felipe.

A gravel driveway curved into the thick green trees, and they walked away from the house. A long, narrow one-story building with a line of windows came into view, like a cheap motel off the beaten path.

"The employees stay here at the barracão. Vera, Yasmin—she's the other maid. Sometimes the guys from the kennels stay here, but neither Levi nor Miguel stays overnight. Daniel does though. His room's on the end. Most of the rooms are pretty small—I couldn't handle living in one for more than a few nights, but Daniel's suite is spacious."

A garage sat to the side of the barracão. Felipe opened the door and stepped inside. "These golf carts are for our... your use. I wouldn't touch Daniel's cart. He doesn't like that." Felipe pointed to the first cart.

A golf cart wouldn't make it very far, but maybe it'd get Cody far enough. He stared at the white vehicle, the plan stirring in his head.

Felipe smacked him in the arm. "Don't count on it. Besides, you didn't see when we arrived. The entrance to the main road has a gate, and Raul—remember him?—he's the only one who can open the gate. Him and Bernardo. And believe me, they won't let you go." Felipe nudged Cody toward the door. "You're not getting out. Uncle Marcos requires pretty tight security on all his properties."

Cody wanted to bang his head against the wall, but maybe Felipe was lying. There might not be anybody at the gate. Hell, there might not even be a front gate.

They left the garage and headed farther down the winding road walled in by trees. The downpour continued, the rain dampening his shoes.

"Why didn't we take a golf cart?" Cody asked, cradling his sore stomach. Since he'd never been in a fight like that, didn't know how long the pain would last.

"Golf carts are for lazy asses." Felipe grinned at first, but it turned into a grimace. "Hold up," he said and kneeled down. He yanked up the cuff of his jeans and adjusted the strap on a holster on his ankle.

Oh great. Not only did he wear a gun, he had a knife too. Cody wouldn't have a chance getting to the phone in Felipe's back pocket.

They continued on, and Cody looked up to the two identical buildings facing each other, similar to the barracão, but with less windows. Felipe strode inside, and Cody followed, passing a front desk and conference room, and going through another door.

A guy hunched over a desk in an office. Cody looked for the tell-tale shape of a holster, and sure enough, he had one on his waist.

"Miguel," Felipe said and spoke in Portuguese, giving Cody a nod. Both guys laughed. "Miguel's our kennel manager. This is," he said with a grin, "Andressa's new boyfriend. I'll show him around the kennels now."

Miguel held up his hand and spit out a bunch more Portuguese. Felipe nodded, his lips pursed. They exchanged spots, and Felipe clacked away on the computer, Miguel standing over his shoulder talking. Cody eyed the room, looking for a phone, but he saw nothing

He might not be in this mess if he'd told Andressa he planned on working in research. Just a few damn words different, and he'd still be in Guatemala.

A good ten minutes later, Felipe got out of his seat, a smile on his face.

"Have fun." Miguel nodded and sat down again.

Cody and Felipe walked out another door, back outside again. He was about to say they forgot their umbrellas, but the sky had changed. Above him was a distinct line, blue sky on one side and gray clouds on the other. The rain had been a temporary relief, but the sweltering temperatures returned.

"What was that about? Inside," Cody asked. A chain-link fence enclosed a large area, which led into several dog runs with doggy doors cut into the wall. "The computer stuff."

"Network issue." Felipe shrugged. "He tried to figure it out but needed the master."

Cody laughed. "You're the resident computer expert."

"I told you, man. I'm a problem solver. Whether it's computers or people, I get the job done."

A white dog ran out of the bushes toward them but stopped at the chain-link fence. He barked excitedly, and soon a chorus of barking bodies joined in.

"They're eight weeks old, getting close to time when they can be adopted," Felipe continued. "They're not big barkers, which is nice, but these guys are puppies, and you're new to them."

Dogo Argentino, Andressa had called them. Cody bent down and stuck his fingers through the fence, getting attacked by a horde of wet tongues.

Felipe strutted to a door and opened it up. One puppy jumped into Felipe's arms and attempted to bite his fingers off while the others rushed for Cody. Felipe laughed and held the small guy close to his face, talking in Portuguese. Little yapping furballs surrounded Cody. He attempted to pet all six as Felipe cradled the one in his arms, scratching its neck.

Go figure. A monster who loved puppies.

"They're skilled hunting dogs, and we place a lot with families." Felipe let the dog down, and the white ball of fur ran to Cody. He scooped the dog up, and the puppy tried licking Cody's face until he held him away. "They're strong, fierce dogs," Felipe added.

"Fierce—for kids?"

Felipe punched him in the shoulder. "It's all in how you raise them. They can be gentle and loving, or nasty and brutal. I've seen them bite a poor defenseless cat in two." He raised his brows at Cody, who rolled his eyes.

A red ball lay off to the side under a tree, and soon Cody tossed it around with the puppies who weren't ignoring him. One little guy ran in circles in the yard, chasing an unseen foe, and for a short time, Cody wasn't thinking about his situation, of Andressa or Felipe.

The panting puppy dropped the ball and headed for a small hut in the corner under a tree. "He's probably getting a drink," said Felipe. A couple others followed.

Cody needed one too. Despite the cloudy sky, the heat was still intense. Felipe headed back for another door, and Cody followed inside, Felipe jabbering about the kennels and the dogs.

"Where's the mom?" Cody asked.

"Probably inside." Felipe nodded to the puppies. "They get plenty of play time every day. Socialization is important. Andressa's dogs are highly prized, and they're bred from champion lines. I'll bring you to see Albina. She's due to have her puppies in about two weeks."

After visiting the pregnant dog, Felipe pulled a piece of paper out of his pocket, studied it, and shoved it back in his pants as he strode down the hall. At another door he knocked and waited for a response.

Inside the room, Daniel looked up from his computer.

"Just showing Cody around." Felipe turned to Cody. "Daniel's office, obviously. Always knock."

Cody went to say hello, but Daniel was facing his screen again. "Shut the door behind you," he said, and they slipped out.

In every new part of the kennel, Cody searched for a phone but saw nothing. Had she really brought him here because he was going to school to be a vet? She'd said they'd had so much in common, but what? If he'd told her he was attending school for anything... anything not related to animals, he might not be here now. Just a few words could've changed everything.

He needed to look around this kennel better. Even though he didn't speak Portuguese, it was worth a try.

There had to be a phone somewhere.

Chapter Nine

Day 3

The rest of the day Cody followed Felipe around, learning about the Dogo Argentino and Andressa's breeding operations.

Outside, a small delivery truck tore down the driveway, and Felipe waved at the driver before it disappeared around the bend, the opposite way of the house.

Cody peered down the road. He had to get to the front gate to check it out. "So you're Andressa's computer tech *and* security? Do you keep in line all the guys Andressa kidnaps?"

Felipe snorted. "No, you're the first. And let me tell you, when she called me and Daniel to Guatemala, he was pissed. Daniel likes… structure, and Andressa bringing home a boyfriend—"

"I'm not her boyfriend." The heat rose to Cody's cheeks, and he clenched his fists. Felipe grasped his shoulders, stopping him.

"I'll tell you something, man to man. Don't fucking mess with Andressa. She will grind your ass to the wall, and there's no way you'll come out alive in the end. Nobody knows where you are, and nobody here will help you, so get over it. You're pretty damn lucky compared to some people around here." Felipe stalked off toward the house.

Cody stood staring into the green trees. The broad and long leaves were so much bigger than the ones at home. The trunks seemed smaller though. What he'd give for a pine tree right now, or the maple trees that filled his parents' backyard. Even leave-less as they were now at home, he'd take them.

"Let's go," Felipe yelled, and Cody gathered the energy to get moving, and soon trudged up the steps to the house.

The cold air hit his wet skin at the same time as the yelling. It was Portuguese, but Cody recognized Andressa's voice. Felipe held his finger to his lips, shushing him, but Cody had already pushed on the door. It swung shut with a bang.

Andressa's head whipped around, but her face lit up with a smile. "Sweetheart, you're back." She slipped over, leaving behind the object of her anger—a girl close to Cody's age wearing the same uniform as Vera. Her head hung, stringy hair in her face, and her shoulders drooped. Andressa glided up to Cody and leaned toward him, holding her head out. "It's proper to give your girlfriend a kiss on the cheek when you see her," she said in a strained voice.

As much as it pained him, he had to do it. "Of course, sorry. I didn't want to get you wet." He gave her a quick peck on the cheek and noticed the broken vase on the floor.

Andressa turned toward the girl, and her smile vanished. "Yasmin came to me with a recommendation, but I'm starting to question Luis's judgment. I've been thinking about firing her."

She flung her hands on her hips and glared at the poor girl. "Clean up this mess. And you'll be paying for the vase. It was a gift from a close friend."

"I sorry, Mees Andressa."

Andressa grabbed Cody's hand and smiled. "Managing a household is tough sometimes. This is the second time she's broken something."

Yasmin was sweeping up the shattered vase when Andressa turned toward her again. "If you keep this up, I'm sending you to Enzo. I won't deal with your subpar work much longer." She swung around to Cody. "I have something to show you before you go get ready for dinner."

She patted him on the butt with a smile. The Jekyll and Hyde routine unnerved him a little, but he did as the queen ordered.

In the office, she held out a newspaper clipping. Three men stood together, one holding a plaque, but Cody couldn't read the words on the page.

"My father is on the right. The mayor just presented him an award for his community service work. We built a clinic to help the needy children who don't have access to medical services. I should've been there, too, to accept the award, but I was in Guatemala with you."

If she'd been there to accept the award, he'd still be in Guatemala sweating over the well project. And then he'd be on a plane flying home.

"My father always encourages us to give back to the community, and I have. Recently I was invited to sit on the board for Amigos Peludos because I've donated a lot of time and money. We're a pet rescue organization. Part shelter but more. We not only work with cats and dogs—we work with exotic animals." She finally took a breath. "There are stupid people who believe wild monkeys would be fun to have as pets, but a few months later they don't want them anymore. We find those poor creatures acceptable homes. Zoos or sanctuaries."

"You work at a shelter?"

She grimaced, adding a shake of her head. "I told you I donate thousands of real. They benefit much more from my money than my time."

Stink up her designer clothes at a cramped, smelly shelter. Of course not. Cody rolled his eyes, hiding it from her.

She pointed to the men in the newspaper clipping. "The mayor and my father are close. They serve on several boards together, and Father was instrumental in pushing forward the development of this new clinic."

"Is he in town?"

Andressa had raved about her dad several times, and it seemed to Cody that his daughter kidnapping an American and keeping him prisoner would get her, and him, into a bit of trouble.

"Yes, but I haven't told him about us yet. He's very protective of me. Nobody is good enough for his princess, and I'm worried he'd question your intentions."

"My… my intentions?" Cody felt like someone had knocked the wind out of him. "You kidnap—"

Andressa smacked him in the face. Cody backed away, his cheek stinging.

"Must I remind you that you wanted to come here? I thought we were done with all this." She snatched the paper from his hands and filed it away in a drawer. "Don't you worry. When it's time to tell my father, he'll understand how much we love each other. He'll learn to love you as much as I do."

"But—"

"We're done talking about this. Go upstairs and get ready for dinner."

She waved him off, and he trudged upstairs. A few more days max, and as soon as he was feeling better, and they left him alone, then he'd be gone.

*

Cody stared at the shallow bowl in front of him: a chicken leg drowning in creamy yellow soup with spinachy-looking bits in it. At least the citrusy smell was good.

"What's this?" he asked.

"Pato no tucupi—it's duck. And it's delicious."

Cody surveyed the rest of the food—white rice, yellow peppers, and more fruit. She always had fresh fruit sitting out on the table.

"I have spectacular news." Andressa took a sip of wine, waiting for his full attention. "Tomorrow I finalize a contract with the local police department. They've finally realized the capabilities of my dogos."

"Your dogs will be police dogs?" He bit down on his lip to hold back the laugh.

"Don't you think my dogs are good enough for the polícia?" She set her spoon down and lasered in on him.

"No, I didn't mean—"

"Thanks for ruining my special news." She grabbed her spoon and quickly took a bite of food.

"Of course your dogs should be working with the police. They're the best. I was just surprised. I thought they were family dogs… you know, pets and stuff." He grabbed his napkin to wipe his damp forehead.

"We're branching out now into new areas. It won't be long before everybody in Brasil will want my dogos."

"I'm sure they will. What did you say this was called?"

Each bite of duck melted on his tongue. Cody stuffed another forkful of the green leafy stuff in his mouth. The acidic flavor was strong, and he'd never had something quite like it.

"This is big for me. Enzo could never have done this. Nobody believed me when I said we should get into breeding, but it led to so much more."

"Who's Enzo?"

"My middle brother. He's got the ego of a king. Father trusts him, but he's the one with problems. He's got no self-control." Andressa shook her head, her eyes cold. "No, I won't talk about Enzo now. You should've seen me today, Cody. I walked into the room full of men and laid it all out there for them. I showed them how well-trained and obedient our dogs are with proper training. How strong they are. And they chose Cachorros do Diamante Negro even though we were the most expensive because they see that our dogos are far superior to those German Shepherds and Boxers."

"What's Cachorros do Diamante Negro?"

Her brown eyes blinked at him, her lips pinched tight. "That's us," she said slowly. "That's my business."

How was he supposed to know that? "What's it mean?"

"Black Diamond Dogs. We're becoming the premier dogo breeder in the country. My competitors didn't think I could do it. *A woman can't run a business like this*, they said, but I've proven them all wrong." Andressa continued to ramble on about some business deal.

Cody rubbed his prickling lips, and a numbness took hold of his mouth. This didn't feel right; he didn't feel right.

The thought pierced his mind. She decided to get rid of him because he was fighting her. He snatched the water glass and took a drink, his throat thick.

Oh crap—it might be poisoned too.

He coughed out the water, and droplets sprayed the table. Andressa squealed and flew back in her seat. She grabbed a napkin and whipped at her face. "What are you doing?"

"You drugged me again. Why? I didn't… I wasn't going to fight you anymore." His face heated, his neck, his whole body. He pushed back from the table, clutching at his throat.

Felipe had said Andressa wouldn't hurt him, as long as he followed her rules.

Andressa laughed. "Relax. You're over-reacting. I didn't give you anything." She stabbed her fork and waved a piece of the green stuff in the air. "It's the jambu. It causes a tingly numbing sensation. It's our specialty here in the Amazon."

"No, my throat. I feel hot." He waved his hand for air in front of his face.

"It's your imagination. Take a drink of water—take my water if you want—and sit down." She reached over for his wine glass and took a large sip. "See. Why would you think I'd poison you?"

I don't know. Maybe because you drugged me before.

He gripped the cold water and focused on the ice cubes. Then he downed the rest of the glass and touched his numb lips. "How long does it last?" His body wasn't heated like it'd been a few minutes ago, and his heart slowed.

"Not long. It's unusual, isn't it? I love seeing you trying new things. Apparently you don't get enough of our foods in the EUA."

No, we're not that lucky. He rolled his eyes inwardly.

They finished dinner, and Vera cleared the dishes away. Andressa didn't say a word of thanks, and when Vera left, her smile turned wicked. "Let's go upstairs."

Cody gripped the side of the table. "Let's watch a movie or something."

"No," Andressa said.

"How about a walk? I'd um… I'd love to see the grounds more."

Andressa glanced at the dark windows. "No. Come with me." She spun around and headed for the steps. Cody didn't move at first until she turned around with a frown on her face. "I said now!"

Each step up was closer to the inevitable. He dragged his feet up the stairs, grasping the railing tightly.

"Don't ruin this night for us. I've been looking forward to making love to you all day." She stopped at the top step, and Cody almost bumped into her. "I'm tired of calling in Felipe."

Phantom pains throbbed from an impending Felipe punch. Each day Cody denied Andressa would mean getting beat, and it'd only be a matter of days before he became piranha food.

Inside the bedroom, Andressa wrapped her arms around his waist and kissed him; he didn't kiss her back. She pulled away and led him to the bed. "This isn't the Cody I remember. Kiss me."

He gave in and kissed her.

"No, you're still not with me." She jerked his shirt over his head and ran her hands over his chest before removing her own top. Her boobs were about busting out of her bra, and Cody closed his eyes, fighting the feelings stirring inside him. "Look at me," she demanded, and when he opened his eyes, she was braless.

He swallowed hard, and she smiled, taking his cheeks into her hands. Her lips prodded him on, and she pushed him backward onto the bed.

"Touch me." She nudged him onto the bed and grinded down on top of him, rubbing him, kissing him. He wanted to throw her off him, to scream at her to stop, but all he saw was Felipe's fist ramming into him relentlessly.

He had to get it over with fast.

It wasn't Andressa's plan though, and she made him pleasure her over and over, just as he had in the hotel room in Guatemala.

Except this time he didn't want it.

Chapter Ten

Day 4

Cody hated himself for giving in to her last night. His performance hadn't impressed her, but she'd been satisfied because, well... he'd given in to her.

He looked at the clock. Andressa's alarm had gone off at five-thirty, and he'd lain there the last hour beating himself up.

The door opened, and Andressa caught him with open eyes. "Rise and shine."

He pulled the covers to his chin, but Andressa swept over to the bed and crawled on top of him, straddling his body. "You should come work out with me. It's a great way to get energized in the morning."

"No thanks."

"We can figure out a routine that works best for your body. I've learned a lot from my personal trainer, so I can find a plan for you too. We can do yoga together." She tugged down the blanket and walked her fingers over his chest.

Not again.

"Meditation is great for the soul." Andressa rolled off of him. "I'm all sweaty, so I'm taking a shower."

Cody needed a shower too, to scrape off the Andressa slime. The water ran forever, and then she stayed in there doing her hair and face. He almost fell back asleep.

"Cody." Andressa's velvet voice jerked him awake, and he realized his mistake. "Cody," she said louder. He didn't want to look her way, but she wouldn't stand for his disobedience, and he'd get to see Felipe's fist again. He took his head out of the blanket.

Sure enough, Andressa stood there buck naked, back arched and chest raised. His eyes followed her curves from her boobs down her hips.

No, no, no, he thought, but his dick sprang to life. She sauntered over, her hips swaying, and ripped the blanket off the bed, getting on him faster than a tiger. If he could close his eyes and drift off to nowhere, it'd be so much better, but Andressa demanded a response, she demanded passion, and he forced it the best he could.

∗

All during their breakfast, a yogurt parfait for her, waffles for him, Cody thought about what he'd say to Andressa. She led him to the attached garage and opened the door. He grabbed her hand before she started the golf cart.

"Andressa," he said solemnly. "I didn't want to tell you this. Didn't want to worry you about my problems, but I thought you should know."

"What's wrong?"

"My mother's sick," he said, staring down at the seat and hoping this lie would work, earn some sympathy so she'd let him go.

"What do you mean?" She leaned forward, all her attention on him. He could do this.

"She has cancer, and I'm worried about her. She started chemo last month. I almost didn't go to Guatemala, and I need to talk to her or my dad and see how she's doing."

"I'm sure she's fine."

"But she's probably worried. This won't help her cancer battle." He flapped his t-shirt to cool down, not sure if it was the Amazon heat or his nerves that made him sweat.

"She'll be fine. The EUA has terrific doctors. Manaus does too. My uncle had lung cancer, but he beat it. I visited him every other day and sat with him. I spent hours there, and soon the cancer disappeared."

"Don't you think it would help my mom like your uncle?"

"Your father is there." She started the golf cart and got ready to go.

"I know, but he has to work too, and—"

"She will be fine," Andressa growled. "You are needed here." She stepped on the gas and roared out of the garage.

"Wait, what if you come with me?"

She laughed. "Did you forget what happened when I was in Guatemala for a few days? Everything fell apart. I can't leave for a few weeks, although I'd love to see New York."

A silent scream ripped through Cody. She had a damn answer for everything.

As Andressa zipped toward the kennels down the gravel road, Cody surveyed the thick trees. He'd hiked the forests in Wisconsin, but they were nothing compared to this. A skunk was about the worst animal he'd ever seen, and even then skunks couldn't kill you. Daddy long legs wouldn't kill you. Or mosquitoes either.

At the kennels, Andressa led him down the hall to the office. Miguel hunched over a computer, and another guy sitting next to him jumped to his feet, eyeing Cody curiously. "Bom dia, Andressa," he said.

"English, Levi." Andressa sighed. "We want Cody to feel welcome here." She nodded at him but made no move to introduce Cody.

Levi's lip curled up in a smirk. "Sorry."

Andressa turned back to Miguel, and Cody watched as Levi's gaze roamed down Andressa's body.

Miguel tossed a pen down on the desk. "Rodrigo's coming by soon."

Andressa spun toward him. "What? Why?"

"Enzo told him to come talk to you. He was supposed to be in town to meet Rodrigo about the money he owes, but Enzo's plans changed."

"Oh, and now I'm supposed to do Enzo's dirty work? If he's doing business in Manaus, he should be here to take care of it." Andressa paced back and forth across the room. "I'm always cleaning up his messes," she muttered and then looked up at Miguel. "Okay, get out. I need to make some calls."

The two guys shuffled out, and Cody checked for the tell-tale signs of guns. He couldn't tell on Miguel, but he saw the outline on Levi's body.

Andressa sat down and pulled out her phone. "Bom dia, papai." Andressa was silent for a moment before launching into a string of Portuguese. Rushed, tense words.

She spoke. She listened. She frowned.

Cody finally took a seat, not knowing what to do. Then she hung up the phone. She stared at the computer screen, and her fingers clicked furiously on the keyboard. He studied the rest of the room. He needed to get a sense of his surroundings and these people before he tried to escape.

The door opened, and Miguel escorted a gaunt man in dirty, ratty pants. Cody almost choked on the BO. The guy blurted something out in Portuguese.

Andressa sneered and turned to Cody. "This is Rodrigo. He is an addict who cares too much about his cocaine. It's why I don't allow my people to do drugs. If they do, Felipe has a nice talking with them before I get rid of them."

The guy didn't react to anything she said, and she spoke a bit of Portuguese to him. He sat down, and Cody cringed. The guy probably hadn't showered in a month.

"Cody, go find Levi. He should be down the hall. I'll be with you shortly."

In the hallway, Cody took a deep breath of fresh air and found Levi in another room, watching a video on the computer. A girl shrieked, and Cody stepped closer. Levi hit pause, but the picture was clear: two naked bodies going at it in bed, two women.

"What do you want?" Levi sniped.

"Andressa told me to wait here."

If Levi was watching porn, he was probably connected to the internet. Cody had to get Levi out so he could send out a message for help.

Miguel walked into the room and burst Cody's hope.

"Tolo," Miguel said sharply and continued on in Portuguese.

"Don't worry." Levi shook his head and hit the play button, the room filling with a girl pretending to be in ecstasy. "See this blonde. I fucked her once. She's just as hot in real life as she is on the screen." He looked to the computer, practically drooling.

"Shut that off. Andressa will be back soon."

"You're mad because you can't fuck girls like this anymore." Levi turned to Cody. "His wife keeps a tight grip on him. Maybe the new girl and her big tits will make him break free. Did you see her yet?"

"Get your ass out of that chair. We have work to do." Miguel folded his arms and glared. Levi shut down his video, and Cody crossed his fingers, hoping Levi would leave the computer on, but he didn't. He logged off.

No more chance to escape.

Chapter Eleven

Day 4

Andressa finally returned to Cody after twenty minutes and ordered him to follow her.

This second building was similar to the first, and she led him into the room with the dog runs. Four adult dogos hung out in their kennels, the other dog runs empty. The smell reminded him of home, of Mom's vet clinic, of all the animals she'd cared for over the years. Dogs and cats and other family pets.

"Braz, Fausto, Caio, Silva." Andressa stopped at the last cage and opened it up. Silva wandered out, tail wagging, and Andressa knelt down and scratched him behind his ears. "These are some of my boys."

"They're the stud dogs?"

Silva's back was about mid-thigh on Cody, and with his cropped ears, short hair, and muscular body, they looked similar to an all-white boxer, but a bit bigger. The puppies were much cuter than the adults.

"They're so much more. They are my champions." Andressa stood. The dog's head was almost waist high, his pointy ears standing at attention.

Cody reached out to pet him.

"Fale," Andressa said.

Silva barked loud, and Cody jerked his hand back. Andressa laughed. "He listens well, doesn't he? He's harmless though." She glanced at the dog. "Abaixe-se."

Silva dropped to the floor and lay down, his head held high. His big dark eyes peered up at Cody. "Go ahead and pet him," Andressa directed.

Cody held his hand out, palm up for Silva to sniff, and then pet his head. The dog was all muscle.

Andressa stepped away after saying something else to the dog, and he followed along with Cody.

"When I took over this kennel, it was nothing. Father put me in charge, and I built this business into what you see today.

"We have two sides. The other side breeds the best dogos in Brasil. Dogos are amazing. Strong and beautiful. They make ideal family dogs, are skilled hunters, and offer loyal protection, but they also make spectacular fighters."

They stopped in the front room. Pictures of adult dogos covered the walls. "Here's Silva. He is one fight away from being a grand champion."

Cody opened his mouth to ask what she was talking about, but she continued on.

"My dogos have spectacular bloodlines, which is why everybody wants them. I have the respect of the dog-breeding community, and now I have an in with the polícia. I won't be training the dogs, but I'll definitely learn about their techniques. It's a profitable business, but this is where I make most of my money. My dogs are the best fighters."

"You run dog fights." A frosty chill spread through him, colder than any Milwaukee winter.

"I don't run them. I win them. Dog fighting is a thrilling sport. To see the power and might these creatures have. It's ridiculous that we're driven underground." Her voice held so much disgust. "My dogs deserve to be fighting in the Arena Amazônia, not in an abandoned building." She adjusted the already-straight picture on the wall.

Cody had no idea what to say. The woman who despised processed foods, exercised religiously, and didn't allow drugs to be used by her employees ran a dog-fighting ring.

"Don't they fight until death?" He'd heard the news stories about gangs and dog-fighting rings. They chained up dogs and tortured them until they were vicious. Rottweilers, Pitbulls, German shepherds. His mother had treated abused and abandoned dogs, sometimes having to put them down because they were so close to death.

She looked at Cody as if trying to figure him out. "No, it's an unfortunate side effect for some dogs, but my dogs don't die. They win."

"But that's cruel."

She threw her hands in the air. "No, it's not. Cruel is when you abuse your dogs. Cruel is leaving them starving in the streets. Our dogs are treated well, given proper food and plenty of time to play."

One building housed dogs trained to be killers while the next held dogs that would be family pets. His stomach turned.

"Aren't you worried those dogs might hurt the kids?"

"Don't be stupid, Cody. They're completely separated. Our fighters aren't around the puppies. And even if they were, they wouldn't hurt them unless given an order." Her eyes glazed over as she stared at one of the pictures on the wall. "Silva is in training for his upcoming fight, and I want you to see him in action."

She led him down the hallway and out the back door onto the grass. At first, everything looked the same as the other kennels, but then Cody noticed the adult dogo with a huge metal chain around its neck. Levi threw the ball, and the dog chased after it, slowly.

Andressa tugged on his arm. "This way."

They stopped at a shelter—four corner posts supporting the tin roof. In the middle was a crude wooden structure surrounded by a worn dirt path.

"This is the catmill," Andressa said.

The catmill reminded him of his childhood, of the fair and riding the small ponies around and around in a circle. A pole stuck out of the ground in the middle, and attached to it was a second pole that ran parallel to the ground. Miguel leashed Silva to the end of the rope attached to the pole, and after a command, Silva lunged forward, trying to get at something in a harness hanging a few feet in front of him.

"What is that?" Cody asked as Silva rotated the catmill around. Wait—Cody focused on the squirming animal in front of Silva. "Is that a cat?"

"Yes. Cats work best. Hence the name." Andressa chuckled.

Silva quickly got to running speed, and Miguel headed over. "He got moving fast today."

"Why is he doing this? Why do you have a chain on his neck?" Cody choked back the bitter tang in his mouth.

"It thickens the skin on their necks and builds their upper body strength." Miguel nodded at the dog. "We start with small chains and build up to larger ones."

"But why?"

Both Andressa and Miguel stared at Cody like he was clueless. "Because it toughens their skin," Miguel finally said.

"It looks awful." Scaring a cat half to death just to train a dog.

"Silva's a strong dog." Andressa looked down her nose as she talked. "The chain is nothing to him. He wants to be out here running and training."

Yeah, whatever.

"True," Miguel said. "When he gets out of his pen, this is the first place he comes."

This couldn't be what Andressa wanted him for, to help train these dogs and take care of them.

"Look at him. Isn't he amazing?" Andressa gazed upon the dog running on the well-worn path. "He deserves the grand champion title." She sighed as if off in dreamland. "Our other dogos will get there too, but Silva is so close."

She rambled on about the dogs in the kennel, but all Cody thought about was the poor cat, how scared it was. He could relate.

Miguel left to go back to Silva, and soon the dog was slowing down. Miguel unhooked him and took off the chain from his neck, but he didn't move, watching intently as Miguel removed the cat from the harness and tossed it to the ground. The cat took off, and Silva stood still, his gaze following the cat's path. Miguel said something, and Silva charged after the cat. In seconds, the dog clamped down on the cat with its strong jaws. The cat squealed.

Cody gasped. "What are you doing?"

Silva flung his head back and forth, the cat screeching in his tight grasp. Cody covered his ears to block out the painful cries as the cat struck the ground over and over, bright red blood matting its gray fur. Cody grabbed his heaving stomach.

"Silva needs his reward." Andressa closed her eyes, her face lighting up. "He'll be my first grand champion. I'll prove Enzo wrong."

Silva dropped the cat's limp body onto the dirt and trotted to Miguel, who gave him healthy praise and petting.

Cody stared at the bloodied lump, feeling dirty, like he had blood on his own hands.

"It's a cat." Andressa's voice held a hard edge. "There are thousands of diseased and starving strays roaming around the city. We're doing the community a favor by getting rid of those feral things."

"But…" They murdered a cat. This wasn't okay—none of it was okay. "I don't even want to be a vet, and you brought me here to train your dogs to be killers? All I wanted was to work in a lab and find a cure for animal diseases. Not be the one to kill them!"

Her eyes narrowed into even slits, and she set her hands on her hips. "Maybe you need to go back to your room for a while. I have work to do." She spun around and trounced away. "And you can walk back by yourself."

Cody took deep breaths, his heart slowing down. It was a trick. Levi would probably follow him. He rushed away before she changed his mind. Felipe had to be around somewhere, but this might be his only chance. He took off down the driveway, hoping the end was close.

Chapter Twelve

Day 4

Cody's clothes stuck to his slick body as he made his way down the road, constantly checking over his shoulder. But nobody followed after him, and he passed by the house, heading toward the highway shown on the aerial photo. No voices, no Andressa, only the screeching of bugs and calls of birds.

Maybe they'd lied to him about the gate. Maybe, just maybe, he'd be on his way to freedom. Andressa counted on him to be compliant, to be afraid of Felipe. The driveway continued to wind through the trees, and Cody hurried, a small spring in his step.

Something rustled in the trees, and he stopped. A rabbit maybe—did rabbits even live in the Amazon? Probably not many since the boa constrictors and anacondas would eat them. A shiver wracked Cody's body. They didn't eat people though.

He eyed the trees, looking for signs of hidden cameras. Felipe hadn't shown up yet, so Cody kept going.

A ten-foot metal gate blocked his escape. Thick metal rods topped by decorative spikes would prove impossible to climb. A stucco wall flanked each side, also impossible to scale. The top of the solid wall had no protrusions, so even if he found a rope, there was nothing to attach it to if he tried to climb over. He peered down the side of the wall, but it was swallowed by the trees, no end in sight. It had to end somewhere.

Two eyes peered out of the window of a small guardhouse adjacent to the wall. Busted.

Cody fanned his back with his shirt, trying to gather his courage. Maybe he could reason with the guy.

Inside the shack, a guy sat stiffly, his suspicious eyes scrutinizing Cody. The room wasn't very big but held a desk and chair, small fridge and air conditioner. Six small TV screens lined one wall, but they were all black.

The man said something in Portuguese. He was the one who held Cody's arms when Felipe had beat him.

"Um. I only speak English. I'm Cody." He held out his hand, but the guy made no move. "I was wondering if you'd open the gate."

Sunlight sifted through the windows, letting in a lot of light, and a good view of all the trees surrounding them. The guy spoke unintelligible words again.

"I don't know Portuguese."

Idiot—Cody chastised himself. This guy didn't understand him. "Gate. Open?" He pointed to the window and slapped his hands together, then pulled them apart slowly. "The gate?"

The guy frowned and spoke rapidly in Portuguese.

"Cody, my man." A gruff voice sounded behind Cody. He jumped, whacking his hip into the desk. Felipe stuck his head into the shack. "You wouldn't be trying to leave, would you? Because I ran into Andressa, and she looks pretty pissed." He crossed his arms— his gigantic biceps bulging.

"I—no. I was just..." He scanned Felipe's tattoo-covered arm, a snake wrapped in leaves and branches. Felipe could wrap his arm around Cody's neck and squeeze the life out of him like an anaconda. It would take seconds.

The guard guy pointed at Cody, rambling on in Portuguese. The grin on Felipe's face grew, and he responded. They went back and forth as Cody stood there, his stomach tightening in anticipation of getting hit.

78

Felipe's lip curled. "Did you really think you could escape? We're in the middle of the rainforest. Besides, Raul wouldn't let you go without saying goodbye."

"No, I wouldn't. I wanted to see what was down here."

"Andressa instructed me to bring you back. Maybe you can go for a swim and cool off."

Oh shit—the river. Cody backed into the corner. He didn't want to die. There were so many things he hadn't done yet, and now they were going to throw him into the river, and he'd be bitten in two by the caimans, just like Silva did with the poor cat.

"I wasn't leaving, I swear. You don't have to throw me into the river." He held his hands up as if it'd prove to Felipe how gutless he was.

Felipe laughed. "Swimming. In her pool. Andressa suggested it because you hadn't been in there yet."

All the breath slipped out of Cody's lungs, and he leaned into the wall. He wouldn't die today.

"Besides. If we were going to throw you into the river, you'd be dead long before your body made a splash."

The hairs prickled on the back of Cody's neck again. Felipe was smiling, but serious.

Felipe waved his hand and disappeared outside. Cody stood there for a few seconds and then shot for the door. As he was about to shut it, Raul spoke. "I'm not dying for you, babaca."

Cody's mouth flapped, and he slammed the door and rushed after a strolling Felipe.

"He knows English?" Cody asked.

"Raul was playing with you." Amusement cloaked Felipe's eyes.

"He didn't look like he was playing."

"Nobody will let you out." Felipe whacked Cody in the arm. "Don't let him fool you. He may be quiet, but he's good. And he's a bit crazy. That's why they kicked him out of the…" He stopped, his brows furrowed. "They threw him out of officer training because he beat the shit out of another trainee."

"He what?"

"Andressa was pissed. We already had his older brother working for us—Bernardo."

"Wait, you mean Andressa's got a guy *in* the police department?"

"She's got a lot of guys. But we had Raul before he went in. The babaca got kicked out, so now he's stuck working the gate. He's not too happy about it either. Which is another reason not to piss him off."

Felipe rambled on about Raul, and back at the house Cody got his swimsuit and towel and headed to the pool. The cloudy sky kept the bright sun away, but not the intense heat. On the stone patio with drink in hand, for half a second he felt like he was at a resort and enjoyed the solitude.

He tossed his towel onto the beach chair, and a movement at the side of the house caught his eye. A woman knelt in the flower garden. Not Vera—the hair wasn't gray—and it wasn't Yasmin. Must be the new girl. Her head tilted up, and she studied him, giving a nod that wasn't quite a hello, but at least she acknowledged him. Yasmin still hadn't looked him in the eyes even once, the few times she'd been around him.

He gave the woman a wave and smile and slipped into the cool water. All his thoughts slowed as he floated on the surface. Andressa was somewhere around, but here he was free.

Back and forth he swam until his body started to tire. Cody climbed out of the water and froze. Felipe lay on one of the beach chairs, his nose in a book. He wore only his shorts, giving Cody a good view of his massive tattoo-covered arms and chest.

Felipe set his book down and grinned. "Andressa thought we should spend more quality time together."

Cody sighed and took a drink of his soda. He needed his brain and time to think, to put a plan together, to watch everybody and learn their weaknesses. Maybe somebody would leave a phone out or a computer on, and while he watched and waited, he'd gather supplies for a journey through the forest. He was safe as long as he didn't do anything dumb.

The door banged, and Andressa sauntered down the steps, two glasses of wine in her hands and a smile on her face. She bent over to set the wine down, and her cover-up fell open, revealing major cleavage.

"Cody and I need alone time," she said to Felipe as she waited for her kiss on the cheek from Cody. He gave her a quick peck, and she untied her cover-up and pulled it off. Holy hell—tiny bikini. Boobs about to pop out. G-string. Cody's shorts stirred, and he tried to settle himself down.

He looked to Felipe, who had the same expression on his face. He was her cousin for god's sake. Of course, then again, she was Cody's captor, so he shouldn't talk.

Felipe gathered his things, then patted Cody on the head. "He's been a good boy."

Cody swatted his hand away. Felipe left them alone, and with the way Andressa was eyeing him, Cody worried she'd climb on top of him right there. He breathed a sigh of relief when she sat on the beach chair.

After a sip of wine, she spoke. "I told Vera to make us a special dinner tonight to celebrate. I didn't have a chance to talk to my father, but Enzo was impressed. He always underestimates me because I'm a woman."

Her hand reached over to Cody's arm and slid up and down slowly. "Enzo's a bit old fashioned. Not like you. I need a man who treats me as his equal, not his conquest."

"You deserve more than that." Cody gave her what she wanted. What she really deserved was a jail cell.

"I'm so lucky to have found you." She stared at Cody with the I-want-to-have-sex look.

"What does Enzo do?" Cody blurted.

"He's head of the Belém operation."

"He breeds dogs there too?"

81

"No." She laughed. "He handles the distribution of their cocaine passing from Columbia through Manaus. He needs to stay away from the product. It'll be his downfall. I'd never put cocaine into my body, never risk my health over an artificial high. I'd prefer a natural high. I keep telling my father about Enzo's issues, but he doesn't listen."

Cocaine. He was almost sure she'd said cocaine.

Andressa rested her hand on his thigh, and he struggled for his words. "Did you say cocaine?"

"Marcos Cardoso came out of nowhere and built up our family name to what it is today. He controls a large share of cocaine that passes through Manaus."

Holy hell. Cody needed to pick his mouth up from the floor. He stared off into the trees, his eyes blurring. She was kidding. She had to be kidding. Was she kidding?

She wasn't kidding.

But her father got the award for community service from the mayor or somebody. He built huge buildings in downtown Manaus. He didn't run a cocaine cartel.

"I thought he was in construction? Didn't you say he built the skyscraper in the picture you have in the office?"

"He's in a lot of things, and construction is his favorite. He's not involved in the cocaine distribution as much anymore. You should see how he's rebuilt the neighborhoods in Manaus—providing inexpensive housing for those who need it. Poverty is terrible in our beautiful city, and my father is doing what he can to fight it. There should be more men like him."

Cody thought he got in deep when he found out about the dogs, but that was nothing. Andressa's family were the ones supplying the cocaine to the gangs who destroyed lives.

"I know you're not dumb enough to ever use cocaine." Andressa patted him on the arm as if it wasn't even a question.

"Of course not. I'd never."

It was the truth. He'd never even smoked pot before, much less taken anything hard.

Barely five minutes ago Cody held hope he'd be able to escape. Andressa was a part of a dog-fighting ring, but the vicious sport was the least of his concerns. She was part of a drug cartel.

He might never get out of here.

Chapter Thirteen

Day 5

Cody spent the next morning at the kennels, but then Miguel left, and Levi got all lazy, so Cody had nothing to do. He grabbed some paper to write out a letter to his parents. Longing for home filled him as he wrote the words, longing for the enthusiastic hug of Mom, the excitement that radiated off Dad when he spoke of some new treasure discovered in the ancient grounds of the Middle East. The laughs of his buddies and their silly inside jokes.

His first try was filled with the truth: how Andressa had kidnapped him and was keeping him hostage, of cocaine and training dogs to kill. But that letter was shredded and now lay in the trash. He scribbled out a second one, and ten minutes after he finished, Miguel returned, with Andressa on his heels.

"I have something for you." Cody held the letter out, covering his inner turmoil with a smile.

Andressa's eyes scanned the page, all the BS about the beautiful and intelligent woman he was living with, her thriving dog-breeding business, and how he wanted to spend the rest of his life in this paradise with her.

Writing it had torn him apart. His parents might actually believe it all, as stupid as the words were. At least they'd know he was alive… and safe for the time being.

Andressa's smile widened.

"Great. I'll send it off for you when I have time." She folded the letter and stuck it in her pocket. He had his doubts she'd even send it. "Now, I have some bad news for you. I need to go into town."

"You're leaving?"

"I'll be back in a while, but Felipe is around to keep you company. Why don't you hang out with him."

Cody could make a run for it. If, and that was a big if—if he got away from Felipe for a bit.

She gave him a kiss and left him at the kennel. His heart raced as he ran over his plan to slip away. He'd have at least four hours minimum she'd be gone. Their drive from the city to her place on that first day had been almost two hours, he figured, not to mention the time for whatever she was doing in town.

The timing was perfect. Felipe was unpacking a computer, and it was almost lunch.

"I'm heading to the house to see if Vera has lunch yet."

Felipe grunted, and Cody saluted him and left. It couldn't be that easy.

Once he got around the bend, he picked up the pace, only stopping at the garage to make sure Andressa's car had left. He was so close he tasted the freedom.

Felipe wouldn't expect him back for at least twenty minutes, and he'd get a good head start in the forest. He'd studied the aerial photo the last few days and figured out the path he'd take to the river. Then he'd follow the shoreline.

He packed a couple bottles of water, some food, and a knife from the kitchen into a small bag, which would have to do for now, then he slipped out the back door.

Cody skirted the side of the house, the grass crunching under his feet. The new girl—Simona was her name—was pulling weeds in the garden, and he'd have to pass on his way to the forest.

Oh god. She might turn him in.

He looked to the trees. Maybe he should wait until another day. But no, he was so close to freedom; he wouldn't give up now.

She glanced up at him, her eyes widening in surprise, and wiped her black hair from her forehead, leaving a smear of dirt. She studied him and his bag. "You going for a walk?" she said in a strong voice he hadn't expected. Her accent was a little different from the others.

"A walk, yeah. Um, in the rainforest."

Simona smiled. "Good luck. If anyone asks, I didn't see you." She hunched over again, and Cody couldn't speak, his throat tight with emotion.

"Thank you," he choked out.

"You'd better go," she said without looking up.

He glanced around the yard, said a quick goodbye, and rushed to the edge of the forest. The trees were thick, but not impassable, and he wandered far enough in to avoid being seen. He'd follow the tree-line around the property and then go toward the water.

The canopy blocked out the sun, but the air was still suffocating. He weaved around a tree with a bunch of small trunks in the shape of a teepee that met about eye level and then formed one solid trunk. If he wasn't in this situation, he'd stop to check it out. But he couldn't spare a second here.

He looked down and froze, his foot hovering over a large silvery web in the grass. He didn't want to see the spider that built that thing. He circled around and kept going.

The river came into view through the trees. He'd keep going until he found a house. Then he'd go to the road. His bare leg brushed against the bark of a tree as the leaves tickled his skin. They might not have poison ivy here, but they had tons of other dangerous plants.

At least the canopy of trees kept out the harshest of the sun's rays, but his pits were drenched, and his shirt clung to his damp skin. He wanted a drink, but he had to conserve water, so he kept going.

He imagined Andressa's hissy fit when she discovered he escaped and brushed something buzzing around his face. Surprisingly the bugs weren't as bad as he'd expected. He heard the noises, and saw a few, but didn't have to slap at his arms all the time like he did in the forests of Wisconsin. No dangerous animals yet either. He scoffed at the warnings Felipe and Daniel had given him.

A weird clicking noise stopped him in his tracks. The noise continued on, and he crept closer. In a small inlet, a bunch of animals moved around, clicking and clacking.

They had long brown hair, and their heads sort of looked similar to a rodent's, but their bodies were the size and shape of a pig: stubby legs with thick bodies, small ears, and narrow eyes. He wound around the trees and stood on the bank, watching the funny creatures. They were far enough in and didn't notice him, and he knelt and cupped his hand to dump water over his sweaty head.

A shot rang out, and Cody fell forward into the cold water. Hands grasped him hard and jerked him out. Something splashed close by as the animals squealed and ran farther into the forest. He was being dragged on his butt, and he struggled to get loose.

Felipe!

"Let me go! Let me go!" Cody yelled, grappling for a small tree, for something to hold on to and pull himself away. If he could get loose, knock Felipe down, he might make it to the water and swim away.

"Get away from the water," Felipe growled. The butt of the gun poked Cody's back, and he stopped fighting. Felipe released him.

"Why'd you shoot at me?" Cody backed away, wiping mud from his face. Scummy, rancid water dripped from his drenched shorts.

"I didn't shoot at you, burro. I was shooting at them." He pointed to the river. Cody scanned the surface. Two eyes seemingly floated on top the water, two dark penetrating eyes attached to a body concealed by the murky water.

"What the hell is that?" Cody focused in on the black shape in the water, at least ten feet long. A croc?

"Caimans. See how they're stalking the capybaras? You're not exactly their target, but if you'd been splashing on the edge of the water, they might've come after you."

Cody jumped back and slammed into a tree trunk. He'd been about ten feet away from a hungry monster. Instead of making it to freedom, he would've bled out on the banks of the river from a missing arm or leg, or who knew what.

"Let's go." Felipe waved, and Cody crawled to his feet, his body trembling.

Andressa was gonna kill him. Felipe had saved him just to bring him back to get his ass beat.

"Just let me go. I won't mention it. I won't go to the police."

Felipe wrinkled his nose. "You think the police would help you? We own the police." He stalked through the trees, gun in hand, and Cody chased after him.

"I'll just go home. Please. She'll kill me."

"No, man. You can handle another beat down."

Cody cringed with a look at Felipe's fists. Felipe turned around and stared at him. "I'll tell you what. You tell Andressa what happened, so I don't have to, and I'll take it easier on you. Not after today though. No more favors. No more Mr. Nice Guy."

"You've been Mr. Nice Guy?" Cody didn't want to see nasty Felipe.

Felipe snorted and skirted a tree. "You don't want to see me go one hundred percent. You won't come back from that."

"Did you see me leave?"

The snicker from Felipe sent Cody even lower. "I came back to tell Vera to send milk along with the food. About then, the perimeter warning system sounded. It works off motion detection."

"You have cameras around here?"

"No. I said motion detection sensors. We have cameras around the buildings, but the sensors picked you up."

"Why are you telling me all this?"

"Because I want to keep you alive. Believe it or not, I don't enjoy hurting people. So you need to know you can't get out of here. I gave you a choice, so make it before we get to the house." He pushed off through the trees, and Cody followed. There was nothing else he could do.

*

After showering and hiding out in the bedroom for a while, Cody spied Andressa in the office and motioned to Felipe, who was camped out on the couch in front of the TV. "I'm ready to tell Andressa," Cody headed toward the executioner.

She jumped up from the desk and hugged him, her eyes weary. "I missed you. It's been a long day, and all I want to do is have a nice dinner and a glass of wine with you."

"The conference call with your dad and Enzo didn't go well?" Felipe asked.

"No." She let out a big breath of air and fell into the seat, rubbing her temples. "They can find another place to keep Enzo's product. I told them not on my grounds. He doesn't want to spend the money setting up additional security." She closed her eyes and took a deep breath. "So what did you do while I was gone?"

"Um, I've got something to tell you." Cody backed up against the wall. She would skin him alive, and he'd end up in the river dead anyway.

"What is it?" She scrutinized his face and then eyed Felipe.

"Well, today I decided to go for a walk. Um, more than a walk. I—"

"Me and Cody had an adventure." Felipe plopped down in the other chair. "He wanted to see the river but got ahead of me. He almost got in between a bunch of capybaras and some hungry caimans. You almost lost him." Felipe chuckled.

What in the world? Cody shut his gaping mouth.

"How could you be so stupid?" She glared at him and then turned to Felipe. "What happened?"

Felipe related the story, leaving out a few pertinent details.

"Well, I'm glad you're safe. Don't go off on your own again." She sat, hands folded on her desk, in lecture mode. "The rainforest can be a dangerous place."

"I won't." And he wouldn't. He had to figure things out better. He couldn't get out the front gate or slip through the perimeter fence, but he would earn her trust until she decided to bring him into town.

His fuzzy head didn't allow him to think it all through right now, but he agreed with Andressa on one thing: the rainforest was dangerous. He needed a glass of wine or two. Maybe a whole bottle.

"Why don't I get the wine ready for you," he said.

"You do that. I have to finish a couple things here and shower. Then I'll be down. Tell Vera dinner will be in an hour."

Felipe followed him out and shut the door behind them.

"Thanks for... you know."

"I didn't do shit. Andressa never asked if you tried to escape. I didn't lie. If she had asked, I would've told her."

"Well, thanks anyway."

"No problem. But remember..." Felipe wound up and punched Cody in the stomach. He gasped and fell to his knees in pain. "This hit was only fifty percent. From now on, it'll be one hundred. And one of these times, something's gonna break."

"There won't be a next time." Not for a while at least.

Felipe stared down at Cody, and then he shot out the front door.

Cody was alone.

Chapter Fourteen

Day 8

One week in captivity, and Cody hadn't found any weaknesses. Nobody left any phones around, no open connections to the internet—they always logged out. Every. Single. Time.

He'd roamed to the other end of the driveway and found a shed in the back, and he'd gone to the gate several times, but somebody was always there. He'd even taken out one of the puppies, under the pretense of playing, and let the thing cross into the trees. Sure enough, Miguel showed up to bitch him out for setting off the sensors.

Getting the other people there to warm up to him wasn't proving easy either. Vera spoke to him occasionally when Andressa wasn't around, but Yasmin hardly looked at him—not like he'd get much out of her with her broken English, and he'd only caught a few glimpses of the other girl again, Simona.

Miguel treated him like an idiot, Levi treated him as a curiosity, and Daniel ignored him.

Felipe on the other hand, hardly ever shut up, always talking about something. At least he made Cody's life more bearable. Ironic considering the hell Felipe had put him through those first few days.

Andressa's alarm rang, nudging Cody toward his daily nightmare.

"Make love to me, Cody," she whispered in his ear. Their morning routine and their nightly routine.

As usual, he forced a smile and his enthusiasm, helped her slip out of her lingerie, and waited for it to end.

He'd once thought it'd be cool to be with a woman who wanted to have sex every day… two times a day, but his opinion had changed.

After Andressa left him to do her morning workout, he lay in bed. He'd bitched so often about getting up and going to class, about the homework and tests, but from now on he'd never take it for granted.

Classes would be starting soon, and his parents would have to contact the school to say he was missing. Dad was probably at the police station in Flores every day, calling the embassy, maybe even hiring a private investigator and doing whatever it took to get Cody back.

He didn't feel like climbing out of bed, but he showered and dressed before Andressa returned, and wandered downstairs to the kitchen.

"Good morning, Mr. Cody," Vera said.

"Morning." No, it wasn't a good morning, and it never would be as long as he was imprisoned here. He glanced out the window to the cloudy sky. He'd swear it rained almost every day, and he was damn sick of it. His captivity and the weather weren't Vera's fault though.

"How do you say good morning in Portuguese?" he asked.

She smiled, spreading much-needed warmth to him. "I seem to remember strict instructions about how this was an English-only home now."

"I know." Cody slumped in the chair and stared outside as the rain pelted the window.

"Bom dia," Vera said.

Cody repeated her words back.

"Boy, if I can learn a few words a week, it'll only take me twenty years to get fluent." He laid his forehead on the table with a thunk. This was hopeless. Even if he escaped, he couldn't communicate with people. Sure, some Brazilians would speak English, but with his luck, he wouldn't find them.

Vera raised a bowl of creamy pink yogurt in the air. "Iogurte. Would you like some?"

"Hey, that sounds pretty close." He grasped onto that tiny bit of familiarity. "Your-gur-tay," he said. "Sure, I'll have some, thanks."

"Very good." Vera smiled and told him the word for the strawberries on the counter.

If nothing else, if Cody escaped to a market, he wouldn't starve.

He sighed at the dark skies out the window. Rain, sun, rain, sun—an endless cycle with little variation in temperature. It got old.

The day flew by as Cody ran the dogs on their treadmill and did other things. Silva was the biggest and strongest of the pack, Lucio, the newest and youngest, lacked the stamina of the older dogs, and all the others were somewhere in between.

Miguel released Cody, and he walked out the door to head to the house. Two vehicles were parked outside. Freedom. He'd drive through gunfire to break through the front gate. The truck would come out battered and bruised, but he'd escape.

Levi about bulldozed him over, and he followed Cody's gaze to the cars. "It won't happen."

"What won't happen?"

Levi smirked. "Andressa had a long talk with us, and quite frankly, I'd prefer to live. So don't be asking me for help."

"I wasn't planning on it." Of course he would've, but he wouldn't admit that now. Cody folded his arms. "I'm not planning on leaving."

Levi snorted. "You won't find the keys, and even if you did, you'd be dead before you got through the gate." He patted the gun on his hip. "You're probably dead anyway once Marcos finds out about you."

"He already knows." Cody tried to act confident, but he really had no idea what Marcos knew.

A darkness emanated from the grin on Levi's face. "Maybe, maybe not. But I can tell you one thing: if he doesn't want you here, you'll be dead and gone. No proof you were even here. Andressa can't save you from him."

The chill raced up Cody's spine as Levi stared him down, face serious as stone.

"Did you hear how he got started? He was in the prison library reading. This guy comes in and starts making trouble. Marcos stands up and walks over all calm-like. Like he's gonna try help the two guys work it out. And he pulls out a shank and slits the guy's throat. Struts away and goes and sits down at the table again while the life is gurgling out of the guy he slit."

Cody was dead. No way he'd get out of Brazil alive.

Levi chuckled. "You can't read the guy. He might be planning your death while telling you he likes your tie."

Cody tried to swallow away the bitterness in his mouth, but the lump made it hard. He didn't want to meet Marcos—he didn't want to die.

No. He wasn't going to die. Andressa wouldn't do something to defy her father on such a level. She had too much respect for him... he hoped.

"Tolo," Levi spit out. Cody had never asked anybody what the word meant, but the meaning was pretty clear now.

"What?" Cody's head snapped up to find Levi scowling.

"Andressa's giving you the fucking world. She brings you into the Cardoso family, and you act like you don't want to be here. This is Marcos fucking Cardoso. They sent him to a Columbian prison, and he took over the whole place in two years. Two short years and he has people groveling at his feet. Doing whatever he wanted. He's the king now, and for whatever stupid reason, his daughter wants you, but you're too dumb to see what she's offering. You don't deserve the shit in her toilet."

Levi stalked off to his car and slammed the door before peeling away. Cody blocked his face from the dirt and rocks shooting up at him. The asshole was full of it, jealous of Cody and trying to scare him. Marcos was probably badass, but if he'd killed someone in prison, he'd still be there.

God, he sure hoped that was the case.

Cody glanced down the road to the house, not wanting to return to the prison warden who now ruled his world.

Chapter Fifteen

Day 8

Cody trudged to the house and found the office empty; he didn't even know where Andressa had been all day. He wanted to ask about Levi's stories, but he wouldn't. She'd laugh and call him an idiot for believing it all.

The cabinet doors below the fish tank were open, and a woman was on her hands and knees half inside the cabinet. Simona. She pulled out a hose and attached it to a drain on the floor inside the cabinet.

She glanced up at Cody, and her face softened into a smile, but she got right back to work. Her weary eyes and the ugly gray uniform aged her, but she couldn't be much older than Cody.

"I'm Cody. We haven't officially met." He moved toward her and held out his hand.

"Simona." She nudged over the stool and stepped up to reach the top of the open tank. Her body remained still as she stared into the water, plastic tube in hand.

Vera padded into the room and glanced at Simona. "Go ahead. They won't bite."

"Bite?" Cody laughed. Simona eyed him, her cute nose wrinkled, before looking back at the tank. Vera wasn't smiling like it was a joke either. "Why would they bite?"

"They're piranhas." Simona grimaced.

"What? Why would Andressa have piranhas?"

"Because she's Andressa Cardoso." The malice in Simona's words was strong, but she clamped her mouth down and looked toward the steps and around the room, but nobody was around. Her body relaxed.

"She's joking, right?" Cody looked to Vera for an answer before walking closer to the tank. He couldn't blame Simona for being freaked out. He wouldn't want to put his hands anywhere near the water either, just in case the piranha were jumpers.

"No." Vera studied Simona. "But they're more scared of you than you are of them."

Simona gripped the hose tighter, holding it above the water's surface.

"Young piranha are actually skittish," Vera continued. "A bit shy. I suggest you finish the job, Simona." Vera spun around and left the room.

Simona bit on her lip and closed her eyes. After opening them, she stuck the end of the hose into the water and squeezed the large bulb attached to the tube. Her eyes flicked back and forth between the swimming piranhas as the vacuum sucked out the water.

"Would you like help?" Cody asked. He was a little taller, and it might be easier for him to handle the vacuum.

The clicking of heels on wood echoed through the room. Andressa marched down the steps, dressed to impress in her usual business attire.

"You're not bothering the help, are you, Cody?" Andressa swooped in next to him and held out her head, waiting for a kiss. He obliged. "Cleaning the tank is a delicate job, and Simona is very clumsy. I wouldn't want her to slip. The piranhas attack anything warm-blooded that falls into the water." She was speaking to Cody but looking at Simona, who continued draining the water. "Let's go to my office."

Before the door shut, the smile fell from her face, and she crossed her arms. Cody felt like a teenager in the principal's office waiting for a lecture.

"You shouldn't be speaking with Simona. She's a conniving bitch and can't be trusted. She exaggerates and often lies, even about minor things. I can't keep all her stories straight. Stories about her father being mayor of their village or how she'd gotten pregnant and kicked out of the house. Or how her mother died in a car accident. It isn't true. She's always looking for sympathy for things she doesn't deserve."

"Why did you hire her then?" Cody clamped his mouth shut at Andressa's expression.

"She owes our family a debt. She's a gambling addict who got way in over her head, and we saved her from some awful people. She owes us her life, but she's nothing but an ungrateful brat."

Andressa stomped around her desk over to the fish tank. The silver fish swam along the length of the tank, and Andressa trailed her finger along the glass, following it.

"Is that a piranha too?" he asked. It had the same shape as the others but different coloring. "Why's it by itself?" The damn things were so ugly.

"Princesa is special. A black diamond piranha," Andressa's voice was low and controlled. "She doesn't play well with others."

The piranha wasn't the only one.

Andressa turned around and smiled. "You've had a busy day. The sun's out now, so let's go get some sun. That's why you traveled south for your spring break after all."

No, he didn't. He went south to help unfortunate people in a poor village.

A half hour later, he lay next to the pool in the oppressive heat. DeShaun would love it here. Lake Michigan was *too flipping cold* he always said. Cody chuckled at his best friend, the loneliness hitting him once again. He'd never get home to see his friends and family.

Andressa talked non-stop, jumping from business matters he knew nothing about to her father's latest accomplishments—the public ones, not the cocaine cartel ones. None of what she said jived with the story Levi told him, but Cody wouldn't come out and ask about her father being in a Columbian prison.

After Vera refilled their lemonade glasses a second time, he had to admit that for being a kidnap victim, he had it pretty easy. Nobody was hurting him—as long as he did what Andressa wanted, and other than fulfilling her twice-daily needs, she hadn't wanted more.

Andressa stretched out on her stomach, her head facing away from him. He followed the curve from her shoulders to her backside, barely covered by the teal triangle of fabric. The bikini bottom tied at the sides at her hips, and he wanted to reach over to tug the knot loose along with the ties to the top. The desire stirred inside him. *Damn, Cody. That is wrong on so many levels.* He leaned his head back and closed his eyes as the shame filled him.

"I should invite everybody over. Carolina's been dying to meet you, but she's been busy and hasn't had a chance to stop by yet." Andressa flipped onto her back.

Cody couldn't get a read on the situation. Carolina was one of the few girls Andressa talked about, but he never got the impression they were best friends. Maybe it was because she was Felipe's girlfriend.

"I keep telling Enzo he needs to stop by, but Father keeps him busy." Andressa studied her nails, probably looking for imperfections.

"Yeah, that'll be great." Meet the coke-addicted brother? No thanks. A slight frown creased Andressa's forehead. "Where's he live again?" Cody asked quickly.

"Belém. My father's given him control over the operations there. It's a tremendous responsibility." She pressed the glass of lemonade against her cheek. "I don't see my brothers as much as I want, and now I'm kind of the only sister, so they all want to take care of me."

"What do you mean you're *kind of* the only sister?"

She huffed, her face darkening. "Emily thinks she's better than us. After college, she told my father she didn't want to work for him. She wasn't proud to be a Cardoso anymore. Of course this happened right after he finished paying for her psychology degree, and then she skipped off to Lima. Good riddance though. She's like our mother was. Self-centered and ungrateful. I'm pretty sure we won't see her ever again."

Cody tried to keep the shock off his face. The anger seethed out of her voice, and his blood chilled, a tough feat in these ninety-degree temperatures.

"She abandoned her family as if we were nothing," Andressa continued. "I haven't talked to her for years, but Father keeps track of her though. He doesn't trust her either."

Holy hell. "So, um…"

There had to be more to the story, way more from the way Andressa was acting, but Cody wasn't sure he wanted to know what the sister did. At least Marcos hadn't snuffed out her life like the guy in prison. Or maybe he'd told Andressa that Emily moved away when she was buried in a shallow grave.

If that's how Marcos treated his family, Cody didn't stand a chance.

He had to lighten her mood a bit. "Maybe she just likes Peru better."

"Do you think this is funny? My sister betrayed our family, and you're taking her side?"

"I didn't—"

"Why can't you be supportive of me? Family is everything, and she renounced the Cardoso name. What kind of woman does that? What kind of woman disavows the family who loves her?" She rambled on about the importance of family loyalty until Cody couldn't take it anymore.

"What about my family?" He clenched his jaw. "What about my mother and father and aunts, uncles, cousins? What about my friends?"

"Do you have to make this all about you?" she snarled. "Why must every conversation lead back to you? You miss your family—I get it. But you made a choice, and you need to live with that choice."

Andressa leaned back and grasped the armrests. "I don't want to talk about her anymore."

Arguing was pointless: Andressa wouldn't quit until she won, or he'd end up being slapped.

"I'm sorry." Cody cringed at his wimpy groveling. He did nothing wrong, but after this time with her, the words just spilled out automatically.

"I heard you had a busy day at the kennels. Miguel said you're picking everything up pretty easily."

Of course she was keeping tabs on him. Felipe was probably lurking around in case he tried to escape too. Cody wasn't dumb. He needed a well thought-out plan. Danger wasn't imminent, so he would play her game, be her boyfriend, take his time, and then he would be gone as soon as he had the chance.

He told her about his day, how much he learned, and how interesting he thought the whole dog-fighting thing was.

And she believed his BS. At least for now.

Chapter Sixteen

Day 11

Cody headed downstairs after showering. Several days had passed, and he considered asking for a black marker to keep track of his days in captivity on the wall, but he was pretty sure she'd give him a big fat no.

He let the kitchen door fall shut behind him. "Bom dia, Vera."

"Good morning to you too." She wiped her wet hands on her towel and faced him with friendly eyes.

Cody was about to tell Vera Andressa would be down soon, but the door flew open, and Andressa marched into the kitchen, surveying the room with her hands on her hips. "Vera, today is not the day to be moving slow."

"I'm sorry, Miss Andressa. Please go sit, and I'll bring your food out in a moment."

"And don't forget the flowers. I see Simona hasn't gotten them yet," Andressa huffed and clutched at Cody's hand. "Come on, baby." She jerked him away, and they sat at the table in the other room.

Within a minute, Vera served the food. Cody dished up a bowl, heavy on the granola, light on the yogurt.

"I have fun news," Andressa said after taking a drink of juice. "We're having company tonight. Enzo will be here for dinner, and my other friends will be by later."

Cody's head whipped up. Enzo—the brother who ran the cocaine cartel? The yogurt in his mouth soured.

Andressa laughed. "Don't look so worried. He might be a little slow to warm up at first, but if I love you, then he'll love you too."

"Does he know how I... How we... I mean, how I got here?"

Andressa's face tightened. "Yes, he knows you decided to move here with me after we fell in love in Guatemala?" Her spoon clinked on the bowl as she set it down. "Enzo knows we just met, and he fully supports our relationship."

Maybe Enzo could save him.

Cody almost snorted. He was probably as crazy as his sister, especially if he knew what was going on. Did their father know too? What about her mother? She'd never said much about their mom, and Andressa had made it clear her feelings for her sister, but he still hadn't put together the whole family picture.

"You never said. How many brothers do you have?"

"Enzo. Jorge's in Bogota handling the Columbian side of the business, and Tito..." She pursed her lips. "He's such a disappointment to my father. No brains and he drinks too much. He and Enzo got into trouble in Venezuela."

"What did he do?"

"Tito slept with the girlfriend of this guy—who wasn't very happy about it. Tito and Enzo beat him so badly, the guy ended up in a wheelchair. Enzo got out of town, but Tito stuck around bragging about what he'd done. The problem was the guy was the son of a city official of Maracaibo. There was no way my father could get him out of his mess." Andressa shook her head with disgust. "And now he's rotting away in prison. He deserves to be there though."

A heaviness settled over Cody. This story just got better and better.

"Enzo will end up like Tito if he's not careful." She waved her hand dismissively in the air. "Enough about them. We have a lot to get done today before he arrives, so go shower and come out to the kennels when you're done."

Enzo wouldn't help him—nobody would, but maybe Cody could get on his good side, make him think Cody wanted to be here. It would make things easier when it was time to escape.

*

Enzo grinned down at his sister, gathering her into a big hug. Then Enzo's head swung to Cody. He stood tall, his dark eyes taking in Cody with a sneer, and spit out words Cody didn't understand. The body language was clear.

"Enzo!" Andressa stomped her foot, the Portuguese sailing out of her mouth. Her hands waved wildly, pointing between the two men. Enzo shot back, and Cody stood there, palms sweating.

The arguing stopped, and they stared each other down. Neither blinked, and the silence hung in the cool chill of the air conditioning.

Footsteps echoed from the foyer, and Daniel said something. Andressa's head tilted, and a smile spread on her face. Enzo threw his hands in the air and stomped off.

She looped her arm through Cody's and tugged him forward. "Don't worry about him. He's acting like an over-protective brother."

Enzo beelined to the bar, pulled out a bottle of liquor, and poured himself a shot. The drink went down, and he took another before grabbing a can of soda and mixing a drink.

"Cody, huh?" He rolled his eyes. "She had to find an American."

Cody scanned Enzo's body, looking for the outline of a gun, but saw nothing. The holster could be on his ankle.

"Where you from? New York or Los Angeles?" Enzo asked.

"Milwaukee," Cody replied, waiting for direction from Andressa.

"Where the fuck is Milwaukee?"

"It's in Wisconsin, Enzo." Andressa folded her arms and glared. "Milwaukee is the largest city in the state of Wisconsin, and it lies on one of the Great Lakes. The metro area is over two million people, and they're an hour from Chicago."

Holy hell—she knew way too much about him, but she had his phone, could scour his social media sites and look up his friends. She'd probably seen pictures of his parents and buddies, knew his address and favorite hangouts. He tugged at the tight collar of his shirt.

"When are we eating?" Enzo glanced to the table with a bored expression.

Andressa frowned. "Pour us wine, and I'll go check on Vera." Andressa spun around and walked away as Enzo smirked at Cody.

"Wine. Can't handle anything stronger, huh?" He headed for the bottles of wine in the corner. Cody watched as he poured the wine and topped his own drink with liquor.

Neither of them said another word until Andressa returned, and Cody handed her the glass.

"How's Simona working out?" Enzo chuckled. Andressa's lips stretched into a thin line as her eyes narrowed on her brother.

"Danilo didn't warn me about her attitude."

Enzo shrugged. "She came cheap."

"Next time, send ugly girls because I'm tired of Levi chasing after them."

"She hot?" Enzo raised his brows, glanced at Cody, and laughed. "Maybe I should ask him."

Andressa slapped Enzo in the back of the head, and he laughed harder.

"Which one is Simona? I can't remember," Cody said. It was the exact answer Andressa needed to hear, and her face brightened. Despite the drab clothes, Andressa made the girls wear, Simona was hot—not to mention her big chest.

Surprisingly, dinner ran smoothly with no more arguments or snarky comments from Enzo. Cody sat silent most of the time while

Andressa and Enzo discussed business. Every once in a while, Enzo would slip back into Portuguese, and she'd scold him and demand he speak English. Then she'd pat Cody's thigh as if to offer reassurance.

"Oh, by the way, I need Felipe tomorrow night," Enzo said.

"What for?" Suspicion clouded her eyes.

"We need to *talk* to a few people." He eyed Cody for a moment. "There's a small group of dealers who moved into my territory. They're working for Vega. Romano's been there to discuss things with him, but Vega's having a hard time understanding how things work. I need Felipe to crack some heads."

"No," Andressa replied without hesitation.

Enzo's eyes narrowed on his sister, his jaw working. "It's business."

"I said no."

"It's family business, and if you want to call Marcos, we'll call him right now." Enzo slapped his phone on the table.

"Fine," Andressa harrumphed. The steam about rose off her face, but she pursed her lips and called Vera for dessert.

Ten minutes later, a loud voice boomed, and Cody spun around. Felipe strutted into the room, his arm hooked around the waist of a thin, short girl.

Andressa headed to the couple, and the two women did the kissing cheek thing. Both girls chatted enthusiastically, and Felipe smiled down at them before giving Cody a head nod.

"Olá, linda." A second guy stepped up behind Andressa. She gasped and flung her arms around his shoulders.

"Tomás?" she squealed and said something in Portuguese.

Whoa—what? His hands gripped her ass as his lips lingered in a steamy kiss.

Something stirred inside Cody, and Enzo chuckled, jolting Cody back to real life. *No. No. No.* He would not be jealous of Andressa.

Finally, their lips broke apart, and she led him toward the bar, babbling in Portuguese as she dug drinks out, and a third guy wandered into the room. She gave him a welcome, minus the kiss.

Cody was forgotten, at least temporarily. He should try leave the room, but she'd get pissed for sure.

"Andressa," Enzo said along with something else in Portuguese, including Cody's name.

Her eyes flew open, and she spun around. Everyone stared at Cody while she spoke in Portuguese, her hands gesturing wildly. He heard his name several times but understood nothing else.

Enzo interrupted her and said something, a stupid smirk on his face.

"Não." She shook her head, then faced Mr. Tall, Dark, and Handsome. Her fingers trailed down his cheek as she spoke to him. She kissed his lips, then drew back.

The guy smacked her in the ass. She giggled and laid his arm across her shoulder. Maybe this guy was Cody's salvation, his freedom. The weight on his shoulders lifted slightly.

"Cody," Andressa said. "I want you to meet everyone." She buzzed through the names, and he repeated them in his head. Carolina was with Felipe, Tomás—his ticket out of there, and the last guy, Luiz.

The group headed to the bar, Andressa staying close to Tomás. Carolina stuck her nose into the vase of flowers sitting out. "These are beautiful, Andressa. Are these orchids from your garden? I didn't see them out front."

"Yes, I put in a second garden. It was a lot of work, but they're stunning, aren't they?"

Cody's lip curled up. He'd been there for almost two weeks, and he hadn't seen Andressa once in her garden. Not even to cut the flowers.

The hour dragged on, and Cody switched to Brazilian beer. He wanted a Bud Light—just one—and to get out of there, but he was forced to listen to conversations he didn't understand. The only good thing was how Andressa remained attached to Tomás, making eyes at him.

If she got together with this guy, Cody could be on his way home. He'd call his parents and assure them he was okay, and he would get back without missing hardly any days of school.

Enzo stepped around the bar and grabbed another beer. Before returning to his seat, he nudged Cody's shoulder. "She told them you're a foreign exchange student. Going to college here for a year."

"Why would I care?" Cody wouldn't react, even if a little jealousy stirred inside.

Enzo grimaced. "You know she's fucking crazy."

Yeah, asshole, I'm living it.

"There was another guy before you," Enzo continued, "but she got tired of him. She fed him to the dogs when he got to be too much trouble."

Felipe lied. Cody's heart thumped so damn hard in his chest, it was about to break through. He held his drink with his clammy hands. He would die right here in this jungle. He glanced over at Felipe and spotted the outline of his gun under his shirt. Felipe would shoot him in the head and bury him in an unmarked grave.

Enzo chortled, drawing the attention of the others.

"What's so funny?" Andressa eyed him suspiciously.

"Nothing. Just told him what happened to your other *foreign exchange student.*"

"What?" She glared at her brother.

"Fed him to the dogs."

Everyone burst out laughing, except for Cody and Andressa, whose nasty look deepened.

"Don't worry." Felipe sniggered. "He was dead first."

Andressa shot her evil eye at him too. They weren't serious. They couldn't be… Everyone was laughing. But after everything he'd learned, Cody wasn't sure.

"Don't listen to them, Cody." Andressa huffed. "There was no other guy."

Luiz clapped his hands together. "Let's get this party started. I'm in the mood for a little more fun."

The group headed to the couches, and to Cody's relief, Andressa snuggled up to Tomás. Now was a great time to escape to his room.

Cody poked her shoulder, avoiding Tomás's dark stare. "I'm going upstairs."

"No. You can stay."

"But I'm—"

"Sit," she said sternly, and Cody sunk down next to Carolina. It barely took half a second for Andressa to forget about him again.

"It's nice to finally meet you." Carolina gave him a friendly smile. "I've asked Andressa a hundred times when I can meet the new boyfriend, but she kept making excuses." She laughed, obviously unfamiliar with the real story.

"It's been a busy few weeks." He shrugged, not knowing what to tell her.

"So, where you from in the EUA? My family considered a trip there years ago, but we didn't end up going. Someday I will. I want to go to New York, but only if we go in the summer. Or Disney World. Felipe promised he'd take me there. Is it true you get to meet the princesses?"

Cody glanced at Felipe. The tough guy who liked to kick ass promised to bring his girlfriend to meet princesses at Disney World. "Um, yeah. You can take pictures with them."

"Happily ever after—what every girl wants, right?" Carolina nudged him in the arm with a smile.

Happy could wait. Freedom was all he wanted. "So what do you do?" he asked.

"I work at an eco-resort."

"Oh, do you manage it?"

"No. I clean rooms," Carolina replied.

"Oh." Not what Cody was expecting.

"There's nothing wrong with cleaning rooms," she said slowly.

Oh crap. "No, I didn't mean anything by it. It's just…" He glanced at Andressa, who was dressed so fancy, and the preppy guys.

Not to mention the cars he saw Enzo and Felipe drive. She was staring at him, and he knew he could get into trouble for insulting Andressa, but he felt the truth was the best way to go.

"Andressa seems to only like the best, and I assumed her friends would all be a little stuck-up too. But you're not."

Carolina chuckled and looked at Andressa, who had a tight grip on Tomás. She leaned closer to Cody and spoke with a quiet voice. "I'm sure Uncle Marcos could provide a more prestigious job for me, but I'd rather find my own and not be in debt to the family." She sighed and glanced at Felipe. "One of us is enough."

"What do you mean?"

The bright smile returned. "I'm actually training with one of the tour leaders. Juan has brought me on the caiman tours, and I've been learning all about them."

Cody had been so close to getting snapped in two by those caiman jaws. Who knew what would've happened if Felipe hadn't come along.

"Like boat tours?" he asked

She laughed. "Yes, tourists really enjoy the piranha fishing too."

Nope, he wouldn't try a water escape, not unless he could build a raft. As long as he was out of the water, he'd be okay. But there's no way to build a raft without anyone noticing, not to mention getting past the sensors in the trees on the way to the river.

"I bet you'd be good with the tourists." It was the truth. She had the personality and spunk.

"I do okay, but I need to learn everything first, learn more about the wildlife and plants."

"Felipe has been teaching me a lot about the dogs. I hope I don't end up getting fed to them, or the piranha, like the last guy."

Carolina pursed her lips, then glanced at Felipe. A small laugh escaped her mouth. "You do realize they were joking. There was no other guy."

Her weary voice made him want to ask more, but if he said too much, Carolina might report back to Andressa.

"I knew that." He forced a laugh, pretending he'd been joking too.

Cody's mouth dropped at the sight in front of him. Enzo was mixing a pile of white powder on a mirror with a razor. He split it several times over and then spread it out into a thin line.

"Carolina, pass it down to Cody." Enzo pointed at him and slid the mirror down.

"No thanks," Cody said. Even if he had the courage to defy Andressa's rules, he wouldn't touch the stuff.

"Don't you want to have some fun?" The spite in Enzo's words burned.

"He can't." Andressa waved her hand at Cody. "Not in my home."

"You let a woman make your decisions?" Enzo laughed, the other guys joining in. "You sure this guy is just an exchange student?" Enzo looked directly at Tomás. "Looks like you've got competition."

"No, no, no." Andressa leaned in to Tomás's neck and kissed him slowly, whispering quiet words in Portuguese to him.

Carolina passed the mirror to Enzo, and Cody looked up to find neither Andressa nor Tomás was paying attention to him, lost once again in their kiss.

Hope was in reach. Tomás was his way out, and Cody was ready to go. He swallowed a drink of beer.

Tomorrow he'd be free.

Chapter Seventeen

Day 11

After three hours of watching others snort lines and drink several bottles of liquor, Cody wanted to climb into bed, but Andressa still wouldn't let him go. Neither she nor Felipe touched the coke, but she drank along with everybody, and the noise level had ridden steadily.

Enzo stumbled over and slumped in the chair. "There aren't enough women here. Did you notice? We need to get more women." Enzo gripped Cody's shoulder. "Let's go."

"Where?"

"To get girls. I should've brought some of my own along, but Andressa would've gotten pissy." He jerked Cody to his feet, led him out the door, and jumped into a golf cart. Enzo could hardly drive a straight line, and Cody clutched the armrest as he swerved sharply. Twice he got too close to the edge of the road. Enzo laughed as Cody ducked to avoid a branch.

Cody's chest tightened when he realized where Enzo was going. They reached the barracão, and Enzo shot out of the golf cart.

"They're probably sleeping. We should leave them alone." Cody remained in the seat.

"Let's go," Enzo growled, a fierce look on his face.

He had to keep Enzo away from them. "Andressa will be pissed if you drag them out of bed."

"Get out of the fucking car." Enzo's menacing stare bore into him, and Cody saw the same buildup of anger in Enzo that he'd seen in Andressa. Enzo took off for the barracão and rushed down the hallway to one of the rooms. He flung open the door and flipped the light on.

"Levante-se," he said to the figure under the covers. She didn't move, and he yelled something else even louder, kicking the bed and yanking off the blanket. Yasmin stared at him with wide eyes and a trembling body.

"Bitches don't listen." He shrugged as if Cody would understand, and went to grab her.

"Hey, what are you doing?" Cody entered the room.

Enzo whipped around and pinned Cody against the wall. His hot, rotten breath turned Cody's stomach, and the hatred poured out of his eyes. "Listen here. This is your one warning. Don't fucking mess with my business."

Something hard pressed against Cody's neck. The light glinted off a steel blade. He couldn't move, couldn't breathe, even though he was shaking inside.

"Do you hear me?" Enzo shouted.

"Yes." He couldn't manage anything else.

Enzo stepped back, and Cody dropped to his knees.

"You may belong to my sister, but she can't protect you from me."

Cody gasped for breath, feeling his neck to make sure he wasn't bleeding. Enzo spun around and raged at Yasmin. She looked at Cody, begging for help, but there was nothing he could do.

She crawled out of bed, and Enzo sailed to the next room where a similar scene played out, but this time with Simona.

"Não." She folded her arms, her big brown eyes full of defiance toward the monster towering over her.

Enzo's face reddened, and he berated her in Portuguese. She shook her head a second time, and he slapped her. Simona backed toward the wall, covering her cheek, tears rising to her eyes. He screamed at her again, and she stared at him, terrified.

"Porra. I hate breaking in the new girls." Enzo shot Cody a look of disgust, then stomped next to Simona. He wrapped his hand in her black hair and yanked so hard that she tumbled out of bed. Her t-shirt rode up her back, and she tugged it down.

His voice remained calm as he spoke to her in Portuguese, but his tone and her pale face sent chills down Cody's back.

She slowly stood, bowing her head. Some of her tears fell to the floor, and she wiped at her wet skin. Even though Cody didn't know her, her fear killed him. He wanted to save the girls from what was coming, but how could he save the girls when he couldn't even save himself?

With shoulders drooping, the two girls in their pajama shirts and shorts marched between Cody and Enzo back to the party.

The darkened room welcomed the four back, but the scene played out much differently than when they'd left. Carolina and Felipe were gone, and Tomás lay on top of Andressa, his head stuck in her breasts. Luiz lay on the couch, his hand down his pants, watching the couple dry hump. She had to be trashed. Andressa had done no more than kiss him in front of others.

Andressa glared at Enzo. "You should maybe talk to me before you drag the help out of bed."

Tomás's hand slid underneath her skirt, and his lips moved up her neck. She giggled.

Cody glanced at a cowering Yasmin. He would soon have his freedom, but Simona and Yasmin were stuck in this prison for who knew how long... Forever maybe.

Luiz jumped off the couch. "Which one's mine?"

"You can have the ugly one." Enzo laughed and thrust Simona toward Luiz.

"Her name is Simona, and she has a lot to do tomorrow, so don't keep her up too late." Andressa whispered something into Tomás's ear, and they crawled off the couch together. She was almost out of the room when she spun around and returned to Cody. "You can wait here until I get back."

All he wanted was to go to bed, to get out of this room. Nothing good was coming.

"But—"

She whacked him in the head. "I said stay here. And if you even think about touching either of those two little sluts, I'll rip your dick off."

Cody staggered back, but by the time she turned around, her smile returned, and she drifted toward Tomás, and they left the room. Her request made no sense, and besides, he'd never touch either of those girls. He stared at their retreating figures as if they'd give him the answers, but there were no answers around here. Ever.

Cody took a drink of beer and almost spit it out when he saw the scene in front of him. A wave of nausea hit.

"Não, não, não," Yasmin pleaded, as a naked Enzo crawled on top of her, her clothes in a crumpled heap next to them. He covered her mouth and pushed into her.

Tears slid down her cheeks and hit Enzo's hand. He wiped it on the couch and slapped her hard. The tears stopped, and she laid her head back and stared toward the ceiling with vacant eyes as Enzo's body slapped against hers. Cody looked away, hating that he was a part of this life, hating that Andressa brought him here.

He smashed his eyes shut, but a yelp made him open wide again. Luiz's hand knotted in Simona's hair as he dragged her toward the couch, his dick leading the way. She slapped at his hands, trying to get free, but he tossed her to the side and yelled.

He kicked at her, and her hands flew up to block her red face as she screamed no.

Cody wanted to turn into Superman, to grab Yasmin and Simona and fly them away to somewhere safe, somewhere with no pain.

Luiz kicked Simona in the stomach again, and she crumpled up on the floor, sobs racking her body. Cody had to do something. A decent man wouldn't have let them get raped.

He planted his feet on the floor and beat down his own terror—they didn't deserve this; nobody deserved this.

He charged for Luiz, a rush of adrenaline coursing through him. Something solid smashed into his chest, and Cody flew backward, smacking his head on the floor. He gasped for breath, unable to take in any air. Oh god—he couldn't breathe. He was going to die.

Calm down, he told himself, his mind clearing. The fall knocked the wind out of him. He fought the panic, and slowly the breath came back to him. Someone kicked his foot, and Cody looked up into the deep dark hatred on Enzo's face.

"Try that again, and you're dead." He twisted the knife in his hand. Cody didn't move, didn't want to breathe.

Enzo trudged over to Luiz and Simona, set the knife on the table out of reach, and knelt down next to her. His hands clamped down around her wrists, holding them above her head. Luiz ripped off her shorts and worked together with Enzo to get the t-shirt off.

She jerked around, trying to fight them until Enzo yanked her hair and pulled back on her head. His thick hand wrapped around her neck, and she stilled.

Simona scrunched her eyes tight, and her body trembled, and Cody shut his own too, the grinding heat and revolting noises choking him. He couldn't bear to watch.

Chapter Eighteen

Day 12

Gentle fingers brushed the side of Cody's head.

"I'm back now," Andressa whispered. "I hope you're not mad, but Tomás and I have a special relationship."

Her face glowed, pushing Cody's grogginess away. Home. The smell of barbeque, the cool winter air—he'd never wanted to see snow so badly and hoped it wouldn't melt before he got home.

"I'm sorry to hear that, but if you want to be with Tomás, I understand." Cody faked a sadness, trying to hide the building excitement. "I guess you'll want me to leave. I'm sure Tomás wouldn't want me around to tempt you."

"No." She patted his shoulder. "Tomás would not approve of you staying, especially knowing how much you love me."

Cody almost broke out into laughter, but then the events from last night played in his head. He shifted on the couch, not knowing how he'd fallen asleep. He needed a shower to scrub off the filth.

"Andressa," Enzo yelled from across the room. "How do we get something to eat around here?"

She looked around, and her eyes rested on Yasmin, wrapped in a blanket in the corner of the room. The poor girl jumped up and scrambled to her clothes, then ran off to the kitchen.

"I'd better go tell her to get Vera. Yasmin is a horrible cook, and I want to make sure she makes something special for Tomás." Andressa patted Cody's head like a child and left for the kitchen.

He relaxed back into the couch. Wisconsin, Mom's cooking and regular food. No more drug dealers or dog abusers or rapists. He didn't want to think about the poor girls being left behind though.

Enzo, Luiz, and Tomás gathered around the dining table, still drinking. The cocaine lay in front of them, and they looked like they'd been up all night long. Luiz's head rolled back, and he let out a moan.

Cody leaned forward and saw the flash of dark skin by the table. Luiz gripped Simona's head as she bobbed in front of him.

The hell Andressa put Cody through was nothing compared to what these girls suffered. He vowed to contact the police once he was safely out of the country. A raucous laugh came from the table as the guys cheered Luiz on.

Cody imagined a knife, slitting their necks, the blood draining the life from their rotten existences. The world would thank him for getting rid of them, but he'd never make it out of this house alive.

A huffing Luiz slapped the bare ass of Simona as she crawled on her hands and knees to Tomás. The bile rose in Cody's throat. It wasn't just the rape, but sharing a girl—passing off all their diseases to those poor women—it made him want to puke.

"Tomás," Andressa screeched, and Cody jumped out of his seat. A torrent of Portuguese streamed out of her mouth, and Cody blinked, trying to focus on her.

Tomás's pants lay gathered at his ankles. Simona crouched between his legs, her chin quivering and eyes wide. Andressa twisted her hand in Simona's dark hair and dragged her away. Simona's head smashed into the table, and tears appeared in her eyes, but Andressa shoved her to the side.

Andressa turned around and screamed at Tomás. All through her rant, he remained still, a bored look on his face. Then Andressa spun around to Simona and kicked her in the ribs. Simona cried out in pain as the guys sat there watching, doing nothing.

"Andressa," Cody yelled. She whirled around and gave him the eyes of death, gulping for breaths of air, then swung around back to Tomás.

"Você!" She pointed at Tomás, spewing more angry words.

He stood and pulled up his pants, zipped up his jeans. No anger. No guilt. Nothing. Tomás folded his arms and said something in a calm voice.

Andressa's body slumped. Her face transformed from anger to agony, and tears hit her cheeks as she choked out her words, but the desperation in her voice didn't sway Tomás. Whatever she thought she had was now gone, or maybe it'd never been there.

Her pain and sorrow enveloped Cody, and for a moment, he felt sorry for her. But then he saw Simona curled up on the floor and imagined all the bruises forming on her skin, the other scarring invisible to anyone but her.

Andressa stared at Tomás, and neither said a word. A scowl formed on her face, and she let out another bitter string of words.

She spun around, and even though her look at Cody only lasted for a second, he saw his freedom slipping out of the room with every stomp of Andressa's heels.

Andressa kicked the guys out and instructed the two women on their day's schedule, going on and on with her demands as she rubbed her temples. Simona hunched over, holding her side on the couch, Yasmin next to her. Both women were silent, now dressed back in their pajamas.

After sending them away, Andressa sunk down onto the couch. Cody didn't say a thing, didn't know what to say after everything that happened. He was still trying to sort it all out in his head.

Andressa winced and stood. "I'm laying down for a while."

She left, and Cody stared at the front door, contemplating another walk to the gate, but the door opened, and Felipe strutted inside.

"Here to babysit me?" Cody sighed.

"Bet you're disappointed Tomás left." He plopped down at the bar.

Cody didn't answer. Tomás stole his freedom because the asshole couldn't control his dick. He wanted to wring Tomás's neck as much as Andressa's.

"What's with them anyway?"

"Ahh," Felipe said, waving his hand dismissively. "We've all heard the story. Girl falls for her brother's friend. They're both crazy fucks. It doesn't work, and it never will, but the girl doesn't get it."

"I can't blame him. She's a complete psycho. They both are." Oh shit. Cody slowly raised his eyes, but Felipe smiled.

"I want to show you something," he said, sliding off the stool and heading toward the fish tank. "Have you learned about the red bellies yet?" He pointed to the piranha.

"Not really. Nothing specific, I mean."

"You ever wonder why a girl keeps piranhas as pets?"

"Many times."

"You haven't met Uncle Marcos yet, have you?" Felipe's voice grew serious.

Cody shook his head no.

"Our world is filled with red bellies. I'm a red belly. Andressa's a red belly. Enzo. All of us. But Marcos Cardoso... he's the fucking black diamond."

Cody tried to remember what Andressa had said about the glitzy fish in her office—the black diamond piranha.

"Watch this." Felipe bent down and dug in the cabinet, took out a fishnet, and opened the top of the tank. When he stuck the net in the water, the fish all scattered, and it took him a minute to catch one.

The piranha flopped around, dripping water as Felipe headed to the office. He opened the top to the other tank and flipped the red belly inside. It darted around the new tank until it found a place to hide in between the grass. The black diamond swam over and circled the smaller fish.

Around and around and around.

Then the predator attacked. The red belly didn't have a chance as the meaner and bigger black diamond chewed him to pieces. As quick as the attack started, it ended, and what was left of the dead fish floated in the water.

Felipe scooped out the fish chunks and then pointed at the black diamond. "That is Marcos Cardoso."

Cody clenched his hands, hoping his sweating pits weren't stinking up the room. He'd known Marcos was dangerous from the way Levi and the others talked, but deep inside he'd wanted to pretend it wasn't true.

There was no pretending anymore.

"I'm ready for a drink. You ready for a drink?" Felipe raised his brows and chuckled.

Cody nodded, unsure the words would come out if he tried to speak. He needed a shot or two. Or ten.

"Drinking makes it easier. When you deal with shit like last night. Enzo's family and all, but..." Felipe shrugged, and Cody hid his surprise. It was nice to know not everybody here approved of rape.

At the bar they each did a shot, and Cody didn't give a damn that it was only eleven in the morning. He stared at the silver flecks in the granite countertop, unable to get the pictures of Simona and Yasmin out of his head.

"Carolina gave you the okay. She's been wanting to meet you, but Andressa kept making her wait."

"She's nice." The guys pretty much ignored him last night—a relief actually, but Carolina talked to him, seemed halfway interested in learning about him.

"She's smart. And gorgeous. Did you see her tight ass?"

"Yeah, nice," Cody said absentmindedly.

Felipe smacked Cody on the arm. "What are you looking at her ass for? I better not catch you staring." He laughed, and Cody shook his head in wonder. "Honestly, I've got no clue what she sees in me, but she's stuck around for two years now."

"Must be your charming personality." Cody hid his smirk, and Felipe burst out laughing.

"Oh, man, did I ever tell you I like you?" He punched Cody in the shoulder, the same spot he hit before. Cody rubbed it. His small bruise was nothing compared to Simona's battered body.

After downing the drinks and watching soccer game re-runs on TV, Felipe disappeared, and Cody went to the kitchen. Vera presented him the grilled cheese sandwich, and as he ate, he listened to her teach him some of the ingredients in Portuguese.

"If there are any special requests for meals, just ask," Vera told him.

"Do you think Andressa will let me go shopping with you?" He half-laughed at his boldness and took his last bite of food. At least when Vera told him no, she wouldn't be a bitch about it like Levi.

"I will add whatever you need to the list, but I don't do the shopping." She gave him a weary smile and stayed silent for a few moments. "I do the ordering online, and the groceries are delivered. I don't leave."

"What do you mean you don't leave?"

She swung the pitcher to the counter and faced him. "I'm not allowed to leave either."

"Wait—what? Did Andressa kidnap you too?"

"No." She lowered her chin, her voice full of emotion. "I'm Andressa's aunt."

"But why can't you leave?"

The door flew open, and Felipe stuck his head inside. "I'm going to the kennels. Get your butt out there after you're done." He didn't even wait for an answer and let the door fall.

Cody opened his mouth to ask her more, but she placed a warm container in his hands. The contents sloshed around inside when he moved it.

"Would you mind dropping off food with Simona at her room? I was about to bring it to her, but if you're going to the kennels, you can."

"No problem. Is it soup?" Vera hadn't given him any for lunch.

"It's Pisca Andina. A Venezuelan soup. Hopefully it'll offer her some comfort."

"She's Venezuelan?" He knew so little about these people he lived with, or more likely the people held prisoner like him. Vera nodded, and he pictured a beat-up Simona in his head. She probably missed home as much as he did. At least Cody wasn't being raped or beat, as long as he followed the rules. "Is she okay?"

Vera twisted the towel in her hands into a tight spiral. "I'm lucky. The pigs are not interested in an old woman like me. The scars in both girls will run deep."

Simona and Yasmin had gone through a night of hell, and Cody had a hunch Vera was hiding her own horrors.

He hustled to the barracão. Simona didn't answer his knock on her door, but he didn't want to leave the food in the hallway, so he opened the door a crack.

"Um, it's Cody. Vera sent me over with food." He heard a quiet response but didn't understand it, so he swung the door open. He hadn't really looked at the room last night and took in the small kitchenette in the hotel-sized room that held only a small table for two, a dresser, a TV, and a bed. Nothing brightened the walls, no personal effects, no color anywhere. The poor girl slaved away all day and then had to return to this restrictive room every night.

The brown lump on the bed shifted with muffled words.

"I'm sorry. I can't hear you. I, um…" The pictures of last night played in his head. Luiz pounding into her. Enzo. Andressa's rage. "I'll leave the food on the table. Do you need anything else? I mean, can I get you anything?"

Simona's head peeked through the blanket, and she slowly crawled out, her bloodshot eyes watching him. Bruises covered her face and arm. Her pajamas hid the rest of her body, but he knew more darkened skin was there. A lump formed in Cody's throat, and he swallowed it down.

"Thank you." She stared at Cody, beaten and broken. He should apologize, say how horrible Enzo and Andressa were, say how she didn't deserve it, but his words would mean nothing because he'd done nothing.

"Let me know if you need anything." *Just don't ask me to save you, because I already failed once.* Cody was worthless.

He shut the door and leaned against it. He had to get a puppy fix. Those little balls of energy with their unconditional love would provide a much-needed distraction, and he needed that distraction more than anything now.

Chapter Nineteen

Day 12

Andressa hadn't come out of her room by lunch, thank god. In Cody's short time there, he hadn't seen her miss much work, but Tomás played her for a fool, and she didn't want to face anyone.

In the kennel office, Felipe typed away on the keyboard, and Cody closed the door. "What'cha doing?"

"General clean-up," Felipe said without looking up. "Making sure the system is running efficiently. Getting rid of the crap Levi puts on here."

"Think you could leave the computer open for me, for a few seconds. You know, so maybe I could send an email to my parents?"

Felipe snorted. "No."

"It was worth a try, huh?" Cody shrugged, and Felipe laughed.

Cody pulled up a chair and sat next to the desk, wondering about Enzo and his father. "So is Marcos really as bad as you said he was?"

"Did you not listen to what I told you?"

Yeah, he'd heard every word. He just didn't want to admit what kind of family he'd fallen in with.

Felipe leaned back in his chair and folded his arms. "I'm grateful to Uncle Marcos for everything he's done for me, but he also scares the hell out of me. He likes to..." Felipe pursed his lips and focused on the computer as he thought. "When someone betrays him, he will make an example of them. When he first got started in the business, he did the dirty work himself. He's not afraid of shit."

Cody dropped his head, his stomach in turmoil. This was his life now. "How many people has he killed?"

"Personally, who knows. Not a lot lately," Felipe said nonchalantly. "But you can bet he's responsible for a lot of dead bodies and unsolved cases."

And Cody would be one of those if he wasn't careful. "What do you think he'll say about me and Andressa?"

"He knows all about you. Andressa wouldn't keep anything so big from him. She's not dumb either." Felipe gave him a wicked grin. "I'm sure he'll love you like his own son. Of course, he left one of his own sons to rot in a Venezuelan prison."

"But Andressa said he couldn't do anything because it was the son of some city official or something."

Felipe picked up the pen on the desk and spun it around. "Oh, he could have gotten him out if he wanted to. Marcos's power extends to Venezuela."

"You're not helping. I was looking for reassurance that he won't throw me to the piranhas."

The laugh shook Felipe's body. "It is what it is. When you meet him for the first time, be yourself, and if he ever tells you to do something that is different from what Andressa said, you do what Marcos said."

"Thanks." Cody rolled his eyes, and Levi's stories popped into his head. "So was he really in a Columbian prison?"

"Marcos? Yeah. It's where he got his start."

"How'd he get out? Levi said he killed a guy there."

"It was a Columbian prison, and he probably paid off someone."

"So, um." How did he say this without insulting Marcos and pissing off Felipe? "Andressa said he's a respected member of the community here."

A small smile graced Felipe's face. "Money gets you everywhere. Money and bribery and threats. Few of the 'respectable' people around here know about his background, and those who do keep quiet. He spreads his wealth around town."

Marcos had bought his way into the local government just as he had the police.

Cody didn't want to hear any more. "I'm going back now. Better check on Andressa." He'd do no such thing, but he'd better make Felipe think he was a good boyfriend.

"Later, man." Felipe's head dipped down, and he started typing away on the computer again.

Back at the house, Andressa's office door was closed, and he wasn't about to go bother her. One part of him wanted to see her embarrassed, to see her suffer for what she'd done to Simona. Andressa deserved everything she got, but he wished Tomás's actions hadn't locked him back in his jail.

Cody was the one in prison when the whole Cardoso family should be there. He opened the bedroom door.

"Shut the door," Andressa screeched.

He jumped at the sound of her voice and slammed the door behind him. The darkness swallowed him whole, couldn't see a thing. He touched the wall to get his bearings. The red numbers of the alarm clock weren't even visible, but a thin outline of light was across from him—the windows.

"Oh Cody, I've been waiting for you to check on me."

"I was busy at the kennels. What are you doing?"

"Come here," Andressa said, her voice weak. "Come lie with me."

He could kill her right now. He could crawl on the bed and wrap his hands around her neck, but it'd get him nowhere. Felipe and the others would catch him and torture and kill him.

Cody shuffled toward the bed, hands out so he didn't bump into anything.

"I have a migraine. And now it's started, there's nothing I can do. I have to wait it out." She tugged him closer, tucking his arm around her warm waist. "My head is pounding."

Good, enjoy it.

"This is all Enzo's fault," Andressa sniped. "He's always getting into my business. He goes and drags my help out of bed without asking. Simona and Yasmin are not his girls. They're mine. And they're so damn lazy, yet he rewards them with a night out." She stopped and tensed up. He hoped the migraine was tearing her head apart. Enzo didn't bring the girls to a club for drinks.

"Rub my head. Sometimes that helps," she commanded.

Screw you! He almost said it, his hand inches away from her neck. But he didn't want to die either, and the sinking feeling inside him told him what he needed to do. Cody reached over and kneaded her head, glad she didn't see his gritted teeth or the fire raging in his eyes.

"Ow, not so hard." Andressa jerked away. "This never would've happened if you would've stopped it. Why didn't you kick Simona out when you saw what she was doing? Were you trying to hurt me? Were you mad because I was with Tomás?"

He stopped rubbing, stunned. "I didn't... No... I tried to stop Enzo, and he put a knife to my throat." Cody touched his taut neck, remembering the blade against his skin.

Her head whipped around, and she scoffed. "That's ridiculous. Enzo wouldn't do that."

"He did too. He—"

"Cody, stop. I don't want to hear your stories." She leaned into him again. "Rub softer now."

This whole family was crazy, and he was stuck right in the middle of their shitshow. He rubbed her head again, lessening the pressure, and Andressa sighed contentedly. "I hope things didn't fall apart at the kennel. I didn't even call out there today."

"It's all good," he said. *Nobody probably wants to see you anyway.* Now if he could only figure out how to give her a permanent headache, they'd give him a damn award.

She stayed quiet. The best part of her migraine was, he imagined, she wouldn't want to have sex—he was free for at least one night.

*

Cody woke in the dark room with no idea of the time. The light framed the windows, but he wasn't about to wake Andressa. He fumbled in his drawers for new clothes, went to another bathroom to shower, and ended up at the kennels.

"What do you want me to do? Andressa still has her migraine, so she didn't give me any directions," he said to Miguel.

"Come with me. Levi didn't show up yet." Miguel stalked to the training side of the kennels, and Cody followed. "They can do the spring pole. Make sure when they're outside, you keep their water dishes full of water."

Miguel dug in the cabinet, pulled out a three-ring binder, and breezed outside to a tall pole with a beam attached at the top. A rope hung down with a spring on the end and a looped rope for the dog to grab onto.

"Check your binder for the time each dog needs to spend on the pole. All you need to do is bring them out here one at a time. Use the word *salte* for them to jump up and hold on to the ring and *solte* for him to drop. They have to hang there according to the times listed. If they drop down, make them do it again. When they're done, go ahead and play catch with them a little before putting them back."

Inside the kennels again, Miguel pointed to the thick metal chain from the door for Fausto. "Put the chain around their neck if it's not already on."

Cody almost laughed. The dogs would never be able to do what Miguel asked.

Fausto slipped through the doggy door and stared at the two men.

"Why do you need to toughen the skin on their necks?" Cody asked.

"The dogs usually aim for the throat when fighting, and we want the skin rough and thick to better protect them."

"That's cruel." Cody shook his head with disgust.

"It's life. Get used to it. Check the binder for instructions." Miguel slapped the binder in Cody's hands and strode away, leaving Cody not knowing exactly what to do. Well, he knew, but really, Miguel just threw him to the wolves. At least the people around Andressa seemed to know English, but the dogs wouldn't, and they probably wouldn't even listen to him.

"Wait," he called after a retreating Miguel. "How am I supposed to time them? I don't have a watch. Why don't you give me your phone?"

Miguel turned around with a smirk on his face. But instead of reaching into his pocket like Cody hoped, he unstrapped a watch and tossed it. "Don't break it," he said before leaving.

Cody put the chain around Fausto's neck, and the dog waited for his command. He led the dog outside to the pole, and Fausto sat right below the rope.

"Salte," Cody said, and Fausto jumped, clamping onto the end. He hung there, and hung there, and hung there. Damn their jaws were strong, and with that ridiculous chain too. Cody said the release words, and Fausto let go. He didn't know how long to wait until getting the dog up there again, so he waited a few minutes and said "salte" again. Fausto leapt into the air and gripped the rope.

"Solte," a voice called, and Levi strutted around the corner. Fausto dropped to the ground. "Is Fausto done?" Levi stole the book from Cody's hands and looked at the page. "Put him away and get Caio." He flipped the book shut and tossed it at Cody.

"He's the smallest one, right?" Cody still wasn't sure what all their names were, and none of the cages were labeled.

"He's just under two years. We tested him not long before you got here."

"For what?"

Levi looked at Cody like he was an idiot. "We gave him an aggression test. You don't do that until they're about eighteen months. It takes a lot of time and effort to prepare a dog." Levi huffed.

"What happens if they don't pass?"

Levi's dark grin lit his face. "Then they're sent in a ring with one of the boys who passed, and they usually don't make it out." Levi chuckled. "Caio did well. He's got the attitude to make it."

Cody slunk away toward the kennels, and Levi unsnapped the bottom piece that Fausto had been holding onto. Cody took Fausto outside and exchanged him with Caio.

Levi was gone when Cody got back, so he waited. Oh yeah, he was supposed to play with Fausto a little too. He'd have to get him later.

The spring on the pole was much higher now, and Cody wondered what Levi was doing. Finally, Levi joined them at the pole. Something small and brown squirmed in his hands.

"What's that?" Cody asked.

Levi held up his prize. A reddish-brown squirrel hung from a small collar. Cody backed away as Levi stuck it on the end of the spring.

"It's a squirrel."

"What are you doing with it?" Cody asked although he knew. Levi was sentencing the poor animal to a painful death. He couldn't not watch as Levi strung up the squirrel, Caio whimpering in anticipation.

"This is how you motivate them." Levi stepped back and told Caio to jump. He missed by at least a foot but didn't need any encouragement to jump again. Caio kept at it, getting closer but never too close. A smirking Levi stood with his arms crossed.

"This isn't the worst of it," Levi said. "You need to toughen up. Maybe we should get you a chain for your neck." He laughed. "Now watch this. This is the cool part."

Levi said something to Caio, and he sat still while Levi lowered the spring. "This is why our dogs are the best. They have control.

We're not stupid streetfighters torturing dogs until they're vicious. Caio, salte."

Caio sprung up and clamped onto the squirrel. The creature squealed, a horrific sound Cody had never heard. It thrashed around, but Caio held on tight, swinging in the air as the squirrel's life slowly drained away. Bright red blood dampened Caio's head.

"Maté-lo," Levi shouted.

Caio jerked the squirrel back and forth, working his jaw. The squirrel screaming intensified, and then it was silent. Caio dropped to the ground and leapt again, blood dripping from his mouth. After a few more attempts, the squirrel's body split apart. Caio flung the dead body to the side and wagged his tail.

"This is how you reward a dog." Levi chuckled and kicked away the bloodied body. The puke surged up Cody's throat. He flung the binder on the ground and stomped away. If the training was this bad, he didn't want to see the actual dog fights, see two dogs tear each other apart.

The rest of the morning Cody played with the puppies, their exuberant barks and wagging tails making it easier to forget about the realities of his life. He didn't know which dogs were marked for dog fighting and which were being sold as pets, and he preferred not to know. He wanted to imagine them all as family dogs, being chased by children and playing catch with a ball.

The whole thing depressed Cody, and he thought about how everything at the compound worked. The men seemed to be able to come and go, but not the women. They were prisoners too, except for the head bitch. And if Cody didn't make her happy, he'd end up like that squirrel, getting ripped apart by a vicious dog.

Chapter Twenty

Day 14

Andressa hid out in her room all day again and never once requested Cody's company. He enjoyed his second day of half freedom, and when he went to bed, she was asleep. She didn't come out of her room the next morning either, and he headed to work at the kennels. Despite her beliefs, the kennels ran fine without her.

Cody couldn't believe his luck when Andressa announced she was taking a trip to Fortaleza, but now he was paying the price: a longer than usual evening of sex for the night before she left.

He lay in bed waiting. Andressa strutted out in blue lacey lingerie, and his gaze fell to her black heels and followed her sexy legs to the garter belt holding her stockings up. She arched her back and stared at him seductively, her long hair swept behind her shoulders. Holy hottie.

His body reacted, and he shifted under the blanket.

"Like what you see?" she purred.

Yes… No… Yes…

What was he doing? It was different when she touched him—he couldn't help it then, but now… He knew who she was, but his body didn't seem to give a damn.

"Most definitely," he managed.

"Now, the best present of the night..." She grinned at him seductively. "Me."

*

Andressa was gone, and he was free. Well, not really, but he was free of her for a short time.

Cody skirted Vera and her vacuum on the steps, and he gave her a wave. The poor woman was always up before Cody, always in the kitchen before seven. There were hours during the day he didn't see her around, but she was often working until eight or nine p.m. Yasmin, Simona, Vera—they were all slave laborers.

At least his life wasn't as bad as theirs.

Cody went into the kitchen to grab a bite to eat. His normal schedule was thrown off since Andressa got up early to catch a flight. She didn't leave without her goodbye sex, much to Cody's disappointment.

He was staring into the fridge when the kitchen door swung shut.

"Can I make you breakfast, Mr. Cody?" Vera asked. "I can make eggs. We have ham too."

"Don't worry about it. I can get it."

"I like to cook. It's one of the few pleasures I have."

"That would be great, thanks."

Cody watched her prepare the scrambled eggs, wondering what she did in her off time, who she was, and what led to her being here. She had a long history that she might not even want to share.

"Can I ask you a question?" he asked.

"You may, but I might not have an answer." She smiled as if she knew he was about to ask something that would get him into trouble.

"How did you end up here?"

Vera stared into the pan for a few moments and then scooped his food onto the plate. She grabbed a towel from the counter and pulled up a chair across the table, her face grim. He didn't move.

"My sister Iris was young and full of life. She fell in love with a man who promised her the world, but she didn't know his world would be filled with darkness and degradation." She wrung the towel, her eyes full of sorrow. "When the children were younger, she wanted to leave, but Marcos wouldn't release her, especially not with the kids. So she stayed."

Vera's face tightened, and she closed her eyes. When she opened them, she looked straight into Cody's face and continued, her voice strong.

"When Andressa was about six, my sister began to collect evidence for the police to use against Marcos, and my husband and I helped plan her escape." She took a deep breath. "But we waited too long, and Marcos discovered what she'd been doing. He executed her and my dear husband, God rest their souls." She made a cross against her chest. "But he gave me the choice. I either had to give him my life or the rest of my years to serve him. Sometimes I think I should've chosen death." She let the tightly rolled towel unravel in her hands, her face lined with years of hard work and pain, something Cody could never fully appreciate.

"I'm sorry," Cody whispered, his gut a twisted knot. What kind of bastard murdered—no executed—his own wife... the mother of his children? And Andressa dragged Cody into Marcos's web of danger.

But Vera was still alive even though she'd betrayed Marcos. Maybe there was hope.

"It is not for you to be sorry." She patted his hand. "We all made choices that got us here in one way or another, and now we must live each day, praying to make it to the next. I was lucky to end up here. Andressa is not as harsh as her father."

"What was your sister like?"

"She was a kind woman who loved her children. She taught me to cook when we were kids, taught me about life."

Cody took a bite of food, listening to Vera talk with a smile on her face. She had so much to say, and he wondered when she'd last had the opportunity to share her memories with anyone.

The door flung open and banged into the wall. Cody jumped, and Felipe snickered. He eyed Vera sitting at the table across from Cody, and she stood and gathered the dishes.

A whole hour had passed without Cody even realizing it.

"So you coming to the kennels or what?" Felipe asked.

"I was just about to. Had a late breakfast." Cody pointed to the dishes and hoped Felipe wouldn't question him more.

"Maybe, Vera," Felipe said slyly, "you can make pé de moleque. Cody might want some."

Vera laughed. "And should I make extra for you too?"

"Make enough for both of us." Felipe turned to Cody. "Andressa doesn't allow the good desserts, but she's not here today, is she?"

"No, she isn't." Vera smiled. She must've learned long ago to hide her true feelings. It was probably why she was still alive.

"Thanks, Vera," Felipe said, heading out the side door, and Cody rushed after him. "We've got a lot to do. Silva's got a fight coming up, and we need to up his training."

"Seriously?" Cody imagined the blood and gore from a fight, much more than a small squirrel or cat.

Felipe punched Cody in the arm and grinned. "A fight, man. Silva is tough. He'll kick ass. I wish you could see it, but Andressa said you weren't ready."

Cody rubbed the sore spot on his arm. Yeah, see dogs rip each other apart—no thanks.

"Grand champion. Silva's almost there." The enthusiasm in Felipe's voice matched his stride, and he gave Cody a run-down of two of Silva's fights.

"How many wins is a grand champion?" Cody asked as they headed through the door. Miguel stared at the computer, didn't even look up.

"Didn't you explain the whole fight thing to him?" Felipe pointed at Cody. "He doesn't even know about Silva."

Miguel shrugged. "He never asked."

"Well, I…" Cody crossed his arms to defend himself. "I don't—"

"Five wins," Felipe interrupted. "Silva is one away, and if he wins this next one—"

"What do you mean if?" Miguel scowled.

Felipe gave him a hard look. "*When* he wins this one, it's not just the title. It's a lot of cash."

"It's the title. His stud requests will jump," Miguel said. "Oh, by the way, Rodrigo is stopping by today."

Levi strutted into the room, speaking Portuguese, and smirked when he saw Cody. "Oh, sorry. Add puppy food to your list."

"Andressa's not around, tolo." Miguel rolled his eyes.

"But her brinquedo might tattle." Levi's lip curled into a sneer.

Cody didn't know what the word meant, but he understood the body language. Felipe might've been a bruiser, but Levi was a grade-A jackhole.

"Being a grand champion isn't an easy feat," Miguel said.

"And we get a nice bonus when he gets there." Levi folded his arms and glared at Cody. "Of course, not the type of bonus I was hoping for. Not since you got here."

"Shut up, Levi." Miguel dug through the drawer in the desk.

"No really. I thought she'd reward me with her hot little body. Slap me silly with those sweet tits. I bet she's all wild and kinky when she fucks. Is she, Cody?"

"Enough already." Miguel turned his back to Levi and shook his head. "You never had a chance."

"I want to know," Levi huffed. "Me and Felipe were talking. Wondering if she swallows. He doesn't think so."

"She's your cousin," Cody accused Felipe.

"No, it's not like that," Felipe started.

"The least Enzo could do is bring some of his girls along for us." Levi practically pouted

"We're done," Miguel said. "I don't need that image running in my head the next time I see her. Let's go, Levi."

Miguel gathered up his things, and Levi slunk out the door behind him. Cody couldn't believe Felipe would talk about Andressa and her sex life.

"I don't know how things work in Brazil," Cody said, "but in America, picturing your cousin having sex is pretty damn creepy."

"Relax, man. She's not my real cousin. Didn't I ever tell you the story?" Felipe said and waited for Cody's reply. "Uncle Marcos isn't my real uncle. I grew up in Belém. My mamãe abandoned me, and my papai worked in a factory until he died. I was fourteen and living on the streets. Tried to rob the wrong person." He shrugged, then smiled. "Actually it was the right person."

Cody sat up straighter. "Who?"

"Enzo. He was in his first year at the university when I pickpocketed him. I almost got away, but one of his buddies nabbed me. Enzo was about to beat me up, but for some reason he stopped and asked me a bunch of questions. Let me go. A week later this fancy guy decked out in a suit shows up and pulls me off the streets, found me a safe place to live, and put me to work. I've been working for Uncle Marcos ever since. And I'm not the only one he rescued."

Cody tried to reconcile the two sides of Marcos: head of a drug cartel with community leader, a guy who murdered his wife and enslaved her sister but rescued lost children from the streets. Of course rescue meant throwing them into a world of drugs, of crime, and cruelty.

"So what's the answer?" Felipe asked.

"To what?"

"Is Andressa a bear in bed or a kitty?" Felipe grinned.

Cody almost laughed. *Kitty.* The word sounded funny coming out of Felipe's mouth.

Felipe continued. "Levi thinks because she's a bitch, that in bed she'd be this soft, quiet thing who purrs when you pet her. But I know she's Andressa, through and through."

Cody stared down at the desk. He'd never been the type to talk about his sex life, and now he was sitting in Brazil being questioned about the woman keeping him captive.

"So does Andressa fuck you, or do you fuck Andressa?" Felipe prodded.

"It's always Andressa." Cody sighed.

Felipe let out a cackle. "I knew it."

Cody thought about what Levi said about Enzo. "I've got a question. Both Andressa and Enzo mentioned his girls. What did they mean?"

Felipe shrugged. "His whore house. He runs a brothel."

No way. It shouldn't surprise Cody though. Nothing should at this point.

"Can we get to work now?" Cody asked. He would stick close to Levi today, try sneak into his car before he left if he had a chance. Or maybe when that Rodrigo guy arrived again. Cody could almost smell the stench of that cokehead who brought animals to Andressa.

When the shelters in town got too full, they paid him to take away the cats and dogs to euthanize them, but he sold the animals to Andressa instead, to be ripped apart by her dogs. Cody would be the caretaker for those animals on Andressa's death row.

He just hoped he wouldn't end up like one of those poor creatures.

Chapter Twenty-One
Day 15

Cody's getaway plan wasn't working. He considered jumping Levi right as he got into the car, but Levi had a gun, and even if Cody was able to knock Levi out, Raul would never let him out of the gate. The only option was to hide in the back of the car, but Levi snuck out when Cody was talking to Felipe.

"You going to the house?" Felipe asked.

Cody let out the air in his lungs, watching Levi crawl into his car and drive away. There'd been no chance of escape when Rodrigo had stopped by either. "Yeah."

"I'll be here another hour or so. We can eat dinner together."

Cody nodded and headed to the house. The billowy clouds covered the sun, but a swim would be refreshing. No breeze swayed the trees—he hadn't yet experienced a windy day, and Cody enjoyed the chirps of whatever birds hid in the trees. He could almost imagine being on spring break with his buddies instead of being held captive here.

He did laps in the pool for a while and then lay floating on his back, thinking about those poor animals in Andressa's back room at the kennel: cats, small dogs, squirrels, and bunnies that Rodrigo had collected for her to use with her dogs. All condemned to death, living the rest of their short lives in small pens.

A movement at Andressa's bedroom window caught his eye. Simona had flung open the curtains and was cleaning the window.

He couldn't see her bruises from down below, but they were probably still there. She had spent the last few days under Andressa's watchful eye, and she always looked relieved to get out of the house.

No matter what type of person Simona was, she didn't deserve what she got the other night. He felt an obligation to give her a kind word, especially since that's all he had to offer. He dried off and headed upstairs to talk to her.

Simona hummed as she swiped a rag across the window, her black braid swinging.

"Hey," Cody said. She jumped and spun around. Her dark eyes darted over his shoulder, and she remained stiff, suspicion marring her dark skin. He had to show her he wasn't a threat.

"I'm sorry. I'll get out of here." She swept up her cleaning supplies, keeping a watchful eye toward the bedroom door.

"You can stay. I'll dress in the bathroom. I just wanted to say hello."

"No." She shook her head, her face tight. "Miss Andressa doesn't allow me to be in a room alone with you."

"Wait—what?" Cody grabbed her arm as she tried to pass by him. "Why?"

She froze, her eyes dropping down to Cody's chest again. Cody wanted to wipe away the sadness filling her face. She pursed her lips, straightened her shoulders, and looked him in the eyes. "Because I am a whore, and I should not tempt you."

Her matter-of-fact voice, void of emotion, almost made Cody laugh. "You can't be serious."

"Yes, Mr. Cody. I am a temptress and cannot be trusted to be alone with you."

"That's dumb. I'd never cheat on Andressa." Or any other woman.

"It doesn't matter what you would do. It matters what Miss Andressa thinks I'd do, and I don't want to give her any reason to think I've done anything."

"But she's not even here. She's gone for a few days. Besides, why would Andressa think you want to sleep with me? Because of what happened with Tomás?"

This conversation was ridiculous. He'd never given Andressa any inclination he was attracted to Simona. Yeah, she was beautiful, but so what.

"No. She ordered me from the beginning to stay away from you." Simona seemed to straighten before him, exuding a confidence he hadn't seen before. "Because she's jealous and spiteful." She challenged him to disagree, but he couldn't. Andressa might have been prettier than Simona, but Simona had something Andressa didn't have.

Big boobs.

A door slammed, and Simona scurried past him with her cleaning supplies, going out the door before he said another word.

The jealous girlfriends he'd had were nothing compared to Andressa.

*

Cody loved his Andressa-free days, but they passed far too quickly. Felipe was around to babysit him—or to make sure he didn't try to escape, and Cody didn't. He needed to prove to Andressa that he was trustworthy.

All along he'd been thinking about this wrong. He needed a serious plan, needed to play Andressa's game. Rash decisions would get him killed, but if he earned her trust, she would allow him to leave, and he'd escape once he was in the city.

He needed to learn about Manaus and Brazil, pick up some Portuguese so he could get where he needed to go. Andressa would never see it coming.

Cody shifted on the couch as he, Felipe, and Carolina watched a mixed martial arts fight. Felipe was raving about all the stars and how he hoped they'd bring back the Ultimate Fighting Championship to Brazil, which happened years ago.

"Enough about the UFC." Carolina laughed. "I think Cody's as bored as I am."

"You're not bored." Felipe tossed a pillow at Cody. "See, he's not bored."

"Huh, what?" Cody pretended he was waking up, sending Carolina into more giggles.

"You've monopolized the conversation, Felipe," Carolina scolded, all in fun.

"He monopolizes every conversation." Cody let out a big huff.

"This shit isn't right. I'm the one in charge here." Felipe faked indignation to his two harassers.

"Of course you are, querido." Carolina winked at Cody, trying to cover her smile. He was still unsure if she understood Cody's real situation.

"I'll need a vacation after this," Felipe said.

"Don't we all," Cody replied. A vacation back to the U.S. Freedom.

"So if we ever make it to the EUA, where should we go?" Carolina asked.

"Try the Midwest in winter. Chicago maybe." Cody would love to dump Andressa in a blizzard, or find a frozen lake, drill a hole, and drop her through.

"Are the winters nice?"

Cody shrugged. "If you like cold and snow."

"No thanks. I'll go where it's warm." Felipe shivered. "Carolina wants to get out of here and travel a bit. Take a vacation."

"Extended vacation. To Belize maybe." Carolina clasped Felipe's hand and looked at him hopefully. "And sooner than later."

Cody shrugged. JJ's family had gone there once, said they'd go back. "Don't know much about it either. I think it's getting more popular for Americans. Get away from Mexico and try something different. Guatemala was nice."

"No, the Cardosos have too many associates in Guatemala. I don't want to live there." Carolina's eyes widened, and Felipe shook his head.

"You moving away?" Cody asked.

"No, she's just dreaming," Felipe answered. "We're never leaving Manaus. Too many opportunities here."

She snorted, and Felipe glared at her, the tension thickening in the air. Her face softened though. "No, Felipe's right. We've got all our friends and family here. I'd miss them too much. It's hard to be so far from family," she added, giving Cody a somber look.

Only the noise from the TV filled the room, and Cody stared at the screen without watching. He hadn't hugged his mom in a long time, had never told her he loved her—or his dad, but now it was the first thing he wanted to do. He wanted to surround himself with the noise of his favorite bar, the chatter of English-only and American music. He wanted Fruity Pebbles and a nice thick steak or a brat off the grill.

He'd get his wish someday, but it would take time.

"So what's the verdict?" Cody asked. "Are you going to tell Andressa I was a good boy?"

Felipe laughed. "How about you get me another beer, and I'll think about it."

*

Cody shifted in the empty bed that night.

What the hell is wrong with me? He banged his head against the wall. His last night without Andressa, and he couldn't enjoy it because he couldn't sleep.

He crawled out of bed and slid open the door to Andressa's balcony. The heat smothered his skin, and he plopped down in one of the cushy chairs. He'd give anything for a crisp autumn night.

Small ripples flowed across the pool surface below.

He looked through the balcony's bars just as a head popped out of the water. Cody jumped out of his seat and grabbed onto the bars to get a better look.

A face peered up at him, the moonlight shining off her wet skin. Simona.

She frowned, then flipped around and started swimming to the other end of the pool, her body gliding effortlessly.

Felipe might show up at any moment. He'd rat out Simona, and Andressa would punish her. She'd get beat. He had to warn her.

Cody slipped through the house and snuck to the back door. Simona continued to swim, and he scanned the yard for any lights or movements.

Nothing.

"What are you doing," he whispered as Simona reached his end of the pool. "Andressa will kill you if she finds out."

Simona laid her arms along the edge of the pool and looked up at him. Her eyes searched his face. "I'm swimming, Cody."

Co-dee. His name seemed to flow from her mouth, the second syllable enunciated. Unlike Andressa, who said his name quickly as if she was in a hurry. But she was. Andressa was always in a hurry, her mind revving at five thousand RPMs.

"You're what?" Cody kept his voice low, scanning the house and yard. A face might show in the window at any moment.

"Swimming." She spoke at a normal level, not whispering like him.

"But if Felipe or Raul catch you, Andressa will be pissed."

"What do you love, Cody?"

"I… uh…" What did she mean? He loved his parents, his friends, and family.

"Our lives are not ours," she continued. "Not anymore. But no matter what Andressa does to me, she can't take away my mind. She can't control who I am inside. I'm tired of living inside my head, and sometimes it's worth the risk to do those things I love. I love to swim." Her smile lit up the dark night, the first time he'd seen her happy.

"Do you swim every night?"

She laughed. "I might take an occasional risk, but I don't have a death wish. Only if Andressa is gone."

In one smooth motion, she pulled herself out of the pool. Water dripped from her slick wet hair down her shoulders and between her breasts.

Holy hell. The dark wet t-shirt clung to her beautiful curves, and he swore she was only wearing underwear. He'd need to jump in the damn pool himself if he wasn't careful.

"Excuse me," she said, brushing by him on her way to the chair to get her towel. He couldn't let her see him drooling over the way her backside swayed.

No wonder Andressa made Simona dress in a dowdy maid's uniform.

Simona wrapped the towel around her body and twisted the water out of her hair.

Say something, stupid. He wasn't a nerdy freshman in high school anymore. He should be able to talk to a hot girl without getting tongue-tied.

"In tenth grade, I won the contest for treading water the longest." He shook his head at his bumbling. "I mean, I like to swim too."

She grinned and glanced toward the pool. "Maybe someday you'll swim too."

She spun around and disappeared into the dark night. Damn, she was gutsy. Andressa popped into his head, her finger wagging at him. The finger turned into a knife, and he saw his own throat being slit.

Cody wiped the dangerous thoughts of Simona clean from his mind. He wouldn't risk Andressa's wrath.

Chapter Twenty-Two

Day 17

"Cody," Andressa squealed. "I missed you so much." She tossed her purse on the table and drew him into a grizzly bear hug. He counted the seconds, waiting for his release.

Finally, she let go but didn't step back. Her arms lay on his shoulders, hands clasped behind his neck.

"Did you miss me?" she asked.

No.

"Of course I did. I was bored to death."

"Felipe said you kept busy at the kennels. You're my good boy." She patted him on the head.

"Andressa, you're back." Daniel stepped out of her office, and the smile slid off her face.

"Can't you see Cody and I are having a moment?" Andressa sniped.

"Sorry, I, uh…" Daniel stared down at his papers. "Come see me when you're free." He turned to flee. "Oh, and Vera's sick today," he said before disappearing into the office.

"Daniel." Andressa snapped her fingers at him, and he popped his head out. "Get Simona over here to do her job." She turned her attention back to Cody. "Can you believe she insists on taking a sick day, on the day I'm coming home no less."

"What is wrong with her?" Cody feigned indignation that would rival Andressa's.

"I know." Andressa nodded her head enthusiastically. "Oh, and Daniel, tell Simona she needs to get started on my laundry and then make a special dinner for me and Cody. I want bobó de camarão."

"I will." Daniel didn't move from the doorway.

"Goodbye, Daniel." She waved him off and led Cody upstairs to the bedroom.

Andressa grabbed his cheeks, and her mint-flavored mouth smothered his, her hands sliding up and down his back and butt. He kept up the charade, the act of wanting her, but he wanted nothing more than to be alone once again.

"Oh Cody." She panted, leaning her forehead against his. She only gave him a moment of reprieve before she stripped him down, shoved him to the bed, and straddled his waist. He fought to maintain control of his body, but it was no use. Her fiery kisses on his neck brought him alive.

He made the correct noises and said the correct words, and she believed he wanted this all. It was better than getting beat. Cody stared off to the door to the balcony. The girl from last night flashed into his head. Simona.

He'd used his ex-girlfriends to get through sex with Andressa, but he'd never thought of using someone he hadn't slept with. But why not? Simona was a sexy woman with a to-die-for body. That chest, her ass. When Andressa kissed his lips, he imagined it was Simona.

Anyone was better than Andressa.

*

"How about this?" Cody held up a bottle of white wine. "I'd like to try this one?"

"You know I prefer red." Andressa sighed, reflecting Cody's feelings inside. He showed her a bottle of red, she nodded, and he opened it and poured two glasses. The dry wine slid down his throat.

"Ten minutes, Miss Andressa," Simona said, sticking her head through the door.

"Hurry it along. Cody and I are hungry."

Cody stared at the swinging door after Simona left, the guilt swallowing him whole. He'd used Simona for sex. Maybe it was only in his mind, but he'd still used her. It was almost like he'd raped her himself.

"What's wrong?" Andressa asked.

His face grew hot. She couldn't read his mind, but she might connect his discomfort with Simona.

"Nothing. Why?"

"Your cheeks are red." She eyed him suspiciously.

"Oh, it must be the wine. It's a little dry for me," he said.

"There's nothing wrong with it. My father gave me this wine."

"Let me try it again." He took another sip.

"Well?" she asked.

He nodded. "You must get your good taste in wine from your dad."

"Yes. Now, sit down. Did I tell you about the seafood restaurant my father brought me to?"

Cody didn't even have time to answer yes before she started talking again.

Dinner went well, until the main course, and Andressa called Simona out to berate her for messing up the food. It was delicious, but Cody kept his mouth shut until Andressa ordered Simona to recreate the whole dish. That would take forever.

He tried to think about what food he'd seen in the kitchen.

"Have you had my world famous sloppy joes?" Cody asked. It was one of Mom's specialties, a bit of home he missed incredibly. The recipe wouldn't be the same, but he could get close to it.

"Sloppy joes? What's that?"

"When you were gone, I thought about making them for you."

"You did?" She leaned forward on her elbows, her lips curling into a smile.

"Fine American cuisine." He winked. "Backyard party favorite. I can whip some up quick so then we don't have to wait for Simona. My specialty just for you."

"Okay." She laughed. "Fine American cuisine that we eat at backyard parties?"

"I'll go kick Simona out, and you can join me."

For a fleeting moment, Cody felt normal, like he was flirting with a gorgeous woman who wanted him, but reality overshadowed his fantasy. He was imprisoned in Brazil by Andressa, trying to keep her from inflicting more pain on an innocent girl.

He went into the kitchen, and Simona looked up in surprise. A whole slew of bowls and spices and other things covered the counter.

"I talked Andressa into something else. You can go," he said.

"Thank you." She sighed at the mess on the counter. "Let me put this away."

"Don't worry about it. I'll take care of it."

She looked about to argue, but then her head swung toward the dining room door, and she nodded.

"Thank you again," she said quietly.

That night she'd been swimming in the pool, she'd asked him what he loved. She'd loved swimming, enough that she'd taken the risk of getting caught. His risk was minor compared to hers, but at least he got Simona away from Andressa, if even for a short time. And in some tiny way, he'd be sticking it to Andressa. She tried to make him forget his old life, but he never would, no matter how long she kept him in prison.

"Hey, Simona," he said. "I love sloppy joes. My mom used to make them all the time when I was a kid."

What a stupid thing to say. She might not even know why he'd say something so random, wouldn't connect what she'd said at the pool to why he was telling her what he loved.

"What are they?"

"I'll tell you about them another time. Good ole American food. I'll make sure there's leftovers in the fridge."

Her smile brightened him inside.

She slipped out the back door, and Cody about jumped when Andressa pushed her way into the kitchen with the two glasses of wine and a bottle stuck in her arms. He forced a smile on his face.

Andressa set the wine down and cornered him at the counter, her arms snaking around his waist.

"You did miss me, didn't you?" she said breathlessly.

"Immensely."

Her wine-flavored mouth covered his, her hands running over every inch of his back until she pulled away. "Now make me this special dinner you were talking about."

Chapter Twenty-Three

Day 20

Things returned to normal, and Felipe disappeared once again, busy doing whatever it was Andressa had him do when he wasn't babysitting Cody or taking care of the computers. The next few days flew by as the guys at the kennel prepped Silva for his fight.

Silva is a champ.

He's the best.

This payoff will be huge.

Andressa's eyes practically bled green the way she spoke.

She'd called Cody to come back from the kennels, and he returned to the house. Simona knelt in the flower bed in front of the house. He shouldn't stop, but he wanted to say hello to her. He, Simona, and Vera were in the same exclusive club—Andressa's prisoners, and talking to her was another screw-you for keeping him here, almost three weeks now.

"You do a great job with all the flower gardens around here," he said. She was the only one ever taking care of them, even though Andressa loved to talk about *her* flowers in *her* gardens.

"Thanks. Don't tell Andressa I love this part of my job," she whispered and then laughed. "The brilliant colors remind me how beauty can thrive in such an awful environment." Her body deflated before his eyes, and he shuttered the urge to give her an encouraging pat on the shoulder. "One of the things I miss the most is going to the Jardín Botánico with my mother. She loved the quiet of the garden, being so close to nature. We used to go once every few weeks when I was younger. I would complain, but she taught me about all the plants and flowers. I'd give anything to be there with her right now." Simona wiped away her dour look and smiled. "And someday I'll get back there."

It was amazing that she remained positive with all Andressa subjected her to. He wanted to stay and talk to her more about the flowers but couldn't.

"I'd better get inside. Andressa's expecting me."

She gave him a wave, and he slipped into the house. Andressa wasn't in the office, but he sat down to wait for her. Hopefully she hadn't seen him talking to Simona.

"I've got a surprise for you." Andressa buzzed into the room and waited for her kiss. "We are doing something special tonight. I can't tell you what now, but you'd better shower." Her bright eyes sparkled, and for a flash her beauty overtook Cody, and he forgot who she was.

It only lasted a second though.

"Come on, sweetie." She ran her finger up his chest to his collar. "Let's you and I go clean up." Her hand dropped to his waist and unbuttoned his jeans. Andressa was a creature of habit, and sex always happened in the mornings and at night but not in the middle of the day. Maybe she was revved up because of the dog fight tomorrow night.

She dragged him to the shower to *make love*, but mostly it was Cody freezing his butt off while she stood under the hot water. Then she made him get dressed in his best clothes and sit and wait in the bedroom while she got ready.

For an hour.

Andressa stepped out of the bathroom in her short lacey emerald-green dress and black heels, showcasing her lean legs. Her hair hung loosely over her bare shoulders, and her makeup was fancier than normal.

No way. It couldn't be. She was bringing him to town. A hundred possibilities flew through Cody's mind along with all the ways to escape. But maybe this was a test. He'd have to play it well and wouldn't run unless he knew with certainty he'd get away.

"Don't forget to wear the cologne I gave you." She handed him the bottle.

"Of course not." He grinned, unable to contain his excitement.

Andressa led Cody downstairs to find Felipe and Carolina waiting for them. The girls did the air kiss thing, and Carolina stepped back. "Gorgeous dress."

"It is." Andressa waved everybody to follow her across the room. "I had a hard time deciding between this one or the royal blue. They both looked sensational."

"Great choice," Carolina said.

"What about me?" Felipe twirled around, the outline of a gun showing through his shirt. Cody had become an expert at picking out the faint line. "Nobody said anything about my clothes. Carolina even bought me a new shirt for this evening."

Andressa let out a long sigh. "Yes, you clean up nicely, Felipe."

He snorted and rushed around her to get behind the bar. "I'll handle the drinks. What are you having, ladies?" He winked at Carolina, and she laughed.

Andressa hardly shut off her mouth during drinks—talking about people Cody hadn't met, but he wasn't listening. All he thought about was this outing. They were going to Manaus.

She trusted him, if even a little. So maybe he could get to a police station or the embassy. The taste of freedom was so close.

But no, not the police—some of them were on her payroll, well, Marcos's payroll, and Cody couldn't risk anything except the embassy. The only problem was he had no clue how to find it.

During a pause in the conversation, he turned to Carolina. "Where was it we're going tonight?"

"To the Brickhouse," Carolina replied.

"Cody." Andressa wagged a finger at him. "I told you it was a surprise." She gave a mock glare to him, then Carolina. "You're lucky he doesn't know what the Brickhouse is."

"Babaca." Carolina jabbed Cody in the arm, smiling.

It didn't matter. This would be his chance. A big crowd at a club would make it easy to slip away or steal someone's phone to make a call. Except he'd never get past the lock screen. Twice he'd gotten a hold of Levi's phone, but he didn't know the password and had never caught Levi typing it in.

Dinner passed painfully slow.

"Why didn't I get invited to eat?" Enzo strutted into the house without ringing the doorbell. Cody stiffened, shutting out the revolting images of Enzo and the two girls and replacing them with Simona's smile. When Andressa wasn't around, her sweet personality shined through. He hoped their outing didn't include bringing her along.

Enzo made himself a drink at the bar, plopped down at the table, and ate straight out of the serving dishes.

"Get a plate." Andressa scowled, but Enzo just stuffed food into his mouth. "This is why I didn't invite you. You have the manners of a monkey."

Enzo grinned. "Is Silva ready to go? I've got big money on this."

Andressa's frown deepened.

Wait—Silva. "Is the fight tonight?" Cody asked.

Silva might wind up dead or severely injured tonight, or the other dog too. Cody almost wanted more time to prepare for the blood and violence—a few hours didn't seem enough.

Andressa threw her crumpled napkin on her plate. "It was supposed to be a surprise. Thanks, Enzo."

He shrugged, his expression revealing his true feelings: he didn't give a damn.

"I thought it was tomorrow," Cody said.

"No. It's tonight." Andressa stood. "Vera, come clear the food away." She spun around and told everyone it was time to go.

They headed out to a big suburban sitting outside the house and piled inside, Enzo driving, Daniel sitting in back.

Down at the entryway, the gate slowly opened, and Cody held his breath like it was a dream, like he'd wake up to find himself still stuck in Andressa's house.

But he didn't, and soon they were speeding down the highway.

Less than twenty minutes later they passed a bunch of houses. Then more. And businesses. When Felipe and Daniel brought Cody to Andressa's house, they'd been in the car for almost two hours before arriving at Andressa's. He was sure of it.

"Is this Manaus?" Cody asked Felipe.

"Yes. You're closer to town than you thought." He snickered.

All this time they were twenty minutes from town and not in the middle of the Amazon jungle. Twenty damn minutes from civilization. He could've walked… If he'd gotten past the alarms and the gate.

He tried to track the turns as they drove farther into town, but it was impossible. Enzo eventually parked the car on the street of an industrial neighborhood, similar to the one Felipe and Daniel brought him to on the first day: dirt streets, crumbling buildings, broken streetlights, and people who might slit his throat without a moment's hesitation.

Cody would risk escape this time though. The moment Felipe turned away, he'd be out of there and on his way home to freedom.

Andressa stopped them outside a graffiti-marred building with broken windows.

"This, Cody, is what it's all about." She swept her arms toward the dilapidated building, and he just nodded. The pungent smell of exhaust and trash filled his nose.

"Let's go," Enzo huffed. "Don't want to be late." He pushed Andressa toward the door. A six-and-a-half-foot scary-ass tattooed guy held it open for her, his eyes wandering down her body.

You can have her, Cody wanted to say, but followed her inside, Felipe right behind him. She strutted down the hall like she'd been here a hundred times; maybe she had. They passed others along the way, a few people greeting her. The smell only worsened, a mix of things he couldn't identify. Cody kept his eyes down to make sure he didn't trip over any of the garbage littering the hallway. Needles were probably hiding under all that mess.

"You're gonna like this, buddy," Felipe whispered, almost knocking Cody over with the nudge.

They stepped around the corner into a large room with fluorescent lights hanging above, illuminating the strange mix of fifty or so people. Half the crowd was Brazil's version of the Hell's Angels, but the other would fit in at a party at Andressa's: people in their twenties and thirties, the women wearing fancy dresses like Andressa and guys all decked out.

Cody moved around Andressa as a guy greeted her. Felipe remained right next to him, barely an arm's length apart. A twenty-by-twenty foot pen, with three-foot-high walls made of rough wood planks, was centered in the room under the bright lights. Rust-red stains covered the gray carpet. Cody's stomach soured at all the deaths that had occurred here.

"Cody, come wish Miguel good luck." Andressa tugged on his arm, and he turned to see Miguel surrounded by the others. Everyone wore big smiles, the death of a dog a happy occasion apparently.

"Silva's all set." Miguel nodded at Andressa. "He'll take Breno down."

Miguel strode away, disappearing into the crowd, and Enzo started talking about the other dog, but Cody blocked his words out, everybody's words. A dog would get mauled tonight for entertainment, for money. Cody's temperature rose, and he wanted to walk around, just to cool off, but he couldn't because Andressa gripped his hand too tightly.

A bell rang out across the room, and Andressa led Cody to the corner where Silva stood next to a scale with someone he didn't recognize. The guy handed over the leash, and Miguel walked with Silva to join what must've been his opponent, a brown brindle dog similar in shape to the dogo. It was the same height but had a few pounds on Silva.

"It's a Presa Canario." Andressa squeezed Cody's hand as they watched the dogs get weighed. "He's a strong dog and a worthy opponent. But I've done my research about this one. Silva will take him."

Miguel took a couple towels out of a bag, and he and the other handler paraded to a makeshift shower. The men exchanged dogs, and each man washed the other guy's dog with soap and water.

These two dogs were going to fight, yet they were right here, hardly paying attention to one another. It didn't match the image of vicious snarling dogs he'd pictured.

"What are they doing?" Cody asked.

"Looking for cheaters," Felipe answered from next to Cody. He wouldn't get a chance to escape with Felipe glued to his side, not to mention Daniel, who stood about five feet behind them.

"Making sure there's no poison on the fur," Andressa said. "It's not common in our professional circuit. Most of the people we fight are reputable, but it's still a precaution. It happens more often in *street fighting.*" She said the words as if it was a lowly form of a great sport.

After the dogs were clean and dry, the men exchanged fighters, and everybody headed back to the crude ring, the whole buzzing crowd shifting toward the fight. The sweat, the smell of beer, the tension filled the air, but Andressa appeared confident that Silva would win.

His white fur gleamed as he strutted around his corner. The referee yelled to the handlers, but even if Cody had been able to understand, he wouldn't have heard with the growing noise. Miguel and the other guy nodded, and the crowd squeezed in, barely leaving any breathing room.

The dogs stood across from each other, behind a white line in each of their corners of the square ring, and the handlers removed the collars. The ref said something, and the two dogs, their bodies pure muscle, sprung toward each other, growls filling the air. The cheering and shouting exploded through the room.

The two fighters attacked, each going for the other's neck. They stood on their hind legs in a morbid dance of snapping jaws and sharp teeth. Silva clamped onto Breno's neck and dragged him down before clambering on top.

They rolled around on the ground, two biting machines, as the crowd yelled and screamed. Silva ended up on top again, and his opponent struggled. Silva lost his grip but quickly got ahold again.

Cody nudged Andressa. "How long does this usually last?"

She kept her gaze on the ring. "Anywhere from ten minutes to maybe two hours. I've never seen one go that long before."

Cody about choked. "Are you kidding?"

She gave him an exasperated look before focusing on Silva again. "Thirty minutes to an hour is normal."

An hour of fighting, of slowly tearing your opponent apart. These people were cruel, and he didn't want to stand here and watch a dog die, for an hour.

The referee yelled, and the two handlers rushed in, tugged the dogs apart, and led them back to their corners.

"Yes," Andressa clapped her hands. "This is good, Cody, very good. They were only fighting ten minutes."

This time the other guy released Breno first, and as soon as he charged off, Miguel let Silva go. Cody swung his head casually to look for Daniel and Enzo, but they were not far behind him, and with Andressa and Felipe flanking him, he'd never be able to run. He needed an opening, a big distraction, because he had no doubt someone would take him down if he tried to run away.

The dogs continued their fighting, grasping each other's necks until the handlers ran out once again and pulled them to their respective corners. A dog fight was a strangely organized thing, not a no-holds-barred fight till the death like he'd been expecting. In a way, it was a bit boring, after the first few minutes at least.

"Why do they keep stopping and restarting?" Cody asked after the men pulled the dogs apart five minutes later. The other handler frowned at his dog.

"Because Breno turned. If a dog turns their head and shoulders away, he's given up. If even for a moment. And after he turns, it's up to him to start the fight again. If he doesn't leave the handler's side, he'll lose." Andressa grinned triumphantly. "Silva has never turned from a fight."

So a dog didn't have to die. Thank goodness.

Miguel paced his small corner, his face tight, but underneath was a smile he was holding in. His opponent, on the other hand, stood still with crossed arms and clenched jaw.

Spots of blood darkened Breno's fur, and Cody wondered if the smell of blood propelled Silva even more. He continued his relentless attack, sinking his teeth into the other dog's neck.

Vicious.

The men separated the dogs once again, but this time Breno didn't leave his corner. The handler screamed at him, but the poor thing cowered, never removing his eyes from Silva's corner.

The referee called out something, and the room erupted.

Carolina jumped up and down, giving out hugs to all her friends—even Cody, but all he saw was the handler driving his boot into Breno's hind end. The poor dog had survived the fight, just to be beaten by his owner.

Enzo wrapped his arm around Andressa's shoulders. "Marcos will be pleased. You've got yourself a grand champion on your hands."

"Yes, he will." She held back her smile, but Cody knew she was screaming inside.

A bunch of people clapped her on the back, congratulating her, and Cody watched the whole surreal scene. This might be his chance to escape with Andressa distracted. He glanced up and didn't see Felipe, and Daniel and Enzo were busy with others.

Half a second later, a hand clamped down on his back. "So what did you think?" Felipe asked. Cody stared at the other handler as the guy yanked on Breno's leash, the collar digging into a gash on the dog's bloodied neck. The man half-dragged Breno as he stomped away, leaving a streak of blood on the floor.

"What's going to happen to him?" Cody asked, not really wanting an answer.

Felipe followed Cody's gaze. "He won't be fighting again."

Why don't you just say it? Cody thought. The penalty for losing a fight was death. For all the shit Felipe had put him through, exposed him to, all the inhumanity he took part in, and Felipe couldn't come out and say the guy would kill his dog.

Andressa said that her dogs never lost, but who knew if that was true, or if it was her deluded ego talking. She'd probably killed some of her own.

"That's how it works," Felipe said, a slight bit of empathy in his voice.

"It's wrong."

Those dogs should have a chance at life, but a normal life wouldn't happen for them. Andressa might not physically abuse her dogs, but he couldn't say the same for the others. So many of these dogs were mistreated and neglected. They were loaded guns, and someone might unknowingly pull their trigger and set them off. They'd be a danger to the people trying to save them.

Maybe it was better that they were put down, although this dog wouldn't die from a gentle shot in a vet's office.

Andressa clutched his arm, her face bursting with excitement. "Let's go, Cody."

He had to wipe those thoughts away and pretend to be happy.

"Where we going now? Out to celebrate?" Maybe he'd get a second chance, unlike the poor dog.

"No, we're going home. I don't think you're ready to hit the clubs yet."

The trust wasn't there yet, not fully, but it would come, and at some point, she wouldn't bring his babysitter along. He'd acted properly and followed the rules tonight, and he would keep playing her game until she was confident he wouldn't run.

He trudged to the car, and they started driving to the compound. His taste of freedom drained like the blood of the dog.

Chapter Twenty-Four

Day 21

The next morning Andressa replayed the whole fight for him. Multiple times.

"I knew Silva was ready for this fight. My training regimen worked. It's not solely the physical aspect. It's food and total well-being." Her eyes narrowed. "Enzo thought he didn't have one more in him. He was wrong."

"No kidding." Cody could recite her stories word for word by now.

"I argued with my father. I said Enzo didn't know what he was talking about, and now Silva proved Enzo wrong." She sat back with a satisfied smile. "The fight was bigger than expected. Word must've gotten out because I earned a lot of money." She smiled seductively, and Cody worried she might drag him to the bedroom.

He spent a torturous two hours *celebrating* with her last night. At least this morning's routine was normal.

"I can't wait to talk to my father."

Cody nodded along. He could definitely wait... like forever.

"You'll finally get to meet him." Andressa clapped her hands together excitedly, and Cody shot up in his seat.

"What?" They were going to see Marcos Cardoso. The cartel leader, the killer... the black diamond piranha. Cody tried to swallow his nerves back. He wasn't ready for this—no way.

"He wants to congratulate me, I'm sure. We'll be leaving at ten for his condo in Manaus, so you don't need to go to the kennel."

Great—two hours to freak himself out over this. He hoped he'd make it out of this meeting alive.

"I've got another surprise." Andressa sidled up to him with a package. "Unwrap it."

He removed the paper slowly because that's how Andressa would want it. The light reflected off a screen. He fumbled for the on button, unable to contain his excitement. "You got me an iPad?"

The internet. He could email his parents, get help, get away from her.

"A thank you would be nice." Her icy voice chilled him.

"I'm sorry. You're so sweet." He wrapped his arm around her waist and hugged her, his freedom feeling within reach again.

Her scowl melted. "I thought you might like something else to do. It's set up for you, and if you want any games or movies, tell Daniel, and he'll download them."

"Wait—why can't I?"

"You won't have access to wi-fi." She stood, and his arm slipped away with his hopes. He'd been stupid to expect that she'd let him use the internet.

"Thanks." He forced a smile and made an excuse to leave. She'd dangled that damn carrot in his face and then ripped it away.

After breakfast, she sent him out to the kennels to retrieve a file, and he took his time driving the golf cart. These small vehicles would never bust out of that sturdy front gate. He grabbed the flash drive from the kennel office and headed back outside, almost taking out a loaded-down Simona. She stumbled to the side and dropped a stack of clean towels.

"I'm so sorry." He scrambled to pick up the towels. "I wasn't paying attention."

"I'm fine." She tried to take the other towels from him, and he shook his head.

"Let me help you." He turned away and held the door open for her. She swished by in her gray dress, and the picture of her dripping wet from the other night invaded his head: the little rivulets of water running down her shoulders, the determination on her face.

He shook the image away.

Cody threw the towels on the table in the grooming room, and Simona gave him a wide smile. "Thanks for your help."

"It's the least I can do. I knocked you down after all."

They stood there staring at each other. Despite her drab, dull clothes, makeup-less face, and hair pulled back, her eyes sparkled. He wanted to talk to her, to go sit in a quiet bar, have a drink, and get to know her, but that would never happen.

"I love Bud Light," he said.

"Bud Light?" She raised her brows as she picked up a towel and started folding.

"Um, yeah. Bud Light. It's an American beer. The stuff here is okay, but it's not the same." *Stop rambling.* "And Lays potato chips with sour cream and onion dip." He sighed. "Andressa would never buy potato chips."

Oh shit. Andressa. He patted the flash drive in his pocket. "I'd better get back. She's waiting for me."

"Thanks again for your help, Co-dee," Simona said. He backed toward the door and waved, but before he slipped out, she spoke again in a quiet voice. "I love hallacas. Every Christmas we'd work together to make our special meal. My aunts and cousins." A light smile hung on her lips as she stared at the towels.

"What is it?"

Her head snapped up. "One of my favorite meals. We make a special dough and add meat and raisins and capers, then wrap it in plantain leaves and boil them. They're delicious."

Cody couldn't quite picture in his head what she meant, but he wouldn't ruin her memory by asking. "It sounds delicious."

"It is. But you'd better get going." She waved him away, and he eased out the door. He'd better come up with a story for Andressa as to why he took so long.

*

Cody tried paying attention on the drive to Manaus with Felipe and Andressa, but they made too many turns, and he soon lost track.

"My father is so excited to meet you," Andressa gushed. "He likes to meet all my boyfriends. But don't let his gruff exterior get to you. He's a teddy bear once you get to know him."

Cody glanced into the mirror to see Felipe laughing silently.

They drove into a downtown area, and Cody gaped out the window. Newer buildings were mixed in with older styles, bright colors among graying concrete. People filled the streets dressed in anything from suits to t-shirts and shorts, and colorful markets mixed with boring office buildings and beautiful architecture, no rhyme or reason to styles, no consistency in upkeep. Half the buildings looked like they needed a new paint job thirty years ago, and the newer buildings still looked old. The weather must be tough on them.

A car zipped in front of them, and Cody noticed the lack of pavement markings. Some streets had them, many did not. Driving here would not be fun.

"Here's my father's building." Andressa tapped on the window.

Cody had just enough time to peer up before they drove into the parking garage. Andressa had said it was a skyscraper, but it was similar to the other high rises around, maybe twenty-thirty floors at best guess, but no skyscraper. There were no skyscrapers from what he saw.

Felipe flashed a card at the gate, and they descended into the bowels of the building. As they walked to the elevator, both Felipe and Andressa flanked him, no way to run. Plus Felipe had the gun— been happy to show it to him before they left.

Baby steps though.

Several elevators lined the wall, and Andressa pranced to the last one, scanned a card in front of the sensor, and a few moments later the doors opened. Inside the elevator, she tapped in a code on a keypad, and the elevator started rising. Other than the ten number keypad, no other buttons were there.

At the top, they exited into a small lobby that held a desk, a computer, some chairs, and a stern security guard. Andressa nodded to him and marched to the large door. She scanned her card again, touched her finger to the screen, and strode in.

Holy hell. The spacy foyer with white marble floors and twelve-foot ceilings was as big as Andressa's bedroom. It opened to an expansive apartment with luxurious furniture, artwork on the walls, and a sense of elegance. Cody had never been in a penthouse apartment, and this one was everything he'd imagined it to be.

"Papai," Andressa called into the open condo. Cody took in the view out the floor-to-ceiling windows, the city below, and the wide river that seemed so close.

"Olá," a female voice said. A beautiful woman in a short skirt and skimpy tank top strolled through the archway. The smile fell from Andressa's face.

"Where's my father?" Her whole body stiffened, her voice tight.

The woman responded in Portuguese, and Andressa's grimace grew at every word.

"Marcos had business to attend to," Felipe whispered. "Big surprise."

"Cody," Andressa said, spinning around. "My father said to wait because he should be back soon. We can wait in his office." She waved for Cody to follow.

"Hi. I'm Cody." He stuck out his hand to the other woman, trying to keep his eyes on her face and not her bulging cleavage.

"Sofia." The woman clasped Cody's hand, but instead of shaking, she held his hand in her palm and ran her fingers over the top of his skin, almost petting him.

Andressa jerked his arm back.

"Sofia is father's personal assistant." Andressa didn't even try hiding her scorn. "We'll be in the office. Felipe, you can wait out here. Cody and I have things to discuss."

They stepped inside the huge office with its imposing wood desk and plush leather chairs. Nothing was out of place.

"You don't like her very much." Cody went to the window, which looked the opposite direction, the whole city laid out in front of him.

"The only reason she's here is because of what's between her legs. But I don't give a damn about her. She's one in a long line of sluts trying to take advantage of my father." Andressa's emotions betrayed her words. "He worked hard for everything he has. He built his empire and this very building." She squeezed Cody's hand. "This will be mine someday. It can be ours."

"That would be nice." Cody hid his disgust, but it wasn't necessary. Andressa was busy staring out the window all dreamily.

"My father will need someone to take over for him eventually. Jorge likes Columbia too much. And Enzo... he doesn't have the business sense I do." Andressa spun him around, leaning his back against the window. Her hands wound around his neck, her lips inches from his. "Can you see us here, Cody? We'll make love every night on top of the world."

She pressed her lips onto his, slowly trailing her hands to his shorts. First the button came undone, then the zipper, and her hands worked him up. She commanded him to undress her, but once they were both naked, she took control.

As Andressa bounced on top of him, he considered throwing himself from the top of this building to end this nightmare.

But he didn't want to die. Besides, there was no way to break the thick glass easily.

No. Cody would continue to gain her trust until it was safe to escape, he'd get to the embassy, and his nightmare would end.

After dressing their sweaty bodies, Cody and Andressa joined Felipe in the family room as he watched a soccer game. Or futebol rather, a name he'd never get used to using.

"Futebol is so boring." Andressa sighed. "Change it to something different."

Felipe flipped through the channels until Andressa told him to stop. Someone was singing on a stage, and he wished they could watch soccer again. She pulled her knees up and cuddled next to Cody. It hit him then.

He'd just had sex in Marcos Cardoso's office. Marcos, the damn head of a cocaine cartel, probably now had a video of Cody having sex with his daughter. What was Andressa doing to him? He wiped his sweaty forehead.

No. She wouldn't do that if there were cameras. Maybe drunk she was a little looser, but not stone-cold sober.

"Someday I'll bring you to the Teatro Amazonas and Casa das Artes. I know one of the artists who is exhibiting there. I'm sure your father would love it."

His head worked overtime trying to figure out why she'd bring up his dad. He'd hardly talked about his parents since he got to Brazil, tried to avoid telling her about them at all, and she rarely asked. The uneasy feeling crept through him.

"What about your mother? Does she enjoy museums and art galleries?" Andressa asked.

"Yes."

"Really?" Andressa grabbed his arm. "I've got so many things I want to show you here. I usually get to most of the productions at the Teatro Amazonas. I've recently gotten involved with their board. They always appreciate my donations."

Felipe yawned loudly.

How many boards did she belong too? Wouldn't they be stunned to find out the queen of charities ran a dog-fighting ring. That'd make the front page for sure.

A door slammed, and Sofia rushed into the room, holding an armful of flowers in a vase. The light drained from Andressa's eyes.

They exchanged words, Andressa's scowl deepening. She jumped to her feet and folded her arms. "My father is unable to make it because his meeting has gone long. I need to leave a note for him, and then we'll go."

She stalked toward the office.

"Good day, gentlemen." With a nod, Sofia left, Cody and Felipe both watching her retreating figure.

"Great ass, huh?" Felipe knocked Cody in the arm. "Don't tell Carolina I said so though."

"Is she really his personal secretary?"

"The old man has lots of *personal secretaries*." He smirked. "This one takes care of his business here. And when I say she takes care of business here, I mean she runs errands and waits around to be fucked. Would be nice to have beautiful women like her waiting on you all the time." He chuckled. "Again, don't mention that to Carolina."

Cody just rolled his eyes.

Felipe's face grew serious. "Don't be fooled by Carolina's small size. She can even kick my ass."

Heels clicked on the marble floor again. "Let's go," Andressa snapped.

Felipe jumped to his feet. "Cody and I were talking. Thinking we should maybe stop off at the bar for a drink."

Andressa directed her angry stare at Cody, and he opened his mouth to defend himself, but Andressa tugged on his arm and led him to the door. Cody would have to wait to meet the head of a drug cartel, and he wasn't sure if that was a good or bad thing.

With Andressa's mood, probably bad. The drive home was silent.

Chapter Twenty-Five

Day 24

After showering, Cody headed into the closet for clothes. "Sinto muito," a voice said.

Simona stood in the door with a bunch of hangers strung across her arm. She took in his almost-naked body, and he gripped his towel tighter across his waist.

"I didn't know you were in here. I'm sorry." Simona backed out of the doorway.

"Your arms are full. Let me get my clothes, and I'll go dress in the bathroom."

"No, I shouldn't be in here. Miss Andressa will be upset." Her eyes followed his chest down to his waist.

"She's doing yoga. Don't worry." He retrieved his clothes and scooted out the door. "She'll be upset if you don't get the laundry put away too."

"True." She watched him head into the bathroom. Cody missed talking to Simona—not that they talked a lot, but besides Vera, she was one of the few who understood his situation, and having an ally was nice.

Fully dressed, he peeked through the door. Simona was still putting away the folded clothes, including his underwear. Vera and the ladies had been doing his laundry all along, but he'd never thought much about it. Not only was Simona folding his boxers into nice smooth squares, but she was responsible for putting away Andressa's slinky lingerie.

Simona probably knew he and Andressa were having sex. His face heated. That was so stupid because of course she assumed it was happening, but he hated for it to be so in-your-face. He hated that anyone knew he was sleeping with Andressa.

He shook off the embarrassment.

"I don't think I've ever said thank you for the work you do," Cody said, leaving plenty of space between them in case Andressa happened to return early.

"It's my job." She shrugged.

"Yeah, but really. I thought my mom was a perfectionist, but you…" He laughed. "I don't think I could ever be so neat."

Andressa wouldn't be too impressed with him if she saw his apartment. The only reason he was so organized now was because he had so few items of his own.

"Well, thank you." She bowed her head. "I do my best."

Cody stared at her dark hair for a moment. "I thought of something new that I now love."

"What's that?"

"Migraines." Mostly Andressa's.

Simona's light, airy laugh filled the room, a beautiful sound. Andressa rarely laughed. She was always rigid and formal, never let loose and be herself. Despite being held captive, Simona still smiled and laughed.

Simona stared at him with a grin. "I'm not sure I can top that."

"Top what?" Andressa's steely voice filled the room, and an emotionless curtain descended on Simona's face. "What are you doing in here, Simona?"

"I'm putting your clothes away." She stacked the shirts, the tension in the room thickening under Andressa's dark gaze.

"I said you're not supposed to be alone with my boyfriend." Andressa stepped next to Cody, her arms folded.

"I'm sorry, Miss Andressa." Simona's hand smoothed out an invisible wrinkle over and over.

"Then why are you here?" The rage in Andressa's voice rose. Cody had to do something. He grabbed Andressa around the shoulders so she was face-to-face with him.

"It's my fault." He draped one arm over her and slid his finger down her face. "I was thinking about you… about this morning… about how I didn't get enough of you." Cody lowered his voice and moved his lips closer to hers. "I knew you wouldn't make love to me if there was a basket of clothes sitting here, so I told her to finish the job." He kissed Andressa's lips, hating how Simona was witnessing the act.

Andressa's mouth curled into a smile. "Didn't get enough of me, did you?" She pecked at his lips quickly, then barked, "Finish up, Simona, and shut the door on the way out."

Luckily, Simona only had a few things left, and soon the door clicked shut. Andressa unzipped his pants, pushing him to the bed. He'd take his punishment, and it wouldn't bother him because Simona got away without a reprimand.

When they were finished, Andressa cuddled in his arms. He realized something then. He hadn't seen Yasmin for a while, and Simona had been around the house more than usual.

"Where did Yasmin go?" he asked.

"I had to get rid of her. She was doing such a lousy job."

The goosebumps rose on Cody's arms. That dog handler had gotten rid of his dog. "What do you mean *get rid of her*?"

"I found a new position for her. I didn't get *rid* of her." She laughed. "You're too much sometimes, Cody."

He laughed along, but he wouldn't put it past Andressa.

*

Cody stood perfectly still on the steps, listening to a screeching Andressa, her voice rising and falling in Portuguese.

A male voice fought back with the same intensity.

He should go upstairs, hide in the bedroom, or slip out the back, but his curiosity wouldn't let him leave. A big smack accompanied Andressa's shrill yelling, and Enzo stormed out of the office toward the front door. Cody shrunk back, but Enzo didn't see him, and the front door slammed.

Andressa stepped out of the room, staring at the door while she rubbed her right hand. Cody slowly and quietly backed up to the top step and then made a noise as if he was just reaching the steps.

"Andressa, there you are," he said as he came downstairs. Her head whipped around, her angry eyes zeroing in on him. "I was …"

Oh crap. He hadn't thought this through. He had to say something good. Her face was tight, her arms folded like she was about to jump down his throat.

"I was going to the kennels, but then I thought maybe you could take a break, and we could go for a swim. The sky is clear."

Andressa huffed. "I don't have time to play, Cody. Some of us have work to do. Get to the kennels."

He slipped out the front door. What had he been thinking anyway? He didn't want to hang out with her. Halfway down the steps, the door flung open behind him.

"Cody," Andressa said, all sugary sweet. "I decided I need a break. I've been working too hard. I'll go with you."

He pasted a phony smile on his face and turned around. "Great."

At the kennels, she dragged him and Levi to the treadmill room with instructions on increasing Braz's training to prepare him for the next fight.

"It's about time you get here," Levi muttered when Andressa was busy digging in a cupboard. "I'm not sure why she brought you to the dog fight and not me." He snorted. "Oh yeah, you're fucking her." He turned on his smile and headed for Andressa, his voice back to normal. "Can we talk for a minute? Privately."

"We'll be right back," Andressa said and disappeared out the door with Levi following.

Cody figured they'd be gone for a few minutes, so he didn't start anything with Braz, but it stretched into twenty. Andressa stuck her head in the room. "Let's go. I need to show you how to be a proper manager."

Outside, Simona stood on the grass, a soldier waiting for orders as Andressa marched up to her.

"I know how much you like working outside, so I have a new job for you." Andressa tilted her head to the side and smiled as if doing a grand favor.

"Thank you, Miss Andressa." Simona's voice was flat.

"Come along, then." Andressa grabbed Cody's hand. He almost pulled back—he wasn't a little boy, but stopped himself. She brought everybody to a big gray bucket, and a puppy ran over. She ignored his nipping at her feet, so Cody picked the dog up.

"The yard needs to be cleaned. Pick up the waste and put it in this bucket. Miguel will show you where to dump it."

Simona nodded and then looked around. "Where's the shovel?"

"There is none. You may use your hands."

"What?" Simona choked out.

"You can pick up the waste with your hands." Her tone had taken on a seething anger, growing stronger by the second.

"Andressa?" Cody's stomach rolled. She couldn't be serious. "She needs a pooper scooper."

"This whore," Andressa said, punctuating every word, "is opening her legs for everyone. And after I told her specifically there is no fraternizing between employees."

"I didn't… who?" Simona shrunk away, waving her hands in front of her face. "I would never have sex with anybody. It's not true." She shook her head wildly.

"Cut the lies. You had sex with Levi." Andressa spun on Cody. "She's been chasing after him, tempting him since she got here."

"But… but… I didn't—"

"We have rules here, Simona." Andressa towered over Simona with ice-cold eyes. "And those rules have a reason." She folded her arms, standing her ground. "Get to work."

"But—"

"Now!" Andressa screeched.

Simona's shoulders drooped as she trudged away with the bucket. She crisscrossed the yard, starting at the bottom of the pen.

"You can't," Cody pleaded. "It's disgusting… It's dog shit. She can't use her hands."

Andressa whipped around. Her eyes shot daggers at him, and her hands fisted. "This is not your business."

"But she—"

"No!" Andressa shrieked. "She's no better than the dog crap in the yard, and it's time she learned her place."

Simona stood tall, determination in her eyes. Then she lowered to the ground, and her hand hovered in the air above the brown pile. With a quick swoop, she swept up the crap. Cody cringed.

Simona stared at her palm and slowly straightened to standing. She tossed the crap into the bucket with her head held high and continued her search of the grass.

"Andressa," Cody begged. "Don't—"

Andressa smacked Cody, and he stumbled backward, holding his cheek. "I told you no. No! No! No!" she screamed as she stomped toward him. "This is unacceptable. Your insolence. I thought we were done with this."

Cody backed away and slammed into the wall, and Andressa shook her fist in his face. "This is my house, and you will do as I tell you."

"Andressa," Felipe called as he ran toward them. "What's going on?"

Andressa stalked away from Cody and grabbed onto the chain-link fence on the dog cage. She gripped it tightly and took deep breaths. Then she spun around and faced them both.

"You need to have another *talk* with Cody." She glowered. Felipe clenched and unclenched his fist of steel several times. This hit would be harder than the last time.

"No. I'm sorry," Cody babbled. "It was a misunderstanding. I was just trying to help. That's not necessary."

"Andressa?" Felipe said.

She scrutinized Cody as he quivered, a scared dog in front of Felipe. Part of him deserved a beating for being such a pathetic wimp, but the other part didn't want a broken nose or anything else.

Andressa rushed to Cody and held her finger in front of her face. "This time I'll give you a break, but not again, Cody. Not again."

She let the heavy warning sink in, spun around, and stomped away. "I'm going to see my father, Felipe. Make sure he doesn't get into any more trouble."

Then she was gone.

Chapter Twenty-Six

Day 24

"What the fuck was that about?" Felipe huffed, staring after Andressa's retreating figure.

Cody's face burned, his whole body on fire. He avoided looking at Simona, who was busy cleaning up the dog crap, and steadied his voice. "Andressa is punishing Simona, and I tried to help her."

Felipe's nose wrinkled as Simona picked up more dog shit and put it in the bucket. "When will you learn?"

"I did." He wouldn't make such a stupid mistake again. As much as he hated to see Simona punished, he couldn't afford to help anyone but himself. They were all trapped in this hell-hole, and if he didn't wise up, he'd find himself in a shallow grave.

"Don't you have things to do?" Felipe asked, and Cody nodded. They headed to the training side of the kennels, and Felipe left Cody to go to the office.

Braz was in full training mode now, complete with a special diet and extra supplements.

"Hey, boy." Cody adjusted the thick steel chain around Braz's neck and scratched in the places Braz couldn't reach. "Ready to run on the treadmill?"

The way these dogs listened was amazing; Miguel had trained them well. Cody's black lab growing up had been a perpetual puppy for most of his life, rambunctious and affectionate but not a good listener despite all the training his mother did.

Braz sat in front of the treadmill looking at Cody, and once he gave the okay, Braz jumped on the treadmill. Cody hooked up the harness and raised the incline. Braz started out at a slow walk, which lasted a few minutes, and then Cody raised the speed little by little until Braz was running.

The treadmill was usually Cody's first choice when helping with dog training. He wasn't about to volunteer for the aggression training, where Miguel or Levi wore protective clothing and a special sleeve so that the dogs could bite at them. No way. And so far nobody had asked him to be the one to sacrifice a small animal to reward the dogs.

Braz finished his run, his long pink tongue hanging out, the Gene Simmons of the Dogo Argentino. Cody missed hearing Dad sing classic rock songs—the man who wore white and black face paint and snuck into KISS concerts in his youth, the man who ran around with long hair and an earring. He grew up to be a history professor. It made Cody smile.

Braz got a drink, and then Cody took him outside to toss the ball around. Simona stood outside the wall to Fausto's pen, her petrified face red and sweaty. She backed away from Braz.

"They won't attack you. They're surprisingly nice dogs." Unless somebody gave them the command to attack.

"I've seen what they can do. Andressa's shown me several times. They're vicious."

He'd watched a practice match between Braz and one of Rodrigo's strays, a dog weakened because he'd survived off scavenged food and then was forced to live in a tiny pen in Andressa's back room. Braz ripped into that dog even though he put up a strong fight, and its death didn't take long. The violence was much worse than the dog fight last week.

Cody took in Simona's damp forehead and offered to get her a drink. She accepted, and he took Braz with to get the water. When they returned, Simona's gaze tracked Braz's movements, but she took the water and gulped down the chilled liquid.

"Is it cooler in Venezuela?" he asked. "I'm not used to this heat." He pressed his own water bottle to his cheek.

"It's just as hot, but we get cooler. And nowhere near as much rain."

Braz shifted, and she stepped back, eyeing him. "I didn't do it, Cody," she blurted, still watching Braz.

He knelt and pet the dog, trying to put Simona at ease. "What do you mean?" He pretended not to notice the brown smeared on her one hand and ignored his rolling stomach. If Simona could handle the putrid stench, he would too.

"I didn't sleep with Levi. He keeps after me, and I keep saying no. I don't know why he told Andressa I did." Her desperation convinced him her words were true. That and he wouldn't put it past Levi to pull such a jerk move.

"Why didn't you explain it to her?" Cody asked. But Simona had tried to deny it. "I mean, why didn't you tell her what he was doing before?"

Simona eyed him funny. "Do you think she cares about me?"

God, no. Cody hung his head. Andressa let Enzo and Luiz rape her. Andressa beat her. Nobody here cared about Simona—well, maybe Vera.

He had to help Simona. Once Andressa calmed down, he'd say he spoke to the guys and found out the truth. Hell, Levi might even fess up to everything if Cody talked to him.

"I'll talk to her. I'll tell her he's lying." He'd make Andressa listen and see the truth about Levi. Cody had a ton of his own stories about how the lazy ass Levi talked smack about women while at work.

"No, I don't need your help."

He glanced at her shit-covered hand, the putrid smell filling his nose, and he opened his mouth to breathe instead. Simona seemed so small and fragile. Somebody needed to stick up for her, and nobody else here ever would.

"I can convince her—"

"No, Cody," she said abruptly. "You will do nothing. You won't say anything to her or him. I want this to go away, so let me do my job."

He stared at her helplessly. There was nothing he could do, so why'd she tell him anyway? He led Braz back into his pen. The dog crap closest to the gate was now gone.

"Um, I'm going to take Fausto out to play a bit. I'll bring him on the other side of the catmill."

Fausto ran out of his doggy door as soon as he heard Cody's whistle. Once Cody closed the doors to the run, and he and the dog were a safe distance away, Simona did her job, not looking so scared. He kept an eye out to make sure nobody was watching. If he got busted helping Simona, he would feel Andressa's wrath, but not as bad as Simona. Felipe would break her bones or leave her bruised for weeks.

"Thank you," Simona said, staring at her bucket of crap. The words built up in his throat again, wanting to apologize for not saving her the night she needed help the most. He needed to say something, anything. He didn't want her to leave.

"Simona, I'm sorry."

"Don't be. You're a prisoner like me."

He was, but he wasn't.

Cody had the run of the house, ate well, swam in a pool whenever he wanted, and had an iPad to waste time with when he was bored. He wasn't constantly degraded or abused. Simona stepped toward him and hid her hand behind her back.

"Someday…" She nodded and gazed off to the road. "Someday we'll be free."

His heart thumped inside. She had faith, unlike Vera, who had resigned herself to live out her sorry life and try stay alive. Cody would keep some hope inside, for both him and Simona, no matter what happened.

*

That evening, Cody sacked out on the couch watching yet another American movie dubbed in Portuguese, trying not to think about that asshole Levi.

Andressa's heels clicked across the floor, and she sat next to him and sighed long and hard. He still wanted to tell Andressa the truth, but he would honor Simona's wishes.

"Vera's got dinner ready," he said.

"How can I eat, Cody?" Andressa flipped off the TV, her jaw set. "How am I supposed to do anything when everybody is against me? My own family. My own brother." She huffed, and Cody held his breath, not knowing if he should ask or stay quiet.

She jumped up, stalked to the bar, and then filled a glass of wine from a bottle Cody had gotten out earlier. She perched on a barstool and stared at him expectedly. He followed her and poured his own wine.

"I have been working with Diego Melo for two years now, and he took him out. He's paranoid. He thinks everybody is after him."

"What do you mean?" And who took him out? And who the hell was Diego Melo? This family was the damn Brazilian mafia— beating the shit out of people when they didn't follow orders.

Her eyes narrowed on Cody. "He's a police officer who's been on my payroll. He's dependable and honest, but Enzo thought he was working for the other side, so now he's gone."

The heat crept up Cody's neck. This wasn't about a beat down. It was murder, and he shouldn't be surprised, but he was. It was so easy for Enzo. Someone disagreed with you, and you murdered them.

"He killed a police officer?"

"Yes!" Andressa threw her hands in the air. "Aren't you paying attention? Sometimes I don't think you're listening to me. I have so much to deal with, and you don't care." She let a long breath out and rubbed her temples. "He didn't talk to me first. He went off an irrational fear. As if I don't keep watch over the police. And my father told me—Me!—that I was wrong. He said Enzo's allowed to take out anybody he wants. This is my life, not his, and he can't keep his damn fingers out of my business."

Cody stared at the wine Andressa was downing. She continued rambling on about how her father let Enzo get away with undermining her authority, but all Cody thought about was the police officer who lost his life.

He chose to dance with the devil, and he got burned. Not like Cody and Simona, who were forced into this big clusterfuck. But then again, maybe the guy had no choice. Maybe they blackmailed him, and he was just trying to stay alive. He might be as innocent as Cody.

"Aren't you listening?" Andressa screeched.

"Yeah. I just—"

Andressa headed toward the stairs with the wine bottle and her glass. "Let's go."

"Where are we going? Vera has dinner waiting."

"You can have the leftovers tomorrow." Andressa stomped off without another word. Cody's stomach grumbled as he followed her up the steps. She would want a massage, she would want Cody to assure her he loved her, and once she settled down, then she'd want sex.

Not long after, they finally reached the last act in bed, and Andressa lay on her stomach underneath him, her legs spread as she waited for him to enter her. It would be so easy right now to kill her.

He ran his hand up her back to her shoulders and rubbed them, slowly working his way to her head. A little pressure on her slim, smooth neck and she would be dead.

"Cody?" Andressa's voice cut through the fog in his mind. She stared at him with questions in her eyes. He was sitting there, staring at her naked back as he straddled her waist. As much as he wanted to, he couldn't kill her.

"What are you waiting for?" she asked.

He shook off the daze and forced a smile on his face. "I was trying to think of something different."

She smiled seductively. "I'm up for different."

He faked his enthusiasm, and when they were done having sex, Andressa snuggled into his arms, blissfully unaware of his thoughts. Lucky for her, Cody wasn't like Enzo.

Chapter Twenty-Seven

Three days passed, and Andressa still bitched about how Enzo was sabotaging her work and her life. Cody listened, nodded his head, and offered sympathy, but he was smart enough to keep his mouth shut about Enzo. If he'd insulted her brother, told her what a jerk Enzo was, it'd come back and bite Cody in the ass at the worst time.

He and Andressa were watching a movie with English subtitles, but he was tired of reading the tiny words on the screen.

"Andressa," a deep voice boomed through the room, and she shot up.

"Papai." Her face wrinkled. "What are you doing here?"

The Marcos Cardoso, with speckled gray hair dressed in a gray suit, strutted into the room. His hard eyes didn't match his smile, and Felipe's words rang in Cody's head. *Marcos Cardoso... he's the fucking black diamond.*

And he was here in Andressa's house uninvited. *Holy shit.*

Cody scanned the room for possible escape, but what the hell would he do? Run? He wouldn't be out the door before Andressa called her goons on him. Cody tried to slow his thumping heart.

She jumped to her feet and ran to her dad, the Portuguese spilling out of her mouth hard and fast. Marcos was shorter than Cody had imagined, looked fairly respectable. Maybe this wouldn't be so bad. Maybe he wouldn't be angry at her and take it out on Cody.

God, he was as delusional as Andressa now. Cody squeezed his eyes shut.

Their conversation bounced back and forth with lots of glances Cody's way, lots of frowns from Andressa, and she seemed to shrink before Cody's eyes. Between the few words Cody had learned and their body language, Marcos was bitching her out. She deserved every damn bit of it.

"Come meet my father, Cody," Andressa said tentatively.

Every step over to Marcos was like walking on hot coals. This man controlled so many lives with only his word: he made men, and he destroyed them. He destroyed his wife, and he wouldn't even give a second thought to destroying Cody. The deep breath Cody took did little to calm him down.

"Papai, this is Cody," Andressa said.

Cody raised his hand, praying it wouldn't tremble. Marcos's firm handshake was as cold as his heart.

"Andressa and I have business to attend to, so she will not be free this evening."

"Yes, Papai." The obedient daughter nodded.

Before Cody slipped away, another voice wafted into the room. Andressa's head flipped around, and her eyes shot open at the two men.

"Andressa," the first guy's voice rang out. Marcos nudged her, and she stepped forward. She responded with a hello in Portuguese, her tense voice matching her stiff body, and forced a smile. Her arms stretched out in front of her. It would be comical, except if Andressa was spooked, that didn't bode well for Cody.

The two men appeared to be about Marcos's age, both dressed in tailored dark suits, gray shirts, gray and black ties. Cody hoped it wasn't his funeral.

The man released her from his hug and swung her arms out, looking at her from head to toe like a child he hadn't seen for years. Cody stood, unsure what to do as the conversation flowed.

Finally, the man let her go and stepped back. Marcos spoke, and she shook hands with the second guy.

"This is Vitor and Carlos," Marcos said. "Two of my associates." He turned to Andressa. "Carlos was possibly interested in financing your expansion plans."

"Oh." Andressa seemed surprised. "Great." But from the way she said it, Cody wasn't sure she was too excited about the idea. She'd mentioned how she wanted to expand the breeding business once or twice but had never told him much about her plans, and he didn't think she'd decided what to do yet.

"So the beautiful Andressa has a man." Vitor eyed him curiously. "I'm not surprised, but I hope you won't mind if we borrow her for the evening."

Andressa flinched ever so slightly.

"I'll get drinks. Cody, can you help me before you leave?" Andressa tugged on his shirt.

"You're not leaving so soon. I want to meet the man who has stolen our Andressa's heart. He will stay with us for a drink." Vitor glanced at Marcos for confirmation, and he nodded.

"Yes, Tio Vitor." She slunk away to the kitchen.

Cody thought he'd have one drink and go, but every time he tried to leave, Vitor would grab his arm and say *one more*. Funny since they hardly included him in the conversation and stuck mostly to Portuguese. Every once in a while they'd break into English, but it didn't last long.

The alcohol and coke flowed freely between the three men, but Andressa sat stiffly beside Cody, almost as if on autopilot. The whole thing was surreal. Cody had always felt weird drinking in front of his parents, even when he was of age, and he couldn't imagine his parents doing cocaine. But then again, he couldn't imagine being the daughter of a drug kingpin either, or being kidnapped and brought to Brazil to help with a dog-fighting ring.

Just before midnight, Marcos turned to Cody. "I think it's time you retire to bed."

"I'll go with him." Andressa stood.

"No, you won't. You have guests to entertain," Marcos said in clipped English. "Goodnight, Cody."

The Portuguese poured out of Andressa's lips, and Marcos's face darkened. He leapt to his feet and slapped her across the cheek. She cowered underneath his waving hand and sharp voice. Cody had wanted to smack her a thousand times himself, but part of him felt bad for her.

No. He refused to let those feelings take hold.

"No matter how old a girl gets, she must respect the wishes of her father." Vitor chuckled, and Cody forced a nod.

She slumped into her chair, her head facing down, and Cody wondered if she'd pissed off Marcos or something, maybe gotten into a tiff with Enzo and was now gonna get a scolding. He'd love to see that.

"Goodnight, Cody," Marcos repeated.

"Um, yeah. It was nice to meet you." He reached out his hand, but Marcos turned a shoulder.

Andressa never once looked up as he left, and he headed to his room, to safety. Soon he climbed into bed and waited, playing around on the iPad for a while. He wanted to know who those guys were.

Cody tried another random password to connect to Andressa's network. Stupid maybe—it was completely useless, but he wouldn't give up.

Andressa didn't show, and by two o'clock, Cody settled in and fell asleep.

*

Cody was surprised he'd slept through Andressa's alarm. He took a look at the smooth blankets on her side. She must not have come to bed last night. Marcos partied like his son.

He lingered in the shower, not wanting to see any of them again, but finally he had to go down. Simona was removing the sheets from the bed in one of the bedrooms. Cody glanced around but didn't see anybody, so he stepped into the room.

"Did Marcos stay here last night?" he whispered.

She startled and spun around. Her gaze flickered over his shoulder to the hallway, her face tense.

"Nobody's out there. I checked." Cody took a step back and continued to watch up and down the hallway. "All clear. They must be eating breakfast."

"I'm not sure. They were gone when I arrived." She gathered everything in a basket and skirted past Cody. He watched her head to the laundry room. She wouldn't risk talking to him right now, so he went downstairs.

Andressa wasn't in the kitchen, but he found her in the gym, kneeling on her yoga mat facing the window.

"Good morning," he said, but she didn't respond. He stepped closer. Earbud cords hung from her ears, and he touched her shoulder. "Andressa."

She almost whacked him with her flailing arms. The damn fanatic couldn't even give up yoga for one morning, even after being up all night. The bags under her eyes were dark.

"When did your dad leave?" Cody asked.

"I don't know," she mumbled, setting herself into a new position. "I'm busy. Go eat breakfast and then go to the kennels. I have things to do."

They always ate together if she was home. He wasn't about to complain though. "Okay, I'll see you later."

She didn't answer, and he left. Vera was in the kitchen and made him breakfast.

"Do you know Vitor and Carlos?" he asked after she gave him his food.

She raised her hands out of the soapy water and turned, studying him. "Vitor yes, Carlos no."

"Andressa called him…" He thought back. "Tio Vitor. Is that uncle?"

"Yes, but he's not her real uncle. Were they here last night?" She wiped off her hands and leaned against the counter, her face dark.

"They didn't show up until the evening, but you must've been gone by then. I think they stayed up all night long. You should've seen all the coke they snorted, and Andressa never came to bed. She's probably gonna crash hard tonight."

"Yes, yes." Vera's head nodded, but she wasn't looking at him. She twisted the towel in her hands, her lips pursed, and then turned back to her dishes.

Cody finished his food and headed out to the kennels. Levi practically flew at him as soon as he got through the door. "Did you meet Marcos?" Levi asked. "What was he like? What did he think of you and Andressa?"

Cody took a step back from the star-struck jackass. "I don't know. He was okay." Marcos didn't even speak to him all that much.

"You met Marcos last night? He was here?" Felipe asked.

"Yeah. With Carlos and Vitor."

Felipe's eyes narrowed, and he looked at Levi. "Cody and I have computer work to do. Get your ass out of here so we can get it done."

Levi gave him a who-me look, but Felipe told him to go. He sulked away, and the door closed.

"How was Andressa this morning?" Felipe asked, his face so serious the question gave Cody pause.

"She's hungover. Kind of pissy."

"I'd suggest you give her space for a few days."

"Hey, I'll give her all the space she wants." Cody laughed, but Felipe didn't join in. "Why?" Cody said tentatively.

Felipe didn't say anything right away, and the seconds ticked by. "You'll learn this eventually, but you didn't hear it from me. Vitor and Andressa have a *special* relationship. They have since she was a teenager."

Andressa's discomfort over Vitor being there with him, all the alcohol she drank, her trying to leave for the night with Cody.

"She screws him?" Cody shook his head, trying to get the image of the old man and Andressa out. Vitor was her dad's age.

Felipe rubbed his temples. "I'm pretty sure it's not her choice. It's her duty." He let the words sink in for a moment. "So if I were you, I'd never bring up the name Vitor around her."

Andressa was Vitor's plaything, and her father allowed her to be abused. It was hard to wrap his head around the whole idea. Maybe in some world, it was justice for Andressa allowing Simona and Yasmin to get raped. Or maybe Andressa's feelings were so deadened, and she cared for nobody but herself. Cody didn't want to think about it all anymore.

"I'm going to find Miguel after I check on the animals in back," he said and headed for the door.

"Give her space," Felipe said again.

"I hear you." He shut the door behind him and dragged himself to feed the sacrifice animals. God, Andressa was just like them, a sacrifice to Vitor. The depravity in this family ran deep.

Cody finished and soon found Miguel rearranging bottles in the medicine cabinet. The dogs took a lot of vitamins and supplements. "Hey, what's the plan for today?" Cody asked.

Miguel stuffed the bottles away and spun around. "Stop sneaking up on me."

"I wasn't sneaking. What do you want me to do today?"

"I'll meet you in the treadmill room. Be there in five."

Cody left to wait, and after Miguel showed up, the morning passed quickly, no thanks to the lazy Levi, who was always trying to get out of work. It wasn't long before Cody went back to the kitchen. A small lunch waited—one plate only, but he didn't see Vera, so he headed to the office. No Andressa. He padded upstairs and found her lying in bed in the dark room.

He shut the door behind him. "Do you have a migraine again?" Crap, maybe she was sleeping. He shouldn't have spoken to her, but it'd be worth getting bitched out to have some Andressa-free days.

"Yes," she said, her voice muffled.

"You need anything?" He played the helpful boyfriend, and he felt sorry for her... a little. She didn't deserve to be abused any more than Simona did.

"No. Leave me alone." Her strangled voice barely made it from under the covers, so he left, not wanting to push it.

Downstairs he stopped to watch Simona cleaning the pool through the window. She set down the brush and slowly made her way to a lounge chair to sit. He followed her gaze across the patio area to a plump bird sitting on the table, the front feathers reddish-orange, and its back bright green and blue. But the orange beak was what caught his attention. It had to be about half the size of the bird, long and thin.

Simona stared at it as it strutted around the table, and when it flew off into the sky, she tilted her head up, a big smile on her face.

Cody cracked open the door. "Do you know what that was?"

"No," she replied, keeping her focus on the sky. He couldn't see the bird though. She glanced off toward the trees. "I'm not familiar with all the birds around here. There's so many, and they're so beautiful. I had a parrot growing up, and we taught him to talk. I've been on the lookout for any of them. Or a toucan. I haven't spotted one yet."

Cody almost laughed. In all this time he'd been here, he'd barely given any thought to the birds. Stupid because the rainforest was filled with unique creatures he'd never see again after he escaped. "They're a lot more colorful here than they are at home."

She smiled knowingly. "I'd love to go on a birdwatching tour. Carolina's company offers them, but that'll never happen." She dropped her head and stared toward her feet. Then she picked up the long handle of the brush and stood. "I'd better get to work."

She turned her back to him and started in on the pool, so he shut the door.

Later afternoon, Cody checked in on Andressa, but she told him to go away. And again in the evening, she snapped at him because her head was throbbing, and it was his fault for asking how she was doing. At ten-thirty he crawled into bed, happy to find her sleeping.

Monday morning she didn't wake him up for sex, and he slept until she returned from her morning exercise and flipped the light on.

"We've got a lot to do today, so get up," she said brusquely and headed for the bathroom.

"Your migraine must not've been a bad one, huh?"

She stopped at the doorway and stared at him with her dark eyes. "No."

The door slammed shut, and seconds later the shower started.

Chapter Twenty-Eight

Cody never thought watching somebody clean a room could be sexy, but Simona had that all down. He'd swear she was adding an extra little wiggle to her butt as she dusted, but no, he was imagining it.

Andressa was in the office talking to someone on the phone, and he was waiting for her to finish up. She hadn't said a word about her dad all week, and Cody was smart enough not to ask.

Simona wiped the dustless shelf. He shouldn't be watching her because if Andressa caught him, she'd tear him a new one. She'd been extra pissy lately.

So instead of watching Simona, or the TV, Cody played another stupid game on his iPad for a bit. Then he brought up the settings folder and stared at the wi-fi connection. Not only did the passwords he tried never work, but he'd searched office drawers and came up with nothing either.

Just for shits and giggles, he tried his own name in the password box again.

Denied.

Simona cleared her throat. "I'm finished in here, Mr. Cody. I'll go now." She stood there, her cleaning basket in hand, looking like she was waiting.

He knew what she wanted. He'd run into her yesterday, and although they only had a few moments, she'd told him one thing: *I love parrots.* He thought about telling her how he fostered dogs when he was a kid, but for some reason, something else popped into his head.

"I love Juicy Fruit," he said quietly. Gum was another thing he hadn't even seen since leaving the States.

"What are you talking about?" Andressa said from behind him.

His pulse flew into warp speed. She'd seen them talking. She would kick their asses. He could handle it, but Simona… Andressa would make her keep working even if she was covered in bruises. He never should've talked to her without looking around.

"Um, that berry. What's it called? Acai. I was wondering if we could get some. They grow down here, right? They're in a lot of juices and stuff in the U.S., and I've wanted to try them fresh."

"They're bitter. You won't like them." She spun to Simona. "What are you waiting for, a thank you?" Andressa snapped. "Go clean somewhere else."

Simona bowed her head and nodded. Then disappeared.

Andressa slid next to him on the couch. "Cody, if you need something, you come to me, or you ask Vera or Daniel. We've talked about Simona enough. She can't be trusted. She tried to take advantage of Levi, and she'll try to steal you away."

"Don't worry about me. I can handle myself." Cody threw up a grin, but Andressa didn't smile.

"I'm serious. She's a conniving bitch, and I don't want her getting her claws into you. I know how you want to help people."

"I don't care about her."

Distract, distract, distract. But Cody's head wasn't thinking clearly enough.

"Of course you don't, but your feelings won't stop her from coming after you."

"She's never done anything or said anything. I don't think she'd dare." He ran his finger over Andressa's ear lightly.

"You're right." Andressa gave him a wicked grin, and he shivered inside. She would beat Simona if she knew they talked often, and he should stop, but he couldn't. He needed her, needed to talk to someone in the same situation as him.

Andressa dragged him into the office to discuss the approaching fight, and Cody's ears perked up.

"It's Braz's turn now," she gushed. "He'll make us proud."

The dread over seeing another dog fight returned. Hopefully this one would have a favorable outcome like the last.

Daniel rushed into the room. "Andressa, we need to talk."

"Can't you see I'm busy," she barked.

"It's important. It's about a problem with one of our employees. I just found out this morning."

Andressa set down her pen, her face darkening. "Sit down."

"It might be better to discuss this alone."

Andressa looked to Cody, then back to Daniel. "Sit."

Daniel pulled out a chair. "I had a long talk with Levi. It seems there's more to the Simona situation than he previously mentioned. She was doing it only because she believed Levi would help her run away."

"That bitch! And she stands in my house acting as if she cares about her job." Andressa whipped out her cell phone and pounded out a text message. She stared at the screen, and Cody and Daniel watched her.

Barely ten seconds passed. "Cody, go to the kennels and get Levi," she huffed.

Simona tried to escape and never told him. Would she have sent the police out to rescue him? She'd lied to him too, said she hadn't slept with Levi, but she must have if she was trying to escape. Why didn't she tell him the truth?

Levi was watching porn again on the computer. No big surprise. Cody wanted to ask him some questions but figured he'd tell Andressa, and she'd become suspicious. They returned to the house, but Andressa shut the office door on Cody.

He eyed the steps, knowing Simona was upstairs. He still couldn't forget the picture of the poor bruised and battered girl after the Tomás situation, and Cody prayed Andressa wouldn't beat her to a pulp. If only he could speak to Andressa before she did anything.

"Simona," Andressa screeched, "get down here right now."

Simona scrambled down the steps and froze when she saw a smirking Levi. Her face fell.

"Get into my office." Andressa slammed her palm onto the wall, and Simona trudged into the room, her hands in her pockets and head down.

The office door banged shut, and Levi strutted through the front door. The shouting started immediately; Andressa didn't hold back, letting the Portuguese go. Cody couldn't see inside the office, but he cringed when he heard the crack of skin against skin. He had to do something.

Cody flung open the door. "Andressa, honey," he said, trying to steady his voice.

She whipped around red-faced, and her dark eyes drilled into him. "Get out," she said in a calm voice. Simona hunched over on the chair.

"I need—"

"I said get out. Felipe's already on his way over, so unless you want to *speak* with him, then you turn around and shut the door."

Oh god. Felipe would hurt her bad. Cody clasped onto the doorknob as Andressa stood glaring at him. Simona's cheek burned bright red, and her dark brown eyes implored him to leave. She mouthed the word "Go."

He had no choice. The front door swung open, and Cody backed away. Felipe thundered up behind him.

"What's up?" Felipe said nonchalantly, as if not noticing the raving lunatic and a girl with red wet eyes in front of him.

Andressa gripped Simona's shoulders and jerked her to her feet. "Take Simona to her room and stay with her until I get there." Andressa thrust Simona forward, and she stumbled. Then she righted herself, stood straight, and marched past Cody toward Felipe.

They watched Felipe escort Simona out the front door. He'd better not hurt her. Of course, it's not like Cody could do anything about it.

Andressa rose up in front of him. "Don't you dare feel sorry for that ungrateful bitch. She tried to run away and stick me with her debt. She brought this on herself. Now get out to the kennels and help Braz get ready for his fight."

Cody turned around and slunk out the door.

Chapter Twenty-Nine

Day 33

Fight night again. Andressa dragged Cody and crew to an upscale condo in downtown Manaus for pre-fight festivities, and Cody had hoped to find an escape, but no luck. Felipe was either next to him or had eyes on him for the whole two hours. Cody wasn't even allowed to piss without an escort.

After the party, they went one hundred eighty degrees to a scummy, half-deserted industrial area. Missing lights darkened the street, and graffiti covered the building walls. They parked the car and followed Tomás and Enzo into another crumbling building. It looked similar to the last, but they were in a different part of town.

Everything played out as did before. The people, the noise, the hulking bodyguard keeping him on a short leash. Cody had no chance to escape.

Miguel and the other handler traded dogs, and Braz came out shiny and wet from his bath. Andressa leaned over and whispered. "Ready to see another champion-to-be in action? I'm giving him twenty minutes to finish the job."

At the ref's word, the dogs jumped from their lines. The two dogs clamped onto each other's necks, trying to force each other down. Cody looked away to watch Andressa, a wide grin on her face. The lure of money brought greed out in not only the poor but also the wealthy.

A dog yelped, and Cody whipped around. The two handlers were pulling the dogs apart, and by the grin on Andressa's face, he knew the Pitbull had turned.

Sure enough, after being brought to their corners, the other guy had to let his dog loose first. The Pitbull charged across the floor with a ferocious growl and latched onto Braz. The dogs gripped each other in a gruesome wrestling match.

Time dragged slowly, and the handlers separated the dogs several times, both turning. Red splotches of blood showed on Braz's white fur, and the other dog slowed down with his limp. Braz turned once again and was led away. Andressa's neck craned, her face growing dim. Miguel spread the fur apart at Braz's neck to show a dark gash of red. Braz stood at his line, ready to attack again though.

Miguel glanced at Andressa and nodded. She relaxed her stance.

Braz leapt over his line, and when he met the Pitbull, they both tumbled to the ground. The Pitbull's giant jaws ripped a piece of Braz's ear out. He yelped and backed away, the red drops of blood dripping to the floor. Andressa swore.

Miguel led Braz to his corner with his bloody ear. He bent down and talked to his dog, but Cody saw a slight trembling in Braz's back legs. A winning dog had confidence, but Braz moved slowly, smearing the drops of blood on the floor with his paws. The ref motioned for Braz to start, and he crossed his line slowly.

The intensity of the crowd increased.

Andressa bumped into Cody, and he stumbled. Her face was a mask of fury, and she muttered angry and fast words to Enzo in Portuguese.

The two dogs rolled around on the floor, and when Braz turned away once more, the crowd roared. A yelling Andressa stomped to Braz's corner.

Miguel's face was taut, the fear in his eyes showing as he tried deflecting Andressa's verbal blows. Enzo reached for his sister, and she whacked at him, but he ripped her away from the ring.

The ref gave the nod, but Braz didn't move. Miguel nudged the trembling dog, but to no avail.

Andressa screeched unintelligible words. The ref said something, and the other handler smirked. Miguel knelt in front of

Braz, rubbed the back of his neck, and said words Cody couldn't hear. Probably a pep talk. *Go fight to your death, Braz. Ignore the pain. Ignore the fear.*

Miguel jumped to his feet and took his place. He patted Braz on the dog's back and gave his command, but the dog remained behind the white line.

Andressa's voice stuck out among the spectators, her rage a deep thunder in a rainstorm of cheers.

Braz didn't move no matter what Miguel did or said.

The ref called the fight, and Miguel's shoulders slumped. A crowd surrounded the handler and his Pitbull, and Miguel yanked Braz out of the ring toward a back door.

Andressa flew after them, Enzo on her tail. Cody followed too and found himself at the end of a dingy hallway. Miguel stood between a screaming Andressa and a quaking Braz. Miguel shook his head, his hands waving as if to ward Andressa off. He glanced back at Braz, the fear etched into his face.

Louder, faster, Andressa shouted, and Miguel's hands fell to his side. He slunk away, past Andressa, past Enzo, and finally past Cody, defeat emanating from his body. He leaned against the wall, his face down.

Braz yelped, and Cody spun around. Andressa stood over him, kicking him in the head, in the neck, Braz's once white head, now red.

"Andressa, stop!" Cody yelled and charged for her, but hands gripped his shoulders and held him back.

"It's too late," Felipe said, his voice empty. "She'll turn on you." He pushed Cody back and leaned against the wall, staring at the ceiling.

Over and over and over her boot slammed into the dog's body, an instrument of death stealing Braz's life.

He didn't fight back as she pummeled him. He collapsed on the floor, and Andressa reared up again. She jammed the stiletto into Braz's back, and it came out covered in blood. She continued to stab the dog, and blood spatters hit the wall, the metallic tang of blood mixing in with the stench of garbage.

The bile rose in Cody's throat, and his whole body wanted to shut down. Her cruelty. The torture. The heat swallowed him up, and he felt lightheaded. Cody turned away, unable to watch those bloody boots finish off poor Braz.

Miguel cringed with each yell from Andressa, but he made no move to stop her. Neither did Felipe, and Enzo stood there smirking. Cody closed his eyes.

Finally, Enzo yelled out Andressa's name. He stomped over to her and quickly and efficiently sliced across Braz's neck with the same knife he'd held to Cody's throat.

Moments later he stalked by with his knife, red drops trailing on the floor.

Andressa jerked Miguel off the wall, yelled something, and pointed the other direction. He responded, his jaw clenched, and shuffled toward Braz.

Andressa looked down at her shoes. "These were expensive." She sighed and disappeared down the hall.

Cody turned his head for one last look and followed the red footsteps. Miguel knelt over his dog. Blood gushed out of Braz's neck onto the floor, a pool gathering. Cody didn't know what to feel, his head in tumult. Grief over the innocent dog's death, but also relief the torture was over. The anger stirred in his belly along with the fear.

He'd known what she'd been capable of, but he'd never seen such unrestrained rage, and now that he'd witnessed a death at her hands, her fury scared him more than anything.

Nothing was said about the dog fight in the days following, and Cody tried to be on his best behavior around the short-fused Andressa. He was happy to be working in the kennel for the day, although Braz's bloody body wouldn't leave his mind. One more time he'd been unable to save someone who needed it. He couldn't save a poor dog's life. How was he going to save Simona or himself?

He'd been organizing the supply room for half an hour now and hadn't accomplished anything.

Miguel stuck his head in the room. "I need you to bring papers to Andressa. We'll need more help later, so come back after lunch."

Cody saluted him, and Miguel attempted a smile. Cody knew Miguel felt like crap by the way his sad gaze latched onto Braz's favorite toys and how he'd tried to hide how he got choked up as Cody cleaned out the kennel. Despite what she claimed, Andressa had no connection with her dogs, but Miguel did.

On the way out of the door, Cody rammed into somebody, a box hitting his stomach. His folder fell to the floor, papers spilling everywhere.

"Sorry," Cody said, surprised to see Enzo righting himself, the box clinking.

"Watch where you're going." Enzo glared at him and pushed past.

Asshole.

Cody gathered his stuff and headed to the golf cart. Simona was walking to the house, a bucket filled with gardening tools hanging from one hand, and Cody stopped, even though he was a little irritated with her. They were both stuck in this place, and she never mentioned she was trying to escape. He shouldn't be mad though. He was Andressa's *boyfriend* after all, even if not by choice.

"Need a ride," he asked.

The bucket thumped to the ground, the tools clanging together. "I'm okay," she said, looking up and down the road. She'd deny him again if he offered to take her, and he couldn't blame her.

"How about I take the bucket? I can set it by the house."

She shook her head but laughed lightly. "Okay, Cody. I give up." She hefted the bucket onto the seat next to him and got in.

He drove off down the road. A bird flew across their path, and he took in its black and white body and red head.

"Did you see that?" Simona asked. "It was so pretty."

Cody nodded. He'd been noticing them a lot more lately. "So are you going to work your magic in the garden?" Gardening definitely was her element.

"Yes." Her face fell, and she stared off into the trees. "I miss working in the garden with my mother. She taught me a lot, and there's so much more I need to learn." She brought her gaze back to Cody. "But I'm glad somebody around here appreciates it."

"Oh, Andressa does. She loves the flowers."

"She does?" Simona's cute nose wrinkled up. "She tells me how horrible they look. How bad a job I'm doing with them."

"No. She likes them." Cody sighed. Andressa couldn't give anyone the credit they deserved. "I'm glad she's not making you pick up dog crap still."

"Me too." Simona laughed. "But there was one good thing about it. Levi doesn't ask me to have sex with him anymore. He looks at my hands and runs away."

Cody chuckled, not knowing how Simona kept up her light side with everything happening around her and to her. He parked at the front of the house, and she told him to dump the tools he was carrying on the grass. A swish of the curtain in the window caught his eye—the office, but Andressa wasn't looking out.

"I'd better get inside." He scurried away.

"Cody?" Simona stopped him on the steps, and he turned around. "I have lots of favorites, but I love passion flowers, and orchids are close behind. It's hard to choose because it's about the color for me. Purple is my favorite."

"Do you have any passion flowers here?"

"Nope, but maybe someday I'll show you one."

"Promise?" He raised his brows.

"I promise." Her brown eyes sparkled, and she swept a few wisps of her black hair behind her ear, leaving a small streak of dirt. He wished they could talk freely or sit by the garden so he could watch her face light up as she told him about her flowers.

He imagined what she'd look like if she cleaned up. If her long hair hung loosely around her shoulders, if her nails were done, if she was dressed in the latest fashions that Andressa wore, Simona would be stunning.

Cody left her standing on the road, wishing Andressa would find out-of-town business to go to. He would love free time with Simona. It was a stupid and dangerous thought, but it was the truth.

Inside, the air-conditioned chill welcomed him, and he brought the folder to the office. Andressa hunched over in her chair, arms folded, with a dark face and suspicious eyes.

"Did you see Enzo?" Andressa spit. "I thought I saw Enzo's car. Did he come out to the kennels?" She clenched her hands, glaring at Cody.

"I passed him on the way out."

"What was he doing there?"

How the hell would I know? Enzo didn't give him the time of day.

"I don't know," Cody said.

Andressa jumped to her feet and stalked around the desk. Cody backed away, and she shot through the office door. Just then, the front door slammed, and Enzo headed their way.

Andressa's eyes narrowed on her brother, and the angry Portuguese spilled from her mouth, but Enzo just sauntered into the office and smirked at Cody.

"Relax. I was bringing Levi a gift."

Andressa chewed him out in Portuguese, but the smile never left Enzo's face.

"It's not for him. It's for a friend." Enzo shrugged. "He knows your rules."

"He'd better damn well know my rules."

"I didn't come here to discuss Levi. I have a business proposition for you." Enzo glanced at Cody with disdain. "I thought I'd talk to you before going to Miguel."

"I'm listening." She folded her arms again, looking anything but open to whatever Enzo had to tell her.

"I thought for the next fight you should try steroids."

Andressa gasped, and her face twisted into a snarl. "No."

"But think of what—"

"I said no. I'm not putting drugs into my dogs." She gripped the edge of the desk, her fingers white.

"The other night was an embarrassment. Do you know how much money I lost?" Enzo sniped.

"Don't blame me for Miguel's mistakes. He put Braz out there when he wasn't ready."

"No, you—"

"Get out!" Andressa screamed, thrusting her hand at the door. "And I don't want to hear about this again."

Enzo stared at her outstretched hand, all smug-like. "Marcos thinks it's a good idea." He turned and strutted out the door.

Fire poured from Andressa's eyes, and her hands fisted.

"I'm not risking the health of my dogs or their future offspring over stupid drugs," Andressa growled to Cody. "Enzo's not even thinking about their viability as stud dogs. Or about my expansion plans. I've got enough people trying to sabotage me, and I don't need my own brother doing it." She spun around and stomped out of the office, slamming the door and leaving a stunned Cody behind her.

Andressa wouldn't give her dogs steroids, but she had no problem stabbing Braz to death with her heel. Nothing in her world made sense.

*

The next day Cody took advantage of the few Andressa-free hours when she visited her father. He found Simona cleaning out the piranha tank, her back to him. Her smooth movements were different from the first time he saw her there. She'd gained a confidence she hadn't had back then, which was maybe why she'd tried to escape.

"Can I ask you a question?" he asked, glad the house was empty except for Vera.

Her head whipped around, and she smiled. "You can ask me a hundred, although I'm not sure we'll have time to answer every one." She set down the cleaning tube and leaned against the fish tank.

"Why didn't you tell me you were going to try escape?"

She sighed and rummaged underneath the tank. "He was being so nice to me. All I wanted to do was use his phone to call my mom, but he wouldn't do it unless I had sex with him. Maybe I should've…" Her voice drifted off.

"He probably would've turned you in as soon as he got tired of you." Cody swallowed the rock in his throat. "He would've used you first."

"I'm used to being used." Her shoulders drooped as her sad brown eyes stared at the fish tank. She'd been through a lot, more than what had happened to her here. Enzo had only added to her scars the night he raped her. "I don't know why I thought he'd help me. I just hoped he would. Help me call my mom at the very least, to tell her I was alive. That I miss her and love her and think about her every day." She looked at Cody. "I should've taken the chance and left. It's too late now."

"How did you end up here?" he said, unsure if he should ask her to share her tragic story.

She focused on the floor, her hair hanging in her face. "When I was eighteen, I thought I was smarter than my mom. I was traveling to Rio to become a model with my boyfriend. He promised me everything, but I was blind. We only made it as far as Belém before we ran out of money."

Cody wanted to hug her, to make her feel better, but he remained in his seat.

"It's a long story, so I'll shorten it. My boyfriend and I lived with his cousin, got into the partying lifestyle. His cousin introduced me to a new type of modeling. All I had to do was get naked for a camera, for the internet, and when you're high, it doesn't seem like too bad of an idea.

"The drugs, the partying, it took a lot of money, and before long my boyfriend figured out how much money he'd make if I actually sold my body."

"You were a prostitute?" Cody tried to hide his shock

"My boyfriend got into trouble with Enzo's crew. He owed them too much money and sold me. Now here I am."

Cody's jaw twitched. The words to his questions bumped around in his head, but he could hardly form a coherent sentence.

"He sold you over a gambling debt?"

"Gambling? No. It was the cocaine. I never knew he was putting us in debt to get it." She shook her head in disgust. "Andressa told me I need to work off the money they paid for me. Even though I was supposed to be the payment. She'll never let me go, not until I'm dead."

She shuffled to the couch, sank down next to him—well, a few feet away—and set her head in her hands. "Andressa knows where my mom lives, knows where she works. She had pictures of my mother, my home, pictures inside my home." Tears welled up in

Simona's eyes, and she wiped them away. "Andressa reminded me of my *debts*. What would I do if they hurt my mom? She's the only family I have. I couldn't live with myself."

Cody wrapped his arms around her, one eye on the door. "I'll help you. I've got a plan. Andressa's starting to trust me. She's giving me more freedom, and once I get the opportunity to run, I'll take it."

"How will you get away?" Her red eyes shattered him into pieces.

"I don't know yet. I have to get to the American Embassy, and I'll be fine. Once I'm safe, I'll contact someone who can help you."

Simona jerked back. "No. They'll go after my mom. You can't. I can't risk it."

He had to do something. He couldn't desert her and forget about her. "Maybe I can send word to your mom."

"If I talk to her, maybe I can warn her, but she won't know who you are. Do you even know Spanish?"

He should've taken Spanish in high school, just on the off chance he'd be kidnapped and brought to Brazil and had to escape to Venezuela. Cody shook his head, both at the ridiculousness of this thought and to answer her question.

Simona sat straighter, determination on her face. "I have to tell her what's going on. Someway, somehow, I need to contact her so she can be safe."

"Does she have anywhere to go?" Was anywhere in South America safe from the Cardosos?

She nodded. "Yes, she has some cousins in Caracas."

Cody put his hand on her lower back and drew little circles with his fingers. He meant to comfort her in the way his mother had so often done for him when younger, but his touch felt like more. Her dark eyes stared at him, and neither of them spoke.

Being this close to her was comfortable, so right, and that scared the hell out of him.

Chapter Thirty-One

Day 41

Andressa snuggled into Cody as they watched TV, but he wasn't thinking about her. Vera slipped through the room with a basket of cleaning supplies. She had been doing Simona's cleaning in addition to all the cooking. Oh god, it'd been a few days since he saw her last. He hadn't thought anything of it until now.

"I'm done with the exercise room, Miss Andressa." Vera hunched over, rubbing a spot on her calf, and Cody noticed the deep circles under her eyes.

"Cody and I want to eat soon. Go start dinner."

"Yes, ma'am." A yawn escaped Vera's mouth, but Andressa's eyes were glued to the TV. Vera retreated to the kitchen.

Asking Andressa about Simona was out of the question. Maybe Simona was sick. If Andressa had gotten rid of Simona, there'd be another woman to replace her.

"I think I've decided what to do," Andressa said.

"About what?"

"Where to expand. Brasília is too far away. I don't want to be making that flight all the time. My father really wants it to go to Belém, but I think I'll choose Macapá. The city isn't as big as Belém, but they're close enough. I think a smaller town might be nice, but also, it's more direct if we want to ship anything down the Amazon."

Or maybe it was because she didn't want to be in the same city as Enzo. She'd been talking more about her plans this past week, and Cody had seen all the information she'd gathered about the two cities and their markets. Any time she'd look at the Belém information, a frown marred her face.

"Macapá sounds like an excellent choice." Her expansion was an interesting idea, something to keep Cody's mind busy until he escaped. He glanced at the kitchen, thinking of Vera. Maybe she would know where Simona was.

"I'm thirsty," Cody said. "Gonna get water. Do you need anything?"

"No."

Cody waited until the kitchen door was closed before he asked Vera about Simona, but she didn't have any answers. He thanked her and returned to Andressa, the pit in his stomach growing. He couldn't imagine where Andressa would've sent Simona, but he hoped he'd find out soon.

*

The next day Cody heard Simona's voice and stopped on the steps. She was back —thank god. He had to find out where she'd been.

"Yes, ma'am," Simona said. Cody inched forward to see Simona with her head bowed. Her normally tidy maid uniform looked wrinkled and dirty.

"After you finish the bathrooms and the laundry, report to the kennels for dog duty. It's your job from now on." Andressa's shrill voice wafted up the stairs.

"Yes, ma'am."

"Get going now. When you're done playing with the dog crap, come back and see me for your next job." Andressa's heels clicked away before Simona mumbled another response.

Cody stayed on the steps and heard the office door close. Simona shuffled up the stairs, and her shoulder brushed his as she passed. She didn't even lift her head.

"Simona?" he whispered, glancing toward the office.

She stopped moving and raised her eyes. The spark was missing, no smile present, and she'd seemed to age ten years in less than a week.

"Yes," she said quietly.

"Where were you? I was worried." He reached out to touch her arm, but she jerked away. Cody noticed a new tattoo on her hand. A circle of three woven strands in the middle of the back of her hand. The word *Meretriz* inside. A line stretched to her knuckles and then formed a ring around her middle finger. A second ring circled her wrist and was also attached to the main circle.

"You got a tattoo?" Cody asked, surprised Andressa allowed her to get one. "I'm too chicken to get one." He laughed at himself, but Simona didn't return the smile. "Where were you?"

"Business trip. Excuse me, I've got work to do." She trudged down the hall like an old woman, and Cody searched her exposed skin for bruises, seeing nothing.

It didn't make sense that Andressa would send her on a business trip—she was the maid, and Andressa didn't involve her in any aspects of the dogs. Maybe later Simona would talk to him when Andressa wasn't around.

*

Cody hardly saw Simona the next few days, and he wouldn't risk sneaking off to talk to her alone.

"Hey, buddy." Felipe raised a beer at him from the bar. "Come have a drink with us."

Cody headed to join Felipe and a guy he didn't know.

"This is Hector," Felipe said. "He came back with us from Brasília. He has dogos too."

Cody shook hands and studied Hector and his preppy looks. A small spark of hope ignited. This was the kind of guy Andressa liked.

Tomás was a lost cause, but maybe if she'd turn her attention to somebody else, Cody would be freed.

"She's buying one of your dogs?" he asked. Andressa hadn't said anything to him about any of this, and usually she was so open.

"No. I brought back a bitch. There's gonna be some sex around here." Hector glanced to the kitchen and laughed with Felipe. Then he jumped to his feet and rummaged in the fridge. "What do you want, Cody?"

Cody tried placing the accent, which was the closest he'd heard to an American in a while.

"Wine," Andressa said from behind him. She laid her hands on Cody's shoulders and waited for him to turn around and kiss her on the cheek. "Open a bottle of Merlot, Hector."

"Yes, ma'am." Hector grinned, a look that would melt most women, but Andressa hardly reacted.

"So you met Hector?" she said. "He brought back Zhara from Brasília. We're mating her and Silva. They should produce strong champions." She smiled appreciatively. "Hector will be with us a short time, and I want you to show him around the kennels. He'll tell you about Zhara since you'll be taking care of her."

"She's staying here?"

"I want to make sure my puppies are given a healthy environment from the start, so we will be taking care of Zhara throughout the pregnancy."

"And don't forget Silva—he deserves a big reward." Felipe sniggered, and Andressa gave him an exasperated look.

Hector poured a glass of wine for Cody and Andressa, and she took her seat beside him. Their talk mostly centered around this new dog, and Cody zoned out for a while.

Vera dashed out of the kitchen to set the table, and he heard another voice. Simona must've been in the kitchen helping make dinner with Vera, which was odd since Vera didn't really need help.

He missed Simona, seeing her smile, hearing her laugh. Missed her talking about the birds she'd spotted when outside.

"I said are you ready to eat?" Andressa poked him in the arm and motioned to the table. The glasses were filled with water, and bread was in a basket. Cody followed the crew to the table, but instead of sitting across from Andressa as he usually did, she told him to sit next to her.

"You don't have much of an accent," Cody remarked to Hector.

"Good ear. I'm from Canada. Lived in Brasília the last ten years. Now I get to visit the sweathole of the world." He laughed. A Canadian. It was the closest thing to home Cody had seen in a long time. A dull ache settled in his stomach. Forty-four days here. His parents wouldn't give up hope yet, wouldn't presume him dead. He didn't want to think about the pain they were feeling not knowing where he was or what happened to him.

"You'll learn to love it here," Andressa said all serious. "Cody got used to the heat."

Not quite. But he forced a smile and agreed with her.

Simona stepped through the doors with a tray of food. She froze, looking straight at Hector, her mouth in a thin line.

"Ah, Simona, how nice to see you again." Hector offered her the same sly grin he'd given Andressa earlier. Simona didn't melt. She didn't smile. "I think I will like it here," he said.

"Are you waiting until our food is cold?" Andressa snapped. Simona trudged to the table to set the food down and refilled the glasses with wine. "You'll be glad to know, Simona, that Hector will be working with us at the kennel for a short time."

Simona nodded, her dark eyes remaining focused on the task in front of her. "Do you need anything else, Miss Andressa?"

Cody couldn't get over Simona's vacant stare. He glanced at Felipe and Hector, but nothing seemed off with them.

"No. We'll call you when we're done."

Simona left the room, and Cody turned to Andressa. "Why is she working tonight? Isn't Vera cooking?" He had to shut the hell up, shouldn't be asking about Simona at all.

214

"Of course she is. Do you think I'd leave the cooking to that fool? Vera was working hard while Simona was gone, so I thought I'd give her a break and give her help. Simona can be our waitress for tonight."

Vera worked her tail off, but it wasn't like Andressa to be generous with breaks. And Vera was still working behind the doors; she just wasn't serving.

"So Cody. As I said, you need to show Hector around our kennels and get Zhara set up in her own space. Santiago and I have been in talks for a while about working together, and I'm excited about this new venture. Santiago's dogs have proven to be champions in the Brasília circuit."

The big dreams of money floated in Andressa's eyes, and Cody refocused his attention on her so she wouldn't notice how distracted he was.

Chapter Thirty-Two

Day 45

Cody walked the road to the kennels with Felipe the next morning. "Okay, so you went to Brasília too?"

"First time there."

"So, um..." *Tread lightly. Make it sound like you're curious.* "What did you do there? Did you and Simona go sightseeing? I'm still trying to figure out why Andressa sent her."

"Who knows. Maybe Andressa felt bad about how she's been treating her lately." Felipe snorted. "Seriously, man. I don't know. Maybe she's from there."

"No—"

That was a dumbass move. He almost said she was from Venezuela. "Andressa said once, but I can't remember where now."

"She didn't talk much on the plane ride down. And then I was off doing my own stuff. Didn't really meet up with Miguel until the last day."

Miguel was sitting with his feet on the desk. Hector got up from his seat on the other side and came around to shake hands with the two men.

"Miguel tells me you practically know it all now," Hector said to Cody.

Cody shrugged. "I'm learning. The breeding part will be all new now."

Felipe's cell rang, and he glanced at the screen. "Ah, the beautiful Carolina. She always has something for me to do." He laughed and typed a message into his phone.

"Girlfriends," Hector huffed. "Who needs them."

Felipe stuck his phone back in his pocket. "No sweet lady down in Brasília?"

"Hell no. There's too many ladies who need loving." He sat on the desk and folded his arms. "I can't believe Andressa doesn't have more girls here. At least she has Simona. She's one spicy girl."

Cody's head whipped around to look at Hector, an icy prickle of jealousy edging through him. The way he'd been looking at her before, the way he was talking about her now, ticked Cody off.

"I took her out to a club. She was rubbing her tits on me all night long. I swear she wanted to fuck me right there on the floor. Could barely get her up to the hotel room before she jumped my bones."

No way. But Simona was acting so weird around Hector—maybe she was embarrassed about sleeping with him, or worried Andressa would get pissed, especially after what happened with Levi.

"I tried to get Miguel to join us. She was all up for a threesome. Wanted two guys at once. I told Miguel I'd even take the back door, but he said no." Hector looked at Miguel as if he was crazy.

"And it'd be the last time I had sex if my wife found out. She'd twist my balls off." Miguel laughed.

"Your loss." Hector shrugged. "She's itching to get with me again. What about you, Cody? Have you hit that girl?"

Heat scorched Cody's cheeks. He was used to Levi's shit talk, but it wasn't about Simona. She was his friend for god's sake—not like he could tell them though. "No. Of course not."

Felipe smacked him on the back in typical fashion. "You think Miguel's wife is bad, you don't even want to know what Andressa would do to Cody if he cheated on her."

Hector chuckled. "What if she was there? Me, Simona. You and Andressa."

Cody almost choked. He couldn't be serious. Andressa would never have sex with multiple people, much less her own maid, but he pretended as if it was no big deal.

"I don't think so. You're on your own." He kept his voice light.

"Too bad because Andressa's got her shit going on. I bet she's wild in the sack. Probably like a bearcat."

"I asked him too, but Cody won't say." Felipe nudged Cody again. "He's too much of a gen-tle-man."

"Not me," Hector said. "I was holding back last night. Simona was so nervous about Andressa knowing about me and her. We're going to hook up before I leave." Hector settled back on the edge of the desk again. "I gotta get me a maid like her. Except I'd have clothing-optional days. No dreary gray dresses."

The guys laughed, and Cody played along. Maybe Simona was trying to use Hector to help her escape. But if she was, she should've made her run in Brasília when she had the chance. None of this made sense.

*

Simona would be spending the night with Hector. The whole situation bugged the hell out of Cody way more than it should. A part of his brain knew there was more to this story because Simona sure didn't seem as if she wanted to be with Hector, but maybe this was an act to throw Andressa off.

He shouldn't be jealous… but he was.

"You're quiet tonight," Andressa said, running her hand through Cody's hair as they lay in bed after sex. He'd spent most of the time imagining he was having sex with Simona, and not Andressa. It was hard to picture Simona being as wild as Hector claimed. Over the last two days, Hector had shared many stories.

"Tired. With everything going on with Hector. Zhara's pretty ferocious."

Nasty was a better word, dangerous. Zhara didn't listen like Andressa's dogs did and often growled with little provocation. Hector had even done a demonstration for Levi with one of the stray dogs; Zhara killed it in seconds. She even snarled at the male dogs, although Hector assured them she'd be accepting once she reached the second part of her cycle.

"I know." Andressa glowed. "Silva's puppies will get my name known. Did I tell you I've been working with local police to get a bigger venue?"

"How do you know which officers will work with you?"

Andressa gave him a proud look. "It's not easy. You get to know them, their families, their history. You get people on the inside. Cultivating a friendly force takes time and energy. Enzo thinks blackmail works best, but he's wrong. You need to make the police officer think they're in control. You need to find their wants. So many of them have so little and dream big."

Like you.

"This will get me closer to my five-year plan. Maybe bump it into completion sooner."

Five-year plan. Cody was a part of it, but he'd been here way too long already. He needed to keep sucking up to her, make her give him her full trust. He was so close, he tasted freedom, and soon he'd be on a plane home to the States.

*

Cody was thankful to Marcos for relieving him of Andressa. He hadn't had many chances to talk to Simona, and he missed her. He waited until she was in the guest bedroom cleaning, the best place to talk with the view of the front drive.

Simona was vacuuming the floor when he slipped into the room, her back to him. He stepped closer to her, and she jumped.

"Oh, it's you," she said, grasping her neck. Her eyes flew to the door in a panic.

"Andressa's gone. Daniel too. Only Vera's around." He was surprised she wasn't a little more glad to see him.

"Oh." She sunk onto the bed, holding onto the cord of the vacuum. Her whole body drooped, like her eyes.

"We haven't gotten to talk much lately."

"I've been busy. Andressa has me working longer hours."

"I know. I'm sorry."

Simona stared off toward the floor, and for the first time in a while, he felt uncomfortable around her. Maybe he should leave... But he didn't want to. Not yet.

"So how was the trip? Did you get to see much of Brasília?"

"Only Miguel's back as I followed him and Hector around. I saw how Hector treats his dogs. Andressa's are lucky." A deep sadness stretched across her face. She'd had a chance to escape and was probably regretting not taking it.

"I heard the club you went to was pretty fun."

"Club?" Her nose wrinkled. "I wouldn't call it a club."

"What do you mean? Hector said—"

Shadows crossed her face. Something was wrong, and he wanted to know... But he didn't.

"So, um, I was wondering. Hector said..."

The asshole was thankfully leaving soon, but he might come back with this new partnership between his boss and Andressa. "Well, are you guys... Is there something going on between you two?"

Simona's mouth dropped, and the cord thunked to the floor. He shouldn't have said anything, but it was too late now.

"I don't care if there is. I mean, we're just friends, but I thought... Well, he was talking about you like there was. That you were hiding it from Andressa. I'm confused because of what happened with Levi." Cody tried to cover his nervousness.

She shuffled to the window and ran her finger up and down the windowsill, her back to him.

"Do you know why Andressa sent me with Miguel?" Her voice was thick with emotion, and every muscle in Cody's body tightened.

"I've been wondering."

She slowly turned toward him. Two times she opened her mouth to speak, but closed it again. On the third, she finally spoke.

"Andressa wanted to show me how lucky I was. She wanted to show me what else was out there and where she would send me if I don't follow her rules." Simona's shoulders sagged.

"What did you see?"

"It doesn't matter. It only matters that I don't want to be a part of Hector's world. Now, I have work to do," she said curtly. She spun around and marched to the vacuum. The noise filled the room, and she pushed the vacuum across the carpet, ignoring Cody.

He went to press the issue, but she spoke again. "I need to finish my work now." Her voice was gruff, her body rigid, and he left the room wondering how much more suffering Simona would have to endure.

Chapter Thirty-Three

Felipe flopped his sweaty body onto the couch. "I need a fucking drink."

"I'm on it," Cody said as he headed toward the beer fridge. He flapped his shirt to get his sticky skin some air. He pulled two cold ones out and returned to Felipe.

Andressa clicked into the room and wrinkled her nose. "Ewww. Get off my sofa. I paid a lot of money for it." She waved her hand at Felipe, and he scooted to the edge so his sweat-stained back wouldn't stink up her precious couch.

"Not my fault. Cody was teaching me about American football. He says I'd do pretty good." Felipe smirked at Andressa.

"Linebacker, definitely," Cody agreed after kissing Andressa's cheek.

Felipe had scrounged up a football, and for a short time Cody had imagined he was playing ball with a buddy.

"American football players are thugs." Her lip curled into a sneer.

Cody stifled his fed-up laugh. She'd watched football a total of ten minutes before declaring it the dumbest sport she'd ever seen.

"But they're rich thugs." Felipe chuckled. "Maybe I should be a football player."

"Don't encourage him." Andressa motioned toward Felipe, and Cody nodded. *Yes, Andressa.*

Yes, Andressa.

Yes, Andressa.

Yes, Andressa.

She planted her hands on her hips. "I hope you don't stink because we need to discuss the party."

"Discuss away." Felipe raised his brows. Andressa was having people over in a couple of nights, and Cody wasn't sure what he should do. Her friends would laugh him out of the room right into a beating by Felipe if he asked for help. It might be best to try get one of them to lend him their phone.

Andressa produced a piece of paper and a pen, then perched on the couch not quite next to Felipe. Cody hoped Felipe stunk.

Fifteen minutes she discussed, item by item, what she wanted Felipe to get and where to find it.

"Yes, ma'am." Felipe stood. "I'll leave you two so you can have your alone time. Let me get out the door first because I don't want to hear that shit like yesterday."

What the hell was Felipe talking about? He and Andressa had sex late at night when the house was quiet. Felipe wasn't here.

"What do you mean?" Andressa threw a confused look to Cody.

"In the kennels. All the giggling."

He slowly stopped at the expression on Andressa's face.

Cody and Andressa hadn't been together yesterday at the kennels.

He wasn't with Andressa at the kennels. At all.

He was with Simona, and she'd been laughing at what he was saying—the first time she'd smiled in days. But they'd just been talking. And it'd barely been five minutes he'd spoken to her.

"A woman giggling?"

Vera didn't go to the kennels, and only one other woman did.

"And Cody was there?" she snapped. Cody froze as if looking at Medusa herself.

Felipe shrunk back like a scolded puppy, but his eyes flicked back and forth between Cody and Andressa. "Well, it wasn't really giggling. Laughing maybe. I saw him but didn't see you. I thought..." His voice trailed off.

"We were talking," Cody blurted. "She was washing up after cleaning the dog crap."

"You had sex with Simona?" Andressa bared her teeth, eyes wide, her body in attack mode.

"Simona?" Felipe repeated quietly.

Cody forced the confidence in his voice. He had to make this right. "No. Of course not. I would never—"

"How could you, Cody?" she yelled and whacked him with a pillow. "I gave you everything. I gave you all of myself." She choked the words out, smacking him again with the pillow. "And this is how you repay me?"

Andressa backed away and collapsed on the couch, sobbing. Oh god, he'd been building up her trust, and now he lost it. He'd never get out of there. Or worse... She'd kill him.

Cody ran to the couch, and it hit him. She wasn't screaming or slapping him. She was crying on the couch as if he really mattered to her. It was so un-Andressa-like. He didn't have time now to think about what that meant because he had to make her believe him. He reached for Andressa's hands, but she jerked them away and slid over. He had to convince her he loved her—he had to save his ass, and Simona's.

"He just heard her laughing. Nothing happened, I swear. I love you more than anything. I'd never hurt you." He needed to be a good actor, as much as his words disgusted him. "Andressa, you are my everything, the love of my life, and the words have been in my heart, but I was scared you didn't feel the same."

She studied him intently. The words he had to say were there, the one other thing that would sway a narcissistic bitch like Andressa.

"She doesn't even come close to you. She's a maid for fuck's sake."

"Watch your mouth." Andressa pulled away from him and glared.

Cody's head about exploded. She was the daughter of a cartel head. She trained dogs to fight to the death. She murdered a dog in cold blood, and she ruthlessly beat a poor woman, and here she was scolding him for saying *fuck*?

"Continue," she said tentatively.

He pushed back the hatred and took a deep breath. "She doesn't have one ounce of the class and style as you. Or the beauty." He scooted closer to her, and she didn't move away. "Or the intelligence and drive. How in the world could I be attracted to someone like her when I have you by my side?" He swallowed hard. "And besides, she has sex with guys like Levi and Hector. I'd never touch a whore like her."

I'm sorry, Simona. She wasn't there to hear him, but he was still an ass for saying such crap. Simona was more of a woman than Andressa could ever hope to be, and he'd insulted her in the worst way.

"Some people go their whole lives without ever finding the one. And I found her. She's right here next to me." If Cody hadn't been so desperate, he'd be laughing at his ridiculousness. It was like all those romantic comedies where the guy spewed forth so much cheese on the screen, and all the girls swooned. "And I'm so sorry I hurt you."

Andressa wiped her eyes, smearing her makeup. "Why were you talking to her alone?" she said quietly.

Dammit. Cody closed his eyes to think. He'd already dug his hole, and now he had to climb out. "She was laughing about Hector and Levi—well, more Levi. She said Levi was like a little kid next to Hector, if you know what I mean."

Andressa searched his eyes. He had to make this good.

He continued. "I'd never hurt you, and I feel like crap for making you think I could possibly be with a slut like her."

Andressa straightened and spoke, her voice terse. "You may not be interested in her, but I think she's after you."

Cody forced a laugh. "She's not after me. She knows I'm yours. I actually feel sorry for her because it must be hard for her to work for such a beautiful and successful woman. You're surrounded by friends and family who love you, and she has nobody." Cody squeezed Andressa's hand. "But you're right. I never should've been in a room alone with her."

"No, you shouldn't have. And you won't again."

"I won't." He wrapped his arms around Andressa.

She snuggled into his shoulder. "Don't ever scare me again. I couldn't bear to lose you. I won't lose you." Her voice held a desperation he'd never heard, a desperation so strong she might do anything to keep him.

"I couldn't bear to lose you either."

Felipe stood in the corner of the room, looking as if he'd just seen a cat and dog mating. He narrowed his eyes on Cody like he knew this was all bullshit.

Or maybe he'd never seen Andressa have an emotional freak-out.

Maybe.

Hopefully.

Felipe turned around and slipped out of the room.

An hour later, Andressa sat at the dinner table, staring at her food. She rubbed her temples before taking a drink of water. She'd probably drag out this whole Simona thing as long as she could.

"Don't you like your chicken?" Cody asked her.

"No, I'm feeling nauseous." She touched her hand to her stomach.

"Are you getting a migraine?"

"Of course I am," she snapped. "Thanks to you and that little slut. What did you expect?" She pushed her plate forward and sighed.

"I told you... we didn't—"

"She's still a whore trying to seduce you so she can hurt me. But I won't let her."

"I won't either, but I don't think—"

"Of course you don't. Because you're blind." She winced and took deep breaths. "I don't need this right now. It's enough that I have Enzo questioning me over mating Zhara and Silva. Did he do the research? Does he know her history? No," she huffed and threw her cloth napkin on the table. "Vera, get in here!" She paused until Vera shuffled in. "We're done eating. Clear everything away."

Cody looked at his barely eaten food, and Andressa grimaced. "Let's go, Cody."

He left the table and followed her to the bedroom. It was only seven-thirty, but she changed into her pajamas. "Get me water and then come join me in bed."

On his way, he thought about the whole mating thing. He hadn't known it was stressing her out, or that Enzo was being a pain in the ass. Everybody else at the kennels was sorta excited about it. Miguel and Felipe because they were looking forward to more champions, Levi because the occasion seemed to allow him to talk about sex even more. Cody had almost asked him if he was gonna jack off when the dogs were mating.

He returned and climbed into bed.

"Shut off the light," she said, and he got out of bed and turned off the light. She made him sit with her through the throbbing for hours, sometimes rubbing her head.

She fell asleep in the middle of the night. His bleary eyes couldn't read the numbers, but he soon followed behind.

Chapter Thirty-Four

Day 54

Cody stood dutifully next to Andressa, pretending to be the perfect boyfriend for the twelve friends of Andressa's who had gathered. At least she'd cooled off over the whole Simona thing, maybe due to Cody's excessive sucking up. He hadn't even looked at Simona once since the other day, well, not when Andressa or anybody else was around.

Simona slipped into the room with a tray full of food, set it down, and approached Andressa.

What the hell? Her choppy hair hung above her shoulders, looking as if she went to a six-year-old stylist.

"Miss Andressa, Vera is finishing the empadinhas. They should be out shortly."

Cody kept his eyes purposefully on one of Andressa's friends.

"What did you do to your hair?" The girl next to Andressa snickered. "I think you should get your money back."

"Maybe you should pay the girl a little more so she can get her hair cut properly," another woman said to Andressa. Even without looking straight at Simona, he saw the uneven length and the big chunk missing from the back of her head.

"It's pretty pathetic, isn't it?" Andressa said, and the group laughed. Simona didn't move, didn't answer, didn't change the expression on her face. "Get on back to the kitchen now."

Simona scuttled away, the yellow skirt swishing as she walked. Andressa might have let Simona wear color tonight, but the dress was at least three sizes too big. Of course, Simona could've worn a potato sack, and she'd still be beautiful.

Cody tapped Andressa on the arm. "I'm going to go talk to Felipe." He said it more like a question, not knowing why he felt the need to ask permission.

"Don't be gone long, baby." She gave him a quick peck on the cheek, and he left her side.

The guys at the bar with Felipe were talking in Portuguese and made no switch to English. Cody was grateful though. He really didn't give a damn about any of these people or what they had to say.

Cody was approaching two long months in Brazil—two fucking months. He never thought it'd be so long, and yet he was still here. He really needed to watch himself with Simona because he had to earn Andressa's trust... Again.

But if he left, Simona would be here alone, with nobody but Vera as a friend.

Felipe punched Cody on the arm. "Wake up. It's a party." He spewed out some Portuguese to the other guys, then turned back to Cody.

"Did Andressa say anything about bringing you into town?" Felipe whispered.

"No." Another chance for him to escape. It was too much to hope for. "Where?"

"Something about the Teatro Amazonas." Felipe wrinkled his nose as if it was a landfill.

"No clue what that is."

"The opera. And she's making me go because she's still not sure about you." Felipe rolled his eyes.

Cody slumped in his seat. He should just chance it and run.

"Maybe she decided to wait after you cheated on her. She let you off pretty easy," Felipe said.

The heat flared into Cody's cheeks, his body a mass of tension. "I did not cheat on her. I never—"

"Relax. I'm just giving you a hard time. I know you don't want to become piranha food." He held his drink to his mouth but paused. "We might be buddies, but Andressa's minha família."

The underlying threat was there. Cody sorta forgot sometimes that they weren't buddies because of how Felipe treated him lately.

"Why'd you even tell her?" Cody couldn't trust Felipe and his allegiance to the Cardoso family.

"Hey, I thought it was you two. Can't blame me for that. I wasn't about to walk in on you and check."

"Next time check." Cody glanced back to Andressa. He mirrored her sickly-sweet smile.

"Toast time." Andressa sauntered over and leaned into him. She brought her arm to Cody's shoulder and stood straight. "Attention, everyone. It's time to make a toast."

The room didn't quiet down, and she clapped her hands together until everyone was silent.

"Thanks everybody for coming. Cody's been here with me for almost two months now, and we are so glad you're finally meeting him. Things have been hectic here, and we really needed a break. So here's to a fun night of friends and lively conversation."

She clinked her glass with Cody's, and the group said something Cody figured was their version of *cheers*. Andressa set her drink down and laid a big wet wine-flavored kiss on his lips.

And she stayed on his lips forever. Finally, she backed off. "Love you, baby," she said loudly.

Anyone within ten feet could hear her.

"You too." He gave the requisite answer. Everybody returned to their conversations, and Cody caught his breath. Andressa was already across the room talking to some others.

"Felipe, why don't you ever kiss me like that," a voice teased. Carolina stood behind them with a dramatic frown, but Felipe didn't move.

"Ahh damn. The ball and chain is here. My night's done." Felipe nudged Cody, unable to hide his smirk.

A smile crept across Carolina's face. "I don't know what you mean, but I'm guessing it's not too nice. Cody, is that an American saying?"

"It's kind of like saying the love of your life." Cody held back his laugh.

Carolina chuckled. "Somehow I don't think you're telling the truth, but I'll let it go this time."

Felipe spun around and hauled her into his lap. They exchanged words, heads close together, before she looked up. "So you and Andressa made up?"

"What?" Cody glanced quick to Felipe. "He told you too? Felipe needs to keep his mouth shut."

"I didn't know." Felipe held his hands up in surrender.

"But you know Andressa." The smile fell from her face, but she wiped away the frown, and her eyes lit up again. "Guess who gets to go along with you to the Teatro Amazonas. It's been so long since I've been there. I guess I needed Andressa to convince Felipe to go."

"I'd rather go to a futebol game than the opera, but I won't complain about a night out with the beautiful Carolina." He gave her a little squeeze on the shoulders.

She blushed but looked adoringly at him before turning back to Cody. "Andressa said you love the opera. Your parents brought you sometimes."

"Love may be overstating it a bit." He'd been there twice with his parents, and he'd even told Andressa he'd almost fallen asleep both times. "It was an experience."

"You disappoint me, man." Felipe shook his head, raising his glass to his lips.

"Oh Felipe." Carolina gave a dramatic sigh. "Not everybody is an uncultured malandro like you." She leaned in and rubbed noses with him.

Cody about choked out his drink in surprise. The enforcer Felipe rubbing noses with his girlfriend.

"I think Andressa wants you." Carolina motioned to Cody, and he excused himself.

Andressa clutched his arm with a frown. "Go check on the pão de queijo. Vera hasn't brought it out, and it should be here by now."

He followed her orders like a good little soldier and retreated to the kitchen.

"Vera, the queen is requesting the pão de queijo." Cody grinned at her, and she laughed.

"Your timing is perfect. I was about to bring them out." She stepped over to a plate covered in the little cheesy bread balls.

Cody's mouth watered for the delicious treat. "Maybe I should test one first. To make sure they're okay."

"Help yourself." She held out the plate.

The door swung open mid-bite, and Simona rushed in. They stared at each other for a moment before she smiled and headed to the fridge. "I need cream to make a drink."

Cody studied the hand holding the fridge door. "I've never seen anybody with a tattoo like that. I mean, one that covers the hand and stretches around the wrist. It's a cool idea." He resisted the urge to reach out and trace his finger along the smooth line. "I didn't get a chance to ask you what the words meant." Meretriz, it said.

Her shoulders tightened. "It means courage." Simona shut the fridge and stared at the back of her hand. "It's a reminder to never give up. A reminder that one day maybe I'll be free." She lowered her head and whispered, "Maybe we'll both be free."

Cody glanced at Vera. "All of us," he added.

Simona's head whipped around, and she stared at Vera for a moment. "Yes, all of us." She smiled softly. "I love the mountains, Cody. What do you love?"

The words *I love you* were on the tip of his tongue. But he didn't mean it like *love*. He loved her determination, her ability to stay positive in this situation.

"I love Lake Michigan. It's huge, and I grew up on it. But I'd love to see the mountains too."

Vera cleared her throat. "Simona, why don't you bring the cream out for the guest who needed it. I'm sure Miss Andressa is waiting."

Simona nodded and disappeared without another word. Cody was about to follow her out, but Vera clutched his arm. "Why don't you try one more before you bring them out? They'll disappear fast."

Cody snatched another bread ball and leaned against the counter. "That they will. Have I told you what an amazing cook you are, Vera?"

"Yes, you have." The gratitude in her eyes was genuine.

Hiding out in the kitchen wasn't an option, so he ate one more bun and prepared to return to the party again. He thanked Vera and disappeared out the door.

Chapter Thirty-Five

Day 55

Saturday morning, Cody's mood was getting better by the minute. Daniel and Andressa were going into Manaus, and Simona would be cleaning the party mess. Only Vera was around the house, for a short time at least.

He finished his work and jogged back to the house. Simona was restocking the bar when he strolled in.

"Guess who's gone for a while?" he said.

"Obviously not you. So maybe Andressa and Daniel?" Cody nodded, and her lips twitched into a smile. "Maybe I'll have help with my cleaning."

"Affirmative," Cody said.

"Then grab that case of beer from the table."

He had his old girl back. Well, she wasn't his girl, but she was acting like she had before the Brasília trip at least.

"I heard a rumor that I might get to go into Manaus again." Cody raised his brows at her, and she brightened. "I'm not sure I can get away this time since Felipe will be with, but supposedly we're going to the opera. It'll give me a better chance to learn about the city."

He needed to pay attention to every turn they took on the drive, figure his way around the town.

"The opera?" Simona rolled her eyes. "Why doesn't she bring you somewhere fun? Like the market or a movie."

He laughed. "I'd love some salty buttered popcorn. Andressa would never approve."

"I wonder if Manaus has an aquarium. My mom took me to the one in Mérida every once in a while. It wasn't very big, but she knew all the names of the fish."

"I haven't been to a zoo or aquarium in a long time."

"You'd love Mérida. It's nestled in a valley in the Andes. There's a cable car that brings you up to Pico Espejo. It's four thousand seven hundred meters high."

Cody chuckled. "I have no idea how tall that is. We don't use meters."

"I don't know either." She shrugged.

Cody thought for a moment. A meter was just over three feet, and she said almost five thousand... he did the math. "That's about fifteen-sixteen thousand feet high. That's mountain-sized."

"It is." She chuckled. "It's a part of the Andes." She leaned against the wall and sighed. "I miss my home."

"I do too." His gaze locked with hers, and they held it, no need to say more.

They finished the stocking and moved onto the next item. He vacuumed for Simona, and pretty soon it was time to eat lunch.

"I don't think we've ever had lunch together before," Cody said, carrying dishes to the table. Even though Andressa wouldn't be back for a bit, he was still on edge. Felipe might walk right through the front door at any moment. Simona would have seconds to grab her plate and glass and get into the kitchen.

"No, we haven't."

They invited Vera to dine with them, and time seemed to fly, Vera talking non-stop about Peru after Cody asked her a question. He'd love to visit the country, but once he escaped, it'd be way too close for comfort.

A quiet lull overtook the table, and Cody stared at the tattoo stretching across Simona's hand.

"When you get back to Venezuela, you can show your mom your tattoo, and she'll know how brave you are."

Simona's eyes misted. She wiped the wetness away, but instead of smiling and talking about her mom, she started sobbing. Then she rushed into the kitchen.

"Stay." Vera waved her hand at him.

Each minute felt like hours as he sat at the table. Five minutes turned into fifteen.

Finally, Vera returned. She trudged over to the chair Simona had been sitting in and sat down. Cody said nothing and watched as Vera twisted her paper napkin into a tight roll.

This was so not good.

"Simona wanted me to tell you because it's very hard for her to say. Andressa sent her to Brasília as a punishment." Vera took a shaky breath. "She sent Simona to provide *services* to Hector."

Cody's throat closed off. She hadn't been embarrassed around Hector. She'd been terrified. He should've known; he probably had, but he hadn't wanted to admit what had happened to her.

First Enzo and his buddies and now Hector. Cody jammed his clenched hand into his shorts, trying to control his anger. "He raped her during the trip? And then he did it again here."

Vera nodded.

Every time Andressa did something, he couldn't believe how cruel she was. But she seemed to top herself every time. Simona never did anything to deserve such torment. A wall of pain slammed into Cody, and he shoved off the table, his whole body tense.

A warm hand lay on his arm. "Simona needs your support, not your anger."

He wanted to pound Andressa into the ground. "How the hell am I supposed to support her?"

His fury was a funnel cloud about to spin into a tornado, and he couldn't control his voice. "How am I supposed to act like nothing's happened? How am I supposed to look Andressa in the eye without knocking her out?" Getting beat would be worth whatever he did to her.

"You do it because it's your only choice." Vera's voice remained calm. "You need to be smart. You need to think and behave like nothing happened. And you need to work on your escape plan?"

Cody's jaw dropped. He'd never said anything, but if Vera knew, then maybe Andressa knew. Maybe she was watching and waiting for Cody to fuck up, and then she'd kill him. "How did you know?"

She smiled wearily. "Because if I were your age, I would have a plan. I've told you before I'm too old, and if I tried to escape, my family would pay the price, but your family is far away. Marcos's reach does not stretch to the EUA."

"I don't have a plan yet, I mean. She was—I was close. She was starting to trust me, but now she's all worried about Simona and me."

"Andressa will trust you. You will find your escape."

Cody looked at Vera's wrinkled face. She seemed so sure of everything, but there was one problem. If he left, Andressa would take out her anger on Simona. The guilt over deserting her would never go away.

"What does the tattoo mean? It doesn't say *courage*, does it?"

"It's for her to tell."

"But she won't even speak to me. She lied to me before."

"I think she's ready to tell you now. Go to her." Vera patted him on the back.

He still had time before Andressa returned, but he took his time walking to the barracão, looking over his shoulder and listening for any noises. He had no explanation for why he was going there if someone stopped him, but he couldn't not go.

He stopped in front of Simona's door, hand poised.

A minute passed before Cody knocked, and when Simona answered, he slipped into the dim room. Simona lay curled up on her bed, hair covering her face. She sniffed and wiped her nose with her hand, the one with the tattoo.

"Can I sit down?" He wanted to rip off the ever-tightening noose around his neck, to be free from this pain and sorrow. Now he'd have to listen to Simona share her burdens, and the noose around his neck would squeeze further.

She nodded, but instead of sitting at the chair and table, he sat next to her on the bed, hoping she was okay being this close to him.

He stared at the word on her hand, *Meretriz*, written in delicate flowing letters. It was a beautiful, artistic design.

"What does mer-eh-triz mean?"

She didn't answer right away, and he decided that if she didn't tell him, he wouldn't ask again to dredge up the painful memories.

"It means whore," she said, her eyes cast down, her voice full of sorrow.

Cody's heart broke all over again. The black swirling lines, the curvy words. Simona had to face that ugly tattoo every day and relive whatever Hector had done to her.

"Did he hurt you?" Of course he had, but part of Cody hoped her past would help her get through it. Maybe being abused by other men made her experience less painful.

No. Rape was brutal, whether you were a prostitute or not. He wanted to wrap his arms around her, to hug the pain away, but didn't want to scare her even more.

"He... he." She sniffed hard. "He made me take cocaine. Tied me up. He had these things. Toys he called them..."

The way she said toys, he knew they were anything but.

"You don't have to say it."

"No, I do." She gripped her blanket tightly. "I couldn't tell Vera what he did to me, but I feel like if I don't say it, it's like it didn't happen. I don't want to remember it, but I don't want it to be like it never happened."

Cody laid his hand on top of hers, and her voice continued, so much pain behind her words.

"He stuck things inside me. Both sides of me. Big things. It hurt so bad, and he didn't care when I couldn't breathe. When he was gagging me with..."

Cody sucked in a hard breath, every nerve on edge. His body blazed, and he wanted to take down everybody who had hurt Simona. If Hector ever dared show up here again, he'd never leave. Cody would spend his life in prison just to take out that bastard.

"I'll kill him." He'd rip the worthless shit apart, piece by piece. "Then I'll throw his body into Princesa's tank." His voice was dark and angry, but he didn't care. Andressa and Hector and everybody else had hurt Simona more than he could ever know, and he couldn't let that go.

She raised her somber eyes to meet his. An empty smile graced her lips. "We'll tie him up and force him to stick his finger into the tank, and Princesa can bite his finger off little by little. Then you can strangle him like he strangled me."

"He strangled you?"

Every word out of her mouth just got worse and worse. Simona had lived a torture he'd never wish on his biggest enemy.

"It's supposed to enhance the feelings for the woman," she said quietly, "but…"

Hector got off on hurting Simona. Cody sat up and stared at her. This gorgeous, soft-spoken woman was so strong. She'd live through so much, and she didn't give up.

"Maybe we can send Silva after his balls," Simona said.

Cody's laugh was hollow. "I'll tell you what. It's your choice, and I'll do whatever you ask." The words poured out of his mouth, but he wasn't sure he could really take somebody's life. Even a man like Hector.

But then again, if Hector was threatening Simona, there'd be no hesitation.

"Then hold me," she said, and he wanted nothing more than to wrap her in his arms and never let go. Simona grabbed her pillow and placed it next to Cody, curling up in his lap like a child. He held tight to her warm body, and for the slightest moment, everything felt normal, felt real. As long as he didn't think about the horror of the situation.

For the next hour, a movie played in his head of Andressa walking in on them. Of her attacking them with a shovel—never mind she wouldn't have a shovel with her. Of seeing Simona's head getting bashed in. Of his world going dark as his own head became like a smashed jack-o'-lantern at Halloween.

But Simona needed him right now, so he didn't move.

He stayed there with her until she was okay and then headed to the kennels for unconditional puppy love. He nuzzled the three-week-old squirming puppy against his cheek, trying to ignore the bloody image of Braz that wouldn't go away. All the original puppies here when he'd arrived were with their new homes, but now there was a new litter from another dog, and one of those might someday end up in the ring, end up dead like Braz.

He enjoyed his time alone until Miguel sent him back to the house to see Andressa. The long hike back took forever, but he had to prepare himself to face her.

Everything's normal. Everything's normal. Everything's normal.

But no matter how many times he said it, his head called him a liar. Bad stuff went down all over the world. He saw what gangs did to decent kids, and he knew kids who got knocked around by their parents.

But this...

First Enzo and now Hector.

His hand trembled at the door. *Settle down.* Andressa was on edge lately, and he didn't need to send her off the cliff; she'd take them all with her.

The cool house chilled his skin but not his heart. Andressa's voice drifted out of the office along with Daniel's. Cody wanted more time to prepare to see her again, but a few hours hiding in the bedroom wouldn't make a difference. He had to face her head on.

He stuck his head in the office. Andressa and Daniel sat, heads bent over a pile of papers. Her face was a sledgehammer to his gut, and the bile rose in his throat. Cody composed himself as best he could.

"Cody, hello." Her bright face darkened his heart. "We got done early."

She left the desk and laid a heavy arm over his shoulder. He kissed her cheek, holding back the cringe. Tonight in bed, he'd have to touch her, have sex with her, and it'd take a herculean effort not to let on something had changed.

Andressa led him to the desk and pulled out colored brochures.

"This is the announcement I made for the new kennels in Macapá. We're still a ways away, but we need to have everything ready."

Cody glanced at Daniel, who wore the same annoyed expression he always wore when Andressa took credit for something that he did.

"We also need to think about expanding the training side. We've got some terrific fighters coming up, and now is the time to invest in our future. Daniel was crunching the numbers, and everything is working out."

Andressa continued to talk, but Cody didn't listen. He had to do something to get Simona out, to get himself out, but what if she wouldn't leave? She was still scared that Marcos and Andressa might go after her mom.

But if he contacted her mother right away and warned her to leave, Simona would go. Somehow they had to make that call, but *how* was the question. The only thing he thought of was stopping somebody on the street and begging to use their phone.

This was one fucking mess, and there seemed to be no way out. It was one thing when Cody was alone, but now he had Simona to think about. He wouldn't leave her behind.

"Cody!" Andressa stared at him, eyes bugging out and hands on her hips. Daniel was looking at him too.

"What?"

She huffed. "Haven't you been listening to a word I've said?"

"Sorry. I was thinking about how I'd much rather be relaxing by the pool with a glass of wine." He gave her what he hoped was a charming smile. "And you."

"Oh, you're so sweet." She wound her arm around his waist and set her head on his shoulder. The stench of her shampoo about made him gag. "I'd love to spend time with you, but we have too much to do today. Tomorrow we'll hang out by the pool. Enzo will be stopping by in the afternoon, but we can have alone time before he gets here."

Goosebumps swarmed Cody's arms. He'd have to tell Simona to make herself scarce.

"Can't wait."

She dropped her arm and pointed to the announcement. "Let's change this wording around. And maybe take this sentence out." She scratched a line through the words on the paper. "And here... I'll work on this a little and get it back to you."

"Yes, Andressa," Daniel sighed.

Cody waited another minute to make sure Andressa didn't need him, and then he left.

Chapter Thirty-Six

Day 58

This kennel project turned out to be a good thing. Andressa studied all her options and planned, and after Enzo told her last week about a state-of-the-art kennel in Belém, she decided she had to see it.

Now Cody had three glorious Andressa-free days, which meant spending some time alone with Simona. But there was only one problem: his chaperone.

Felipe tossed the suitcase on the bed. "I'm having company tonight. I considered crawling in bed with you, but Carolina smells better." He looked Cody up and down with a smirk. "And I'm pretty sure you're not up for the things I want her to do."

"I don't want to hear your sex stories. I don't even want to hear the two of you." He got enough of that with Levi and his porn videos or hearing Enzo talk about the girls in his brothel.

"Too bad because she's a screamer." He laughed.

Maybe if Felipe was *occupied* with Carolina, Cody could slip away. Andressa trusted him more now. He hadn't tried to sneak off, not even when they were in town for the third dog fight.

Cody reached to his back pocket, pulled out Andressa's list, and announced he was going to the kennels.

Too many prying eyes followed Cody that day. Simona was on shit duty, and he did his best to stay away because Andressa probably paid the guys extra to watch him more closely.

After a long day at work, he ate dinner with Carolina and Felipe.

"How do you like the acarajé?" Carolina asked. "It's Felipe's special recipe."

"Wait—he cooks?" Cody asked. Not this bruiser. "What is it?"

"Beans," Felipe said with a shrug. Cody took another bite. It looked kind of funky but tasted good.

"I told him he should go to school to be a chef." Carolina patted Felipe's arm lovingly.

Cody about spit out his food. She was crossing the line of incredulity. Felipe in a white chef's hat and apron. No way.

Felipe wore a sheepish grin. "I still think about it sometimes. Maybe I'll ask Marcos for a loan to start up a restaurant."

"No!" Carolina snapped. Cody's head jerked up. He'd never heard such venom in Carolina's voice. Felipe stared at her with the same surprise on his face.

Her voice softened. "I mean no. You can do it on your own. Then you won't owe anybody anything."

Felipe pursed his lips. "You're probably right."

"What kind of restaurant would you open? Cody asked, trying to dig out of the oppressive air. He should've known Felipe liked to cook. The guy hardly shut up.

"Italian maybe?" Felipe shrugged.

"Are you kidding?"

"Actually, he's not," Carolina said. "He ate at an Italian restaurant when he was younger, and ever since then, he's been obsessed. We go to Tutto Italia so often that they know us by name now."

Felipe laughed. "I haven't really put too much thought into it. Besides, I'd have to train under a professional before starting my own restaurant."

"Maybe you should." Carolina squeezed Felipe's hand, but he stared off into the air behind her.

Marcos had a hold over other people, including Felipe.

Cody hung with them for a bit, but when Carolina and Felipe snuggled up on the couch, he gave them a goodnight and headed upstairs. He stepped to a window in one of the unused bedrooms.

The road stretched into the trees. The barracão were so close but yet so far. He wanted to picture Simona sitting among the flowers in her garden, inhaling their sweet scent.

Felipe's laughter rumbled down the hallway, and Cody flinched. The bedroom door was shut, and it's not as if he was doing anything wrong.

A door slammed out in the hallway, but Cody remained in the room for a short time to be safe. Then he slipped out.

Was Simona lonely in her tiny room? Was she thinking of him?

He couldn't get her out of his mind, and his thoughts switched to things he shouldn't be thinking about. Her soft skin, the way her face lit up when she smiled, the way she looked at him—or at least the way it felt like to him.

He would never treat her like Hector did, like any of those men who used her for sex. He would treat her as she deserved: like a lady.

*

Felipe and Carolina kept Cody up for a while, but not for the reasons he'd originally worried.

"Thank god," Cody muttered when silence overtook the top floor of the house. He assumed the couple had been watching TV and something damn funny because every five minutes or so, Felipe would let out a roar of laughter. He never heard Carolina, but Cody had watched enough TV with Felipe to know that's probably what they were doing. No screaming as Felipe had claimed.

He wanted to see Simona, but he couldn't risk getting caught, so instead of sneaking to the barracão to see her, he lay on his bed and stared out the window, thinking of her.

Cody woke with a start and stared bleary eyed at the clock. Two a.m. He closed his eyes, but the sleep had slipped away into the dark night.

Damn. He reached for the remote but paused to look toward the windows. He should shut the curtains so the bright light didn't wake him in the morning.

At the window Cody gasped. Little ripples spread out across the pool. Simona glided smoothly across the surface. She was insane. Felipe and Carolina were in the house, right on the other side of that upstairs window. He glanced to the room they were in.

Cody rushed out the door as silently as he could. Felipe might wake any moment. Things had changed with Simona, and Andressa would severely punish her for even the tiniest infraction. She shouldn't risk her life, no matter how much she loved swimming.

The stifling heat smacked him when he snuck out of the kitchen door. He waited at the poolside until Simona reached him. She was swimming laps and didn't even notice him there, so he tapped her on the back when she flipped around to swim the other way.

She popped out of the water with startled eyes. "Cody?"

"What are you doing? Felipe will hear you."

"He won't. He sleeps like a bear."

"No, he doesn't. You don't know that. Get out." He tugged on her arm, but she jerked back.

"Carolina told me. Don't worry, Cody."

Cody pictured Simona's bruised and bloodied face once Felipe got done with her. He made a grab for her shoulder but missed.

"It's too risky." Catching Simona swimming might've resulted in a small punishment before, but now was different.

"It's okay. I talked to Carolina. If Felipe wakes, she'll distract him."

"How? Why would she help you?" He'd never even seen Carolina talking to Simona.

"Carolina is a good woman." Simona splashed a bit of water at him. "Come swim with me."

Even if Carolina was helping Simona, there was no guarantee she'd keep Felipe away. He might not even wake her when he got out of bed. Cody looked to the house, imagining Felipe charging out the door.

"He's sleeping," Simona assured him.

"But he might wake up."

"But he probably won't. And even if he did, and he found us, Carolina would help us out."

"He won't lie to Andressa."

"Cody, please." She tugged on his hand.

He remembered the first time he found her swimming. She'd wanted to feel free. He wanted that too, wanted to be with her under the bright starry sky.

Despite everything in his head screaming no, he stepped into the water in his clothes and followed her lead, doing laps, swimming as many different strokes he knew until finally she got out of the pool.

She dried off and handed him the towel. "Don't you feel free?"

The anxiety over being found gripped his chest. "Not really." Not until he was out of Brazil.

"Well then, I will feel free for you."

Once he peeked around the side of the house and saw the shades drawn on Felipe's window, and saw no other movement, he grabbed her hand, and they headed toward the barracão. They remained silent until they got to the safety of the building.

They hit the hallway, and he felt as if he was walking his high school girlfriend back to her house, wondering if he should go for a goodnight kiss and if the parents were inside watching.

He was a long way from high school though.

Cody took in her small, empty room. A ceramic bowl with ashes sat on the table, but the only other personal item was a cup with flowers in it. She wasn't a smoker, and besides, the ashes looked too big to be cigarette ashes.

"Maybe we should brave the Amazon," Cody said, leaning against the wall. "Swim it." All they had to do was get far enough away and find their way into town. The only worry was getting past the sensors. Maybe if he deliberately set them off in one location and they snuck away from the opposite side, they might have a chance to get to the river.

He'd been stunned when Vera told him people often swam in the Amazon, that it was relatively safe and how there was little chance of being attacked by piranhas. Manaus even had a public beach where people swam all the time.

Simona stared at him with the look a parent gives a child when they have to explain something over and over, and Cody knew why: Andressa would get to her mother before she did.

"Someday we will. Hopefully soon," she said softly.

"What?" He jerked upright.

She wrapped her hands around his. "I've talked to Carolina and asked her to send a letter to my mom to warn her."

If Simona could warn her mom, they could get out of there. "Oh my god, Simona—this is—"

"No." Simona put her fingers to his lips. "Not yet. She's not ready. But I understand. She's scared like me. She's scared for Felipe, for putting him in danger."

Every ounce of hope floated away. Andressa would never let them go. He'd be married to her and having kids and celebrating their tenth wedding anniversary, and Simona would still be her punching bag.

Simona stared into his eyes with a knowing look. "Someday we'll be free."

He hated that she was the one reassuring him, that she was the stronger one.

"I know."

How did she not give up with everything they threw at her? Simona was so beautiful, inside and out.

The heat of her body warmed him, the smell of the pool water. Her lips were so close, right there in front of him. All it would take was leaning forward a few inches.

Hector's face flashed in his head and all the other unknown men who forced themselves on her. Cody shrunk back.

He glanced at the bowl of ashes again. "Were you burning something?"

Simona slid the bowl over and stared down into the darkness. "It's my journal. I don't dare keep my actual thoughts around in case Andressa goes through my things. She searches every once in a while. It helps to write my feelings out, but as soon as I write them, I burn them."

Cody stuck his finger into the ashes, blackening his skin. These were Simona's thoughts and dreams, maybe her nightmares. "What do you do with the ashes?"

"Bury them in the garden." She grinned.

Just like she buried her pain.

He didn't want to leave, but he had to. "I'd better get going." Cody stared at his feet. "I don't want to."

"I know." She squeezed his arm, and they sat for a few moments. He had to get out of there, had to escape, but he wouldn't do it without her.

Chapter Thirty-Seven

Day 66

"When you run Caio on the catmill, add another five minutes to his run," Miguel said. "I'm going to the vet for supplies."

"No problem," Cody replied and glanced at his to-do list, not asking why Miguel was doing Levi's job. "I've got everything else done. I'm taking off soon."

Miguel nodded and disappeared out the door. Cody finished in the office and got the dog hooked up and running. Caio's fight was approaching, and Miguel was getting edgy.

After Cody finished with Caio, he headed back to the house for lunch. Vera was sitting at the table, her hands folded. He glanced toward the office door, but it was shut.

"Simona wants to talk to you in the kitchen," Vera said to Cody, her face grave. She took a stack of cloth napkins to the table. "I'll be out here. If Andressa comes, I'll tell you and hold her off."

"Okay." His insides churned, but he wouldn't not go.

Simona hunched over the table, her hands clasped in her lap. The tears dripped down her face onto the table, but she made no move to wipe them. Cody didn't see any bruises, and he hadn't heard Andressa complain about anything with Simona lately. At least anything out of the ordinary.

He glanced at the door and pushed the worry away. Vera would alert them.

"What's up?" he said, immediately feeling stupid.

"I don't know what I'll do. I..." She wiped her pained eyes with her free hand and uncurled her fingers.

Cody stared at the white thing in her hand. He recognized it, but his brain couldn't put the words together. The thermometer thing, except there were no numbers. The blue thin lines showed in the little window. The thing seemed to pulse in her hand, growing bigger, ticking like a bomb.

He shook his head and focused on the lines.

She couldn't be.

He looked at her stomach, then back to the pregnancy test.

Oh god. Andressa might accuse him of being the father. He swallowed the bitter taste in his mouth, disgusted with himself. This was about Simona, not him.

"Are you okay? How are you doing?" he asked.

"I'm fine." She didn't take her eyes off the white stick in her hands.

"Who's the…"

The look on her face stopped him. She folded her knees to her chest and wrapped her arms around them tight, rocking back and forth and staring at her window.

"It was him?" he whispered, unable to say Hector's name.

A nod, barely there, but he saw it. She closed her eyes and continued her slow motion. *Be a man*, his dad shouted at him.

He knelt in front of her and put his hands on her legs. She stopped moving and lowered her feet to the floor.

"It'll be okay. Everything will be okay." It was complete bullshit, but it was all he had to offer at the moment. "Come here." He tugged on her hand, and she slid off the chair, collapsing into his arms. The tears streaming down her face echoed all his fear and pain. Andressa would be furious. All he could see was a nine-month pregnant Simona on her knees, scrubbing the floor or trying to clean out the piranha tank.

No, Andressa wouldn't even allow a baby, which was maybe a blessing to have an abortion.

Simona's crying tapered off, and she laid her head on his shoulder. He couldn't even comprehend the fear and worry invading her mind.

"I can talk to her," he offered. "But wait, she'll wonder how you got the test. Where did you get the test?" Cody had been through all Andressa's drawers and never once saw any pregnancy tests.

"Carolina got it for me. But no, that'll make it worse. Andressa will think you're trying to protect me, and she's already paranoid."

"It's not your fault. You need to tell her it was him." He didn't say the word rape even though he wanted to. Hector had raped her, yet Cody was the one having a hard time saying it out loud. He'd never dealt with the pain and the horror of rape, never seen a loved one go through it, never knew any women who'd been raped... Not that he knew of at least. They probably hid their pain like Simona.

"She'll say I wanted to get pregnant to get out of work. How can I raise a baby with her? What future does this baby have?"

"You want to keep it?" How... why? "Won't you get an abortion?"

She stared at him with damp eyes, her lip quivering. "No," she whispered, her hand resting on her belly. "This is a baby. He's innocent, and no matter where he came from, I can't kill it like it's nothing. What if she forces me to get an abortion?" Simona's face crumpled once again, and Cody held her tight. "She can't kill my baby," she choked out.

"She might not." His words meant nothing though. "Is there somebody who can take care of the baby?" God, he was an idiot. Andressa didn't allow Simona contact with anyone in the outside world.

"No."

Carolina. Maybe she could find somebody to take it.

He looked at Simona's wet face and her red eyes. This wasn't the time. He tipped up her chin so she would look at him.

"We'll get through this."

We.

The words just slipped out. He couldn't deny his feelings even though they might get him killed, but he had to hide them.

Cody kissed her forehead, and she held him tight. They sat still, unmoving. He didn't want to let her go, but every second ticking by was a better chance of getting caught by Andressa.

"Can you be there when I tell her?" Simona asked. "I don't want you to say anything. Maybe it'd be better if you also tell me how dumb I was, so Andressa doesn't know. But having you there will help me."

"Of course I will."

He couldn't protect her, but he would be there for her if she wanted. It was all he could do right now.

*

One week passed; maybe Simona was waiting for the right moment to tell Andressa, although there'd never be a right moment.

He and Andressa were finishing dinner, and Simona stepped through the door. "May I please talk to you, Miss Andressa?"

"Can't it wait until after we're done eating?" Her plate was clean, and Cody barely had two bites left.

"Okay, I'll—"

"Never mind. Dinner is ruined. What do you want?"

Simona played with the lowest button on her shirt, her eyes twitching as she stared at Andressa.

"Do you remember when I went to Brasília?"

"Yes," Andressa said, eyeing Simona suspiciously.

"Well, Hector…" She let go of the button, and her hand clenched into fists. Even though she wasn't looking at Cody, he sent every type of good thought to her he could. "We were together, and I'm pregnant."

Cody gritted his teeth. Hector raped her, took away her choice, and all because Andressa presented her to him.

Andressa pursed her lips and reached for her wine. She took a sip. And another. Then swirled the wine in her glass as if looking for answers.

"I knew your whoring around would get you into trouble." She remained rigid. "First Levi and now Hector."

"I'm sorry. I didn't mean to... I didn't want to."

"I'll have to call out a doctor to take care of it. The money is coming out of your wages."

Wages? Cody almost scoffed at the absurdity.

Simona backed up until she hit the wall, her eyes watering and voice quivering. "I don't want to get an abortion. Please don't kill my baby."

Andressa slowly rose to her feet, her arms folded, and towered over Simona. "And how do you think you'll be able to keep up with your work? You're hardly able to perform your duties now. This house looks as if a child cleaned it."

Cody scooted his chair back to stand, but he saw the fear in Simona's eyes. She asked him to stay quiet, and he would.

"I don't know. I'll figure it out."

"You can't have a baby here, and I'm not paying for your mistake."

For half a moment, Cody wished it was that easy, that Simona would get an abortion, but the heartbreak on her face showed differently. As hard as her life would be, she didn't want to get rid of the baby.

"I'll look into doctors." Andressa scowled. "It'll cost extra to have them come out here." She studied Simona for a few more moments. "You may go now."

Simona trudged out of the room. Cody waited for Andressa to say something first.

"This is the thanks I get for providing a decent place for her to work. After that baby's gone, I should tie her legs together."

Cody gathered the courage to say the words he needed to. "Maybe you should let her have it. If she can give the baby to someone to adopt, it might make her a better worker."

"Doubtful."

"No, I'm serious. Think of how grateful she would be to you. You saved her baby and helped find a proper home for it. Helping her baby will motivate her, make her appreciative of the wonderful things you do for her."

Andressa's brows lowered as if she was seriously considering it.

"And I bet you know a ton of people who would love to adopt a baby. Imagine how you could change their lives. It's worth considering."

"Well, I can think about it." She sighed.

Her words gave Cody hope, something he had little of these days.

The next day Andressa studied Caio's training plan. "This looks good," she said to Miguel. "I made some changes with his diet, so he'll be in top performance."

"Yes, I'm sure he will be, but…" Miguel's eyes flitted back and forth between Andressa and Cody. "I was talking to Dr. Abreu, and he assured me—"

"Stop!" Andressa pounded on the table. "Did I not make it clear over and over? I am not contaminating my dogs' bodies with drugs."

"But it's—"

"Out." She pointed. Miguel hesitated but then slunk out the door.

"How many times do I have to repeat myself? We will not use steroids." Andressa leaned back in her seat and sighed. "It's like working with children."

Cody glanced at the door. "Why does he want to? I mean, does it really make that big of a difference?"

Andressa stared at him as if he was dumb. "No, it doesn't. And it's not worth hurting the dogs. It's the lazy way out. Miguel doesn't want to put in the time and effort, but I'm not pumping my dogs full of chemicals because he doesn't want to do his job. I don't need this distraction right now. First it was Simona and now this."

Cody bristled. "What are you going to do? Did you ever think of firing her?" Cody knew you couldn't fire a slave, but maybe if he put the thought in Andressa's head, she might consider letting Simona go.

Andressa stared at the pen as she rolled it back and forth, and Cody waited for her to work out whatever was in her head. Her eyes lit up bright and wide. "Maybe it's time," she said and marched to his chair. She swung her leg over him and straddled his lap, the desire burning strong in her eyes. Her hands wound around his neck, and she leaned in. "It's perfect. We can get married before the baby comes. This will be the start of our new life together. This little girl will have such a wonderful life."

Married... Little girl... They didn't even know the sex of the baby yet.

"But—"

"You were so right. I *can* find the perfect parents for her baby." Her face flushed with excitement. "Us. This baby deserves a better life than that whore can provide. She deserves better."

No. No. No. Andressa was crazy.

Fucking crazy.

"Us?" he asked.

She grasped his shoulders and kissed him hard, passionately. "I won't have to ruin my figure, and we'll have Simona here to take care of it."

Her hands slipped under his t-shirt and down into his shorts. He willed his body to ignore her touches. Only a lunatic would steal a baby from a mother and make her help raise the child.

But the lunatic was before him. On him, making his body do things despite his repulsion.

Andressa.

*

A few days later Cody stared at the pink and white striped walls in the bedroom. His stomach was in constant flux lately. They were stuck, unable to make an escape plan until they talked to Carolina again, begged her for help, but she hadn't been around at all.

Simona had been surprised at how well Andressa was treating her. She didn't know the real reason why, but Cody did, and he hadn't had the heart to tell her the truth about Andressa's vile plan. A forced abortion would devastate Simona, but this wasn't much better.

Andressa stepped behind him in the doorway and wrapped her arms around his waist. Her chin rested on his shoulders. "What do you think?"

"Simona will love it." In just a couple days, Andressa had painted and furnished the bedroom into all things baby girl and kept it hidden from Simona.

Andressa didn't even know it was a girl

"I don't care what Simona thinks. I care what you think." Andressa scowled at him. Cody almost snorted. She'd never once cared about what he thought.

"It's beautiful. You have a knack for decorating."

Andressa smiled brightly. Not only had she decorated this room, but she'd been rambling on about baby names. All during bedroom talk though; she hadn't announced her plans to anyone yet.

"Miss Andressa," Simona said from the hallway.

Andressa released Cody and spun around. "You're late. I told you to be here at two." Cody glanced at the clock. Exactly two minutes past two.

"I'm sorry. I was helping Vera in the kitchen."

"That's not an excuse." Andressa sighed. "Come in. Cody and I wanted to speak with you." Andressa waved Simona into the room, and she froze when she stepped inside. Her eyes took in the pink striped walls, the white crib and changing table, the plush recliner in the corner. Simona's face filled with confusion.

Andressa led Cody to the recliner and sat down, patting the big armrest. He perched on the side of her chair as Simona stood before them.

"Cody and I have been talking. We've decided that we will be adopting your baby."

"What, no!" Simona backed away and grabbed the windowsill with one hand, her face pale.

Andressa folded her arms and shot her a grimace. "My baby deserves better than to be raised by a whore like you."

Simona looked to Cody for support, but he didn't know what to say, what to do.

"But it's my baby," she pleaded. "You can't take him away."

Andressa slapped Simona. "This is not your baby. This is my baby. You are mine, and if you didn't want to get pregnant, you shouldn't have opened your legs for Hector."

Cody grasped the chair to hold himself back. Yelling at Andressa now would only make this worse.

"Miss Andressa." Simona sunk to her knees and wiped her wet eyes. "Please don't…"

Andressa's face hardened into pure contempt. Twisted and dark as the night she'd beat poor Braz to death. "If you prefer, we can send the baby to his father."

Cody gasped. "How can you—"

"Shut up, Cody. This is none of your business."

This was his life. She would force him to marry her, to steal and raise another woman's baby as their own.

"What is your choice?" Andressa's hard-edged voice sliced through him. Simona hung her head, the tears dripping from her red face. Hector wouldn't want a baby. He'd sell it to the highest bidder, and with the quality of people he associated with, the baby didn't stand much of a chance.

"I choose you," Simona's quiet voice said.

"Of course you do." Andressa sneered.

"I am arranging for a midwife visit to make sure my baby's okay. I expect you to care for this baby as if it's your own. Do you understand?"

Simona nodded.

"I said, do you understand?" Andressa punctuated each word sharply.

"Yes, ma'am."

Andressa smiled in satisfaction. "Now get out of here and get back to work. And no mention of our exciting news until we announce it ourselves."

Simona stood still, her cheeks wet and splotchy. For half a second, her eyes connected with Cody's, and his heart sank. Hollow eyes stared at him, eyes with no hope. She trudged out of the room, her shoulders drooping, and her head bent.

"Oh Cody," Andressa sat on the chair with him again, a dreamy look on her face. "I can't believe we'll be parents."

Married to Andressa. With everything going on, he hadn't focused on the marriage part. A picture flashed in his head of a seventyish him and Andressa sitting on a porch in their rocking chairs, watching a bunch of demented Cardoso grandchildren running around.

"Neither can I," he said, laying his head on her shoulder. She sighed softly, and he knew he'd made the right move. More than anything he had to convince her he was all in. Then he and Simona could make their escape before Andressa stole the baby.

Chapter Thirty-Nine
Day 80

Cody finished showering after a swim in the pool. It was nearing the end of May and getting close to three months in Brazil. He should've been done with classes by now, started his summer job. Now he'd have to make up the whole semester when he got back.

If he got back. Things had seemed so much easier when he was only worried about himself, but now he had two lives to worry about. No, three.

The house had been quiet with Andressa at the kennels, but now the music played from the bedroom. He dressed and opened the door.

She was laying out dress clothes. Oh god, she was making him elope this weekend. He couldn't get married, not now, not to her.

No, she'd talked about the big white wedding with hundreds of guests. She wanted the spotlight on her for the day, and she wouldn't give up the experience for anything.

"Cody." She spun around. "Great news. I wasn't sure until recently, so I didn't want to ruin the surprise for you. My father is coming for dinner."

"What?" Oh no, Marcos. Cody hadn't thought about him in a while with all this other crap going on. He didn't need this right now. He didn't need this ever. It was bad enough that a psycho from hell wanted to marry him, but he would also have a brother-in-law who was just as bad and a father-in-law who was ten times worse.

"I'm having a hard time keeping in our news, but I can't tell anyone until after I speak with Father. He'll be so excited."

No.

No, he won't.

"It's the start to a special weekend. Tonight dinner with my father. Saturday, a special night too. We'll meet our friends in town so we can share the big news. It'll be a celebration."

"We're going into Manaus?" Maybe he should make a run for it. Andressa would never expect him to leave now.

"This is the great part of not being pregnant myself. I don't have to give up my wine." Andressa grinned.

What was he thinking? He wouldn't leave Simona behind.

"Sounds like fun."

Andressa babbled on about their plans: dinner and clubs and who would be there. He dutifully put on the dress shirt and pants she required. At least Andressa didn't make Cody wear the suit coat. He already felt as if he was going to his own funeral.

Not long after, he was sitting with Andressa, sipping wine while waiting for her father. Cody had to give credit to Andressa for one thing. Even though she still made Simona work her butt off, she was providing her with better food, and plenty of it, and even had scheduled a visit from a midwife. She never once asked Simona how she was doing though or how she felt. Thank goodness Simona didn't have morning sickness.

Cody glanced at Simona, who waited by the kitchen door for Andressa's next request. She didn't know about Andressa's marriage plans. He should've told her. Why didn't he tell her?

A door shut, and Marcos strutted into the room.

"Papai, you're here." Andressa jumped out of her seat and hugged her dad.

Cody trudged over to them and offered his hand. "Hello, sir." Marcos just stared at his hand, so he pulled it back. This was not a good sign.

"Simona, open a bottle of Havana Cachaça for Papai."

She scuttled to the bar, and Andressa led her dad the same way.

"Now what do I owe this surprise dinner invitation to," Marcos said, making Cody wonder if he ever smiled. "You sounded very urgent."

"I have wonderful news." Andressa grasped Cody's hand and squeezed. "Two things, actually." She looked at him, a grin from ear to ear. If only it wasn't Cody's life she was affecting. "Cody and I got engaged."

She thrust her hand toward Marcos's face. Cody's mouth dropped at the ring on her finger. A ring he'd never laid eyes on.

Marcos held her hand, looking at the enormous diamond.

"Congratulations are in order then. Welcome to the family, Cody." Marcos patted him on the back, but his voice betrayed his words.

"Thank you, sir." Cody looked over Andressa's shoulder to see Simona's gaping mouth. She closed her eyes and shook her head, and when she opened them again, her expression was blank.

"Marcos, call me Marcos."

"Everything fell into place," Andressa gushed. "Cody is learning so much at the kennels. He's such an asset, and I'm lucky I found him." She glanced at Cody fondly. "We're having the wedding in six months, but that's not it. We've decided to have a baby."

"A baby?" Marcos's brows rose, and he eyed Cody.

"I know it seems fast, but this is the right thing for us. Simona got pregnant and doesn't want the baby, so we decided the best home for the baby would be here with us."

Andressa had her whole story planned out, an explanation for everything.

"You don't want a baby in your life. You need to travel and have fun and not get tied down at such a young age."

"I'm twenty-eight now. Somebody has to be the adult in this family. Enzo sure isn't the one." The scorn in her voice was strong, and Marcos smiled wryly.

"You will finally be a grandfather," she said. "Can you believe it?"

"I guess I am." He sighed. "But if it makes you happy, that's all I want."

"Thank you." She wrapped her arms around Marcos and hugged him.

Later at dinner, Vera placed the last dish on the table. Every time she brought more food out, Cody studied her and the way she looked at Marcos, how she reacted to him.

"Can I get you anything else, Miss Andressa?" she asked in a cool voice.

"More wine." Marcos tapped his empty glass.

"Yes, sir." Her voice was steady, and she grabbed the bottle of wine from the table and refilled his glass. Marcos murdered his own wife, Vera's sister, yet she did not appear afraid.

"You may go now," Andressa dismissed her, and Vera disappeared into the kitchen. Andressa glanced at the door. "I hate to bring up business during dinner, but I need to talk to you about Enzo. I have a special job I need done, but I'm afraid he's getting sloppy. His habit is out of control, and I need more of a professional."

Cody squirmed in his seat. But this couldn't involve Simona since Andressa was determined to take her baby. It had to be something different... He hoped.

Marcos folded his hands and frowned. "I'm dealing with it."

"But do you realize how bad it is? He's using every day. He almost got caught with that body. If that officer hadn't already been under our service, Enzo would be in jail."

Cody's ears perked up. Andressa hadn't told him about any Enzo fiasco.

"I'm aware of what happened, Andressa." Marcos's voice cut through the tension. "What is it you need?"

"I have someone who is not paying up. This has been going on for a while now. If he's doing business with me, he has to fulfill his side of the bargain. I need him in the hospital, but I need him alive. Enzo goes too far; he can't control himself once he gets going."

"Who?"

"It's Paulo. And I need to show him the importance of staying true to our family, so I want to keep it in the family. Felipe is…" She pursed her lips.

"Who's Paulo?" Cody asked. Both Marcos and Andressa looked at him as if he'd spoken out of turn.

Andressa narrowed her eyes at Cody. "He's my cousin, and he begged me for a job. He wants the Cardoso name behind him, and at first he was okay, but now he's taking my generosity for granted."

"What about Felipe?" Marcos said.

Andressa shook her head. "Carolina is making him soft. She's trying to pull him away from us."

"Felipe would do anything for you," Cody stammered, unsure why he felt the need to defend Felipe.

"I know he would if I told him to. But he's been begging me to let him work full time at the kennels, with the dogs." Andressa patted Cody's hand. "He enjoys hanging out with my Cody."

"Felipe would do well in that setting." Marcos nodded as the pride surged through Cody. He was having a good effect on Felipe, if even a little.

"He's an intelligent guy, and he has a slow fuse. He doesn't hit out of anger, which is Enzo's problem, and Felipe knows when to quit."

"But if his heart isn't in it," Marcos added.

A sigh slipped out of Andressa's lips.

"He's proven himself. I think you should consider letting him be at the kennel full time," Marcos folded his hands as if it was his decision and the matter was settled. And maybe it was.

"I will."

Cody paid attention to the rest of their business discussions, but couldn't stop thinking about their outing in Manaus. Knowing he'd have the ability to escape, but that he couldn't leave Simona, would be torture.

Chapter Forty

Day 82

While Andressa dressed in the bedroom, Cody slipped down to the kitchen to see Simona. She and Vera were preparing drinks and appetizers for the pre-party, and he couldn't get over her coolness earlier.

"Vera, can you excuse us for a few minutes?"

"Yes, Mr. Cody." She took a tray of food and headed out the door. Time was limited, and Cody had to spit it out, but Simona kept moving, putting the fresh fruit on the plate.

"It doesn't mean anything. This engagement stuff. I didn't... It was Andressa. All her. I don't even know where she got the ring from."

"I know," she said, her voice listless. She returned to her food, placing each piece on the tray. Cody was at a loss, but he couldn't blame her for her despondency. He hadn't seen her smile once since the night Andressa revealed her plans, and he wanted to see Simona's bright eyes again, to hear her laugh, but she had accepted her fate and resigned herself to the job.

And that scared him.

"This doesn't change anything. I still—"

The door swung open, and Vera stood in the doorway. "I'll send Simona out to help you with drinks." Vera smiled at whoever was on the other side of the door and stepped all the way in. "Simona, Andressa's guests are here."

Simona pushed the fruit aside and shuffled out the door without giving Cody a second glance. The door swung shut.

"She's still in shock," Vera said quietly.

"What can I do?" Cody felt helpless, hopeless.

"Nothing. Give her time to figure it out." She gave him a swat on the shoulders. "Now get out there and entertain your guests."

Your guests. His and Andressa's guests. His stomach churned.

He slipped out of the kitchen and almost ran into Felipe, who was stuffing food into his mouth at the table. Felipe glanced at the kitchen and toward Simona, then back to Cody.

"Andressa's going to kick your ass for eating before she's down here," Cody said.

"Don't worry. I'll tell her you said it's okay." Felipe jabbed Cody in the arm and laughed.

"I'm sure you will."

"Cody," Carolina said, rushing over to him. She wrapped him in a hug. "How are you doing?"

"Spectacular." His word dripped with sarcasm, but Carolina wouldn't know it.

This would be another nightmare. An evening celebrating his ridiculous engagement with Andressa's so-called friends. Cody hoped it didn't drag.

*

"You're looking sexy." Felipe smirked as he climbed into the limo an hour later. Cody rolled his eyes. Most of the people in the limo he recognized, but some were new faces. Andressa was going all out tonight.

Cody dreaded the moment of her big announcement, which would make everything feel more real. It put a deadline on their plan to escape too.

The chatter grew louder with every new couple they picked up; one more and they would head to the restaurant. The Portuguese swirled around him, but he didn't mind being ignored.

"I heard Marcos stopped by the other night," Felipe said. "What did he want?"

Andressa would rip him a new one if he let the secret out. "Beat's me. Business stuff."

"Did they talk about Enzo?" Felipe lowered his voice even though it was unnecessary since nobody was paying attention to them.

"Something about some trouble he almost got into."

"It was nuts." Felipe shook his head like he was dumbfounded, and Cody knew whatever Enzo did was bad—really bad. "Did you hear what he did?"

"He beat a guy to death." Andressa had only given him a few details.

"He was so high he didn't even realize he got caught. All over one of his girls. A low-life pimp stole her away, and Enzo went there to get her back. Everything got out of control, and Enzo started beating on him. Slit his throat and watched him bleed to death. He was fucking the whore when the police showed. Neighbors called it in on the noise. The officer found them covered in blood, in the same room as the body. Enzo and the girl."

The space closed in around Cody, the air stuffy. Life was nothing to a man like Enzo, Cody's future brother-in-law if Andressa had her way. "He cut his throat?"

Felipe stared hard at Cody, and he realized he was holding his own throat.

"Enzo was covered in the guy's blood," Felipe continued. "The officer who found them will live a nice life now thanks to Marcos."

"What happened to the girl?"

Felipe shrugged. "I don't know, but she's probably pretty fucked up after seeing that shit. Plus, Enzo wouldn't have been too kind to her for leaving."

Cody paled. Simona had lived in a world like Enzo's, being used and abused by men. "That's horrible."

Felipe studied Cody's face. "Never said it was a pretty life."

Cody wanted to ask Felipe why he did it, why he was a part of the Cardoso clan, but he kept his mouth shut. Felipe would rat him out without a moment's hesitation.

Felipe leaned back into his seat and smiled. "You're not thinking of slipping away from Andressa tonight, are you?"

"No," Cody said a bit too emphatically. "You may not believe me, but I love Andressa. We might not have started out right, but she's going places, and I want to go with her. She's got awesome dogs, and I'm starting to think she should break into the American market."

"What an easy way for you to get home." Felipe smirked.

"No. I'm serious. It's big money in the States." He forced the enthusiasm into his voice. "I talked to Andressa about it, but I have to do a little more research for her." It was actually Andressa who broached the subject with him; Cody had no clue about anything having to do with dog fighting in the U.S.

The Academy should give him an award for his act.

"Wouldn't Mexico be better?"

"I don't know much about Mexico, but I know the U.S. I can find out what cities would be the best to go to. Chicago or LA or maybe Detroit. It'd probably be best to find a city overridden with gangs and police issues." Cody about kicked himself for saying Chicago and Detroit. Those cities were way too close to home.

The limo stopped abruptly downtown, and Cody looked out the window to see the river not far away.

"Everybody out!" Andressa yelled, and a bunch in the group cheered.

She led the way into the building, holding Cody's hand. Andressa looked sexy as hell in her short, tight red dress and black heels, with her cleavage showing but not busting out. Classy as always.

They stopped at the maître d, and he brought them to a table in a back room. Cody checked out the restaurant: waiters in tuxes, crystal and china, soft candlelight, and patrons in suits and dresses.

They filed into their seats with Andressa at the head and Cody to her left. Carolina sat on his other side with Felipe next to her. No sooner had they settled, then a swarm of waiters descended. Water glasses, bread, and wine was poured.

Or champagne Cody noted when he saw the bubbles.

The waiters disappeared, the door shut, and Andressa clinked on her glass. Once the group quieted down, she stood.

"Thank you everyone for coming. I'm so happy to have my closest friends here to share in my wonderful news."

Cody's heart thumped loudly, and he worried somebody would see through his thin facade. He had to get his Academy Award face on again.

He looked to her, not knowing if he should stand up, but she didn't acknowledge him, hiding the ring she had now slipped on.

"So you know Cody and I have been together for several months now, and it's been a whirlwind of fun and special moments. Cody fell in love with not only me but also Brasil. And…" She finally looked down at him. "He asked me to marry him!" She squealed in such an un-Andressa-like way, holding her hand out for everyone to see.

The room buzzed with chatter and shrieks from the women, congratulations and more. Cody sported the biggest, phoniest smile on his face. He caught Carolina's eyes for a second—long enough to see her surprise, but she flipped the switch and smiled joyously along with everyone else.

"Cody," Andressa said, squeezing his shoulder. He stood next to her, and she raised her glass of champagne in one hand and wrapped her other arm around his waist. Everybody followed with their glasses. "I want to say how happy I am that you came into my life. I now know all the things I was missing out on. I love you, and I can't wait to spend the rest of our lives together."

I came into your life because you made me. Cody's face ached from the forced smile.

"Your turn," Andressa mouthed.

Cody took a deep breath. "Andressa, when we met in Guatemala, I never imagined I'd someday be marrying you. This relationship took me by surprise, but you've shown me so many things I never knew existed. You've made me a better man, and I'm so glad I found you."

"Oh Cody." Andressa pulled him into an embrace, their kiss earning whoops and hollers.

"A toast," someone said. "To Andressa and Cody," another chimed in, and everybody clinked glasses.

Cody looked around the smiling table. Felipe grinned along with everyone else, but his eyes… Cody knew he knew.

"How did you ask her?" the girl next to Andressa asked.

Damn. He should've had a story ready.

Andressa beamed. "He was so sweet," she said. "He surprised me with reservations at Mauricio, and then we spent the evening at Teatro Amazonas. The night was perfectly wonderful, and at the end of the evening, he got down on one knee—it's an American thing—and opened this lovely velvet box and said the sweetest things about how special I was and how I'd changed his life." Andressa touched her chest, her face flushed.

Where the fuck had that come from? Andressa probably believed the stupid-ass story herself. Cody clenched his fists under the table, taking every ounce of strength to keep the smile on his face.

He focused on his glass of champagne and thought of Simona. She was the reason he was doing this. The beautiful, broken Simona. It killed him that he had to return to Andressa's when this night was done, but he'd never take the chance of leaving Simona behind. There was no way he'd get to her if he took off now. They had to leave together.

"Then he asked me to marry him, and I said I would." Andressa continued on about how much Cody loved her. Her attentive subjects smiled and nodded and ohhed and ahhed.

He glanced at the exit for the hundredth time. The doors might lead to his freedom, but Simona would be locked in even tighter. If Andressa only knew he was thinking about another girl at her engagement party, a woman who was stronger and more beautiful than Andressa could ever be. He didn't just want to help Simona escape; he wanted to be with her, to take care of her.

Dinner soon turned into dancing. The group bypassed the line to get in, and after they had drinks, Andressa dragged him onto the dance floor. Gone was the ladylike woman at the restaurant, replaced by a drunk and slovenly Andressa.

Her hands were all over his ass, and she constantly ground her boobs into his body too. Only him though. She danced with several of her guy friends, but there always remained a respectable amount of space between them.

At least she won't cheat on me. The thought made Cody laugh. Maybe she had a couple redeemable qualities, except they didn't absolve her of all the other shit she pulled.

They ended up back at the table with friends. It was impossible to talk unless you were shouting into the other person's ear, but somehow Andressa seemed to be conversing with everyone just fine. Cody glanced at her animated face, his future wife.

He shook off the image, disgusted with himself.

It wouldn't happen. Not in his life.

Chapter Forty-One
Day 83

Andressa slept soundly the next morning, but Cody woke at six-thirty. He doubted she'd be up until ten with all the alcohol she drank. He shut the door quietly and went to get something to eat. He hit the bottom of the stairs, and a duster clattered to the floor.

"Cody, what are you doing here?" Simona gaped at him.

"What do you mean what am I doing here?"

"You were in Manaus," she said, her face still looking shocked.

"We didn't stay over."

Simona picked up her duster, her eyes cloudy. "No, I mean why didn't you run away? You could be free right now."

She thought she meant nothing to him. She was nothing to so many people, but she wasn't nothing to him. He'd never in a million years desert her, but all Simona knew was being used and abused.

He clenched his hands and steadied his voice. "I couldn't leave you."

She sniffed away her tears, and her trembling body fell into his arms. "I thought I'd never see you again." Her choked words spilled out through the sobbing.

"Oh god, no. Never. I won't ever leave you. Simona, I…" He pulled back and looked into her sad eyes. "I love you."

"I love you too," she whispered, hugging him so tightly he could barely breathe. The ramifications of their words were clear to both of them. Andressa wouldn't let them live if she found out, and yet he held on as the seconds ticked by. He didn't want to let go of her or the tiny baby inside of her.

A door clicked behind them, and Cody pushed her away. Daniel rounded the corner and stared at Simona's wet face.

"What's going on?" he demanded.

They were busted—just like his bones would be when Daniel told Andressa.

"I sprained my ankle." She sniffed. "It hurts." Simona bent down, rubbed her ankle, and grimaced. "I tripped coming down the stairs." She stepped away with a limp, a cringe on her face.

Cody let out the breath he was holding.

Daniel sighed. "Okay. You go to your room. You can have the rest of the day off. I don't think Andressa will have much need for you today."

"Thank you." Simona faked a limp as she hobbled away.

"Should I just head to the kennels this morning?" Cody asked Daniel. "Andressa didn't give me any direction. She's still sleeping."

Daniel glanced at Simon's slow-moving figure. "Why don't you help Simona to her room. Did you eat breakfast yet?" He waited for an answer, and Cody shook his head. "Then come see me after you eat breakfast."

Daniel left, and Cody helped Simona out the door. She kept up her limp until they were safely inside the barracão. He followed her into her room and shut the door. They wouldn't have much time.

Simona wrapped her arms around his neck and leaned into his chest. He felt her wet eyes against his skin. "You should've left," she repeated over and over. "I don't know if you're brave or stupid, but whatever it is, I love you so much."

"I love you too." He'd never felt so strongly about any woman. He didn't just want to protect her; he wanted to hold her hand and listen to her talk about her home or the birds she loved or whatever. He wanted to watch her sit in the garden and care for her flowers. He wanted to bring her home to his family. He wanted to share his life with her. "You have to promise me that no matter what happens, you won't give up. We," he said, accenting the word strongly, "will get out of here."

"I promise," she whispered. Cody stared into her hopeful eyes, a nervousness taking hold. Three lives depended on him for their freedom, and the pressure was a noose about to tighten. He had to get them out of there.

"I'd better go." He released her and stepped back.

"Wait." She wound her arms around his neck again, smelling fresh, like soap, her touch so natural. Her lips pressed into his, firm and unyielding. It was a kiss he wanted to repeat over and over.

He broke it off and opened the door to leave. Just before he shut it, she whispered once more. "I promise."

Chapter Forty-Two
Day 84

Another dungy, dirty building. Another sadistic cheering crowd. Another win for Andressa's dog.

Caio had his first fight and came through practically unscathed. The other dog fared worse: a deep gash in his neck, fur matted with blood—a triumph in Andressa's eyes.

Cody would never get used to this.

Andressa showered Caio with hugs and praise as the other dog hobbled away, a pissed off owner jerking the leash. That dog was now on death row.

"Oh Cody," Andressa squealed. "We did it!" Her arms wound around him, and she kissed him among the noise of the crowd.

Not too long after, they were at a trendy bar surrounded by Andressa's friends. She hadn't dragged him out to the dance floor, too busy retelling her win to the friends who were not at the fight.

Carolina scooted up to the table. "I need a drink, Cody. Come with me."

His stomach flip-flopped. Now was the time to talk to her. Carolina never told Felipe about Simona asking for help, so he had to take the chance and trust her.

He glanced at Andressa, but she was talking animatedly with someone else. He started to follow Carolina, but Felipe grabbed his arm. "Where you going with my girl?" He narrowed his eyes at Cody, and Carolina laughed.

"The waitress is too slow, and I noticed your drink is almost gone."

"She's the best. Didn't I tell you?" Felipe grinned, whacking Cody on the shoulder.

"A hundred times." Cody laughed along with them.

"We'll be right back." She smiled sincerely, a tenderness in her eyes. They weaved through the crowd, Cody's heart thumping along with the beat of the music until they arrived at the bar and put an order in.

He patted his back pocket out of habit, the action was still ingrained in him. "I don't have a wallet."

Carolina chuckled. "I got it." She looked at the table, and all humor left her face. After another glance at Andressa, Carolina shoved something into his hands. He rifled through the colorful bills, which included some American hundreds "This should be enough to get you out of here. We'll go dance later, and then I'll tell them you went to the bathroom."

Cody started to open his hand, but she squeezed it tight, pressing her shoulders next to his to block any view open to Andressa. "No. It's about a thousand dollars, mostly Brasilian real. Just get out of the country first, and then you can figure out how to get home. I'd go to Peru."

The money burned his hand. It was so tempting. So, so tempting... but Simona.

"I can't." His stomach soured. This was his one chance, and he was turning it down.

"What, why?"

The bartender placed two drinks down. Carolina said something to him, and the bartender walked away again.

"Why won't you go?" she demanded.

If he admitted why and Andressa found out, Simona would be dead. He stared deep into Carolina's eyes. She was willing to give Cody a thousand dollars. She was risking her life to help him. Or maybe she was setting him up, testing him. Maybe she'd turn around and rat him out to Andressa.

No. Carolina wouldn't do that.

"I can't leave Simona. And the baby."

"That was you?" Her tan faced blanched.

"No, not by me. Hector raped her and…" He didn't have time to explain the whole story. "Andressa sent her to get raped by this guy for punishment, and she's pregnant. Andressa's already decided she's taking the baby. We're going to raise it as our own, and I know if I leave, she'll take it out on Simona. She'll punish her. She's already suspicious of us."

If Carolina was setting him up, he was sunk. He didn't quite admit his feelings for Simona, but Carolina could probably read him easily enough. Nobody had offered to help him, Andressa's grip so tight, and he had to believe Carolina's motivations were honest. He'd find out soon enough.

"That's why you have to get out now."

"I can't." He shoved the money into her hands. Keeping it wasn't an option. There's no way he could explain it to Andressa. The bartender set several shots down, and Carolina threw money at him. Cody looked to the table. Andressa was watching them. He smiled and picked up the shot to show her and then pointed at her and him. "We have to go back," he said.

Carolina stuffed the money into her purse, her face dark, and grabbed the drinks. "What will you do?"

"I don't know yet. She's worried about Marcos going after her mom. She won't leave until she knows her mom is safe." The table was approaching too quickly, and Cody let the smile grow on his face again. "And I can't abandon her." Before they reached the table, Cody whispered, "Does Felipe know?"

"No," she said, smiling along with Cody.

"For you." He presented the shot to Andressa, and they clinked glasses before swallowing down the hard liquor. It burned his throat.

"Carolina got it for us because…" He glanced her way. "I forgot my wallet." The music was so loud, and it's not like anyone would hear them, but he was trying to get a message across to Andressa. She looked him over, her head tilted to the side. Maybe he shouldn't have been so forward. Maybe she'd think he wanted money and would use it to escape.

"Thanks for the drinks, Carolina," Cody said. He hoped he got the double meaning in his gratitude. If she'd been willing to do this for him, she was definitely ready to call Simona's mother; they just had to coordinate somehow. Wait—Simona's mom. He should've mentioned the letter thing. Or maybe Carolina could call her. If he got her alone again, he'd mention it specifically.

"Well, we need to celebrate your win tonight." She leaned in and gave Andressa a hug.

If Carolina got him and Simona out of there alive, he wasn't the only one who deserved an Academy Award.

*

The next day Cody watched the black diamond swim back and forth in its tank as Andressa pored over a spreadsheet. It never ceased to amaze him how much money passed through her hands.

She had the perfect scheme set up. Most of her expenses for the dog fighters' training were covered under the normal breeding expenses, but none of the income was shown. She had a crapload of money going tax free.

"Andressa." Daniel stuck his head in the door and frowned. "We need to talk." Andressa waved him in, and he looked at Cody but didn't try send him away.

A brown bag thunked on the table; Daniel stuck his hand inside and pulled out several dark glass bottles. Andressa's face hardened.

"Levi showed me Miguel's secret stash. Said he'd been doing it for the last few fights."

"I told him no." Andressa's cold, hard voice left no doubt in Cody's mind; this wouldn't end pretty for Miguel. She pursed her lips, fingering the bottle, and with every passing second, her anger grew.

"Where is he?" she growled.

"In the office."

Andressa shot to her feet and stomped out of the room.

"What's she gonna do?" Cody asked Daniel. He shrugged.

Andressa bypassed the garage and stalked to the kennels incredibly fast for a woman wearing heels, and Cody and Daniel could hardly keep up. She threw open the office door with a bang, and Felipe practically fell out of his seat in surprise.

The Portuguese flew out of her mouth, her face tight with fury, and she flung the bottles at Miguel's chest. They bounced off and clattered to the floor. Miguel backed his chair away from her.

"Andressa, pare," Miguel cried. "Não era—"

"Não!" Andressa smacked him and started her tirade again, all up in his face. She finally allowed him a chance to speak, and it seemed as if he was trying to defend his actions, but Andressa would cut him off at every turn. Cody needed a translator to tell him what was going on. Felipe and Daniel stood off to the side watching, and Levi slipped in the door, a smirk on his face.

The arguing continued until Cody heard a word he recognized.

"Enzo?" Andressa repeated, her body stiffening.

"Enzo." Miguel nodded and continued in Portuguese. Cody crept to the corner where Felipe stood.

"What's going on?"

"Shush," Felipe smacked him in the arm. Andressa's voice ticked into a higher screech, and Cody felt an odd satisfaction of Andressa being screwed over by her brother.

"Daniel," Andressa yelled, and he jumped into action. Miguel stood there staring as if he didn't know what to do, but Daniel gripped his arm and tugged him toward the door. Levi scooted out of the way, and Andressa stomped after the two men. Levi shuffled out the door, and Cody shut it behind him.

He wanted to follow the crew, but he'd get better information out of Felipe. "What'd she freak out about?" Cody asked.

"This shit isn't good." Felipe huffed, and Cody waited for more, but Felipe walked behind the desk, picked up the brown bottles, and stared at the labels, shaking his head.

Cody didn't know if he meant Enzo or Miguel.

"Miguel's been using steroids since Braz lost," Felipe continued. "Enzo put him up to it and has been paying him extra to do it without Andressa knowing. The branco is rotting Enzo's brain. He doesn't think Andressa knows what she's doing, but he's wrong. Enzo doesn't know much about running a business. He saw one loss and got worried. He doesn't understand you win some and lose some, but as long as you're doing more winning, you're okay."

Felipe rubbed his temples.

"What'll happen to Miguel?" Cody asked.

"Not much since Enzo's behind it all. He's out of here, but Andressa won't touch him. Lucky for him, otherwise we'd be feeding him to the piranhas." Felipe attempted a wry smile, but Cody didn't laugh. "If you know what's good for you, you'll stay away from Andressa for a while."

"You don't have to tell me twice." Cody sighed. He took off to get some work done and found Levi sitting on his ass watching TV. Not a surprise. "Did you feed the dogs yet?" Cody asked him.

"You can do it."

Andressa would need somebody new to replace Miguel, and Levi wasn't the guy. He'd have to talk to her about this. She wasn't around the kennels as much, so she didn't witness Levi's laziness. Miguel had been dumb to cross Andressa, but he'd been a competent manager and trainer.

The rest of the day was spent training and playing with the dogs, and at six Cody headed to the house. Dinner was seven sharp, and he'd better be there and ready.

Chapter Forty-Three

Day 89

Things were okay for a few days, and once again, Cody found himself driving with Andressa to see Marcos. Just her and him this time, no Felipe. She spent most of the time bitching about Enzo, and hopefully that busty Sofia wouldn't be around to make her mood worse.

Cody didn't have a set escape plan yet but had two ideas he needed to think about. The first was to just brave the river and swim as far as they could. The other was a bit riskier and might involve Carolina if she were willing.

Andressa reached across the seat and grabbed his hand. "This whole thing got me thinking. You do so well with the dogs, and I know your heart is set on becoming a veterinarian, so maybe you can go back to school someday."

"That'd be nice, but only if it's what you want." There's no way in hell he'd be around in a few years.

"I think getting rid of Miguel is a smart decision. His work has been subpar for a while, and he was starting to bring this organization down."

What a crock. Miguel kept her program running, did everything she asked. Well… except for the steroid thing.

"This is a wonderful opportunity for you. You've been doing a lot for us, and I'd love to see you take on more responsibility."

No, no, no. He couldn't discipline the dogs like Miguel had. And doing the actual fights… No way.

"But Andressa, I don't know anything about dog fighting. I can't do Miguel's job."

She frowned, but Cody had to stick up for himself. "I don't think I'm cut out for Miguel's job, but I can do the kennel side."

She looked at him skeptically. "You're too soft. You need to toughen up."

What she really meant: You need to learn that a dog's life has no value. You need to flick a switch and be able to kill a dog you raised just because it disappointed you in a fight.

"But that's what you love about me, don't you?" He grinned and then nudged her foot until she smiled. She was eating his bullshit up. "We complement each other. You're the tough, smart chick, and I'm the softie."

"Oh Cody." She got all googly-eyed, her voice warm.

"I don't want to seem lazy because I love working with the dogs, but if I took over Miguel's job, I wouldn't have much time for you." The absurd thing was, having less time with her was exactly what he wanted.

Andressa covered his hand with hers, and she beamed. "You're right about that."

The car dropped them off, and soon they stepped into Marcos's luxurious apartment.

"Andressa." Marcos crossed the room and gave her a kiss on the cheek. He shook Cody's hand and gave him a greeting. "Your brother is not here yet, so please come have a drink."

"Of course he isn't." Andressa frowned. Marcos led them to the family room and poured three glasses of wine, the fourth empty.

"Thank you, Father." Andressa took a big sip and gripped the stem of her glass tightly. "Before Enzo arrives, I want to talk about changes we're making. Cody and I had a long talk. I've decided to split Miguel's position into two. Cody will handle the breeding side, and we'll look for somebody to handle the training."

"What about Levi?" Marcos asked.

Andressa shook her head. "No. Levi is lazy. He doesn't have the diligence or the dedication. He's always had a bit of an attitude, but since things were getting done, I didn't question Miguel."

Oh please. Andressa wasn't aware of his laziness until Cody told her, and Felipe backed him up.

"Perhaps firing Miguel wasn't in your best interest."

"Yes, it was." Andressa straightened in her chair. "He had a problem following orders, and—"

The door opened, and Enzo strutted in. He greeted the others but didn't glance Cody's way. Andressa folded her arms and eyed Enzo as he filled his glass with liquor.

Andressa glared at Enzo.

Enzo stared down Andressa.

Cody held his breath.

Andressa shot to her feet and spewed an angry torrent, waving her hands and releasing a pent-up fury. Enzo stretched on the couch, a half smirk on his face. He interrupted her tirade every once in a while but didn't act as if he was in the middle of Hurricane Andressa.

Marcos broke in, his voice firm.

Andressa's face fell. She tried to argue with her dad, but he shut her down every time. Marcos continued to talk, and Cody studied Enzo. He lost his smirk, but he certainly didn't look unhappy like Andressa.

"Now that everything is settled, let's go eat dinner." Marcos led them to the dining room, stuck his head through a doorway and spoke to someone, and then took his seat at the head of the table.

A woman glided through the door with a tray of food. Cody couldn't help but gape at her long, lean legs leading to a skirt that barely covered her ass, and boobs about to pop out of the top of her cheesy French maid uniform, one right out of a Halloween costume catalog.

Enzo smacked him in the arm and chuckled. "I told Andressa she needs girls like this, but she can't handle the competition."

"I don't want sluts at my house." Andressa sneered at the girl, who didn't react.

"Andressa," Marcos growled. "You'll treat my help with respect. Cody, if you need anything, let Monica know." He spoke to the girl and patted her ass before she left, a smile on her face.

Andressa slumped in her seat, and Enzo leaned over and whispered. "Don't you want to fuck a woman like that every day?"

Cody didn't answer. Instead, he tried to convey his disgust to Andressa so she wouldn't bitch him out later.

Marcos reverted to Portuguese, but Andressa didn't participate in the conversation, and at the end of dinner, he heard his name. His head whipped up to find Andressa's wide-opened mouth.

"Não." She shook her head, offering what he figured was some kind of defense. Enzo laughed silently from his side of the table.

Marcos held his palm up, and Andressa stopped. "Cody. It's time we get to know you better since you'll be a part of our family. Andressa will return home, and the three of us are going out."

Enzo smirked.

What did they want with him? Where were they taking him? He'd never be able to defend himself against these two.

"We have things we need to do tomorrow." Andressa's strained voice kept Cody on edge.

"And I will get him back to you." Marcos's steely eyes stared down his daughter, and she sighed. Cody let out his breath. He'd live to see tomorrow.

"Not too late," she whined.

"Don't worry." Enzo winked.

By the end of the hour, Cody kissed Andressa goodnight at the door. She looked at him with a sad, defeated face. Maybe they were going to take him out and beat him or torture him so he'd leave Andressa. Maybe it was like gangs who jumped prospects to get them in or made them commit crimes.

"I'll see you tomorrow, won't I?" Cody clutched at her hand.

She blinked her wet eyes. "Do you love me, Cody?"

"You know I do." God, she was freaking him out.

"Be good then. My father and Enzo are bad influences. Don't get into trouble."

Drugs. It had to be about drugs.

"I'd never do coke. I love you, and I'd never hurt you." He pulled her into a hug, and she snuggled in.

"I'll miss you," she whispered.

"I'll miss you too." He held her until she pushed back, her face now masked.

Cody returned to the other two men. He wasn't about to snort coke with them... well, he'd do it if it meant not getting his ass beat, but hopefully it wouldn't come to that.

Enzo jumped to his feet and rubbed his hands together. "Let's get this party started."

Marcos chuckled. "But first, a toast to my future son-in-law." He handed Cody a full glass of wine. "To a long and happy life. May you always know the right thing to say." He held his glass to Cody's and clinked.

Wise words for dealing with Andressa.

Marcos looked to Enzo.

"I've got nothing." Enzo laughed. "Oh wait, don't fucking get caught."

Cody had no intention of cheating on Andressa. Although that wasn't true; his mind had already betrayed Andressa with his thoughts of Simona.

Marcos whisked him off to a limo, where two more men joined them. They picked up some others and headed to an upscale bar, a private booth in the corner, and a waitress who only attended to them. Marcos tossed around his money as if it was nothing.

One drink. Two drinks. Three.

Enzo pretty much ignored Cody, especially after one of his buddies joined the group, but Marcos kept Cody talking.

They made a second stop at another bar, and Cody watched Enzo suck down a shot once again. He lost count of the drinks Enzo had, and before long Enzo was leading them to yet another place. Cody had no idea what time it was, but at least these bar changes gave him a break away from the liquor. His head was fuzzy, and he wasn't walking straight.

He followed the animated crew through the front door of the newest bar, another building in downtown Manaus. This wasn't a bar really, more like a conference room with girls in slinky dresses serving drinks.

A private party at a hotel. Was that where they'd come? The room was huge but was furnished with couches and coffee tables and pub tables. Plus a bar in the corner. All sorts of people milled around talking and drinking. A few had plates of appetizers in their hands, but Cody saw no food sitting out.

Marcos greeted a ton of people as they passed, and then Cody saw somebody he recognized.

"Vitor." Marcos did the man hug thing and stepped back.

"Ahh, Cody. So nice to see you again," Vitor said. Cody shook hands with him, trying to stop his rolling stomach. Vitor molested Andressa at a young age, with her father's permission. "I hear congratulations are due. My little girl doesn't belong to me anymore."

"Guess not." Cody shivered and covered it with a laugh. Part of him doubted that marrying Andressa would put an end to her relationship with Vitor.

"Welcome to Minha Casa. I think you'll like it here."

"We had to save the best for last." Enzo grinned.

"Oh, is this another club?" It wasn't really like a bar though with its bright fluorescent lights and cozy furniture. Clubs were dark with flashing lights and loud music.

"It's my house." Enzo swept his arms out.

"Oh, you live here?" But wait, Enzo lived in Belém. But he had to have an apartment here. This was no apartment though.

"It's Cody's first time here." Enzo nodded at Vitor.

"Ahh, my son. Let's go get a drink and get settled in. Our friends are in the sala vermelha." Vitor laid a hand on Cody's back and prompted him forward.

Marcos led the way through a door and down the hall to a smaller version of the room they'd been in. Not as many people filled the space, and there were way more women than men.

He did a double take. Every woman in the room was buck naked. He blinked his eyes. No, some were dressed, but most were naked.

"It's a beautiful sight, isn't it?" Vitor whispered in his ear. He whistled loudly, raised his hand in the air, and snapped.

A bunch of girls ran over, the naked ones, with boobs bouncing. All shapes and sizes and colors. One... two... three... four... Cody tried counting but gave up. His head wouldn't handle it. Twelve or so women stood in front of them, backs arched and smiles on their faces.

"These are my girls, Cody, and as our guest of honor, you get to pick first." Enzo slapped him on the back.

Cody's mind reeled. He was in one of Enzo's brothels. These were prostitutes. Like Simona had been except she'd been on the street, which was worse. But was it worse?

Marcos looked on him like a proud father, although Cody's mind was not where Marcos probably thought it should be. Cody wasn't admiring Enzo's offerings; all he wanted was to get out.

And Andressa. This was what she meant. She hadn't been scared he was going to get high or that they'd kill him.

"We've got Minh from Vietnam. Elea from Kenya. Dasha from Russia. We're a fucking international delight." Vitor chuckled at his own joke and introduced every single girl. They took a step forward when he called their names, heads held high, chests jutting out, and Miss Universe smiles on their faces. "And if you don't care about where they're from, because we sure as hell don't, just look at those bodies. Your girl at home doesn't have the big tits, so maybe you want something more fun."

Vitor stepped behind a girl with a giant chest and fondled her boobs. "Feel free to check them out first." Vitor's hand slid down past the girl's waist, down between her thighs. Cody held back his disgust as Vitor slipped his finger inside the girl. She smiled vacantly. "They don't mind."

Vitor grinned, and Cody about gagged. These women had been with so many men, might even carry diseases, none of which were their fault.

Simona entered his mind again. There were so many things he hadn't thought about, things he never considered. She'd been subjected to the same filth these women here were. Men like Vitor had taken advantage and hurt her.

"Take your pick," Enzo said.

"I... I..." Pick a girl. For what?

"He's nervous. First time, Cody?" Enzo laughed along with the other men.

Marcos slapped his son on the back of his head playfully. "He's more of a gentleman than you. Maybe he wants to talk to the girls first."

Cody was drowning, unable to swim out of this shark tank. Were these girls forced into these jobs? Of course they were. No girl would willingly choose this life. Depravity ran strong in this family, and those without the iron will got run over or tossed away.

He didn't know what to do.

Chapter Forty-Four

Day 89

"You don't have to choose now," Vitor said.

Choices. Cody didn't want to choose any girl. Andressa probably never chose to have sex with Vitor either, and Vera didn't choose to serve her murderous brother-in-law. Nobody had any choices.

"Plenty of time. Fuck them all if you want." Marcos laughed. "I can assure you Pilar and Rosine are top notch."

That grossed Cody out on so many levels. He spotted a couple talking in the corner. She looked like Yasmin. A naked Yasmin. He couldn't quite tell if it was her and wiped his sweaty palms on his pants.

Vitor snapped his fingers again. "Dasha, take Cody for a drink." He turned back to Cody. "She's a feisty one. And she speaks English well. You might enjoy her."

Cody nodded and stepped toward the girl who answered to Vitor.

"Hello, Cody, how are you this evening?" she said with a strong Russian accent. She led him toward a bar in the corner, and he kept his eyes away from her naked body.

"Um, good." His head was still trying to figure this all out. Marcos and Enzo might be setting him up so Andressa would reject him.

But no. This was their life, and they expected him to take part.

What the hell would he do if they pushed him off toward a private room? He couldn't have sex with this woman.

Cody averted his gaze from the couch they were passing; a woman was sucking off a guy in a suit. And it wasn't just the men. A clothed woman snorted a line of coke and made out with one of the naked prostitutes. Another couch held a couple going at it, oblivious to the other people right next to them.

He couldn't look anywhere without feeling dirty.

Cody blinked his eyes to clean them, but then they arrived at the bar. He was safe.

But he wasn't. The woman behind the bar was naked too.

"What's your pleasure, Cody?" Dasha asked.

"Huh?" He backed away. She wouldn't go down on him right here, in a room full of people. Would she?

"What do you want to drink?" she asked, and he relaxed.

"A whiskey sour." It was the drink Enzo had been feeding him all night long.

She gave the bartender their order.

"Wait, no." He couldn't have any more liquor. "Beer. Just beer."

Dasha corrected the order, and the bartender left.

Andressa would kill him if anything happened with Dasha, but Marcos and Enzo might kill him if nothing happened.

Oh my god, Simona. If he even touched one of these girls, she'd hate him forever, and that scared him more than Andressa.

The naked bartender slapped two glasses of beer on the bar.

"So, um, where are you from?" Cody struggled for something to say. "Where in Russia, I mean. I've never been there, but my parents have."

"Moscow."

Great. Something he knew about.

"No kidding. That's where my parents went. I love how the city is laid out. The rings. It'd be fun to go there someday." Except once he got home, he'd never leave the country again.

"The rings?" she asked.

"Um, the roads," he said, studying her confused face. Moscow was known for their unique road system. "Are you really from Moscow?"

She shook her head sadly. "I'm from Kazakhstan, but most people don't know where it is, so Vitor makes me say Russia."

"Do you miss it?"

"I grew up in Aktau. It's on the Caspian Sea. I miss the sea and the rocky cliffs and the seasons."

"Me too. The seasons I mean. This rain-all-the-time thing sucks. I never thought I'd say it, but I miss the snow."

Dasha laughed with him, a real laugh.

"I miss my family," he added, and his smile fell as he stared at his beer. He missed them more than anything.

"I do too," Dasha said softly. "I would go back in an instant if I could."

Reality knocked Cody to the ground, and he became aware again of where he was and who he was with.

Vitor slung his arm over Cody's shoulder. "So how is my girl treating you?"

"Very well. She seems like a nice girl."

"Then why don't you bring your drinks back. Marcos is waiting for you."

Cody glanced at Dasha, but she had a phony Miss America smile back on her face. They followed Vitor to a quiet set of couches in the corner. Enzo, Marcos, and another guy were sitting with prostitutes in between them.

The third man, Bruno, slid a tray of white powder toward Cody, but he shook his head. Enzo snickered and said something to the guy in Portuguese. They both laughed.

"So, Cody," Marcos said, leaning forward. "Andressa seems to believe in your business instincts. Tell me your thoughts on the whole steroids thing."

Cody's mouth went dry. He didn't want to piss off Enzo, but he couldn't go against Andressa either. There's no doubt Enzo would share that with her.

He cleared his throat. "Well, I wasn't in veterinary school yet, so I don't know how steroids affect the dog's body, but I know it messes up the human body. I'd be concerned with the short-term effects as much as the long. Stud fees for your champions would be enormous, and steroids might affect the bottom line."

"I seem to remember Andressa arguing as such." Marcos looked to Enzo.

"They can quit the steroids before it's time," Enzo spit out. "The dog will be okay."

"No, it can have long-term effects too," Cody said.

"Didn't you say you weren't a vet yet?" Enzo glared, his jaw tight.

"So where did Miguel go?" Bruno asked.

"He's coming to Belém with me. Andressa's such a tight-ass bitch." Enzo huffed. "I don't know how you fucking live with her."

"Enzo." Marcos's warning came out loud and clear, just as Cody was opening his mouth to support Andressa.

For god sakes he'd sunk low. Now Enzo had him defending Andressa. Things were so not right in the world.

"Your little girl's growing up." Bruno smiled at Marcos, then laughed. "I'm not sure how she ended up engaged to an American though."

"Why don't you tell him the story, Cody," Marcos said.

"We met in Guatemala. I was there with Engineers Without Borders to build a well system for a village."

"And how did that go?" Bruno asked.

Cody was dumbstruck for a moment, not knowing how to answer. It didn't go because Andressa kidnapped him.

"Yes, how did that go, Cody?" Enzo leaned forward on his elbows, enjoying Cody's discomfort.

"Very well. They were a deserving village. I've heard Marcos is very generous to the people of Manaus, and I hope to continue in his steps."

Marcos nodded, buying Cody's crap, and his life depended on his ability to sell that crap. Unfortunately, he didn't have a fucking clue what Marcos did and didn't know. Felipe had assured him he knew. What a fucking mess.

"That's one of the things I love about Andressa," Marcos said. "Her generosity and kindness." Funny words from a brutal son of a bitch.

Enzo rolled his eyes.

"You could learn some lessons from Cody," Marcos said, the stern look given to his son.

"He's a saint. Just like Andressa," Enzo sniped.

"It seems that Cody was a suitable find," Vitor said. "Marcos was telling me earlier about the suggestions he made on the new kennel upgrades."

"It's a kennel." Enzo sneered. "A monkey can run it. You don't have to keep dogs in line like we do here. They don't talk back." He glared at one of the girls, and she looked to the floor.

"The care of the dogs might be easy," Marcos said, "but Andressa's formed great contacts with the breeding. Plus, we need to have legit businesses on the front. Her business degree did her well."

"Andressa suggested I finish my school here so I can maybe go to veterinary school." Cody enjoyed seeing Enzo all pissed off. "Even if I don't end up becoming a vet, I really want to get my college degree."

"Everyone should earn a degree from the university." Marcos stared hard at his son. Nobody said a word, the tension tight.

Enzo jumped up. "Let's go, Minh."

She hesitated, and he yanked her to her feet.

Bruno said something to Marcos in Portuguese, and they both laughed. "Cody has no brothers or sisters, so I'm sure he's not used to sibling rivalry."

Especially when it came to two psychopaths.

"No, I don't. Didn't Enzo go to college?" Cody asked.

Marcos snorted. "He wasted years of my money partying."

Bruno brought up his time at college, and the topic of conversation changed. The time passed slowly. Vitor was up and down, but Marcos and Bruno seemed content to sit and talk with Cody.

A short time later, Enzo returned without Minh. He plopped down on the couch and did a line before scooting up to another girl. "Get me a cachaça."

She did as ordered, and he downed it quickly.

"Do you want another beer, Cody?" Dasha asked, her boobs rubbing into his shoulder. He'd practically forgotten about her, but now he felt the heat from her body.

"Sure. Same as before, please."

"Get me a cachaça too," Enzo commanded.

"Yes, sir." She rushed off and returned in record time.

After another half hour or so, Marcos turned to Cody. "We'll be leaving in about an hour, so it's time."

Dasha tugged on his arm, and he looked at her.

Oh.

Shit.

"Um…" It was best to turn her down politely in the other room. If she told Marcos, so be it. That was better than having a confrontation here. "Okay, yeah, let's go."

Cody ignored Enzo's smirk as he walked away.

Dasha led him down a deserted hallway lit by the harsh lights on the ceiling, the noise and music from the previous room blocked away. This was it. He had to hope she wouldn't put up a fuss when he said no, and he prayed she wouldn't tell Marcos.

He was caught in a giant spider web. If he went left, Marcos would eat him alive. If he went right, Andressa would.

Dasha stopped at a door that hung open, darkness behind it. "I picked a nice room for you."

Cody wiped his wet palms on his pants. "Thanks."

A king-sized bed flanked one end of the room, complete with vibrant purple bedspread and mounds of girly pillows.

A plush couch and coffee table faced a large screen TV on the wall. "We can watch porn if it helps you," Dasha said.

Cody headed over to the mini-fridge in the small kitchenette. Beer and liquor and soda and more. He opened a bottle of water, and the chilled liquid cooled his parched throat. He downed half the bottle before he realized it.

Oh damn, maybe he wasn't supposed to drink it. He glanced up with wide eyes to a laughing Dasha. "Have whatever you want," she said.

"Thanks." His face grew hot, and he studied the ceiling and the walls, checking for a camera. Other than the TV, nothing hung on the walls.

"What are you looking for?" Dasha asked.

"Do they have cameras in here?"

She shook her head and hopped onto the bar stool, her boobs spreading out over the counter. "Our clients demand privacy."

This was so fucking ridiculous. The laughs spilled out of his throat from deep inside, and Dasha looked at him as if he was having a mental breakdown, but he couldn't help it.

"I'm not the psycho, believe me. Marcos is a psycho, and Enzo's a psycho, and Andressa's a psycho, but I'm about the sanest one around here." He finished off his water. "Who the hell brings their future son-in-law to a brothel? Who kills a low-level pimp because his girl ran away on him? Who kidnaps a random stranger and brings him to Brazil and expects him to fall in love and marry her? Who thinks any of this is right?"

Cody sunk onto a bar stool and banged his head on the table. He lay still, the only sound Dasha's breathing.

Dasha. His head whipped up. She was gaping at him. Holy shit. Had he really said that aloud?

"Please don't tell him I said that. He'll kill me." Marcos would kill him. Enzo would kill him. Andressa too. They'd all kill him.

"Who?" she said softly.

"All of them. Any of them."

Marcos and his deranged offspring would escort him somewhere deep into the Amazon. They'd tie him up to a tree, and each take turns. Marcos would cut off one hand, Enzo would cut off the other, and Andressa—well, he knew which appendage she'd cut off.

Then they'd leave him to bleed to death, the bugs would swarm him, and the animals would scavenge off his rotting body. Cody shuddered.

"Did you come here on your own free will?" he asked Dasha.

"To Brasil, yes. Here…" She shrugged sadly. "No."

That was enough for Cody. He didn't want to hear another sad story like Simona's; he was teetering on the edge of sanity as it was.

"I don't want to have sex with you," he said.

"I figured that out a while ago."

No woman should be stuck in this life. All the men and women she was forced to please, clients who demanded privacy, people with money and power. Dasha was a high-class whore with wealthy clients, but she wasn't much better off than a girl like Simona who hooked in the back alley of a dirty street.

"Please tell Marcos we did though."

"What did we do? What's your story?" she asked.

Cody thought for a moment. It had to be believable.

"Okay, maybe first you… you know… gave me oral sex." His face ran hot, but all he thought was how stupid he was. He was sitting with a naked hooker in a private room of a brothel, and he couldn't say the word blow job. When he got back to the States, he'd have some stories to tell his friends.

"Blow job," he continued. "You did that first. Then we had sex. Plain vanilla sex because that's what they'll believe I did since I obviously looked like a kid on his first day of school out there."

"Vanilla sex?" She laughed.

"Missionary position. You can tell them that."

"Cody, they won't grill me on our positions and your style. Although I have a feeling this is a special case."

The skin prickled on the back of his neck. "What do you mean?"

"Vitor doesn't usually take an interest in our dealings with clients, but you're marrying his Andressa. I picked up enough to know he's…" She touched her finger to her chin. "He's checking you out. Andressa is important to him."

His own little sex toy given to him by her father.

"You speak Portuguese then?" he asked.

"I'm not great at speaking it, but I understand it."

They sat quietly. Cody wasn't sure what to say now.

"Do you get a break after this? I noticed Minh didn't come back to the room after Enzo left with her."

Dasha shifted in her seat, eyeing him quietly. Cody waited.

"Minh won't be returning to work tonight. She has bruises and scratches that will need to heal."

"Enzo beat her up?"

"Enzo likes things rough, and when he's drunk and angry—"

"It's my fault." The heat of the room suffocated Cody. It was him who pissed Enzo off. Marcos comparing Cody to Enzo, Andressa to Enzo.

"Don't blame yourself." Dasha patted his arm. "It's not the first time, and it won't be the last."

Cody trudged to the fridge and grabbed two cans of beer. The first went down as quick as the water. He sat and drank and thought of all this shit that was now his life. He'd chosen to go to Guatemala, he'd chosen to go to Andressa's hotel room, and he'd said the words that got Minh hurt.

His fault. All his fault.

He felt Dasha's warm hand on his arm again. A squeeze.

"Cody." Enzo pounded on the door. "Wrap it up."

He looked at Dasha, and she patted his hand again, repeating his story back. They messed up the bed so it looked used, and then he stepped out to face the crowd.

Chapter Forty-Five
Day 90

Cody slunk into the silent house at five a.m. Andressa wasn't in the bedroom or anywhere else, so he went to get a drink from the kitchen. Andressa sat outside, staring toward the pool. His heart thumped as his head tried to figure out what to say.

He opened the door, but even though the click was loud in the dark night, she didn't look back. He held his breath and shuffled toward her.

"Andressa?" He set his hand on her stiff shoulder, but she didn't move. "Hey, what are you doing up?"

He knelt in front of her and took in her wet eyes. She blinked a few times, and her gaze hardened. She put her hands on his shoulders and shoved him. Cody rolled back-assward, his head knocking on the concrete.

"Bastardo," she screamed. "How could you do this to me?"

He scrambled to his feet, rubbing the back of his head. "I didn't do anything. What are you talking about?"

"I know you were at Minha Casa. I know you were with a whore." She pounded on his chest with her fists. Cody tried to grab her wrists, but it was as if she had six arms, and he couldn't get a grip.

"I didn't do anything," he yelled.

"Enzo told me you had sex with one of his girls."

She would kill him. Felipe was probably already on his way here, and he'd end up in a shallow grave.

"Andressa, stop." He shoved her away with all his strength, and she stumbled backward. At the edge of the pool, she seemed to hold still as if an unseen hand was holding her up. Then she splashed into the water. She popped up, sputtering and swearing, and wiped her eyes with her wet hand.

He hadn't meant to push her in. He'd been so close to gathering her trust, and now Enzo fucked it all up. There was nothing left to do. She'd either believe him, or she wouldn't.

"Listen to me. Nothing happened. Yes, I was in a room with a girl, but I told her no. I let Enzo and your father think something happened."

"But he said—"

"I don't care what he said because it's not true. You know how he lies. And I got the feeling he doesn't want us together. He'll do anything to split us up."

"Why should I believe you?" She crossed her arms and glared, but her voice softened. He couldn't let up now.

"Because you know me, and you know him. We went in the bedroom and talked. Her name is Dasha, and she's from Kazakhstan. She's just a working girl there to do a job, but it didn't happen with me." God, if Andressa checked out his story with her, Dasha wouldn't know she was supposed to tell Andressa the truth.

He stretched out his hand, but she stalked to the steps. Water dripped from her body as she got out of the pool. It would've been comical if it wasn't so serious.

"Why did you tell Enzo you had sex with her?"

"Because I didn't want her to get into trouble."

Andressa tugged on his collar, then inspected him, sniffing his neck. She released him and shuffled to the chair, her body soaking the seat. Cody trudged over to her and sat beside her, her wet clothes chilling his skin.

"I'd never hurt you, Andressa. I love you."

She lifted her head to meet his gaze, and he continued. "The whole time I was there, all I wanted was to come home to you. Those girls are…" He had to play it right. "They're nothing next to you. Sex with a prostitute isn't worth losing what I have with you." He stroked her hand, waiting for a response.

"You really didn't do anything?" she asked in a small voice, amazing him with her brokenness. He'd seen it that one time. She had real feelings; she had pain. The emotions warred inside him, wanting to hurt her and tell her he did it, but he couldn't.

"Of course not. I'm a one-woman man. I always have been. And now I've found the perfect woman, nobody else compares."

Andressa snorted. "I'm not dumb. Enzo's girls are beautiful."

"Maybe, but they're not you. There's so much more to life than looks. I noticed how gorgeous you were in Guatemala, but it was the things you said, the stuff in your mind, that attracted me to you."

"Oh Cody. I love you." She leaned in and kissed his lips, falling into him. "I shouldn't have worried. You'd never betray me."

She settled into his lap and held on tightly to him, and Cody sighed in relief. Now all he had to worry about was Enzo and Marcos finding out the truth.

*

Andressa seemed to enjoy having this information that her father and Enzo didn't have, and now she had a brand new project: a wedding to plan before Simona had the baby. Cody didn't know how she was getting things done with all this wedding talk, but her new spreadsheets and everything else kept her occupied.

Cody worked at the kennel, the time dragging. Andressa and Daniel would be back at two, and Cody hadn't had time to see Simona. Now he was eating lunch with Levi.

"I can't believe she brought in a loser from Bolivia." Levi crumpled up his napkin and threw it on his plate. Cody rubbed his temples, closing his eyes and wishing Levi would disappear. Since Andressa had announced her replacement for Miguel, Levi had bitched about not getting the job.

"He's been around dogos his whole life, been fighting them for years." Cody considered dropping hints to Andressa to replace Levi too. Even she was growing weary of his laziness. Miguel had let him get away with a lot.

"Still, she should stay within the family." Levi huffed, and Cody rolled his eyes. Levi was no more a part of the Cardoso family any more than Cody.

"I'll bring the dishes to the house." He gathered everything onto the tray.

"Why? Vera will be back."

Because he needed to see Simona.

"Need fresh air." Cody tossed the garbage and took the tray to the house. Stolen moments like these were the only times he saw her.

After stopping in the kitchen, Cody searched the whole house, unable to find her. Passing through the family room, he heard a clink from behind the bar and checked it out. Simona was on her hands and knees in front of the wine rack.

"Getting into the wine again?" Cody peeked over the bar.

Simona laughed. "I wish." She smiled at him, but he saw the anguish in her dark eyes.

He rounded the bar and sat next to her. He took her hand, so warm, so small, and held it in his. "Let's ask Carolina for help again. She offered me a thousand dollars, so I'm sure she'll help you, especially with the baby now. She can just call your Mom."

"I don't think she knows Spanish."

"Aren't they really close though?"

"They're similar but a little different. I picked up the Portuguese once I got here, but when I tried to speak it to my mom, she had a tough time. She got the basics of what I was saying, but this would be so confusing to explain, and Carolina speaks so fast. My mom would never get it. Or she might think it's a joke."

"I'll ask her first, and if she can't, then we'll have to do the letter. Once we get out of here, we can go to Venezuela and make sure your mom is safe."

Her face tightened. "I don't dare imagine it because what if it doesn't come true?"

"It will. Don't think like that." Cody cupped her cheek. "We'll escape, and your baby will have a free life." He slid his hand on her still-flat belly. "Can you feel anything?"

"No." She chuckled. "It's still too early. I'm only about two months along."

He stared into her deep brown eyes. "I can't believe you have a baby in there. You're going to be a mother." She would be an amazing mother, a courageous woman who wouldn't give up. "He's very lucky to have you."

"It could be a she." Simona smiled.

"Or twins." He shrugged, then laughed, but it fell away. She'd talked of seeing her mom again, but would Simona want to stay with her? An emptiness filled him even though he hadn't lost her yet.

He would lose her. She would stay in Venezuela when he went home.

"The next time I see Carolina, I'll ask her if she'll send the letter to your mom. We'll have to figure out a way to sneak it to her, but I'm sure she'll help us."

"She'll help us." Simona laid her lips on his for a quick kiss and then wrapped her arms around Cody's shoulders. "I just know she will."

Chapter Forty-Six

Day 99

Cody waited in the bedroom, blocking out Andressa's voice as she gave Simona instructions. Any minute Simona's midwife would be here for an ultrasound. The doorbell rang, and Andressa hurried out of the room.

"Are you nervous?" Cody asked.

"I'm trying not to get attached." She smiled warily. She wasn't as convinced they'd get away as Cody was.

"I'll throw out a suggestion to Felipe to bring Carolina over." That wasn't unusual since Felipe knew Cody liked Carolina. "I'll talk to her then."

The voices carried down the hallway, and Andressa escorted a woman into the room. She couldn't have been much older than Andressa herself.

Andressa introduced the midwife, Clara, and directed Simona to lie on the bed while Clara unpacked some equipment from a large rolling bag.

"You're nine weeks along, right?" Clara asked.

Simona nodded as Andressa said yes.

"And you've been eating healthy and have been taking the prenatal vitamins?"

"Every day," Andressa responded. "I got the brand you recommended, and we eat healthy in my home, so there was no need to change her diet. I'm sure she'd be eating badly if she lived on her own though." Andressa laughed.

Cody watched the whole process, fascinated by everything. He'd never seen an ultrasound before but had figured it was something they had to do in a hospital or clinic. But Clara had her own little computer and other equipment. Simona shivered when Clara put the goopy stuff on her stomach, but soon all eyes were on the screen.

Clara droned on as he looked at a baby. Granted, it was no more than a blob, but it was a baby.

Their baby.

For the first time he felt a connection to the tiny piece of life in Simona's stomach. It could be his; he could be a father. He wanted to be a father to Simona's baby. He wanted to be with her.

Cody clenched the footboard and held tight. He had to talk Simona into coming to the U.S. with him. He'd even marry her in Venezuela if that's what it took. The thought of losing her, losing the baby inside her, left him hollowed out.

Even if she wasn't ready to give him an answer, he needed to know she'd at least consider it.

"Cody?" Andressa said. Everybody was staring at him. "Do you have any questions?"

"Uh, no. I think you guys covered it all."

Andressa frowned at him. He'd probably get bitched out for not showing enough interest, but if he asked something they already talked about, she'd accuse him of not listening. Maybe he needed to go for the sympathy factor.

"It's overwhelming," he said. Simona shifted on the bed, distracting him, and he slid closer to Andressa and wrapped his arm around her waist. "All of it. I'm lucky to have you here to explain it to me." Cody looked to Clara. "Andressa has been reading a ton of baby books and sharing it with me."

Andressa's lips quirked into a smile. "True. I don't have many friends who have babies, so it's all new to me."

As much as Andressa was reading up on having babies, she was leaving Simona in the dark. Andressa shoved those special baby vitamins at her, told her what to do and what to eat, but shared little information with Simona.

Andressa wrapped things up with Clara and sent her on her way, and Simona returned to work. He had to speak with her, but he needed to figure out how to get close without Andressa seeing.

*

Several days passed after the ultrasound, but Cody wasn't able to see Simona alone. Felipe either. Not until Andressa dragged him and Felipe to an orchestra concert with Carolina. She was the one he needed to talk to though.

All night he waited for a second alone with Carolina, and he didn't get it until late evening when they wandered into a bar for a nightcap.

He glanced around the crowded bar as they looked for seats. He had to create his opportunity because it'd never appear on its own.

"Over here." Andressa waved them to an open table. She settled into her seat, but Cody stayed standing. "Sit down." She motioned just as Cody nudged Carolina's arm.

"It's pretty busy. It'll take forever to get a server. We'll go get drinks."

Andressa frowned and checked out the bar. "They'll be over."

"Ahh, but Cody was telling me about a delicious drink he used to have at home, and I want to try it."

"Um, yeah," Cody said. "They won't know the name here, so I'll have to tell them how to make it."

"What is it?" Andressa perked up.

"I don't want no frou-frou drink." Felipe plunked down into a chair, and Cody laughed. Even Felipe was picking up words from Cody now.

"I got it. No frou-frou drink." Cody glanced at Andressa and grinned. "You'll have to wait and see."

That pacified her, and he and Carolina took off for the bar. He waited until they were a safe distance away, and the words erupted like a volcano.

"Simona won't leave until her mom has been warned, so we want to send a letter. She needs to hide from Marcos. Will you help us?"

"Of course I will. I'll do whatever I can."

The people in front of them moved away from the bar, and the bartender looked at them, presumably asking what they wanted.

Cody's mind blanked. He had to come up with something good. Carolina leaned in toward the guy and put in an order. She flipped around as the bartender walked away. "What do you want to get?"

"Um, damn." He thought hard, and one thing popped into his head. Andressa liked coconut. "An Electric Smurf." He waited for Carolina to chuckle but then remembered she wouldn't know what a Smurf was. "Tell them coconut rum, blue curacao, pineapple, and Sprite?"

The bartender returned with Felipe's beer, and Carolina explained the drink. After he left, she turned to Cody. "You have Simona write her letter. I can also hide money away and tell you where to pick it up. Just tell me when you're ready."

"How? I can't exactly call you."

"I'll find an excuse to come to the house. Felipe wants to be there when the new guy arrives, and I want to meet him too."

"Jaime should here by Wednesday, I think." Cody wanted to put the glass of cold beer on his hot forehead. He'd have to slip the note to Carolina with Andressa around.

Three drinks clunked on the counter, and Carolina dug in her purse.

"I'm such a loser." Cody sighed.

"What are you talking about?"

He couldn't shutter the grimace on his face. "I'm here at a bar with a beautiful woman, and I can't even buy her a drink."

"Cody." Carolina laughed, her face bright pink. "Maybe you should talk to Andressa about getting your own money."

He forced a smile, pushing down the crap inside. He couldn't buy his own drinks, he couldn't save himself, and he couldn't save Simona. Not without help.

Andressa had taken away his manhood, but he'd get it back.

Chapter Forty-Seven

Day 105

A few days later Cody headed to the kennels. He rounded the bend and saw Simona carrying a basket full of clean towels. Damn that Andressa. She'd better not be making Simona work so hard when she was farther along in the pregnancy.

He jogged to catch up with her. "Hey, let me help you."

"Thank you." Simona handed over the basket.

Cody eyed the road and lowered his voice. "Carolina will help us. She'll mail off the letter and even give us some money when we're ready. You can write out your letter, and I'll hold on to it until Carolina shows up." If Andressa found the letter before he got rid of it, she'd kill him. She'd kill Simona. "I don't know what day she'll be here, but have it ready by Wednesday. She'll probably show up to see Felipe."

Simona nodded and opened the door to the kennel. Levi pushed through the doorway and stopped to eye Cody, then Simona—except his gaze stopped at her chest.

"She spreading her legs for you too now?" Levi smirked. Simona's face reddened, and she stared at the ground.

Cody flung the basket to the side and swung his fist toward Levi's stomach. Levi let out an "umph" and backed away. He straightened up as Cody shook his throbbing hand. Levi looked as though it hardly affected him though.

"It's called being a gentleman, you jackass. Maybe if you were more of one, Andressa would've given you Miguel's job. Now hold the door open for Simona so she can do the job Andressa wants her to do. And if you're lucky, I won't tell Andressa about all the crap you pull."

Levi stared at him as if he was about to argue, but he pushed open the door and held it.

Simona picked up her basket and walked inside, and Levi stormed away. Cody wouldn't take this shit from Levi anymore. Andressa had to know what kind of liability Levi was.

In the room, the basket of towels thumped to the floor, and a warm hand touched his arm. Tears gathered in her eyes.

"Sometimes I wish…" she started in a strangled voice. "Sometimes I wish this would all go away. That I wouldn't have to worry about the baby anymore. It's not like you. You can go home and return to your normal life, but I can't. It won't ever be normal again." She sniffed, her other hand spread out on her belly and a guilty look on her face. "There are times I don't want it."

Cody wiped the tears from her cheeks. "That's normal. Nobody could blame you." The baby would forever remind her of what she'd gone through, yet she wasn't willing to throw it away. Her strength was amazing. "You are the most incredible woman I know. You're tough, and you're brave, and even though you've had some doubts, you'll be an awesome mother. So don't you forget that."

Simona threw her arms around his waist and squeezed him tight. It was the moment he should ask her what her plans were, but he was scared of what her answer would be. He gathered his nerves and pulled back, staring into her dark eyes. How could he ask her to give up her mother again, a mom who could help her raise this baby, when she'd been stolen from her too? There was no way he would stay in Venezuela with her.

"Will your mom help you with the baby when you get home?" There. He'd asked, but he hadn't. Of course her mother would help her out and love the baby, but he couldn't risk hearing her say no, she wouldn't come with him.

Her face clouded, and her lip quivered. "You don't want me to come with you?" Her voice was light yet filled with pain. She had wanted to go with him, and now she thought he was throwing her away too.

"No, Simona," he said. She shut her eyes tight, and the tears started again. "No, I mean yes. Oh god, that's not what I mean." He grabbed her hands and held them to his chest. "Yes, I want you to come with me. I want that more than anything. I thought… I didn't want you to feel like you had to go. I wanted it to be a choice. But…"

This moment had been huge, and he fucked it up.

He steadied his voice. "I was terrified that if I asked, you might say no because of your mom. I love you more than anything, and I never want to let you go."

"I love you too." Simona leaned her body into Cody's and kissed him deeply. Her touch filled him with everything he never knew he wanted. She was his, and he promised himself to never give her up. They would get away from Andressa, make sure Simona's mother was safe, and then go to the U.S. and make a new life together.

Cody broke away, left breathless by her kiss.

Oh shit. He scanned the windows for any movement, his heart beating wildly. Levi was lurking around somewhere, or somebody else could've walked in on them. They couldn't risk being caught…

Not now when they were so close.

Chapter Forty-Eight

Day 106

Cody stared at the closed office door. Andressa was going to throw a fit. Lucio had thrown up twice yesterday. Cody figured the dog had just gotten into something, but today they found more puke in the kennel, and he could hardly coax Lucio out.

He knocked.

"What?" Andressa barked. He should walk away, but she'd get even pissier. Cody slowly opened the door to Andressa's ice-cold stare and Levi's emotionless face. He only hoped Andressa was firing him. "We're a little busy here. What do you want?"

This was a no-win for Cody, and he had a feeling who'd be blamed.

"Lucio needs to see a vet."

"Can't you take care of it?" she snapped.

He wasn't a vet, and it wasn't as if he picked up that knowledge through osmosis from his mom.

"No. He's been vomiting since yesterday, and he's lethargic. He didn't even go for his food. He doesn't act like he's in pain, but something's wrong. I don't have the training to diagnose whatever it is."

"Is Simona still out there?" She folded her arms and waited for Cody's answer. Why was she asking about Simona? She had nothing to do with the dogs, other than cleaning the kennels.

"I don't know."

"Get back out there and take care of Lucio. I'll call in Dr. Ribeiro if I have to." Andressa waved him off with a flick of her hand, and Cody backed out of the doorway.

He trudged down the road toward the kennels, thinking about Simona and whether they'd even let her into the U.S. He was ready to do anything, to marry her if necessary, in order to get her to freedom. He wanted to spend the rest of his life with her, and he hoped she felt the same way.

A car roared in behind him, pelting him with gravel. Felipe damn near hit him and then had the audacity to grin as he got out of the car.

"Are you trying to kill me?" Cody shook his head at the overgrown child.

"Nope. I'd have Carolina to answer to, and that girl scares me sometimes." Felipe kept a straight face as he said it but broke out into a smile. Cody laughed at him. "Which, speaking of the she-devil... She said she had something to give you."

The hairs prickled up on Cody's neck. She wouldn't have told him.

She couldn't.

"Uh, what's that?"

"Rice kris-pees."

Cody let out a sigh of relief. Maybe this was her way of trying to see him.

"She got Rice Krispies? Do they sell them here?" Few of the Brazilian versions of American foods were exactly the same, but there's no way someone would mess up Rice Krispies... Or maybe they could.

"I don't know. She's been experimenting with American desserts. I don't like it. Her taking over the kitchen."

Cody chuckled at Felipe's face. "Hey, if she's making desserts, what are you complaining about?"

"You've got a point." Felipe shrugged and headed into the kennel.

"Come check out Lucio. He's sick or something. Andressa needs to call a vet." Cody led Felipe to Lucio's kennel, watching out for Simona. He shouldn't bother. It's not as if he'd talk to her in front of Felipe anyway.

*

An hour later Andressa still hadn't shown up, but Cody had cleaned the puke in Lucio's kennel because Levi would never do it.

"So this is the list?" Felipe waved a piece of paper in the air. One good thing about Miguel, he'd kept meticulous records. So even though Cody hadn't learned everything yet, all he had to do was go back into each dog's file to figure things out, with Felipe's help on the translations.

"Yes. I think Andressa said the next fight is not too far off, and these tests will help determine which dog is ready. Cesar or Gil."

"Should we place a bet? I'll take Cesar. He's pretty damn vicious." Felipe raised his brows.

"I've got no money. Maybe for the plate of Rice Krispies because once you eat one, you'll want the whole pan."

"They're not that good." Felipe laughed.

"Okay then. No bet."

"Oh, I'll do it." Felipe smirked. Cody would enjoy eating the Rice Krispies in front of him. Cesar might be bigger, but he didn't have the strength and agility of Gil.

Cody's head snapped up at a loud noise, a woman's angry rant.

"Is that Andressa?" Felipe asked, looking in the same direction as Cody. They couldn't see anything, but the noise was coming from the other side of the kennel.

"Yeah." Cody took off toward the sound. He rounded the corner and froze. Felipe slammed into him, and Cody stumbled forward, feeling as if he got the wind knocked out of him.

Simona's small body lay hunched over on the gravel road as Andressa kicked her in the back. The sharp point of Andressa's toe slammed into Simona, and she yelped.

"Andressa, stop!" Cody ran, arms outstretched. Andressa was going to kill her. He shoved Andressa away from Simona and held her tight. "What are you doing? Quit it."

"Let me go," Andressa screeched, her dark hair filling his mouth. Arms were everywhere, her fists pounding on Cody's chest, but he held her back as Simona writhed in pain. He didn't see any blood, but she was sobbing, shaking, her hair sticking to her wet face. He couldn't tell if it was bruises or dirt that marred her skin.

Oh god, the baby.

"Stop!" he yelled, forcing Andressa farther away. "You'll hurt our baby. Please don't hurt our baby."

Even though her arms slackened, he kept hold of her wrists. She turned her red face up to his, her breath slowing, and shot daggers at him with her eyes.

"She's a piece of trash." Andressa's voice was low and menacing, and Cody used all his strength not to turn around and check on Simona. Andressa jerked one arm away and pulled something out of her pocket. "Look at this, Cody. Just look."

She waved the paper in his face, and he stepped back, taking the sheet. Simona's handwriting. His pulse raced as he skimmed the letter, looking for his name. She couldn't have mentioned him because Andressa wasn't mad at him. Simona stared up at him from the ground with her bloodshot eyes, her lips trembling.

He got to the end of the letter without seeing his name, but it was damning. The letter explained in detail what Andressa had done, how she was keeping Simona captive, and how Simona said she would escape before the baby was born. He had to fix this, but how? The first step was to keep Andressa from hurting Simona or the baby.

Andressa fixed her angry gaze on Simona, and his heart broke. Tears streamed down Simona's grimy face, her clothes smudged with dirt. Bruises were probably forming on her skin right then, but at least there wasn't blood.

"She was running away again and stealing my baby."

Cody shivered at the hard edge in Andressa's voice. He was at a loss, not sure of what to say. He grasped her hand. "But you were hurting our baby. She's a human. She's not a dog."

Andressa's eyes narrowed even more as she studied his face. "You're sleeping with her."

"No!" Cody yelled. "Why do you always go back to this? I've never touched her." Andressa's free hand struck Cody, and his legs faltered. "Andressa, stop it! I'm not sleeping with her!" He gripped her shoulders and stuck his face into hers. "You're hurting *our* baby. You could've killed her."

Andressa stared at him. Felipe and Levi seemed frozen in place, and Simona whimpered on the ground, so he shook Andressa's shoulders. "Please don't hurt our baby."

"Our baby," she repeated back to him as if a light clicked on in her head.

"Yes," he sighed, grasping her arm tightly. "I want this baby with you. I want to marry you. Why can't you see that?"

"She is out of here as soon as the baby is born," Andressa spat, glaring at Simona.

"That's fine." He rubbed her shoulders to get her to calm down. "We don't need her. As you said, her work is subpar at best."

"You and Felipe can take her to her room. Levi, you're coming with me to see Lucio." Andressa stomped off without another word, Levi following.

Cody dropped to his knees, his heart thudding in his chest. "Are you okay?"

Simona opened her eyes to show him a depth of pain he'd never felt. She couldn't lose hope, not now. They had to get out of there.

"I'm okay," she whispered. Cody wrapped his arm around her shoulder and slowly helped her to sitting, her face wincing the whole way. He felt Felipe's presence behind him but didn't look up. Little rocks were embedded in her cheek, and he wiped them away, leaving small red gouges in her skin.

Cody looked toward the direction Levi and Andressa had left. That asshole had something to do with this, but how had Andressa found the letter? He couldn't ask with Felipe here.

"Let's get you back to your room." Felipe reached down and pulled Simona to her feet. She gasped and hunched over, her face contorting in pain. "Oh fuck. I'm sorry," Felipe said.

Simona bit back her tears and straightened. Before Cody did anything, Felipe started to lead her to his truck, a flinch in every step.

Cody clenched his hands and steadied himself. He'd need all his self-control to hold back around Andressa. It was more important than ever that they escape.

Felipe drove to the barracão and helped Simona to her room. Furniture was turned upside down, her sheets lay crumpled on the bed, and all of Simona's things lay scattered on the floor.

Felipe righted the chair.

"I'll make your bed so you can lie down." Cody skirted around Simona as she slumped in the seat. "Felipe, will you go get Vera, please?"

"Sure." He glanced back and forth between Cody and Simona before slipping out of the room.

"How did she know?" Cody asked as soon as Felipe was gone. He stretched the mattress pad over the bed quickly.

"I'm not sure. She came out of nowhere and started yelling about how I wouldn't take her baby away."

Cody held her pillow in his hands, bringing it to his nose and sniffing. It smelled like Simona. "She was talking to Levi right before. Did you tell him something?"

"Of course not," she snapped, closing her eyes and wincing.

"I'm sorry. I know you wouldn't. I just don't know how she'd find out." Cody tossed the pillow onto the bed. "Here, let me help you lie down."

After she settled in, he ran to the bathroom to get a warm washcloth. Back at her bed, he sat by her side and wiped off her forehead and dirty tear-stained cheeks. The baby wasn't that big yet, and Simona's body took the brunt of the attack.

It would be okay—it had to be.

"I'm sorry," he sighed. "This is all my fault. I should've taken the letter from you as soon as you wrote it."

"No." She shook her head. "And I won't let her stop us. I should've never insisted on writing it. We should've just tried to escape. Now I've ruined it all and put my mother in danger."

"We'll get out." It was the only thing he cared about at this point. They both fell silent, and Cody continued cleaning her face.

"Are you okay?" Vera's voice made Cody jump. She rushed into the room, Felipe behind her.

"Yes." Simona closed her eyes and pulled the blanket to her chest.

"Gentlemen, she needs her rest. Felipe, fix some tea and bring it out for us."

Cody almost volunteered to do it, but Felipe's suspicious eyes already scrutinized him. Felipe trudged out, and Cody followed.

"I'll check on Lucio again," Cody said because he had no idea what else to do at the moment.

Chapter Forty-Nine

Day 108

Andressa spent the afternoon in her office while Cody worked at the kennels. He didn't want to think about what she would do to Simona after the baby was born because it scared him too much. It wouldn't matter anyway; they'd be long gone by then.

Act normal, he kept telling himself; Felipe couldn't know anything was wrong. They worked through the testing, and the results were as Cody predicted. Gil would move up to the pre-fight training.

"Looks like I'll get all those Rice Krispies. Sucks to be you." Cody bent down and scratched Gil behind the ears, forcing a grin.

Felipe rolled his eyes and called Gil, pitching a ball across the yard. "So, did Simona say anything else? What's this all about?"

Cody shrugged, keeping his eyes on Gil as he ran back. "She wrote a letter to her family. Said Andressa was keeping her captive, that she was gonna try escape before the baby was born."

Gil returned, and Felipe tossed the ball again "Why? I thought she didn't want it. Andressa said she'd tried to abort it."

Cody's head swung around. Simona would never do such a thing. She wanted her baby more than anything. "Oh yeah. We're lucky Andressa stopped her. I've always wanted to have kids. My parents were the oldest in their families, so most of my cousins were a lot younger than me. What about you and Carolina? Any wedding bells in the future for you?"

Oh god, quit rambling. Cody hid his cringe.

"She thinks I need to grow up first." Felipe snorted.

"She's right." Cody grinned.

Felipe gripped the ball in his hand and fired it at Cody. He spun away, but the ball hit him in the side.

"Asshole!" he yelled as he scooped up the ball and hurled it back. He took off for a tree to avoid being hit again. For ten minutes he cleared his head of Simona and Andressa and got in a good game of dodgeball. He just wished he could've enjoyed it more.

*

The plates were set. The wine was poured. Everything was normal.

But it wasn't.

Felipe waited patiently, drinking beer as Andressa spoke to Vera at dinner. "We need privacy. You can wait in the kitchen until I call you back."

"Yes, ma'am." Vera scooted away.

Cody hadn't had a chance to ask her about Simona, not even one second to slip into the kitchen.

As soon as the door closed, Andressa put on her serious face. "I wanted to discuss the Simona situation with you, Felipe. I can't trust her anymore. I never should've trusted her after the first incident. I've been thinking today about how to handle the problem, and I've got it figured out."

She scooped food onto her plate and passed the bowl to Cody. Then grabbed another.

"What's that?" Felipe asked.

"Can I dish up my food first?" she admonished him with a scowl. They waited, Cody about on the edge of his seat. She was in control—she was always in control.

He took a bite of chicken to help hide his emotions. Chew. Swallow. Bite. Chew. Swallow.

"I've decided to have Simona wear an ankle bracelet equipped with GPS. She has work to do, and I can't be there all the time to make sure she's not sneaking away with our baby. Raul and Bernardo will be in charge of monitoring her, but I'll be able to check in on her with an app on my phone." She grinned, so proud of herself.

"An app?" Cody asked. Crap, what if she made him wear one too?

"Rafael Barbosa will be delivering the unit in three days. Until then, I'll need you here, Felipe, to keep an eye on her."

"No problem. Can I get one of these things so I can track Carolina?" He laughed, but Andressa glared at him, and he shut it down.

"This is very serious. It's the second time she has tried to run away. This time with my baby. She's lucky she's still alive."

A silent shiver racked Cody's body. The only thing keeping Simona alive was the baby in her stomach, but that baby wouldn't stay there forever.

"What about after the baby's born?" Cody asked. *Stay calm. Act normal.* He took a sip of water to cool his burning body.

"I spoke with Enzo today, and he has room for her at Minha Casa. It's perfect really. She can pay me back much quicker than if she stays here, and he'll keep her in line."

The blood drained from Cody's face. Andressa was sentencing Simona to life in a brothel, getting beat by men like Enzo and Vitor if she did something wrong.

Andressa wouldn't... She couldn't...

His stomach twisted into a tight knot.

But she would.

He had to get Simona out of there.

"So what do you want me to do?" Felipe asked. "Stand guard at her door at night? Watch her while she works?"

"Basically, yes. I visited her earlier and told her she can have a day off. She's got some nasty bruises on her body and needs to take better care of our baby."

Andressa put those bruises there. Cody gripped the edge of the table, biting down on his tongue. Her cruelty was never-ending.

"You can go home after dinner, but when you return, bring your bag because I want you here until I get her GPS unit." Andressa sipped her wine like nothing was wrong.

Simona was a fucking prisoner.

The thought almost made Cody laugh. She'd always been a prisoner, but now, keeping her locked up, having somebody watch her 24-7; it was worse than prison.

"You sure it's okay for me to leave for a bit?" Felipe asked.

"I said yes. She was complaining about cramps, and she can barely walk straight. I think we'll be fine." Andressa was quiet for a moment. "But why don't you stop at the barracão before you leave. Tell her you'll be standing watch outside the front door. She won't come out."

"Okay, I'll do that. I think Cody will miss working with me though if I'm standing guard for her the next few days." Felipe grinned.

"He'll get by," Andressa answered for him. "And once you're back full time, we'll need to prepare for Jaime's arrival."

Felipe left, and Andressa laid her hand on Cody's arm and let out a dark laugh. "You want to know the funny thing about all of this? There's nobody there to get her letter."

Oh god, Andressa killed her mom already. Cody tried to relax his tense body. "What do you mean?"

"When she tried to escape last time, I checked on her mother again. She'd died not long ago in a bus accident. A semi-truck smashed into the bus she was on, and it killed four people."

Simona was going to freak. Her mother was the only important thing in her life, the one thing that kept her going. This would break her.

"But why didn't you say anything?"

"Because I was waiting for the right moment to share it with her, and I forgot. We've had so much going on, but I can tell her now. I'll have to dig out the article for her." Andressa chuckled.

Three days until Simona got an ankle bracelet. He needed to find Carolina. It was now or never, and he'd get Simona out of there or die trying.

Chapter Fifty

Day 108

That night Andressa snuggled up to Cody while they watched TV, talking too much for him to pay attention though.

"A friend approached me to do a talk for their women in business organization. I agreed to do it. It's a wonderful opportunity to get our name out into the community."

"Sounds like a good idea," he said with no emotion.

"Andressa." Felipe stepped into the room. "I think you need to come out to the barracão."

"What's wrong now?" Andressa sighed.

"Simona. She's bleeding a lot. Her sheets are covered in blood."

"I'm sure it's nothing." She stood and headed for the door. Cody jumped up behind her, his chest tight. It wasn't nothing; Andressa had beat Simona badly. *Please don't let her lose the baby*, he repeated over and over as they rushed to the barracão.

"What's going on here?" Andressa stormed into Simona's room, the unmistakable smell of sweat and blood hitting Cody's nose.

Vera held a sobbing Simona at the end of the bed. The clean end. The one not covered in blood. Oh god. Cody squeezed his eyes shut, his nose burning.

"You need to call a doctor," Vera said calmly. "She needs help."

"She's fine." Andressa folded her arms. "It's a little blood."

"I don't think so." Vera stroked Simona on the back. He hated not being able to go to her, to hold her, to comfort her with what little comfort he had. How many times could his heart break for someone? It was endless.

"The bleeding has stopped," Vera said, "but she's lost a lot of blood."

It was so much blood, way too much blood. There was no way the baby would survive. He fought the growing panic. It was probably already gone.

"Felipe, go get new sheets," Andressa directed. "Cody, go get a wet washcloth and towel. Vera, get something to clean this mess."

Simona wiped her eyes and stared at the floor, unaware of what was going on around her.

Cody slunk away before Vera released Simona. He got the towels from the bathroom and raced back. Andressa was talking, and Cody stopped outside the door. Losing the baby would devastate Simona, but he wouldn't give up hope. He knew nothing about babies. Maybe it was possible the baby was still alive.

But the bloody scene in front of him revealed otherwise.

"I know what you're doing. You'll do anything to keep me from adopting your baby. This changes nothing. You'll just be heading to Minha Casa sooner. Do you understand me?"

Cody peeked around the doorway. Andressa towered over a beat-down Simona cowering on the chair.

"I said, do you understand?"

Simona raised her face to Andressa, her dull red eyes unfocused. "Yes, Miss Andressa." Her fragile voice was barely audible.

Someone else entered the hallway, and Cody scooted into the room, not wanting to look as if he was spying. "Here's some towels." He laid them on the table, but Simona didn't look at him. Didn't even react.

"Sheets." Felipe tossed them on the bed and backed away.

"You may go." Andressa waved Felipe away and paced up and down the small open space in the room. "This blood better come out. Couldn't you have made it to the bathroom? It's down the hall." She glared at the bloody sheets on the bed.

Vera rushed into the room, and Andressa sent Cody off, telling him to wait in the house for her.

Time seemed to slow as he lay in front of the TV, not seeing what was happening on the screen, not hearing the voices in the show. Simona had lost the baby. He would lose Simona. He had no hope left to grasp on to.

Andressa returned in a half an hour, but it felt like forever. She slid onto the couch next to him, and every nerve in his body screamed at her to move away, but he stayed still.

"Simona has been more trouble than she's worth. I had such plans for this baby, and now they're all gone." Andressa huffed. "Choices, Cody. We all have choices to make, and she has consistently made the wrong ones."

Simona never had a choice. Not once since she was sold off by her boyfriend. So many people used her, abused her, and she kept fighting. And now, she lost her baby, the thing that was keeping her going. Cody's throat tightened, tears gathering in his eyes.

Andressa squeezed his thigh. "I'm sorry. I know this baby meant a lot to you. I don't want you to worry though. She'll pay for what she's done." Andressa's voice was so cold, as cold as her heart. "I talked to Enzo," she continued, "but he won't take her until he checks her out himself. He doesn't believe me when I told him she was okay." She shook her head with disgust.

Andressa was a monster, and he had to sit next to that monster as if nothing had happened. He had to follow her up to their bedroom and climb into bed with her.

Amazingly, she didn't ask him to have sex that night, but he tossed and turned in bed. Every thought was about Simona, every pain in his chest for her. He had to see her; he had to let her know how sorry he was and how he would get her out of there no matter what.

*

At three a.m., Cody was still wide awake although Andressa had fallen asleep hours ago. He rolled out of bed and padded to the door.

327

She wouldn't wake up. He could go see Simona for a bit and get back into bed before she awoke.

The starry night lit the way, and he snuck into the barracão. Without a knock, he entered Simona's room. A small light was on, allowing him to see the two sleeping women on the bed. Vera lay propped up against the headboard, a bunch of pillows underneath her, with Simona curled up next to her.

At least she had Vera. That woman had done more for Cody than he could ever thank her for, and knowing he'd be leaving her behind pained him. He wanted to take her with too. Maybe he should ask her if she wanted to go. The three of them could get away.

Cody crept to the bed and shook Vera lightly. Her eyes popped open. "Mr. Cody?" She looked around, her voice as anxious as her eyes.

"How is she doing?"

"You must get out of here." Vera gripped the blanket and pulled it higher on Simona's body.

"Andressa's sleeping. She's been sleeping for hours. I had to make sure Simona was okay." He swallowed back the lump in his throat. "How is she?"

"She's surviving." Vera stared at the girl in her lap, and Simona stirred, blinking her eyes at Cody. Vera sighed. "I'll let you two talk."

She slid out from beneath Simona, and Cody took her place. The door shut, and Simona set her head in Cody's lap. He ran his fingers up and down her bare arm, not knowing what to say.

"I'm sorry." It was all he had. No sorries would ever be enough for what Simona had gone through. She took a deep, ragged breath. He couldn't see her face but knew the tears stained her cheeks.

"You have a few days before Andressa sends you to Enzo. I'll make sure Felipe brings Carolina by. I think she was coming tomorrow anyway. We'll have to leave. We might have to go to the river and swim."

His gut wrenched. He had to tell her the truth about her mom.

"I know." Her lifeless voice drained him. "We just need to get across the border into Venezuela, and then we'll be okay."

Cody bit his lip, preparing to break Simona's heart once again. She loved her mother so much.

"We shouldn't go to Venezuela. We don't need to." She gave him a questioning look. *Do it now. Just spit it out.* "I was talking to Andressa, and she admitted to looking up your mother. I'm sorry, Simona, but she's not there anymore."

Simona gasped. "Andressa killed her?" More tears sprung to her eyes.

He squeezed her hand tightly. "No, she didn't. Andressa found out she died in a bus accident. Several people were killed along with your mother."

"She might be lying?"

"I doubt it. She brought it up, and at some point, she was going to tell you."

Simona leaned back and wiped her wet eyes. "Instead of going to Mérida, we'll head toward Ciudad Guayana. Hopefully there'll be a smaller town on the way that has an American Embassy, but I'm not as familiar with that part of the country."

"We'll figure it out." Their stop might include a justice of the peace, but he wouldn't bring that up until necessary. He wanted Simona to see a doctor before they left, but they couldn't risk stopping in Manaus. "You'll love the U.S., although you might have to get used to the cold." He smiled, and she laughed.

"As long as you have warm jackets and boots, I'll be okay."

"We will be okay," he said, nodding. Someday, when she was ready to have a baby again, he would be right there with her.

Cody's eyelids were made of lead, and he closed them for a few minutes. He needed to get back to Andressa's bed, but he didn't want to leave Simona... Not yet.

Chapter Fifty-One

Day 109

"What the hell is going on here?" Andressa screeched.

Cody lifted his head from the pillow.

Oh shit. Simona shifted on the bed, the bed he was in. Andressa filled the doorway, her face twisted in anger, hands on her hips. He jumped out of bed.

"It's not what you think. I was comforting her."

"I knew it!" Andressa stomped into the room and slapped Cody. "I knew you were cheating on me, you liar. This was your baby, wasn't it? That's why you're so upset." Andressa gasped. "You were trying to help her escape?"

"No, I… It's not like that. We didn't…"

"Quit lying to me?" she shrieked. "You've been lying to me this whole time." Her eyes narrowed, a darkness taking hold, her voice deadly. "Don't think you'll get away with this."

Andressa spun around and stalked out of the room.

"Wait!" Cody chased after her. "It's not my baby. We never had sex."

She stopped and twisted around. "But you wanted to. You wanted to have sex with her."

No words came. For once he wanted to tell her the truth.

"Bastardo." She slapped him again and ran for the house. He had to make her believe he didn't want Simona. They'd survived so much; he couldn't die now. Oh god, she was going for a gun.

"Andressa, stop!" he screamed, but she sprinted into the house and to the office. She grabbed her phone, and Cody stood, stunned, trying to figure out what she was doing.

"Felipe, get your ass over here. Cody betrayed me. He's sleeping with Simona." Her face wrinkled up. "Now," she yelled and slammed the phone on the desk. The venom shot out of her eyes. "You could've had everything. You had me, and you gave it up for that trash. You gave up your life for nothing." Andressa's eyes grew wide. "Nothing!"

"I never wanted you. You kidnapped me. You forced me to stay here," he yelled.

Andressa pitched the phone at him, and he ducked. It smashed into the piranha tank, creating a small crack. It was so freeing to see her shock and disappointment. He wouldn't quit now.

"I never loved you. Nobody could love you."

She snatched the letter opener off the desk and hollered, racing toward him. Cody raised his hands to catch her wrists, the opener coming inches from his face.

Her scream drilled his ears, and she jabbed at him with her weapon. He shoved her away and tried again to grab her wrists, but she moved so fast. Her hand swung down to stab him in the balls, but he jumped out of the way.

She lunged again, and this time he seized both her wrists. She kicked at him, but he managed to get the opener away and flung it out the door. His body was on fire from all the hits and kicks, but the adrenaline was flowing.

"Quit fighting me." He gripped her shoulders and shoved her backward. Her head hit the fish tank with a crack, and she fell forward, a spider web of lines spreading in the glass.

Cody caught her before she hit the floor. He knelt down to find her pulse. Still beating, but she was out cold. This was their chance, but they'd have to get away before Felipe arrived.

He stepped over her to the door but stopped. The silver piranha still swam around the tank. He plucked the stapler off the desk and smashed it into the glass. Again and again. The glass shattered, and Cody leapt aside as the water poured out, soaking Andressa. The piranha landed on the floor and flopped around.

Cody hopped over Andressa and dug in the drawer for her car keys. They'd drive through the gate if they had to. Smash into it over and over.

He ran for the barracão and found Simona in her room, dressed. "Let's go. I knocked out Andressa. I don't know how long she'll be out." He jerked on her arm, and she squealed.

"Oh fuck." Cody swooped her into his arms and ran for the garage. He looked up to find three buttons. The first one didn't open the garage door, but the second one did. He roared out of the garage and down the driveway.

The first one might be the main gate. "Duck down. Maybe Raul won't see you." He wouldn't let Cody go, but if he saw the car first, he'll think it's Andressa.

Before Cody hit the guard shack, he slowed down and hit the first button.

The gate started to open. All he had to do was drive slowly. By the time he got close enough to the gate for Raul to see, it'd be too late. They'd be through, and Raul wouldn't stop them.

The gate was three-quarters open, and Cody stepped on the gas. But before they got through the gate, a truck pulled in front of them.

Felipe!

The truck blocked the way to freedom. Cody stared through the windshield at the man who would kill him.

"Get out of the car?" Raul yelled, a gun trained on Cody's head. Everything they'd almost had, the freedom, was gone. And they were dead. Simona had lost her baby and would now lose her life.

They would be piranha feed.

"Stay here," he told Simona and crawled out. By the time he was out, Felipe was standing there too.

"What's going on, Cody?" Felipe said, glancing at Raul and his gun. Cody felt Simona slip behind him.

"He didn't have permission to leave. Andressa didn't contact me, and she's not answering the phone."

"Where's Andressa?" Felipe growled.

Nothing was left but the truth. He was dead anyway.

"She attacked me in the office. I fought back and knocked her out."

"Did you fucking kill her?" Raul yelled. The gun pointed at Cody's head, so close that Raul wouldn't miss.

"No. She just got knocked out. She was still breathing. She's not dead." They were so close now, so close to freedom. They couldn't die now.

"Go check on her," Felipe said.

"What?" Raul glared at Cody.

"Go make sure she's okay, then call me. I'll take care of him right here if she's not alive." Felipe removed the gun from his holster and pointed it at Cody.

"I didn't kill her, I swear," Cody stammered.

"Maybe we should kill him right now," Raul leered.

"Are you a fool?" Felipe huffed. "And what would Andressa do to you if she knew you took that away from her."

Cody closed his eyes. Andressa would be the one to pull the trigger. They'd hold him and Simona until Andressa was okay.

Raul holstered his gun and took off down the road.

Felipe didn't take his eyes off Cody.

"I didn't mean to hurt her. She was trying to kill me, and she's going to kill Simona. She already killed her baby, and now she'll send her to Minha Casa. Let her go. I'll stay back. Please, Felipe!"

"Shut the fuck up, man," Felipe whispered. He stared at Cody, a look of a man who was about to make a dangerous decision. Cody prayed Felipe wouldn't shoot them.

Felipe raised his gun, and Cody closed his eyes, waiting for the bullet to rip through him.

"Get in the truck," Felipe yelled. Cody opened his eyes to find Felipe waving at him, his gun holstered. "I said get in the truck."

Simona grabbed his arm and ran for the door. What the hell was going on? What was he doing?

Felipe charged for the truck and jumped in the front seat. "Crawl in back. Get down. Nobody can see you." He stomped on the gas, and the truck reversed to the highway and then jerked forward down the road.

"What's he doing?" Simona whispered. Cody opened his mouth to ask, but Felipe had his phone out, talking rapidly in Portuguese.

"What's he saying?" Cody asked.

"Shush," she said and listened. "He's talking about money and meeting us someplace."

Felipe threw his phone onto the front seat.

"Where are you taking us?" Cody asked, the landscape zipping by fast. They swerved around a slower car, and Felipe sped up.

"Shut up. I'm thinking." He sounded scared.

They drove in silence, just the roar of the engine.

"Okay, this is the deal. You can come with us to Boa Vista, and then you're on your own. You got it?"

Cody raised his head to talk to him, but Felipe yelled to get back down.

"Where's Boa Vista?" Cody asked.

"It's north of here. That's it then. We're not taking you with us."

"We?" Cody whispered to Simona.

"Carolina," she said softly.

"Do you know where Boa Vista is?"

"It's on the way to Venezuela. Don't worry," she assured him. He'd keep worrying though, all the way until he arrived home in the U.S.

They drove for fifteen more nerve-wracking minutes until Felipe pulled into a parking garage, up to the third level. He parked the car and glanced around.

"What are we doing here?" Cody asked.

"Get out."

"Wait, what? You're not leaving us here?" Did he change his mind? Simona spoke Portuguese, but still. Andressa might find them.

Felipe whipped his door open and jumped out. He threw his arms around Carolina. Cody opened the door and slipped out, Simona behind him. Carolina had a large backpack on and another bag in her hands. She finally released Felipe and wiped the tears in her eyes.

"Let's go." Felipe led them to a car parked down a few spots. They all crawled in, and Felipe took off for the exit. Cody and Simona crouched down once again.

Everything started to click in his head.

"Are you doing okay?" Carolina asked.

"I'm fine," Simona said in a shaky voice, and Cody stared at her stomach. Damn, he'd forgotten all about the miscarriage. The baby would have to come out. She had to get to a doctor.

"Do you want to go to a hospital?" Cody picked up her hand and squeezed. "They can drop us off there instead."

"No," she said. "We need to get somewhere safe first. Cody stroked her hand. Her body would heal, and those were the only thoughts he would think from now on.

"Have you been planning this?" Cody asked Felipe.

Nobody answered him right away, and Carolina and Felipe exchanged quiet words.

"This… no." Felipe sighed. "But in this business, you always need to have a back-up plan in case shit goes down."

"It's always been my plan," Carolina said. "I didn't expect it to happen this way either. I wanted to leave, but now they won't just let us go."

Felipe was as good as dead if the Cardosos ever found him. Cody couldn't worry about him; he had his own concerns.

"It'll take us about twelve hours to get there," Carolina said. "We'll get you heading off to Venezuela, and then we'll go to Guyana on our way to Be—"

Cody heard a whacking sound.

"We'll be in Guyana," Felipe said. "Give them their money."

Carolina dropped a bag behind the seat, and Cody grabbed it. Inside he found stacks of bills. At least a thousand U.S. dollars and a bunch of Brazilian real too.

"That's in case something goes wrong," Felipe said.

Cody's gut clenched as he stared at the money. They'd have to sneak across the border or bribe somebody to let them pass. He had no clue what this trip held for them. They had no back-up plan, no I.D., nothing.

"Go ahead and sit up," Felipe said, and Cody rose to see the city disappearing behind them, a long stretch of highway in front of them.

Simona squeezed his hand. "We'll be fine. We can get through anything, as long as we stick together."

He had to believe in her words because he had no choice, but as they left Andressa in the dust, leaving all the darkness and depravity behind, he knew one thing was for sure: he'd never stop looking back.

Epilogue

A few months later

Milwaukee, Wisconsin

Cody flipped the sizzling burgers and took a drink of his cold beer. Only one weekend left before his last semester of college started. Simona had been wrong about slipping back into his old life. It had been easier than he thought.

Well, maybe a few things changed. He spent more time at home with his parents, and he wasn't as interested in partying the single life with his friends. But his life had changed for the better. He was married with a beautiful woman on his side, thriving under the freedom she now lived, and she fit right into his life: his parents loved her, and his friends admired her.

He couldn't blame them because he did too.

"Those burgers done?" Dad patted Cody on the shoulder.

"Just about." He readied the plate to pile on the burgers. Laughs spilled from the group of women sitting at the table, loudest among them was Simona. She placed her hand on her swollen belly as she laughed. Five months pregnant. Cody thought it was a miracle she hadn't lost the baby, but the doctors had said she'd only lost blood. It had seemed like so much that night, but the doctors gave her the okay once she got to Venezuela.

"Your mom has already warned the staff she'd be taking time off in January." Dad chuckled.

"I'm sure she has." She'd had a hard time letting Cody out of her sight when he returned. She'd probably be even worse with this baby.

Dad didn't ask a lot of questions, unlike Mom. They knew Simona's baby wasn't his, but they didn't know the full story about her past. His parents would understand, but that was Simona's story to tell, not his, and she wasn't ready yet.

Every day he thanked God for what he had, his parents, his family, and Simona, because he knew others were still trapped. The guilt over leaving Vera behind was strong, and he wanted to know what Andressa did about Felipe's betrayal, or if they'd made it somewhere safe.

He'd never know because he'd never set foot in South America again, would never contact anyone, never look them up.

Simona was right. They had to move forward because that was all they could do. Move forward and never look back.

Acknowledgments

This story was started in 2013, many years ago. I took a bit of a break on writing it and then got back to it and finally finished. But then the editing and all those other steps in the self-publishing process took a long time too. But I finally made it.

There's so many people along the way who offered support and advice, including my writing friends, the Beta Girls. Thank you to Rachel Schieffelbein and Jolene Perry for your help with making my story better. And ditto to Theresa Paolo, especially for answering a hundred questions about all those little pesky publishing things.

Thank you to Lyn, who helped with some of the translations. I won't put her full name here because she might get blamed for things that are not her fault, since I didn't have her read the whole story and check everything.

Thank you to my terrific cousin, Carol Kees, who has read this and a few other of my books and has given me wonderful compliments and other story advice.

Thank you to my wonderful family.

And lastly, thank you to all my readers. I'm happy to finally be able to share more of my stories with you.

About the Author

Reading has always been a big part of Suzi's life. She even won the most-pages-read award a few times in her junior high English class many, many years ago. She started many writing projects as a kid but never actually finished anything, and then she took a big break from writing that lasted well into adulthood.

She's written in a variety of genres, including horror, suspense and thriller, and has even dipped into fantasy slightly with her fairytale retellings. She's also published contemporary young adult novels under the name Suzi Drew.

In addition to writing, she works as a freelance editor, which means she gets to read at work too. Outside of the writing world, she enjoys spending time with her family and friends and her sweet and fluffy dog.

To find out more about Suzi,
go to SuziWieland.com

Also by Suzi Wieland

Thriller Novels
Black Diamond Dogs

Horror Novels
House of Desire

Horror and Suspense Novellas/Short Stories
Shallow Depths
(Un)lucky Thirteen
Long-Term Effects
The Silent Treatment
A Story to Tell
Panne Dora Pass

Twisted Twins Series
Glenda and Gus
Two for the Price of One
A Hard Split

Fairy Tale Novellas
The Down the Twisted Path Series
The Whole Story
An Unwanted Life
Killing Rosie
The Perfect Meal
When the Forest Cries
In the Queen's Dark Light

Please visit SuziWieland.com
for more information.

Printed in the USA
CPSIA information can be obtained
at www.ICGtesting.com
CBHW021728111224
18825CB00027B/358

9 798330 498550